the Witch's Daughter

ALSO BY IMOGEN EDWARDS-JONES

The Witches of St Petersburg

the Witch's Daughter

Imogen Edwards-Jones

HEAD of ZEUS

An Aria Book

First published in the UK in 2023 by Head of Zeus,
part of Bloomsbury Publishing Plc

9 7 5 3 1 2 4 6 8

A catalogue record for this book is available from the British Library.

ISBN (HB): 9781838933289
ISBN (XTPB): 9781838933296
ISBN (E): 9781838933319

Printed and bound in Great Britain by
CPI Group (UK) Ltd, Croydon CRO 4YY

Head of Zeus
First Floor East
5–8 Hardwick Street
London ECIR 4RG

WWW.HEADOFZEUS.COM

To the handsome Kit Craig and the wonderful Annabel
with love

AUTHOR'S NOTE

This is a work of fiction – although many of the facts are as is, this is not entirely as it was. I have taken many forms of poetic license. Also Russian dates present all sorts of problems. Until 1st February 1918, Russia used the Old Style Julian Calendar which meant that it was 12 days behind the West in the 19th Century, and 13 days behind in the 20th Century. Many sources don't differentiate between the two calendars. Some slip between both. Others don't bother with either! I have tried to use the Gregorian New Style Calendar as much as possible in this novel for clarity and efficacity. But I am sure some errors will have slipped through the net; I hope it does not spoil your enjoyment of the story.

CAST OF CHARACTERS

Grand Duchess Militza Nikolayevna – second daughter of King Nikola of Montenegro; she was one of twelve children, only nine of whom survived into adulthood.

Grand Duke Peter Nikolayevich – cousin to Tsar Nicholas II of Russia, married to Militza.

Princess Marina Petrovna of Russia – eldest daughter of Grand Duchess Militza and Grand Duke Peter.

Prince Roman Petrovich of Russia – only son of Grand Duchess Militza and Grand Duke Peter.

Princess Nadezhda Petrovna of Russia – the younger daughter of Grand Duchess Militza and Grand Duke Peter; her twin sister Princess Sofia Petrovna of Russia died at birth.

Grand Duchess Anastasia (Stana) – third daughter of King Nikola of Montenegro.

George Maximilianovich, 6th Duke of Leuchtenberg – Stana's first husband.

Grand Duke Nikolai Nikolayevich (Nikolasha) – brother of Grand Duke Peter Nikolayevich, commander in chief of the Russian army, viceroy of the Caucasus, and cousin to Tsar Nicholas II; second husband to Stana.

Tsar Nicholas II (Nicky) – reigned as the last Emperor of Russia from 1894 to 1917.

Tsarina Alexandra Fyodorovna (née Princess Alexandra of Hesse-Darmstadt; also called Alix) – Empress of Russia.

Their children:

Olga

Tatiana

Maria

Anastasia

Alexei, the Tsarevich

Dowager Empress Maria Fyodorovna (née Princess Dagmar of Denmark; also known as Minny) – widow of Alexander III, mother to Tsar Nicholas II.

Grand Duchess Elizabeth Fyodorovna (Ella) – elder sister of the Tsarina; married to Grand Duke Sergei Alexandrovich, uncle to the Tsar.

Grand Duchess Vladimir, Maria Pavlovna – one of the richest women in all Russia.

Grand Duke Vladimir Alexandrovich – husband to Maria Pavlovna and uncle to the Tsar.

Count Felix Sumarokov-Elston (Count Felix Yusupov) – married to Princess Zinaida Yusupova, the richest woman in all Russia; father of Prince Nikolai Felixovich and Prince Felix Felixovich.

Prince Felix Yusupov – married to Princess Irina Alexandrovna, daughter of Xenia (Tsar Nicholas II's sister) and Alexander Mikhailovich (Sandro); one of the murderers of Rasputin.

Prince Dmitry Pavlovich – son of Grand Duke Paul Alexandrovich of Russia, grandson of Tsar Alexander II of Russia, first cousin of Tsar Nicholas II; one of the murderers of Rasputin.

Anna Vyrubova (née Taneyeva) – the Tsarina's best friend.

Dr Shamzaran Badmaev (otherwise known as Dr Peter Badmaev) – apothecary, philosopher, and purveyor of fine drugs; born in Tibet.

Grigory Yefimovich Rasputin (Grisha) – man of God, hierophant, and holy satyr from Siberia.

Yekaterina Konstantinovna Breshko-Breskovskaya (otherwise known as Catherine Breshkovsky) – rebel, political prisoner and 'Grandmother of the Revolution'.

Bertie Stopford (Albert Henry Stopford) – antiques dealer, diplomatic courier and best friend of Grand Duchess Vladimir, whose jewels he smuggled out of Russia. He served time in Wormwood Scrubs for homosexuality and died in 1939. He is buried in Bagneux, France.

Prince Oleg Konstantinovich of Russia – fiancé to Princess Nadezhda of Russia; a poet and considered the cleverest of his seven siblings, he was the only member of the Imperial Family to die on the battlefields of WW1. He was twenty-one years old.

After witnessing an admirable performance of the Revolution with the keenest enjoyment, the intellectuals wanted to fetch their warm fur-lined overcoats and return to their fine comfortable homes: but the coats had been stolen and the houses burned.

Rosanov – *The Revolution and the Intellectuals*

There is no more Russian nobility. There is no more Russian aristocracy... A future historian will describe in precise detail how this class died. You will read this account and you will experience madness and horror...

The Red Newspaper (Petrograd)
No. 10, 14 January 1922

Paris for lunch, dinner in St Petersburg.

Kaiser Wilhelm II

PROLOGUE

31 August 1914, Znamenka, Peterhof

Militza and Peter sat down to breakfast, at opposite ends of the highly polished dining table and drank their coffee in total silence, save for the ticking of the large, baroque mantel clock. The clock stood on an equally large baroque table between the two sets of French windows that looked out on to the immaculately curated garden, the avenue of evergreens and the Gulf of Finland beyond. The sweet smell of cut grass floated in on the warm, late-summer breeze that wafted through the open doors. A soft-shoed butler served the Grand Duke Peter Nikolayevich his buttered toast and black cherry jam, while the Grand Duchess Militza Nikolayevna was content with her usual raw eggs. It was an old habit. The Grand Duchess Vladimir, the self-appointed doyenne of all things fashionable, had once been overheard extolling the virtues of such a healthy breakfast and soon the whole court, including the Tsarina herself, had followed suit. Militza no longer knew what Tsarina Alexandra, Alix, had for breakfast, or for lunch for that matter – those days were long gone. But she had kept up the habit all the same. What better way to start the day than consuming the ancient symbol of new life?

She cracked open two eggs into her glass, splitting the shells with her long, sharp thumb nails. Puncturing the two yolks with a silver fork, she whipped them into a light froth, tapping and tinkling the sides of the glass as she did so. She looked down the length of the table. Her husband would normally complain, in jovial tones, about the noise and her 'filthy habit', but today he was silent. He was reading a pile of dispatches from the front. They'd arrived overnight, bound in black ribbon, sealed with red wax and encased in a leather envelope. His pale eyes were unblinking behind his slightly smeared spectacles, his mouth was immobile, his lips, below his stiffly waxed upturned moustache, were tight, only his left hand was shaking. Militza picked up the glass, opened her throat, and swiftly swallowed the medicinal cocktail back in one.

'Everything all right?' she asked, dabbing the corners of her mouth with a white linen napkin.

Peter did not reply. He wasn't being rude, he just didn't appear to hear her. She glanced down at the folded newspaper next to her on the table and smoothed it flat. *Grand Duke Nikolai Nikolayevich leads from The Front!* proclaimed the headline. *Two Russian armies poised to take Eastern Prussia*, read the subheading underneath. She continued further down the page. The Germans were amassing on their western front, the Russians were lunging over the border, they outnumbered the enemy two to one. Victory was inevitable...

'I see your brother is marching the troops out earlier than expected,' remarked Militza, nodding at the newspaper. 'I thought they didn't have enough guns or, more's the point, enough boots? Isn't that what you said? Not enough equipment? Not enough training? But they seem to have launched an attack anyway. Extraordinary.' She shook her head. 'Peter!'

'Sorry.' He looked up from his papers, his face blanched, his eyes red and brimmed with tears. 'Fifty thousand,' he mumbled, shaking his head. 'Fifty thousand. How is that possible?'

'Fifty thousand what?'

'Dead... Russian dead. Ninety-two thousand taken prisoner. Cavalry, Cossacks, horses. Five infantry corps, four cavalry divisions, a whole army... annihilated.'

'In one battle?'

'It appears so.' His voice was barely audible. 'The Germans are calling it the Battle of Tannenberg, revenge for their loss five hundred years ago.' He shook his head again. 'And what revenge...'

'Mama, Mama, Mama!' Cries and footsteps clattered down the parquet corridor. 'Have you heard! Have you heard?'

Nadezhda burst through the double doors into the dining room; the sudden draught blowing the papers in front of her father off the table and up, swirling, into the air. Dressed in a white chiffon day dress, her long dark hair hanging loose around her shoulders, her normally pale cheeks were pink from running.

'Oleg is here, and he's told me everything! They shot the wounded in cold blood as they lay stuck in the mud, they put bullets through the heads of the horses. Thousands of screaming men and horses, driven into two huge swampy lakes to drown. It took them eight hours to kill them all. They were twitching and moaning, stuck in the quagmire, unable to move.'

'Oleg,' nodded Militza, smiling, fighting to maintain her composure as her heart beat wildly in her chest. 'How very lovely to see you.'

'Grand Duchess Militza Nikolayevna,' replied the young man bowing in the doorway, his hand placed across his chest. 'Grand Duke Peter Nikolayevich.' He bowed again, turning towards the other end of the table.

Dressed in his scarlet and blue guard's uniform and tight, red-striped breeches and knee-length highly polished leather boots, Oleg's face still shone with the golden glow of youth. His blond hair, shorn against his head, only emphasised his earnestness and made him appear younger than his twenty-one years. Nadezhda stood next to him, her sharp features quivering with indignation and outrage.

'Tell them,' she said, taking hold of his arm. 'Tell them what you told me.'

'You can keep your stories, Oleg,' said Peter, getting out of his chair. 'I have urgent matters to attend to.'

'Papa!' Nadezhda fixed her father with a glare.

Of their three children, Nadezhda was most like her mother. Not physically. The eldest, Marina, was more like Militza in appearance, with the same black hair from the Black Mountains of Montenegro. Nadezhda was dark too, but she had the look of her father, tall and slim like a reed in the wind, she hailed more from the Russian north than the temperate climes of the Balkans. But Nadezhda had her mother's heart, her mother's soul, her mother's gifts, and the same black eyes.

Peter sat slowly back down, his papers still scattered all over floor.

'Oleg had a telephone call this morning from his brother Kostya at the front. Did you know five Konstantinovich brothers have enlisted in the war?'

'I did.' Peter nodded.

'Much to his mother's misery,' added Militza.

'Anyway, what did Kostya tell you, my love?' prompted Nadezhda.

Oleg paused. Although he had known both Militza and Peter his entire life, their country estates – Znamenka and the Konstantinovsky Palace – were close to each other and, as children, his large family of eight siblings, including six brothers, were always back and forth, playing tennis, swimming in the waves, climbing trees, putting on plays with Marina, Roman and Nadezhda, but what he had to say was so appalling, he did not want to upset his future parents-in-law. His engagement to Nadezhda was unofficial, but he was determined to marry her. Even if he did have to wait the two years, that everyone had insisted on, until she turned eighteen.

'Go on,' nodded Militza.

'It was as if the gates of hell had swung open, so Kostya said, and all that is evil and pestilent was released,' he began, glancing from one end of the table to the other. 'There were thousands of them, our soldiers, our army, stuck in the mud, unable to move, exhausted by the struggle, or by the loss of blood, or the agony of their wounds. Our boys baked in the sun, their mouths gaping, their eyes frying, with nothing to drink. The Germans left them to die. But three days later some of them came back, out of compassion, pity, or most likely irritation. The moans and cries were travelling across the plain and they could not sleep. They came to find the bodies still twitching and the horses still breathing. Mostly the wounded were too tired to plead for their lives. A bullet through the brain would put an end to their pain. It took the Germans eight hours to kill all our soldiers, wandering between the corpses, picking off them off one by one, as they clung to life, caked in mud, just about breathing.'

'Tell me it isn't true,' whispered Militza, rising out of her chair.

'Papa?' Nadezhda looked at father.

Peter shook his head. 'It's all in there.' He indicated to the papers on the floor. 'Our appalling defeat. So many Russian lives lost. Of the 150,000 who went into battle only 10,000 souls returned. And General Alexander Samsonov...' He stopped. The story was too painful to tell.

'What happened to the general?' snapped Nadezhda.

'He was so ashamed of the defeat, and the loss of his men, he walked into the woods and shot himself,' continued Oleg.

'Killed himself?'

Militza covered her mouth in horror. Samsonov was a hero in the Russo-Japanese War. Samsonov was the commander of the fiercely loyal Semirechyenskoe Cossacks. She'd met him at court, they'd dined together at the Yacht Club. He'd made her laugh.

'He's a true man of honour,' added Oleg. 'He went off on his own. His troops only knew what had happened when one shot rang out.'

'What a terrible waste of young men,' said Militza. 'What a terrible waste of lives.'

'What has the great Uncle Nikolai got to say about this?' asked Nadezhda, staring hotly at her father.

'Nadya,' hushed Oleg.

'What?' Nadezhda spun around. 'My uncle, the brilliant Grand Duke Nikolai Nikolayevich, is in charge of this war. He's commander in chief of the whole army! My uncle's in charge of all the bloodshed. *He* chose that we fight the Germans.'

'The Tsar chose to enter this war,' corrected Peter. His voice was quiet and yet clear.

'And your big brother is helping him,' hissed Nadezhda, her face flushed with fury. 'There's only one person who can stop this horror. One man.' She raised her slim index finger. 'One person who truly understands the Russian people and how they suffer. Rasputin!'

'We don't talk of *that* man in this house.' It was Peter's turn to glare at his daughter.

'We're the only house that doesn't!' Nadezhda's pretty little mouth curled with disdain, her reddened cheeks burnt bright.

'Don't talk to your father like that,' admonished Militza.

'Don't talk to me like I am a child!'

'Then don't behave like one.'

'Go to your room!' Peter stood up.

'I am sixteen years old!'

'If I have to repeat myself the consequences will be dire.' Peter pointed his finger slowly and directly at the door.

'Not as dire as this war!' Nadezhda turned around and marched out of the dining room, slamming the door behind her.

Oleg remained. Rigid with embarrassment, his lips

were pursed, his eyes, as clear and as blue as a Siberian sky in winter, were wide with astonishment. He knew his beloved had a hot head and a passionate heart, that's why he'd fallen so deeply in love with her in the first place, but he'd never seen her behave as petulantly as this. Maybe the families had been right to make him wait two years. Maybe she was a little too childish for marriage just yet. Although, now, with the advent of war, with everything else in such a state of flux, one less uncertainty might have been comforting.

'I apologise for my daughter's lack of patriotic fervour,' said Peter, as he bent down to pick up his papers.

'Allow me, sir,' said Oleg, kneeling down next to him.

'It's her *fervour* we should be watchful of,' retorted Militza, reaching for her small dark blue glass bottle on the table and squeezing some steadying cocaine elixir into the pipette before releasing the drops directly in her mouth. 'And you, Oleg, I presume will be staying with us a little longer?' she asked, again patting the corners of her mouth with her linen napkin.

'I have my mobilisation papers.' He smiled.

'But you're not long recovered from pneumonia and pleurisy. You've only just returned from Bari. And your parents are only just back from Germany, and we all know how difficult that journey was. Stuck behind enemy lines, as war was declared. How is your father?'

'A little better,' said Oleg. 'Still confined to his rooms.'

'And you are still so very thin.' She looked him up and down.

'But well enough for the front.' Oleg stood up and smoothed down his trousers. 'I want to fight for my country.

I want to fight for the Tsar and Mother Russia. The people need to know that the Imperial House is not scared to send its sons in to battle. And I am not scared to die.'

'No one is scared to die, until they stare death straight in the face,' replied Militza.

'"It is not death that a man should fear, but he should fear never beginning to live."' Oleg was pleased with his erudition.

'Marcus Aurelius.' Militza nodded, acknowledging his quotation. 'All very noble, I am sure. But it is those left behind who truly feel the pain.'

Oleg's pale face and clear blue eyes shone, bathed in the morning light. His soul was so pure, his spirit so guileless and his innocence so luminous he could easily, Militza thought, be taken for an angel. Not worthy of this dark depressing world full of war and death and misery. She smiled. What a beautiful soul he was.

Little did she know that this was the last time she'd ever see him alive again.

Oleg was to be mortally wounded less than one month later. His riderless horse would be found pawing the ground next to him on the muddied, bloodied battlefield, his broken body brought back from the front as they fought to save his life. He would be returned to his parents in a coffin, pulled by a gun carriage, covered in flowers. The only member of the Imperial family to be killed in battle during the whole of the war.

'I am so happy,' he'd said, with his dying breath as he seeped gangrene and putrefaction. 'It will encourage the troops to know the Imperial House is not afraid to shed its blood.'

★ ★ ★

Nadezhda's scream on receiving the news of her beloved's death was so long and loud and piercing Militza imagined it to be the sound of a soul being wrenched in two. Such was her grief, such was her misery that Nadezhda took to her bed and did not rise again from it for six whole months. Just as the war ravaged Russia, so heartache consumed Nadezhda; it ate away at her body and sucked her flesh of all its force. She lay like a husk in the crepuscular darkness of her bedroom, hovering between life and death, tormented by the throes of Limbo, haunted by the images of the battlefield and the screams of the dying. And all the time Militza prayed. She and Stana chanted and mixed herbs and tinctures and called upon Spirit and the thousands of wise women who'd come before them to help. Those mavens of the soul who'd been burnt, ducked and drowned, they asked them to rise up and come to their aid in their hour of need. Just as they had begged the Four Winds once before for help, they called on all that they knew, all that they had, to save her.

Nadezhda called for Rasputin in her delirious sleep. Even Peter suggested they contact the Mad Monk, ask him to come to their aid. He owed them that much. But Militza would rather dance with the Devil himself than abase herself in front of that man. If Spirit wanted to take her daughter, the combined forces of her and her sister Stana would be powerless to stop it. What would be, would be.

Who, having raised his hands against the Lord's Anointed, will remain unpunished?

1 Samuel 26:9

CHAPTER 1

30 December 1916, Petrograd

It was dark; dawn would not raise its head and the moon resolutely refused to show its face, as the *droshky* pulled up outside the palace on Petrovksy Embankment. Militza had said nothing to the driver. She'd kept her eyes down, while her scratched, freezing hands shook uncontrollably on her lap. Her back was rigid and her black sable-lined cloak draped closely around her face. She tried not to move. She wanted to remain as anonymous and as unmemorable as possible, a vague shadow of a figure for whom Dr Stanislaus de Lazovert had hailed a taxi at 6 a.m.

He'd been the only one brave enough. The others had thrown themselves into the shadows as the *droshky* appeared through the gloom, moving slowly and silently, its wooden wheels slicing its way through the snow-covered street. Militza could hear them panting with fear, she saw the flashing glint of terror in their eyes as they flattened themselves against walls and doorways on Petrovsky Prospekt, desperately hoping not to be seen. But it was the doctor who stepped forward into the streetlight and mumbled something along the lines of 'allow me' before cupping his leather-gloved hands and hollering.

The driver was half asleep. His frost-blown nose was just visible over his scarf. His tired horse snorted clouds into the silence. The driver coughed and eyed her up and down as the doctor said the address and, on seeing the cloak and the shine of her jet evening bag, he immediately demanded double the fare. They were all at it these days. Bread was triple the price and vodka was impossible to find; even the most basic of supplies had to be bought on the black market. The good doctor agreed the price because Militza couldn't speak – her mouth was dry, her cracked lips were parched and her heart was pounding uncontrollably in her chest. What had she done? Try as she might she could not unsee what she had seen. She climbed unsteadily up the steps into the small carriage, sat rigidly on the black leather-buttoned seat and closed her eyes. But the horror, his face, those pale eyes, the sign of the cross and the look he'd given her as he slowly sank into the depths of the freezing Neva, weighed down by the sodden fur of Prince Yusupov's coat: they were images imprinted on her soul. No matter how tightly she shut her eyes, they would not disappear. Every night she would see them. Every night she would see his face and hear his whisper. And, she knew it then, he would haunt her forever.

'Right here, please,' she said, rapping the roof of the carriage with her knuckles.

'I could take you in,' he shouted down, straining his head to glance in through the steamed-up window.

'The street is fine,' she mumbled, opening the carriage door. 'I don't want to wake the house.'

She pulled herself off the seat and stepped down; her

frozen toes could not feel the snow through her sodden silk slippers.

'Thank you,' she said, careful not to catch his eye as she fumbled through her handbag. She pulled out some roubles that immediately sprang through her fingers and tumbled into the snow. 'Sorry.' She bent down slowly, hardly able to move. The strain of lugging the body, wrapped up in a curtain, and throwing it over the railings of the bridge, had taken its toll. Not that she had done much of the heavy lifting. Vladimir Purishkevich, Lieutenant Sergei Mikhailovich Sukhotin and Dr Stanislaus de Lazovert had thrown the corpse off the bridge, while Militza and Prince Dmitry Pavlovich had looked on. But the panic before – loading the car and tearing the blue curtains off the wall of the Yusupov Palace – had exhausted her. She was now cold and stiff and it was hard for her to move. She realised, also, as she scrubbed about in the snow picking up the furls of money, that she had lost her gloves. Black kid. Monogrammed. In golden thread. Her distinctive initials were sewn into the backs of the wrists.

'Here,' she said, handing the fistful of money up to the driver. 'Take it all.'

He didn't need telling twice. His heavily mittened hand snatched the wad of roubles and shoved them quickly into his greatcoat pocket. He didn't even count them.

'Good night,' she said.

'Is it?' he replied and, with a shake of the reins, he was off.

Alone in the street, Militza stood, staring into the darkness. She inhaled the cold, sharp air deep into her lungs and then slowly exhaled. The enormity of what she had done was only just beginning to hit her. The Devil was dead. The horned satyr she and Stana had called upon all those years ago, when desperate and demoralised, that Holy Monster of depravity who'd been carried to them by the Four Winds, was no more. Why was she not more relieved? Elated even?

Fate had dealt her the cards and she had snatched at them with both hands. She'd met Oswald Rayner in the Yacht Club for a reason. He'd drunk too much cognac and told her the game was afoot and Prince Yusupov was planning to pull off the most important political assassination of the century with some wine and cakes, like a child in a fairy tale. Fate had brought her to the palace that night and Fate had made her pull the trigger.

She slowly pushed at the wrought-iron gates of the palace. Black and embossed with the Nikolayevich coat of arms, they squeaked in the cold. A dog barked his response from over the other side of the wall. She ran swiftly across the courtyard. Should she ring the enormous doorbell and wake the house? Or hope the door to the entrance at the side was open?

It was almost 6.30 a.m.; the kitchen maids were surely up. Militza tried the handle to the side door and thankfully it turned. She slipped quickly through the double doors and, silent as a shadow, made her way along the unlit corridor towards the hall. All she had to do was fly up the stairs to her bedroom and pretend that she had been there, asleep, for the whole night. If she could only make it there, unseen, she'd have an alibi, even if the *droshky* driver were to remember her. No one would doubt the word of a Grand Duchess.

The hallway was dark; the servants had yet to turn on the lights. Militza slowed her pace and rose up on her toes; she lifted her snow-dampened skirts and held her breath, terrified to make a sound. She approached the long divan at the bottom of the stairs; she had a foot on the bottom step. Suddenly, something leapt up in the blackness. A giant dark shadow with whip-long hair and a rustle of skirts sprang from the divan, throwing a thick cloak to the floor. Militza flattened herself against the marble banister, her heart pounding, her eyes firmly shut, not daring to look.

'Is that you?' hissed a voice.

There was a click of a lamp switch and a bright blinding light. Her sister Stana was standing by the divan still wearing the dark green silk dress she'd worn out to dinner at the Yacht Club the night before. Her long black hair hung in strands around her shoulders, her face was as white as wax and just as luminous. She had clearly not slept and had been waiting all night, coiled like a cobra, for her sister to return.

'And?'

'And what?' replied Militza, dazed by her sister's appearance.

'Has he gone?'

'Who?'

'Rasputin.' Stana stepped forward and grabbed her sister by the shoulders, staring feverishly into her black eyes. 'Did you throw him into the river?' she whispered, gripping the shoulders even tighter. 'Did you drown him? Is he dead? Did you make sure the water filled his lungs and the ice froze his blood and his breath left his body? Did you make sure the ripples closed over his face and that he shall never... ever... be made a saint?'

'I did.' Militza was shivering. With cold? Or the memory? 'I watched him sink, I watched him open his eyes and smile. And worse...'

'How can there be anything worse?'

'I watched him forgive me.'

'I don't understand.'

'He forgave me, you, us... both of us. He made the sign of the cross as he sank into the depths. I heard his soul scream as he disappeared down into the deep.'

Stana shook her head. 'So he went to the Devil.' She stared at her sister. 'The Beast was happy to collect one of His own.' She inhaled deeply. Her mouth hardened with resolve. 'So that's it then.' She smiled. 'It's over.'

There was a noise at the top of the stairs and the two sisters looked up. Standing on the landing in her white lace nightgown, her dark hair tied loosely at the nape of her neck, was a beautiful young woman. Nadezhda. She looked like a ghost. Her pale skin and sharp features shone in the half-light from her upstairs bedroom. She stared down at her mother, a frown on her eighteen-year-old face.

'What are you doing?' she mumbled, as if still half asleep.

'Why are you awake?' responded Militza, keeping her tone light, hoping to reassure her daughter and send her back to bed.

'I couldn't sleep.'

'Oleg?' asked Militza.

'Not tonight,' she replied. 'Tonight was different, Mama.' Her eyes were wide and glassy. 'Tonight I had a terrible feeling something had happened... It was as if I was gasping for air, struggling, drowning and so terribly... terribly cold. It was a horrible dream, Mama, truly horrible.' She placed a fine hand on the white marble staircase and began to walk down. 'What's happened?' she asked, taking in the scene below her. 'Why are you up? Why are you both dressed? What did I miss?'

'Nothing, my love,' reassured Militza.

'Nothing,' agreed Stana. 'We've just been out, and we are back very late. They had some gypsy dancers at the Yacht Club and your mama and I could not resist. It's been so long... what with war... we thought...'

'Gypsy dancers at the Yacht Club? How bizarre. Was Rasputin there?'

'No.' Militza could feel the sudden rush of blood to her cheeks at the mere mention of his name. 'Why would he be there?'

'Only he loves gypsies, he loves dancing. Life. I'm surprised.' She shrugged. 'Oh, what a horrible dream that was,' she added with a shiver. 'So very vivid, Mama, it really was, as if I were drowning in the river just outside there.' She pointed towards the locked front door. 'Weighed down by a giant fur coat.'

Suddenly the double front doors burst open with a smash and clatter of broken glass and the hammering of wood on wood, as a tornado of wind and snow tore through the hall. Nadezhda screamed, her hair flew around her face, her white lace nightie swirled around her knees in the maelstrom. Both Militza and Stana stood stock-still, their fists clenched, their eyes fixed at the entrance, too terrified to move. Surely he couldn't be back? Surely he was dead at the bottom of the river, never to resurface? Surely not even he could cheat death for the fifth time? Gutted by a whore, beaten by a priest, poisoned by cakes, shot through the head and drowned. The wind swirled up and up, through the house, rattling the chandeliers that sang like tinkling glasses at a ball. The curtains bellowed and ballooned and a lamp crashed to the floor. Nadezhda's high-pitched screeching continued to echo and bounce off the marble columns and porphyry pillars in the hall.

'I do apologise,' came a voice from the threshold. A silhouette of a man swiftly removed his hat. 'I only gave the door the gentlest of pushes...' He walked urgently towards them. 'How are you? Are you all right? What happened? Did you—'

'Mr Rayner!' Militza interrupted, raising her gloveless hand sharply in the air, for fear the man might say more. 'I don't believe you have met my daughter? Nadezhda.'

'Your daughter?' Rayner looked confused as he slammed the front doors and scanned the snow-scattered, darkened hall. His hair was immaculately parted down the middle and greased flat over his skull. His white shirt, just visible below his buttoned, fur-collared coat, looked freshly laundered and ironed. Unlike Militza and Stana, Oswald Rayner appeared to have gone home to change after the murder.

'Yes.' Militza smiled tightly, rubbing her scratched and scraped hands together before clasping them behind her back. 'My daughter.'

'Mama! I am not dressed for visitors,' replied Nadezhda hotly, pulling the frills of her nightdress tightly around her neck.

'Princess.' Rayner bowed, fiddling nervously with his brown felt hat. 'How very delightful to make your acquaintance.'

'Sir.' Nadezhda smiled briefly, before glancing furiously across at her mother.

'Now run along, dear, and back to bed,' said Militza.

'But—'

'But nothing,' insisted Militza, waving her hand dismissively.

Militza's reply was sharp and Nadezhda knew better than to respond. Her mother was not someone you crossed, even if she were still wearing an evening gown at six forty-five in the morning and had cuts and scrapes on her hands. Her mother's appearance was posing more questions than answers. But it could wait. She turned to go back up the stairs.

'Rasputin is missing,' blurted Rayner.

'No!' Nadezhda gasped as she paused on the third step. She looked back at her mother, whose face remained inscrutable.

'Missing?' Militza's voice was barely audible.

'Bertie Stopford left me a message at five thirty this morning.'

'Five thirty?' asked Stana, glancing across at her sister and then at Rayner.

All three of them were thinking the same thing.

Grigory Yefimovich Rasputin was surely dead by 5.30 a.m. on 30 December 1916. Militza had fired the bullet into his brain, right through his frontal lobe, using Oswald Rayner's gun. The only .455 Webley revolver in all of Russia. Standard issue for British Secret Service. Standard issue for a British secret agent. Rayner: the fluent Russian speaker. The spy. Best friend of Prince Felix Yusupov in whose palace Rasputin had been shot. Best friends since

Oxford University, best friends since they both joined the Bullingdon Club, the only 'murderers' to do so in its entire history, since it was founded in 1780. She had shot him and then helped the Grand Duke Dmitry Pavlovich shove the bound and hooded body, wrapped in Yusupov's fur coat and the blue velvet curtain ripped from the walls of the Yusupov Palace, into the car. The car that wouldn't start properly, the car that stopped and stalled all the way to the Bolshoi Petrovsky Bridge. But what time did they get to the bridge? Was even he alive then, despite the shot through his head? What time did they throw him over the railings into the frozen river? What time was it when his bloodied galosh flew off, the one they left on the opposite riverbank? What time was it that she watched him sink to the bottom of the river, weighed down by the coat? When she saw him open his pale blue eyes and stare into her soul and make the sign of the cross as he disappeared into the depths?

'Five thirty,' confirmed Rayner. 'Bertie has some friends in the secret police and they said he went out last night after midnight and has not returned. Yet. His daughter called them, worried, or was it her friend? Anyway, he's missing.'

'He's probably drunk. Have they checked the Islands?' asked Nadezhda. 'He so loves going there. He's there a lot. Or maybe church? He could be praying, praying for Russia?'

'Go to bed,' hissed Militza in the direction of the stairs.

'I am only trying to help,' protested Nadezhda.

'I am sure you are,' replied Stana. 'But your mother is tired and now she is very worried about her friend.'

'Friend!' Nadezhda laughed. 'Everyone knows Mother despises Rasputin and has done so for years. Ever since he banished you and Uncle Nikolasha to the Caucasus. Actually, even before then. You hate him. You all hate him. You all despise him, you want him dead, everyone knows that!'

'Your mother doesn't despise Rasputin,' retorted Stana, her hands on her hips, her long dark hair Medusa-like on her shoulders. 'Now go to bed.'

'It's only because you don't understand him, no one does really,' said Nadezhda. 'You're all too blind. You, most of Petrograd and the entire city of Moscow hate him too. In fact, every soul, all the way to the striking sailors in Vladivostok, can't stand him. He's the most hated man in Russia.'

'I'm sure he'll be found soon. He's probably asleep somewhere,' said Militza through tight lips. 'Now, you go back to bed and rest, and perhaps Mr Rayner might like to join us for a cup of coffee, or tea, or something a little more fortifying on this cold morning. I most certainly need a little something. It's been a very long night.'

'I would be delighted,' replied Oswald Rayner, with a curt, polite bow as he looked Militza directly in the eye.

And so the three conspirators retired to the Blue Parlour for refreshments.

It was about 12 p.m. when the telephone calls started. The rumour mills were clearly working overtime. Everyone knew Militza was staying with her sister Stana at the palace on Petrovsky Embankment. It was a new palace, built by Grand Duke Nikolai Nikolayevich as a wedding gift for Stana. Large, Italianate, with a view of the Neva and the

Winter Palace the other side of the river, they had all been living together while their husbands, Nikolasha and Peter, were in the Caucasus, helping with the war.

And the calls were numerous. Militza and Stana refused to take them. Militza instructed Natalya, her long-serving lady's maid, to say that she was unwell and not available to postulate on the sudden disappearance of the Tsarina's friend. Brana, the crone whom the sisters had brought with them from Montenegro all those years ago, was dispatched to find a bottle of Vin Mariani in the cellar, a cocaine-laced wine that Militza had ordered in case of fatigue. For both she and Stana found themselves immensely fatigued. In fact, Militza was numb. For someone normally so sharp and bright, the broken woman sitting on the divan, staring into the flickering fire, deathly grey and with a tremor in her shoulders, was unrecognisable. Stana was only marginally more animated. Oswald Rayner was worried, deeply worried. In his limited experience, getting away with murder required a little bit more verve than this.

'Ladies,' he hissed, as Brana left the room, having served three large goblets of Vin Mariani. 'We must come up with a plan.'

'What do you mean?' asked Stana, picking up her glass of wine. 'There were no witnesses. We shall be fine.'

'My good lady,' replied Rayner, taking a cigarette out of a small silver case, 'there are always witnesses to a murder.'

'Don't be foolish, Mr Rayner,' she retorted with an irritated shake of her head. 'My sister and I dined at the Yacht Club last night and came straight home. It's dangerous to be out in Petrograd these days, what with the war and everything – why should we do anything else?'

'Of course, of course, of course you did,' he agreed, sucking speedily on his cigarette. 'Wise, most wise. Stick to that. Keep it simple. I like it.'

'It was anything but that,' mumbled Militza, draining her glass of wine.

'But what?' asked Stana.

'Simple,' she replied.

The slate grey sky had already succumbed to darkness when, at about 3 p.m., the Honourable Albert Stopford burst through the doors of the Blue Parlour on the first floor of the Nikolayevsky Palace on Petrovsky Embankment. A tall, slim, elegantly dressed Englishman with thin mousy hair, a long sharp nose and large limpid eyes the colour of the English Channel, he bristled with energy and wit and although he'd only recently arrived in the city, he was already inordinately popular, especially with the inordinately grand Grand Duchess Vladimir who simply would not, could not, go out to dinner without him.

A famed dancer of the cotillion and the French quadrille, pedigreed and penniless, Bertie was a man of few obvious means but extensive connections. And no one quite knew what he was doing in Petrograd at the height of the war. He was reportedly an antiques and jewellery dealer specialising in Fabergé and Cartier, which was possibly why the Grand Duchess Maria Pavlovna Vladimir enjoyed his company so much, for there was little else she loved more in the world. And Bertie was an ace at helping her dispose of her dear departed husband's palace-load of money. Although this by no means explained his close friendship with Oswald Rayner and his numerous other powerful contacts at the British Embassy. Truth be told, Bertie Stopford was one of those Englishmen who put a great deal of effort into appearing to be a great deal more foolish and frivolous than they actually were.

'Rayner!' he exclaimed as he walked through the door. 'Your Royal Highnesses.' He bowed beautifully, swiftly smoothing his moustache between his right thumb and forefinger. 'I do apologise for this intrusion and for persuading your servants to allow me up here. They were hugely reluctant, but I am afraid I have been searching the city for my friend here. I have been to Donon's, the Yacht Club, the Villa Rhode and an all-too-brief luncheon at the embassy with Sir George Buchanan and General Hanbury-Williams, which is no mean feat, may I say, as they are not the sort of chaps who would settle for two courses and a kummel. But I have news. News that cannot wait. Rasputin is dead!'

'Missing,' corrected Rayner.

'No. Dead! Most certainly dead and Prince Yusupov and his lover Prince Dmitry Pavlovich are in the frame.'

'His lover?' queried Stana, a little astonished.

'Lover, madame, yes.' He nodded slowly and bowed again just in case. 'My friend in the police is adamant. There were shots fired. There is blood all over the courtyard next to the Yusupov Palace. They tried to explain it away. That they'd shot a dog. A hound. A beautiful hound. But my friend in the police said there was too much blood in the snow for a hound.'

'But it might not necessarily be Rasputin,' suggested Rayner.

'Oh, but it is. Yusupov admitted as much, and anyway Felix was the one who sent a car to collect Rasputin from his apartment at midnight last night to meet Princess Irina at the palace on Moika.'

'But who'd believe such a thing? Irina is in the Crimea, I saw her only recently,' said Stana.

'Precisely!' declared Bertie. 'A trap!'

'A trap indeed,' muttered Militza.

'They were not alone,' continued Bertie. 'There were others. Carousing was heard. *And* there were women.'

'Women?' asked Rayner.

'Two,' he confirmed, sticking two fingers in the air, by way of illustration. 'Two women were seen leaving the palace in the early hours. They are keen to identify them, obviously.' He tapped his two fingers together. 'Two.' He glanced across at Stana and Militza, who stared back at him. Their dark eyes were blank. 'I do apologise,' he nodded slowly, lowering his eyes, contemplating a further bow, 'but I have been assured by the police that, on account of their clothing, they were ladies of the night.'

'Ladies of the night,' repeated Militza, a frown flickering across her face.

'Prostitutes,' explained Bertie. 'A couple of old prostitutes.'

'Prostitutes?' Stana's voice betrayed her surprise.

'Prostitutes.' Rayner nodded enthusiastically. 'Most likely those old gypsy whores you can pick up at the Rhode.'

'I do apologise,' Bertie said again. 'Such language... but it gets worse.' His voice fell to a whisper. 'The Tsarina has been informed and she is distraught, she's had to be sedated. A whole vial of Veronal. She is inconsolable. After all, he was her only friend, after Anna Vyrubova obviously, but she is stricken by grief, screaming and wailing apparently, terrified about what will happen next.'

'What will happen next?' asked Rayner.

'What Rasputin said? What he predicted would happen?' He looked at each of them, an eyebrow raised in expectation. 'In the letter?'

'What letter?' asked Militza.

'The letter!' Bertie found it hard to conceal his delight. 'The letter he wrote to the Tsar?'

'Rasputin wrote a letter to the Tsar?' asked Rayner.

'Full of predictions,' added Bertie. 'I have a copy. My friend in the police.' He tapped his trouser pocket and pulled out an envelope. 'Here. It was intercepted and they made a copy, several copies, in fact.'

'Really?' Stana sounded surprised.

'Of course.' Bertie shrugged. 'What do you think the secret police are doing outside his apartment all day, if they are not reading his post and making copies? Anyway, here it is. This is what he predicted about his own death before the year was out. Before tomorrow, in fact. Tomorrow is New Year's Eve. Obviously.' He cleared his throat, flapped out the paper in front of him and began to read.

'I feel that I shall leave life before January 1st. I wish to make known to the Russian people, to Papa, to the Russian Mother and to the Children what they must understand. If I am killed by common assassins, and especially by my brothers the Russian peasants, you, the Tsar of Russia, will have nothing to fear for your children, they will reign for hundreds of years.

But if I am murdered by boyars, nobles, and if they

shed my blood, their hands will remain soiled with my blood for twenty-five years and they will leave Russia. Brothers will kill brothers, and they will kill each other and hate each other, and for twenty-five years there will be no peace in the country. The Tsar of the land of Russia, if you hear the sound of the bell, which will tell you that Grigory has been killed, you must know this: if it was your relations who have wrought my death, then none of your children will remain alive for more than two years. And if they do, they will beg for death as they will see the defeat of Russia, see the Antichrist coming, plague, poverty, destroyed churches, and desecrated sanctuaries where everyone is dead. The Russian Tsar, you will be killed by the Russian people and the people will be cursed and will serve as the devil's weapon killing each other everywhere. Three times for 25 years they will destroy the Russian people and the orthodox faith and the Russian land will die. I shall be killed. I am no longer among the living. Pray, pray, be strong, and think of your blessed family.'

There was silence in the Blue Parlour, save for the gentle crackle of the dying fire.

'They haven't found a body, have they?' said Rayner, injecting his voice with a little optimism.

'Not yet,' agreed Bertie, plucking a cigarette from the silver box in front of him. 'My Grand Duchess Vladimir thinks it's only a matter of time. But the real question is, who actually killed him? If they are related to the Tsar, if they are noble, if they are royal, if they are a boyar, then, that is what Rasputin predicted.'

'What nonsense,' said Rayner. 'Superstitious nonsense.'

'Prince Felix Yusupov is of noble blood, he is a prince *and* he is related to the Tsar by marriage to his niece.' Bertie's index finger was raised by way of correcting his friend.

'What if it wasn't him?' asked Rayner.

'Well,' replied Bertie with a shrug as he lit his cigarette, 'let's hope they are not of noble birth.' He exhaled. 'Because that would be bad. Awfully bad.'

They sat in silence contemplating the fate of Russia, the fate of the Tsar and his family.

'Do you remember the words of Papus?' Stana turned slowly towards her sister; her eyelids flickered as all the blood drained from her face.

'No,' Militza whispered under her breath.

'"Rasputin is a vessel like Pandora's Box,"' began Stana, her hands shaking on her lap as she spoke, '"which contains all the vices, crimes and filth of the Russian people. Should the vessel be broken we will see its dreadful contents spill themselves across Russia."'

Pursued by the wild and vulgar throng
By the greedy hounds, crawling around the Throne,
His greying head has been forever laid low
By a tool in the hands of an obscure Freemason.

Murdered. What's the use of lamentations,
Or sympathy, which are, obviously insincere.
It's either laughter or curses over the corpse
Or a solitary, burning hot tear.

Found in the Tsarina's papers, written in her own hand

CHAPTER 2

January 1917, Tsarskoye Selo

News of Rasputin's disappearance spread through the city like wildfire. Telegrams flew back and forth, fuelling speculation. Telephones would not stop ringing. Messengers were sent from palace to palace. Rumours were rife. The truth was rationed. Newspapers were censored, risking huge fines for mentioning the possibility of his demise. The Tsarina was heard frantically to be offering a large reward for any information concerning his whereabouts. Prince Felix Yusupov and Grand Duke Dmitri Pavlovich were being firmly touted as the principal players in the disappearance/murder. Prince Yusupov was alleged already to have written a letter to Alexandra protesting his innocence. The Tsar was on his way back from the front, abandoning the campaign due to the crisis, taking the 4 p.m. train from Mogilev. And Anna Vyrubova, the Tsarina's favourite, closest and indeed only, friend, and perhaps the most ardent of Rasputin's already fervently ardent admirers, claimed that as she slept an icon had fallen off her bedroom wall and knocked over a portrait of the Mad Monk himself. This was taken by all who heard, as a sign.

Yet the following day the Grand Duchess Vladimir held a luncheon for thirty-four of her closest acquaintances at her great palace on the Embankment. It could have been construed as a celebration had the invitations not been issued a few days previously. For, in the absence of the Tsarina at the heart of the city, Grand Duchess Maria Pavlovna Vladimirovich had created an alternative court at the Vladimir Palace, where she entertained her own entourage with huge generosity. Militza and Stana would not normally be invited to such an intimate event, but these were not normal times. The city was breeding factions. Better to unite behind the common enemy than to fight amongst themselves.

The sisters hesitated as they drew up in their sledge in front of the imposing granite palace decorated with lions' faces and innumerable coats of arms.

Should the vessel be broken. Should the vessel be broken. The words would not leave Militza's head. What had she done? What 'vices, crimes and filth' were about to spill across Russia? She was struck by such a terrible sense of foreboding she could barely breathe. She'd hardly slept. Had it not been for a hefty draught given to her by her old nursemaid Brana, towards the early hours her eyes would never have closed. Maybe sleeplessness would have saved her from the terrible visions that stalked her fitful slumber. It was hard to know which was worse.

'Just keep calm,' Stana whispered to her sister, taking hold of her gloved hand. 'No one knows anything.'

'I'm not sure I can,' Militza whispered back. She looked up at the palace.

'It's all rumour and conjecture. Remember what Mr Rayner said last night? Keep it simple.'

'You're right,' agreed Militza. 'It's only silly superstition.'

She climbed out from under the warm fur blanket into the biting cold wind, blowing straight off the frozen Neva. It was enough to ice the bones and chill the soul. The skies were clear blue. A pale sun shone. But the temperature was sixteen degrees below zero.

As they walked through the entrance to the palace, past the Gothic gargoyles and into the hall, they came across a buoyant Bertie Stopford being brushed down in the vestibule by a footman dressed in the distinctive scarlet livery of the Vladimirs.

'What a beautiful day!' he exclaimed, rubbing his hands together as the footman removed the dusting of snow that had blown on to his shoulders. 'Have you heard the news?'

'What news?' asked Militza, as calmly as possible. Handing over her mink wrap, she tensed a little, fighting the dual waves of fear and irritation. Much as she enjoyed the company of the Hon. Mr Stopford, his desire to be first with every twist and turn of current events was as annoying as it was alarming.

'Only that the Grand Duchess Elizabeth Fyodorovna has sent two telegrams of congratulations. One to Felix's mother, Princess Zinaida Yusupova, and the second to Grand Duke Dmitri himself, praising the patriotic actions of both Prince Felix and Dmitri.' His moustache twitched with delight. 'Apparently, she was also asking after all the gory details. Can you imagine? The Tsarina's own sister! Praising the assassins... Good news travels fast, even if you live in a nunnery, apparently!'

'Apparently.' Stana smiled.

'Did you also hear that even Grand Duke Nikolas Mikhailovich went around to Dmitry's apartment last night where Felix was dining and praised the murderers!' he added. 'He called them patriotic heroes! The saviours of all Russia!'

'Uncle Bimbo?' asked Stana, handing over her fur. 'But he hates the war as much as Rasputin did— does,' she corrected herself.

'He clearly hates Rasputin more,' replied Bertie.

'How does *he* know anything?' asked Stana, glancing across at her sister.

'Felix telephoned him at five thirty, just after the murder, or so he claims.'

'Five thirty? Just after the murder? Uncle Bimbo is always prone to exaggeration,' muttered Militza.

Felix had done no such thing. He'd passed clean out in the snow at the sight of Rasputin's blood. Like a drunken sailor on his way back from a bar, he'd had to be taken to his rooms to recover. Or was that later? Was the Holy Satyr still alive at 5.30 a.m.? Or had she executed him by then? Militza shivered. A deep chill slithered down her spine.

'I think this might be a bit of an English luncheon,' Bertie added, warming his hands at the large sandstone fireplace. 'The British ambassador is coming, plus Lady Georgina, General Hanbury-Williams and a few others... Ah! There you are!' He turned and bowed so low and deeply, Militza feared he might never stand upright again. 'Your Imperial

Highness Maria Pavlovna! How are you? Looking radiant and fragrant... Today even the sun is shining!'

'We are not yet sure of *that* fact,' replied the Grand Duchess Vladimir, swooping down her marble and gilt staircase.

'It's only a matter of time!' he replied. 'He is surely murdered, and the body can't be far off.'

'He could yet still be found asleep under a table at the Villa Rhode,' said the Grand Duchess as she puckered her lips and kissed him on the cheek. 'It's been known.'

'The whole of the city is looking for him,' Bertie continued.

'He could be in Pokrovskoe,' mumbled Militza, muddying the water, already murky with claim, counter-claim, news, gossip and superstition.

'Why on earth would he travel back home to Siberia at this time of year?' The Grand Duchess stopped in her tracks and looked Militza slowly up and down, a puzzled expression creasing her middle-aged face.

'It's possible,' ventured Militza.

'He must be dead. Surely? No one goes east at this time of year. Far too cold. Far too difficult. And anyway, Felix and Dmitri are claiming credit for it all. It's just you and the Tsarina who still think he could possibly be alive. And Lily Dehn, but she's a fool, and Anna Vyrubova and she's an idiot.' She paused. 'What's your excuse?'

'Experience,' replied Stana, stepping forward. 'He's disappeared for days at a time before, hauled up in some drinking den, surrounded by acolytes, the secret police are always losing him. Rasputin—'

'Please do *not* mention his name!' The Grand Duchess raised her hand in the air. 'I can't bear it. It's all we've heard for months, years. It's all too ghastly. He's called "The Unmentionable" in this house. Now,' she smiled, 'shall we go upstairs and have a little glass of champagne to celebrate?'

Upstairs in the Raspberry Parlour, with views across the Neva and the Peter and Paul Fortress beyond, the disappearance of the 'The Unmentionable' was on everyone's lips. The Grand Duchess Vladimir's three sons were exchanging theories as to where he might be. Her youngest, Grand Duke Andrei Vladimirovich, had just come back from two months at the front and seemed to be relishing the conversation, after weeks of mud and misery in the windswept north.

'So, do you have any theories?' he asked Militza, taking a large gulp of his Cristal champagne.

'Other than his being found in an alcoholic stupor somewhere? No. He could have left town.'

'I would have thought you'd know more than most,' he continued, drinking again from his glass.

'And why is that?' Her flute of untouched champagne quivered in her hand.

'You have been friends for so long, you were the one who introduced him to the Tsar and Tsarina. He came through your house, as your brother-in-law, Uncle Nikolasha is always loath to remember.'

'That was a long time ago.'

'But you were *all* his champions!' He snorted.

'Relationships change,' Militza replied.

'Maybe if you asked your tarot cards, or tipped a table or two, spoke to some spirits, you'd find out where he is!' He chuckled at his own joke and took another sip of champagne.

'Those bubbles appear to be going to your head,' snapped Militza.

'Everyone playing nicely?' asked Bertie, sensing the frosty atmosphere in the corner of the room.

'We were just admiring the view across the river,' said Militza, smiling.

'Oh, I never tire of it.' Bertie exhaled loudly. 'No matter how many times I have been in this beautiful room. And there are many... Oh, Ambassador... Sir George... I believe you know her Imperial Highness Militza Nikolayevna, very old friends of "The Unmentionable".'

Sir George stepped forward, a tall, slim, immaculately dressed fellow with the regulation aquiline nose, heavy moustache and watery grey eyes of an Old Etonian member of the British gentry.

'Indeed,' he replied, nodding politely whilst readjusting his monocle. 'We have met a few times before. So, where do *you* think the scoundrel is?' he asked.

'He could be anywhere,' she replied.

'"They seek him here, they seek him there"; he's more elusive than the Scarlet Pimpernel,' said Sir George. 'I thoroughly enjoy a mystery. Don't tell anyone but I am an ardent admirer of a good detective novel.'

'But alive? Militza's the only one who thinks so,' said Andrei, drinking more champagne.

'I am not sure if that's possible,' said Sir George. 'Not according to the police report that landed on my desk this morning.'

'Police report?' Militza blinked rapidly.

'The one I told you about,' confirmed Bertie.

'It's quite basic, just the arrivals and departures from the

Yusupov Palace. And the times the shots were fired. The blood in the snow, the dead hound. And the departure of two women—'

'The prostitutes—' added Bertie.

'Prostitutes!' chortled Andrei, his cheeks flushed with booze. 'I don't think Felix and Dmitry like that sort of thing!'

'They were probably for The Unmentionable,' suggests Bertie. 'Bait? He did like that sort of thing.'

'He liked most things,' agreed Andrei.

'I thought Prince Felix's wife Irina was the bait?' added Sir George.

'But she is in Crimea,' interjected Militza.

'Hence the prostitutes,' nodded Bertie. 'But it's all just like I said, when I wrote home ten days ago, I warned there would be a tragic *dénouement*. We were warned, weren't we, Sir George?'

'A tragic *dénouement*?' Andrei looked puzzled. 'I'm not sure how tragic it is.'

'But a *dénouement* nonetheless,' corrected Bertie.

'Indeed. You British appear to be remarkably informed. It's almost as if you lot have got something to do with it?' Andrei laughed.

'I assure you, sir, the British do not meddle in the affairs of another sovereign state,' declared Sir George brusquely.

'Everyone!' The Grand Duchess Vladimir clapped her hands together with a flourish and the room fell silent. 'Just to announce the police have found a galosh!' Stana immediately glanced across at her sister. Militza gripped her glass of champagne a little tighter. 'A galosh has been spotted on the ice under Petrovsky Bridge on Malaya Nevka. His daughter is on her way to see if it does indeed belong to "He Who Shall Not Be Named".'

'Well, there we are then, the body cannot be far away.' Sir George nodded, smoothing the corners of his moustache. 'I shall inform His Majesty the Tsar of this development this evening.'

'You are seeing the Tsar this evening?' asked Militza.

'We are allies, my lady, in this war,' he replied. 'We have much to discuss.'

Talk of the galosh dominated the luncheon, as did theories as to how the murder occurred. The more the guests imbibed, the more grotesque the stories and elaborate the scenarios became. Hoots of laughter circled around the table along with a heavy silver bowl of glistening beluga caviar. It may have been blisteringly cold outside and the middle of a war, but standards were standards. While the streets of the city teemed with the shivering poor queuing for bread, Grand Duchess Vladimir still managed to procure her annual six barrels of caviar and her six prime sturgeons delivered as soon as the winter sleigh tracks were open by a convoy from the Caspian Sea, led by a Cossack sergeant.

Bertie scooped a large spoonful on to his plate.

'Forgive me, Militza,' confided Bertie, nodding politely at the footman, 'for I simply cannot resist caviar. I'd eat it for every luncheon and dinner if I could. It's Russia's ambrosia. It is one of the things I pine for most when I am in rainy old London. We just don't get the quality and, frankly, the quantity that you do here.'

'No one quite has the quantity of the Grand Duchess Vladimir,' replied Militza.

'My Grand Duchess is generous to a fault.' Bertie grinned and helped himself to a pile of warm blinis. 'Can you believe the letters copied by the secret police? It doesn't bode well to have Felix and Dmitri as the assassins, does it?'

'Just superstitions.'

'But you Russians love your superstitions. I can't keep up with them half the time. What's the one when you spill the salt?'

'You spit the Devil in the eye over your shoulder, three times.'

'That's it. Spit at the Devil three times. Talking of devils, the embassy was absolutely pre-warned that something might happen to "He Who Can't be Named" but the plots were too numerous to monitor. Even so, those two are the most unlikely of criminals, don't you think?' Militza remained silent. 'Well, everyone knows what a lotus-eater Felix is. He's not the sort of chap ever to get his hands dirty. He can barely stub out a cigarette. A game of tennis is about as physical as he gets.'

'He is one of the finest tennis players in Russia,' said Militza.

'He learnt on the fields of Oxford, of course. Or should I say courts. He is always clever enough to lose when he plays the Tsar, though,' replied Bertie. 'Otherwise, he would never have been allowed Irina's hand in marriage.' He laughed. 'So maybe he *is* smart enough to have killed the Devil. Anyway,' Bertie continued, slathering another blini jam-thick with caviar, 'I've heard Felix has gone to ground today. All enquiries at the Yusupov Palace have been met with the same intelligence: he's gone south to Crimea.'

'You stay remarkably well-informed for someone who deals in jewels, Mr Stopford.'

'You flatter me, madame!' He grinned. 'I have eyes and ears and I listen. I also spend a lot of time in the Yacht Club drinking gin and talking, mainly to my old and dear friend Mr Rayner.'

'Oh, Mr Rayner,' said Militza, nodding.

'He was the one who told me there was a plan afoot to get rid of "Dark Forces".' Bertie raised his rather fine eyebrows in a conspiratorial fashion.

'Dark Forces?'

'The Unmentionable.' He glanced up and down the table. 'By the British.'

'The British wanted, want,' she corrected herself quickly, 'to get rid of Dark Forces? The Unmentionable?'

'Oh yes.' He nodded and then leant over to whisper into her ear. 'But not in a way that would ever come back to us, of course.'

'Of course.'

'Plan it; but get someone else to do it. That sort of thing. You know, by proxy, as it were. To keep you lot in the war.'

'Of course.'

'*He* was trying to persuade the Tsarina otherwise.'

'Everyone knows that.'

'And what with the Tsar at the front and that madman Protopopov around, it was only a matter of time before she decided to rule in his place, with *him* at her side. And the last thing anyone needs is Protopopov. Everyone thinks he's suffering from syphilitic insanity, but we all know it's simply an addiction to cocaine. He sobs and twitches if he doesn't get any. Which is not ideal in a Minister of the Interior. It doesn't get more insane than his idea back in October – or was it November? – when he asked the richest bankers in Petrograd to buy all the bread in Russia and distribute it amongst the poor. We all know he simply got the job because he paid Rasputin!'

'Bertie!' came a shrill voice from the other end of the table. 'If you mention that name again, you'll have to go and sit in the drawing room all on your own!'

'My Grand Duchess,' he bowed his head, 'I am most awfully sorry. I sincerely promise it won't happen again.'

On the way back in the sledge, Militza felt her shoulders relax a little, her head listed sideways, and she half-closed her eyes. The luncheon had managed to allay some of her deepest fears. The jolly way the news of Rasputin's disappearance had been met made the whole situation – the dreadful, protracted murder, his escape from the palace, his running like a dog only to be shot like one – into something of a party anecdote. Perhaps it was just the palpable relief that he'd gone. And no one cared precisely where. His shadow had loomed so long and large and had been so menacing and all-encompassing. The dictatorship was over. *De mortuis nil nisi bonum* clearly did not apply to the corpse of Rasputin.

It was Nadezhda who woke Militza with the news that they'd found the body. The police had been cutting holes in the ice for the last two days near where the galosh had been found, but with no success. It was only on the morning of the third day after Rasputin had disappeared that a policeman spotted some frozen fabric sticking up out of the ice, about two hundred metres downstream from the bridge. The body had frozen solid and had to be chipped away until it was freed, then pulled from the river, like a giant ice-cube.

'Oh, Mama, I can't tell you what they found!' Nadezhda was sitting on Militza's bed still wearing her white nightdress, despite the clock edging past 11 a.m. Her thin hand hovered over her mouth as she whispered.

'... and his hands were above his head. They were loose, untied, he'd freed himself. But his fingernails were all broken and scraped, as if he'd been scratching at the ice, trying to get out of the water. Can you imagine, Mother? He drowned. Rasputin drowned.'

'Praise God,' said Militza, rapidly crossing herself.

'What do you mean, "Praise God"!' Nadezhda's dry red lips parted, her black eyes febrile.

'Praise God and rest his soul, is what I was saying.' Militza smiled and patted her daughter's hand. 'Praise God and rest his soul.'

'How long do you think he was under the water before he drowned?' asked Nadezhda, her hand trembling. 'I'd hate to think that he might have been in pain.'

'Drowning is like sleeping,' Militza reassured her. 'He would not have felt a thing.'

'But before?'

'Who knows what became of him before that? But the Lord was indeed merciful and kind, that he was taken by the water, by the ice. He will never be a saint, sadly. A drowned soul according to the Orthodox religion can't be beatified. But Grisha was too much a man of the people to need such frivolities. He was from the earth, and so to the earth he shall return.'

'They didn't manage to get him into the coffin they brought for him,' said Nadezhda. 'His arms were frozen stiff over his head. He was taken in a lidless box to the morgue to defrost. Thankfully, some of the faithful managed to save the water that surrounded him. They gathered the miracle water in pails. Here.' She held a small glass jar of cloudy, brown river water up to the light. 'I shall never let it out of my sight, I will carry it with me, always, for it will bring me the greatest of good fortune. And I need that...'

'Your misfortune is over,' said Militza, squeezing her daughter's forearm. But even as the words left her mouth, she knew them to be untrue.

The clouds were gathering. The embers of discontent and revolution were being feverishly fanned in the *traktirs* and slums and doss houses of the city. The shadows on the streets were increasingly malevolent and a sense of impending doom dragged its heavy feet along the pavements, through the dark narrow passages and across the frozen canals. There may only have been a pane of glass that separated Militza from the stooped silhouettes in the street, but it could equally have been a gulf as wide as the Siberian Steppes. At night, as she tried to sleep, she had the same vision, over and over again – Nevsky Prospekt, teeming with a shouting, marauding horde, pitchforks in their hands, guns in their belts, slogans flapping in the breeze. Hundreds of them. Possibly thousands. Shoulder to shoulder as they marched.

Their grins were toothless, as they forced their way towards her. There were screams and shouts and blood-curdling cries. But worst of all was the staccato sound of machine-gun fire and the thud of corpses in the street. Was the vessel broken? Vices, crimes and filth.

'This war can't last forever. Soon the Tsar will realise the error of his ways, that no one wants this war, that no one wants young Russian lives to be lost at the front and we shall return to normal.' Nadezhda nodded determinedly. 'By the way, the police found tyre tracks in the snow,' she added. 'They apparently propped the body up against the railings and lifted his feet and pushed him over into the river, his body hadn't cleared the bridge properly. He hit his head on the way down to the water and they found blood splattered on the piers.'

'Are you sure?' said Militza.

'Perfectly.' Nadezhda looked puzzled.

'Oh, it's all so distressing,' replied Militza. 'So many awful details. I don't want to recall any of them. Hear them.'

'I know,' agreed Nadezhda. 'According to his daughter his right hand was poised, his fingers were together, as if he'd died making the sign of the cross.'

They tried to keep the funeral a secret. The atmosphere in the city was beyond febrile. The newspapers were still not allowed to report on the identity of the corpse dragged out of the river. But everyone knew. Everyone had a theory. And still the rumours circulated. The autopsy of the semi-thawed body was held in the middle of the night, by gaslight because the mortuary had no electricity. A zinc-lined coffin was purchased by the Petrograd Governor-General from Martynov's Funeral Parlour for five hundred roubles (a generous 10 per cent off the original purchase price). The Tsarina herself was said to have sat, dressed as a nurse, with the body all night long. But still no one knew where they might bury Rasputin. It was too dangerous to send the body back to Siberia for fear of inciting riots along the way. To bury him in Tsarskoye Selo also would be problematic, as if he'd been elevated from peasant pauper to the royal family itself. Finally, it was Stana who found out where they were to inter the swine. Neither she nor Militza were invited. Nor indeed were any members of Rasputin's family. Not his wife, Praskovya, nor any of his three children.

It was a cold, slate-grey morning as they sat in their automobile, on the roadside, opposite the half-finished church. By way of some gruesome compromise, they'd chosen this dank patch of ground on Anna Vyrubova's estate, where Grisha himself had, only a few months ago, laid the first 'consecrated stone'. They'd erected a small military tent next to the grave and constructed a wooden walkway from the path to the graveside, above the frozen mud. It was so bleak, desolate and despairing a resting place that Militza almost felt sorry for the man.

At about 9 a.m., the royal party arrived. Nicholas, Alexandra, the four grand duchesses, the rotund Anna Vyrubova – his most pious and fervent admirer – and Lily Dehn, confidante of the Tsarina and a fellow member of the *Rasputinki* fan club. There were various other commanders and military men. The Tsarevich Alexei was nowhere to be seen. He was presumably too ill, his blood too weak after another haemorrhage to attend. Draped in long black robes, the Tsarina and her daughters looked more like a procession of weeping nuns than royal mourners. Beside the shallow grave, the ceremony was presided over by Father Alexander Vasiliev. While he prayed and lamented, they stood immobile, silhouetted against a steel sky, buffeted by a hard wind from the east. As the coffin was lowered, Alix gave each of the mourners a snow-white lily-of-the-valley, and they threw a stem in turn upon the coffin. As the shovelfuls of mud began to rain down, thundering loudly against the lid of the zinc-lined box, the royal party departed, disappearing into the grey light of the morning.

Militza and Stana did not leave their automobile. Covered in blankets, they stared in silence through the increasingly fugged up windows. Neither of them knew what they were expecting. A murder of thousands of crows to explode screaming and cawing into the sky? A celestial choir singing incantations of joy as they floated through the woods? The Holy Satyr was gone. He was made of flesh and bone after all. They'd manifested him all those years ago. Rasputin. In a moment of terrible weakness and desperation, in a final last-ditch attempt to hold onto what political power they had managed to claw, grasp, for themselves, they'd taken wax and dust from a dead man's grave plus the soul of an unborn child and, using all the power of their sisters before them, they called upon the Devil and the Four Winds. And the Devil had surely answered. Rasputin came just as they'd made him. Just as they had fashioned him in wax and dust – part baby, part monk, part holy satyr. But instead of doing their bidding and being their faithful, loyal, obedient servant, he'd stormed the city; he'd wreaked havoc in St Petersburg as he tap-danced along those damp watery streets. He'd caroused with the gypsies, he'd gorged on prostitutes and he'd danced with ladies of the court. He abased them in bedrooms, in parlours, over the arm of the fetid daybed in his foul apartment. He'd exerted every ounce of influence he could over the Tsar and his pitiful wife. But worst of all, he'd turned against them, Militza and Stana. He'd briefed against them. He'd counselled against them. He'd been most disloyal. The monster had turned on his mistress's makers. And now, there he was. Six feet under, in a zinc-lined coffin, with a bullet through his brain and his lungs full of water. They were victorious.

'So,' exhaled Stana, breaking the quiet.

'From the Four Winds he came, and to the Earth he is sent,' Militza whispered. 'May his spirit never rise. May he stay below this sod, may his soul never see the light.'

'Dead, buried, and forgotten.'

'Mostly forgotten,' added Militza.

'Amen to that.'

Do you mean that I am to regain the confidence of my people, or that they are to regain my confidence?

Tsar Nicholas II to the British Ambassador,
Sir George Buchanan

CHAPTER 3

February 1917, Petrograd

Food shortages were everywhere. The army had taken fifteen million men away from the farms and villages. The unharvested crops had rotted in the fields and there was no one to sow the seeds for the following year. Famine was crawling through the slums, taking the young and the weak. At the Nikolayevsky Palace the kitchen was complaining to the upstairs butlers that there was no salted bacon to be had, and only a very poor choice of boiled ham available on the streets. And what there was, was very over-priced indeed. Inflation was running at 300 per cent, an egg cost four times it had the year before, and butter was five times as much. Desperate souls were stealing the crosses off the graves of the poor for firewood. And still the war continued, and still the losses mounted up, and still the Tsar, since the death of Rasputin, weak with fatigue and indecision, stayed in Tsarskoye Selo chopping wood for his daily exercise, playing dominoes with his staff, bezique with his wife and reading Sherlock Holmes aloud to his children.

Meanwhile, the scandal of Rasputin's murder continued

to shock the city. While Felix seemed to be preening like a peacock, basking in the glow of his new-found fame as the 'Saviour of Russia', Prince Dmitry Pavlovich appeared to have aged overnight. He was spotted out at the Yacht Club, Donon's and the ballet chain-smoking, drinking heavily and wringing his hands like some latter-day Lady Macbeth, swearing blind he didn't have blood on his soul. Speculation mounted that the two princes would be charged with murder. The police had no right to enter a house when a member of the Imperial family was present, or indeed arrest a member of the Imperial family, so it could only be at the Tsar's, or more like the Tsarina's, behest that they were being investigated for the crime at all.

'We must not draw attention to ourselves,' said Stana as they drank tea in the Blue Parlour.

'Equally, we can't let poor Prince Dmitry go to prison,' replied Militza. 'For something...'

'No, you're right,' confirmed Stana. 'But how do we persuade Nicky to call off the hounds if we don't want the pack to turn on us?'

Eventually the sisters decided on a two-pronged attack. The first was to approach Grand Duke Alexander Mikhailovich, known to all as Sandro. Married to the Tsar's sister Xenia, he was close enough in the family to warrant an audience with the increasingly isolated Nicholas and he was also a mystical Freemason who mistrusted the status quo and who, on the odd occasion, had been seen to attend the Black Salons. Famous for their table tipping and tarot, these were hosted by the Countess Sophia Ignatiev and regularly frequented by Militza and Stana. But despite his eloquence his appeals to the Tsar fell on deaf ears and were met with a blank expression and the words, 'Very nice speech, Sandro. However, nobody has the right to kill, be it a grand duke or a peasant.'

Next, the Grand Duchess Vladimir was persuaded to circulate a letter to be sent to the Tsar in support of dear Dmitry. *You, who were his Guardian and his Supreme Protector in infancy and boyhood, well know how deeply he loved You and Our Country.* It was an excellent letter and many of the great and the good added their signatures – including her four children, Queen Olga of Greece and a great many uncles, aunts and cousins of the Tsar himself.

She had yet to hear back from the Tsar when she, Militza, Stana, Nadezhda and the garrulous Mr Stopford all gathered together at Nikolayevsky Station at two o'clock on Friday morning, nearly two months after the death of Rasputin.

The Grand Duchess Vladimir had decided to take her personal ambulance train, Number 1, to help evacuate some of the wounded from the front, along with some doctors, nurses and her priest. Militza, Stana and Nadezhda had volunteered to help. Ever since the Tsarina and the four Grand Duchesses had taken up nursing at the start of the war, all the ladies of the aristocracy had become experts in first aid. It was the height of fashion to attend courses held by the Red Cross. Many of the capital's chicest ladies had their own hospitals. Ballrooms had been converted, old palaces had been given over to the wounded, everyone needed to be seen to be doing their bit. Militza and Stana had their own little hospital at the guard house of the imperial fortress on Inginernaya Ulitza, 8. Bertie Stopford was hugely involved in the Anglo-Russian hospital on the corner of Nevksy and the Fontanka. The beautiful crimson neo-baroque palace, decorated with giant stone carved statues of Atlas, was the epicentre of the British ex-pat war effort. Owned by none other than Prince Dmitry Pavlovich, the palace had been given to him at the beginning of the war.

The train journey to the front was to take some ten or twelve hours, followed by another, of twelve to fourteen hours, on the way back. The Grand Duchess Vladimir always insisted they travel more slowly on the return. Not only would it give the priest more time to talk to and bless the dying, but it meant the injured would be less rattled and bumped on the poorly maintained tracks.

The train was already in the station when Militza, Stana, Nadezhda and the faithful Brana arrived. The old nurse was something of a reluctant passenger on these trips. She found the suffering of the young men unbearable and the ostentatious largesse of the Grand Duchess Vladimir equally so. It was hard work. Not that she was ever afraid of that. Better to stop the war, she thought, than have these flamboyant mercy missions swooping in and out of the battlefield to assuage the guilt of the aristocrats at court. Brana had tried to back out of previous trips, but Militza had always insisted she came. And she could never deny Militza. She'd known both sisters since their birth; she'd been instructed to look after them by their mother Milena, Queen of Montenegro. Not that Militza ever needed looking after – even as a young girl she was powerful. And Brana's knowledge of herbs, tinctures and pain relief was invaluable on the train, she knew that, especially when the doctors were busy elsewhere. So she came, despite herself.

'I know you don't want to be here,' said Militza to Brana

as they walked along the platform together. 'And I am grateful and so is the Grand Duchess Vladimir.'

'I am not here for you or the Grand Duchess,' replied the elderly woman, pulling her woollen scarf tightly around her sharp old cheekbones. 'It's the young men I'm here for. Like lambs to the slaughter. It's an injustice, that's for sure.'

'Better keep your views to yourself. There's a good girl.' Militza patted Brana on the shoulder. She was getting rather outspoken in her old age. 'Just here!' she said to a footman with a click of her fingers. 'And careful with that bag.'

Piles of boxes on the platforms were being loaded by the Grand Duchess Vladimir's footmen, all dressed in her familiar red livery. Bandages, swabs, tourniquets, ether and small bottles of morphine and some hypodermic needles; quite how the Grand Duchess had managed to procure such supplies was something of a mystery.

'I see you have your box of tricks,' said Grand Duchess Vladimir, watching her footman load Militza's two large leather-bound medicine cases containing over seven hundred individual bottles of everything from laudanum to citric acid, from cocaine elixir to henbane and belladonna drops.

'I thought it might be helpful,' replied Militza.

'It most certainly is,' she agreed. 'You never know what you might encounter. Last time we picked up 492 soldiers, twelve of whom were dead before we even left the station. Ah, Bertie, I see you have supplies too!'

'Thirty bottles of vodka, one hundred and fifty packets of cigarettes and three bottles of cherry brandy I found behind the bar at the Astoria Hotel,' he confirmed. 'They were good enough to give me one for the war effort, the other two I had to buy myself.'

'Where did you get so many packets of cigarettes?' asked Stana, carrying a box of bandages.

'The concierge,' replied Bertie. 'They're the same all over the world. They can get their hands on anything, for the right price!'

'Are we all nearly ready to depart?' asked the Duchess. 'There's a hot samovar in carriage number four, for anyone who would like tea.'

'Two minutes,' replied Militza. 'I have left my wrap in my automobile.'

As she walked along the dark platform, through the frozen fog, back towards the street and her waiting chauffeur, she saw the silhouette of a young man. His head was bowed, his shoulders rounded against the wind, and his coat hung open as if he didn't care about the cold, or the night, or the freezing fog. He looked familiar.

'Dmitry?'

He spun around, showing a face white as wax, his eyes wide with fear. 'Who's that?' he hissed into the shadows.

'It's me, Militza.'

'Have you come to kill me too?'

'No.' She stopped in her tracks, horrified.

'What are you doing here then?'

'Me? I'm here with a hospital train. Travelling to the front. You?'

'How very noble. How ironic, that you're free to walk the streets and I'm being banished to Persia!' He laughed, a little hysterically.

'What, right now?'

'In the dead of night. With no one to say goodbye to me. That's what happens when you're a murderer, apparently.

Not that I would know. Because I'm not one. But that's the plan!' He laughed again. 'Get rid of me, in the middle of the night. No fanfare, no send-off, they don't want to provoke any unrest.'

'Oh, Dmitry!' she took a step towards him.

'Don't.' He raised his hand. 'I know it's better this way. I know it's better for me. It is better for you and for Stana. I only wish I could feel stronger and happier about it. It had to be done. We both know that.'

'But—'

'Shh.' He put his finger to his lips. 'Don't worry. I shall be fine. History will be kind to us, Militza, I know it will. And when all this is over, let us drink champagne together in Paris.'

'Paris,' she whispered.

'Paris,' he repeated. He nodded slowly and in the weak light of the platform lamps, Militza could see his eyes were full of tears.

'Grand Duke!' barked a voice from behind him.

'Yes, sir!' he replied.

'Your train is on platform three, ready to depart.'

He turned and gave Militza the briefest of waves and put his finger to his lips one more time. 'Don't breathe a word.'

And with that he was gone. Militza stood, staring into the fog. Would history really be kind to them? She sighed. Had she made a terrible mistake? What vice and filth and crimes would be released?

A whistle blew from the other end of the platform.

'All aboard,' yelled the driver into the darkness.

Her wrap would have to wait.

Back on the train, Militza did not breathe a word, not

even to Stana. The news would get out quickly enough. Dmitry had too many people fighting his corner for it not to. She also didn't want to put his life in danger. She wondered if a similar fate would befall Felix. She wasn't so worried about him. He was married to the Tsar's niece and he was the richest man in Russia; he had more money than God, he had more money than the Tsar, and certainly more palaces and land. Whatever happened to him, he'd be fine. He also didn't seem to care, announcing his notoriety in every drawing room in Petrograd and delighting in it, elaborating as he went. But Dmitry? Exiled to Persia. How long for? Young men didn't live long out there, on the edge of the empire. There were spies and assassins everywhere. She wondered if he would ever see Russia again.

Militza took off her fur-edged hat and placed it in the luggage rack above her head. Looking at herself in the blackened windows, she swiftly tied a white scarf around her head. She was here to work; she could think about Felix and Dmitry and the investigation when she returned to the city. She smoothed down the front of her black dress and, checking for her long white apron in her bag, started to walk down the train.

Twenty-eight of the twenty-nine carriages of the Grand Duchess Vladimir's Number 1 train had been given over to rows and rows of wooden slatted beds. They were four to a cabin, one above the other, with room for doctors and nurses to move in between. The whole party knew these beds would be full to capacity on the way back, so they should sleep as much as they could on the way out; it would be all-hands-on-deck and standing room only on their return. The remaining carriage was not filled with beds, but was something of a makeshift restaurant car, with a samovar for tea and some plates of cold meats, pickles, brown bread and slices of *salo*, or cold pig fat. It was regarded as a delicacy, although not something that either Militza or Stana could stomach.

As the train pulled slowly out of the station, the party gathered in the restaurant car for glasses of hot sweet tea and a small selection of *butterbrot* and pickles, provided by the Grand Duchess Vladimir's chef. Bertie insisted on cracking open one of his bottles of cherry brandy and adding a slug to everyone's glass of tea to help them sleep. The atmosphere in the carriage was one of nervous apprehension. All except Nadezhda had been to the front to help collect the wounded before, but each time they left the city, each time they crawled along on the tracks towards the fighting, the situation appeared to have worsened. The number of injured were multiplying and their conditions had considerably deteriorated. Perhaps it was the length of time they were waiting for help, lying in the mud, screaming in agony, drenched in trenches filled with stagnant urine, corpse-water, lice, rats and the blood of their fellow soldiers. As soon as they opened the doors of the train the smell of gangrene gas, the high sweet stench that grabbed at the back of the throat and watered the eyes, would fill the carriages, as would the moaning, the weeping of boys for their mothers, the crying out of names of loved ones. Then there would be the acrid aroma of alcohol as the doctors drenched their limbs, followed by the sound of screaming and sawing, all through the night, as they amputated as many infected arms and legs as they could, all the way back to Petrograd.

It was 3 a.m. by the time one of the young doctors suggested they might go to bed. And it wasn't long before the rest of the group followed suit. No one undressed, for no one was really going to sleep. They all lay there on the thin horse-hair mattresses, rocking to the rhythm of the train, staring at the ceiling or the bunk above them, waiting with a sense of foreboding and dread for what lay ahead.

Militza woke and sat up in her bunk just as the dawn was breaking over the horizon. She pressed her cheek against the cold windowpane. The countryside was still black, an etched outline, with little or no detail, but as the pale purple of sunrise shifted through orange and then blue, the full extent of the chaos and destruction became apparent.

It was the mud that shocked her first. She was used to grey skies and a scarcity of green during the endless winters in Petrograd. There was never any light nor colour during those dark winter months. But this, this was extraordinary, as if the landscape had been ploughed. The trees were devoid of leaves, the bushes were smashed, broken and bent and the tracks, the roads had all turned to mud. The small houses that they passed were mostly destroyed, the roofs had collapsed, the windows were broken. Fences were down, gates were off their hinges. Occasionally, along the nearby road, there might be a peppering of chickens, a lone horse and cart, a few soldiers walking together. Some were barefoot, others in their shirtsleeves in the cold, with only a few weapons between them. Was this the broken vessel? Was this what she had done?

Militza sat there in silence, while her sister and daughter still slept, and wept. This was a graveyard, pure and simple, crowded with lost souls. If she closed her eyes, she could hear them scream.

'Oh, Mama!' exclaimed Nadezhda, sliding off the top bunk. 'Look at this terrible place.'

'I've seen worse,' replied Militza, swiftly flicking the tears away from under her eyes. 'It's not that bad. War is never good for the land. Or the people.'

Nadezhda stared. 'I have never seen anything like it.'

'No.' Militza smiled weakly at her daughter.

'Do you think Oleg was shot in a place like this?'

'Of course not.' Militza touched her daughter's elbow. 'Oleg was shot in the summer; he lay down in the flowers and the long grass. He was in the Elysium fields.'

'But he was shot in battle,' Nadezhda corrected. 'They found his unseated horse.'

'I know it wasn't as bad as this. He had lilies and roses on his coffin.'

'He did.'

'Lilies and roses... It was nothing like this. I promise.'

And yet, Oleg had died of gangrene, the infection from his wounds, but not from his wounds themselves. Had he not been in the mud, swimming with pestilence and plague, he might have survived, but the water and the mud seeped into his wounds and, like the tens of thousands of other young men before and indeed after him, he was killed by the filth of his uniform.

'Are we nearly here?' asked Stana stretching out on her mattress. 'I feel we are about to arrive.'

'I think we have another half hour before we get there.

Perhaps we should all have some tea,' suggested Militza. 'It might be our only chance.'

Back in the dining car, all remnants of last night's supper had disappeared and the tables where they'd sat, eaten their bread, pig fat and cooked meats, were now covered in white cloth.

'Good morning, Your Highnesses,' declared Bertie smoking a cigarette and flicking his ash at his feet on the wooden floor. 'I trust everyone slept well?'

'Good morning, Mr Stopford,' replied Stana.

'The samovar's hot.' He nodded towards the large golden churn steaming in the corner. 'Do help yourself but stay away from the operating tables.' He nodded at the row of tables in the middle of the room. 'They are trying to keep them clean.'

'Good morning,' announced the Grand Duchess Vladimir walking to the carriage with exaggerated ebullience and her arms wide open. 'Everyone ready for the fray?'

In the cold light of the grey day, devoid of her finery and extensive, expensive jewels, the Grand Duchess Vladimir appeared older than she was. Now in her early sixties, her pale blue eyes remained sharp. It was the rest of her face that had grown pinched and dull with age. Yet her energy and her enthusiasm, spurred on by friendship with Mr Stopford, still appeared boundless.

'I am wondering if it might be better if each of us took charge of a carriage. The priest and the doctors can be called upon when required.' She smiled. 'What do you think?'

'Good idea, my Duchess,' replied Bertie, with a grin, as if they were discussing the rules of engagement at a cocktail party.

'And you, Bertie—'

'Yes, my Grand Duchess?'

'You can go up and down the train handing out cigarettes.'

He nodded. 'Apologies in advance.' He bowed to Militza, Stana and Nadezhda. 'But I'm afraid I shall be the most popular person on the train.'

'You most certainly will be.' Nadezhda laughed.

'Do you think you can manage a whole carriage on your own?' Militza asked Nadezhda.

'I can,' she replied, standing tall as if to emphasise her determination.

'Excellent, your father's daughter, I see. There is also a team of nurses, six dancers from the Mariinksy Ballet and some from my own hospital here to help anyone who needs it. And my footmen can carry hot water up and down the train. You don't have to cope on your own, that's the important thing.'

As they drank their tea in silence, the train began to slow down. It advanced at a walking pace, gingerly, slowly, almost as if it were picking its way through the mud. Bertie smoked cigarette after cigarette, staring out of the window, stubbing them out on the floor. Even the Grand Duchess Vladimir, who persistently complained of a bad heart, smoked one, which Militza had never seen her do before. The brakes squeaked again; the train slowed some more. A small station came into view with a wooden roof and flaking turquoise paint on the outside walls – it might have been a joyous place to have alighted, once. But now it was most certainly not. Rows of tents had popped up like mushrooms, there were carts, horses, soldiers, more carts, piled high with soldiers, passed out on top of each other like music hall drunks. Were it not for the bandages and the blood, they could have been asleep. And the noise. The cannon fire, the sound of bullets, and the cries and moans of all those men.

As they pulled into the station, they saw the platform, covered in bodies and blood and uniforms. Lines of stretchers lay flat on the ground. Some were being carried between two men, there were others piled into the back of open carts. Nadezhda was expecting chaos, fighting, shouting, soldiers climbing over each other to get on the train. But there was no such thing. It was orderly, respectful, kind, and not at all what she had imagined. Each man was treated with dignity as the peasants deposited their charges at the station. There were some walking wounded, jovial young chaps trying to make the best of broken arms, bandaged eyes, wounds to their shoulders. Others were not responsive and their arms hung off the sides of the stretchers, swinging in time to the steps of the men carrying them. Many of them were naked; their shirts or trousers had been ripped away, torn clean off their flesh by shrapnel. Few of them had boots. No one would waste leather boots on an injured soldier. They'd been removed as soon as they'd left the battlefield. No one needed shoes to board a train.

It took about five hours to load the men. Moving each soldier gently to a bed, noting down their names and where they came from. The Grand Duchess was thorough.

The smell was overwhelming at times. Mud, filth, death and putrefaction all jostled for dominance in the airless carriages. Soon Militza, Stana and Nadezhda's beds were full up. The Grand Duchess's footmen ran up and down the train with buckets of hot water, and the cleaning and the dressing began. Both Militza and Stana worked quickly, efficiently washing and changing dressings, calming, muttering, talking, distracting, casting as much of a spell as they could. Brana was in charge of the travelling chest of tinctures and potions, grinding and mixing, administering and injecting. Endlessly injecting. The principal request was for pain relief.

Nadezhda, on the other hand, was horrified by what she saw. She was petrified by indecision and revulsion. She didn't want to touch open wounds, or naked bodies. The smell of sweat, the matted knots of pubic hair. She had only kissed one man and had never seen male flesh before, let alone touched a young man's naked thigh. She stood, her teeth gritted with determination, and prayed for guidance. For the Lord to help her help them. But once she started gently washing wounds, gingerly finding out names, ages, stories, all she could think of as she cleaned and bandaged was Oleg. Beautiful Oleg. The Blessed One, for that's what his name meant. Holy. Blessed. If only she had been able to help him. If only she had been there, to wash and clean his wounds and tend to him, he might never have died, and she might now be married. How she missed him. How she still loved him. The golden soul with the Siberian blue eyes. She sighed and even sang a little as she dressed wounds. And with each of them, she furtively brought out the jar of cloudy muddy Rasputin Water that she'd placed in her pocket. Her mother would be furious if she knew. But Mother didn't know everything. While she worked, she dipped her thumb in the jar and drew a small cross on each forehead. One young man, who'd been unconscious with pain, woke up to the sight of her face, her clean warm towels and the cross on his forehead and asked if he was in heaven already.

Meanwhile, Bertie was making himself hugely popular, continuously walking the length of the train, handing out his contraband. He was followed by the priest who was administering communion and listening to last testaments. It was surprising how many wanted letters to be written. Letters they would never read, sent to loved ones who could not decipher them. But still Militza sat with them and wrote down their words, mumbled through parched, cracked lips, eyes glazing over as they remembered where they were born, and how happy their lives had been until now.

'How are you?' asked Bertie, as Militza walked towards him. He was leaning out of an open window taking in some air. She was looking for Brana; a young guard's officer was crying out in pain.

'Tired,' she admitted for the first time that day. 'Have you seen Brana?'

'Isn't it sad,' he said, shaking his head, before lighting yet another cigarette. 'I've just watched two chaps die. They went out like watches running down – they just stopped breathing. There was simply no more fight left.' He paused. 'And in carriage fifteen there's a soldier, shot in the spine, who's with his beautiful young wife. She is dressed as a man, a volunteer for the Field Telephone Service. She cut her hair short, put on a uniform and followed him into battle. That's true love,' he said, smiling.

'It is,' agreed Militza.

'Good evening,' said a young doctor, walking towards them. His face was shining with sweat, his brow was heavy with exhaustion and his large brown eyes were haunted. His white tunic was covered in blood. 'May I have one of those?' He nodded towards Bertie's cigarettes.

Bertie handed him the packet of Players. 'Here, please take the whole thing.'

'Thank you,' mumbled the doctor, putting a cigarette in his mouth and letting Bertie give him a light.

'How is it?' asked Bertie.

'Worse than last time.' He exhaled. 'I am not sure how much more of this Russia can take. How many more fathers, husbands, lovers and sons can we lose?'

'It's millions so far,' said Militza.

'The Riga push cost us ninety-five thousand men,' said the doctor. 'There was no artillery to support them, or Red Cross to collect the bodies. They all froze solid where they lay.'

'Ninety-five thousand?' Militza whispered.

'More. I came across a thousand dead last week. Poisoned gas. The masks were still in storage, so the poor sods had urinated on their handkerchiefs and tied them around their faces. Needless to say that didn't work.'

'What a terrible waste of young life,' said Bertie.

'It's the mothers of the millions that I worry about. When their sons come home in coffins and there's no one to plough the land, no one to bring in the harvest, no one to sow for next year. Where will sorrow and anger take them?'

'To the gates of the palace,' replied Bertie, exhaling. 'The Tsar hasn't walked beyond those walls in months. He doesn't know anything. He doesn't see anything. He's got no bloody idea. Too busy drinking tea with his wife. Meanwhile the streets of Petrograd seethe. A fire is burning and it's being fuelled by the petrol of revolution. How many times have you heard them sing "La Marseillaise"?'

'Once or twice,' said Militza.

'I lie in bed at night, and from my hotel room window that looks out on to Nevsky I can hear it being sung in some alleyway, in some part of the city, every single night.'

'Not long now,' agreed the doctor, before grinding his cigarette butt into the carriage floor. 'Not long at all.'

They arrived back in Petrograd in the early hours of the following morning to be met by a fleet of ambulances sent from the Anglo-Russian hospital. They waited patiently most of the morning, shuttling back and forth with the wounded. Others, those who could walk aided or unaided, were transported to the same hospital by the few trucks that were at the Grand Duchess's disposal. By luncheon the train was empty, and all the soldiers had been processed.

'So,' said Bertie, standing on the platform, rubbing his hands together. 'A quick luncheon at the Astoria, a nap and the British mission are at the opera tonight, if you'd care to join us? I know Sir George would be delighted to see you.'

Militza stared at him. Her dress was covered in blood. Her body was shaking with exhaustion, her head was heavy with the images, the sounds, the cries and the acrid smells she had just experienced. Those poor young men, those poor young wives, the children, their mothers. The hell. The opera!

'I am not sure,' she replied.

'I know what you mean,' Bertie concurred. 'I have never been a huge fan of *The Queen of Spades*.'

Bread! Bread! Bread!

Down with the German woman!
Down with the war! Down with the Tsar!

The women of Petrograd

CHAPTER 4

March 1917, Petrograd

It started in the north of the city. The Vyborg District. Nadezhda and Brana were in the market at Sennaya Ploshchad when they heard. They wouldn't normally have travelled so far into the slums, but they were looking for herbs to restock the medicine chest after the train trip to the front and none were available anywhere else, and probably not even there. They were taking a chance. Everyone was taking a chance these days, walking the streets, leaving their houses, trying to find food. The atmosphere was tense, foreboding hung in the air, and no one looked anyone else in the eye.

'There's nothing to buy. I'm cold. I want to go home. Everyone's staring…' muttered Nadezhda, as she walked past yet another empty stall, warily side-stepping two gaunt-looking women, their wide eyes searching the empty tables.

'Just a few more minutes,' replied Brana.

'You've said that already.'

'There are usually *some* herbs here.'

'I don't know why Mama bothers with all these

silly old-fashioned tinctures in the first place. It's so unsophisticated.'

Brana stopped in her tracks. 'Enough!' She raised her rough leathery hand. 'Don't dismiss what you don't know.' She could feel her weathered cheeks flush a little. She wouldn't normally contradict the mistress's daughter, but Nadezhda had been on the train, and she'd seen those young men and how the herbs had helped.

'Why would I want to know?' Nadezhda shrugged, turning to look down at the hunched elderly woman with her pinched lips and thin woollen headscarf wrapped tightly around her wizened face. 'The whole witchcraft thing, the table tipping, the tarot. It's provincial. It's embarrassing.'

'It saved your life once.' Brana's tone was matter-of-fact, her stare was direct, her grey-filmed eyes didn't blink.

'No, it did *not*. Don't be so foolish!' Nadezhda laughed a little at the thought. 'God did that.'

They carried on in silence, scouring the stalls in the snow, Brana finally spotting a sprig of rosemary and some bunches of sage in the far corner of the market, just as a young woman came hurtling towards them, shouting at the top of her voice. 'The women from the textile factories are marching! They are chanting for bread, yelling "Down with the war!", "Down with the Tsar!", "Down with the German woman!"'

They'd had enough of the food shortages, the rising prices, the casualties, the deaths, the endless war; and now they'd downed tools and headed out on to the streets. It was a holiday to honour women, not that that mattered, not that anyone cared about much any more. There was nothing to celebrate. They were starving, they were exhausted, weak, enfeebled, and they wanted one thing only: to be able to feed their children and then – possibly – themselves.

It began with a small group, a few women, marching down the street with their home-made banners, but then they chanced upon the early workers' shift, coming out of the factories, and their numbers swelled as the day progressed. They started in their hundreds, but by 10 a.m. they'd grown to 20,000. By midday they were 50,000 and still they were marching. They were heading south, towards the Nevksy Prospekt, towards the Embankment and the Winter Palace. The young woman in the market was urging others to join them. She was handing out leaflets: 'Down with the bourgeois.' 'Down with the rich.' 'Down with the Tsar.' 'Down with autocracy.' Her angular face was earnest, with a scarf tied tightly under her sharp chin, and her pale eyes were on fire.

'You!' she said, pointing to Nadezhda, who was rigid with fear as she stood as close to Brana as possible. How she regretted putting on her fine boots today; how she hoped no one would notice her expensive, fur-lined gloves.

'Me?' Her stomach lurched.

'Can you read?' she asked, looking Nadezhda up and down.

Nadezhda hesitated, she looked at Brana. She hid her gloves behind her back. What was the right answer? The young woman didn't look threatening, and she was on her own, but you could never tell these days. 'Well—'

'Well, what?'

'Yes.' Nadezhda's voice was quiet. She didn't whisper her response so much as mumble it.

'Good,' replied the girl, grabbing at the leather satchel

she had slung across her chest. 'Here.' She pulled out a magazine with a graphic image of a young woman in a headscarf, with her fist in the air. Written in Cyrillic across the top was *Rabotnitsa* – woman worker. 'Take that,' she said. 'I'm not wasting it on the illiterate.'

'Thank you,' Nadezhda replied, looking down at the magazine. She felt a quiver of excitement that this young woman had picked her, of all people, out of the crowd. They were kindred spirits, modern women fighting for freedom. 'But it says here that it costs four kopeks.' Nadezhda reached in her purse to pay.

'Don't worry about that,' replied the girl. Then, clenching her fist and punching the air she grinned at Nadezhda and cried, '*Vive la révolution!*'

A few women in the market joined in. 'Revolution!' they replied, punching in the air.

Nadezhda smiled and, making a fist, punched the air in return. '*Vive la révolution!*'

'Oh, Brana! Did you see that? Did you see?' asked Nadezhda on the way home. 'Isn't it incredible? Incredible! I agree with all that they're saying. Down with the war, down with autocracy, and bread for all!'

'I did.'

'But don't you agree with them? You of all people must agree with them? You of all people must side with the poor.'

'I'm not sure you should bring that paper into the house,' said Brana as they walked home. 'Your mother won't like it.'

'I don't care what my mother thinks!'

Nadezhda's cheeks were flushed with excitement as she marched along the pavement, arms linked with Brana, clutching the magazine to her chest. Her footsteps were light. There was a spring in her stride as she picked her way along the frozen, snow-clogged pavements. Normally, she would have hailed a *droshky*, or ridden the tram, but today she wanted to walk, see the city, breathe in the smouldering stench of revolution. She felt alive for the first time since Oleg died. The colours of the street were brighter, even the grey, dank, freezing day did not touch her soul as it normally did. She was happy, she met the stares of others. Blood was pumping through her fine veins.

She breezed into the palace and up the stairs to the Blue Parlour, where she found her older sister, Marina, sitting by the fire, wrapped in a shawl, sewing a sampler, her little French bulldog, Mignon, with a yellow bow around his neck sitting next to her.

'Good God,' proclaimed Nadezhda flopping on the divan and letting the *Rabotnitsa* magazine slip out from under her arm. 'Have you been here all day? Sewing away?'

'Not the whole day.' Marina looked up. With her black eyes and heavy brows, she could only be a daughter of one of the Black Princesses – or the Black Peril, or the Black Pearls, or the Crows or the Cockroaches as her mother and aunt were called by the more malicious members of the court. 'I went to the Yacht Club for luncheon with Mother and Aunt Stana.'

'How exciting.' Nadezhda rolled her eyes a little.

'It was, actually,' she replied, putting down her sampler. 'Mr Rayner was there, and Olga Orlov. And everyone was talking about the banishment of poor Dmitry. He spent fourteen hours in his carriage without food or drink, apparently, and cried all the way to Persia.'

'He shouldn't have committed murder then, should he?' replied Nadezhda, tucking her hands between her knees. 'Poor lamb.'

'I swear you like Rasputin despite all the harm he's caused this family,' replied Marina. 'Or perhaps even because of it...'

'Think what you like.' Nadezhda shrugged.

Marina paused. 'Uncle Bimbo turned up at the club.'

'And what was his thrilling news? He'd found another place where they served sturgeon and peaches and the dancing girls were very fine?'

'No.' Marina looked a little put out. Her sister's mouth was curling unpleasantly, and she was aggressively spitting her words. 'He said Felix has also been exiled to one of his estates.'

'He's spoilt for choice.'

'Apparently it's the worst one, the small yellow manor house in Rakitnoye, Belgorod, right on the border with Ukraine.' She giggled slightly. 'It's got that black earth he abhors.'

'How lucky to have so many different earths to choose from!'

'What's wrong with you? Why are you being so mean?'

'I saw the revolution today! Look!' Nadezhda waved the radical magazine in front of her elder sister.

'Well, it didn't get very far, did it,' replied Marina. 'They broke some glass, stole some bread and were stopped by the Cossacks and the soldiers who fired on them.'

'They fired on women? Who were marching for bread?'

'Only in the air.'

'But they fired?'

'Didn't you hear that in the cheap seats?'

'No.'

'Anyway, the Tsar's gone back to the front to fight the Germans,' she continued. 'Papa and Uncle Nikolasha are both still in Tiflis and are not returning anytime soon, and the Grand Duchess Vladimir is off to Kislovodsk, to take the waters, apparently – she's finding the tension in the city too exhausting for words.' She picked up her sampler. 'It's amazing what you learn at the Yacht Club. Anyway, what do they want?'

'Who?'

'Your new Revolutionary friends. Bread? Peace?'

'Blood,' replied Nadezhda, picking up her magazine and leaving the room.

Little did she know as she lay in bed that night seething, listening to the music and tinkling of champagne glasses downstairs as her mother and her aunt entertained the British ambassador and his wife, that the rest of the city was seething with her.

They festered, boiled, plotted and planned. They cut flags from red cloth and painted slogans, sang songs and discussed the future and the end of the bourgeoisie. They waited until the early morning, when the dignitaries were fast asleep, working off their fat dinners and hangovers from the night before. As dawn broke, they rose.

The generals had underestimated them; the government officials had dismissed them. They would never do so again. For that morning tens of thousands started out, marching through the workers' districts, waving their banners, demanding an end to the war, an end to poverty, they shouted for bread, democracy and revolution. Although quite what the latter was, no one quite knew. At the Alexandrovsky Bridge, there was a pause. Several hundred Cossacks and soldiers were standing in their way; they were armed and could fire at any point. But instead, they smiled and stood aside and let the marchers cross. By lunchtime they had crossed the Neva and were heading towards Nevsky Prospekt. With its wide boulevard and beautiful shops, it was the ideal place for a demonstration.

Nadezhda was at Aux Gourmets when she heard them singing down the street. Militza had gone to meet Bertie for a cup of coffee at the Astoria Hotel and Nadezhda, having accompanied her mother, had grown so tired of the conversation – all about what was going on at Tsarskoye Selo, which of the Grand Duchesses had a cold, or was it measles – that she'd left to see if she could buy some sugared almonds, anything, in the capital's usually bustling and most luxurious delicatessen.

Famous for having lobsters on ice and fish in aspic in its expansive window displays, Aux Gourmets was usually equally sumptuous inside. Among the potted palms and shining duck-egg blue tiles, there would be English lamb shipped from Ostende via Paris, milk-fed suckling pigs from Moscow, and wheels and wheels of Brie. But today, as Nadezhda pressed her nose against the glass, the window displays were bare and, as she looked through the doors, the shop was empty save for a few triangles of cheese on the counter and some curled cuts of cold meats. The prices were beyond most of the inhabitants of the city.

It was the 'Marseillaise' that she heard first, and the sound of whistles and drums, hammering a beat for pounding feet.

'*Marchez, marchez!*'

'*Aux armes, citoyens!*'

'*Liberté, liberté, chérie!*'

There were thousands of them, blocking the avenue, their red banners waving against the cold blue sky. They were singing with their fists in the air, and faces beaming, moving as one. It was intoxicating. The police were nowhere to be seen; they'd abandoned their posts long ago. In amongst the crowd were soldiers, still wearing uniform, who'd put down their weapons rather than putting down the crowd. The few Cossacks on the street simply watched, their *nagaikas* – short whips – by their sides, their swords in their belts.

Nadezhda watched breathlessly, her eyes wide, her mouth gaping. She held tightly on to the granite corner between Nevsky and Bolshaya Morskaya, too scared to join them, but too transfixed to leave. They were thronging past her, chanting, marching, the nails on their boots drubbing the pavement. She could smell them as they thundered past – sweat, dust, dirt, desperation, dignity, stale *samogon* and cigarettes. Vodka sales had been banned and there were rumours that all the grain had disappeared to make moonshine – *samogon*. Maybe that was true, but Nadezhda didn't care. She gripped the firm stone of the building, for fear she might swoon. She felt her feet start to move to the beat of the drum.

'Nadezhda Petrovna!' came a voice behind her. 'Is that you?'

She turned around. 'Nikolai Vladimirovich? What are you doing here?'

The sight of Prince Nicholas Orlov dressed in his red guard's uniform, his face flushed, his green eyes shining, his normally well-coiffed thick dark hair ruffled and hanging across his face, was something of a shock. Charming, witty and a little wild, Prince Nicholas was Marina's friend. The only son of Fat Orlov and Princess Olga Orlov (otherwise known as Flesh and Bone, due to Fat Orlov's corpulence and his wife's extreme thinness), Prince Nicholas was an ebullient, urbane fellow, famed for his exquisite mazurka and excellent horsemanship. He was seven years Nadezhda's senior, most of the discerning ladies of Petrograd were madly in love with him, and she was amazed he even knew her name.

'Gosh,' he said, taking a step back and running his hands through his thick hair. 'When did you get so grown up?' He grinned a wide smile.

'I've just turned nineteen years old,' she replied, hotly.

'And I have been in the Caucasus,' he replied. 'Forgive me.' He picked up her gloved hand and kissed the back of it. 'I have no manners at all. How are you? How's your mama? Your dear sister? Your brother? I know how your uncle is, my father has been with him in Tiflis for months! He is *all* I hear about. But I am not sure they know all this is going on.' He paused and, still holding her hand, stared at the marchers over Nadezhda's shoulder. 'Are you thinking of joining them?'

'No.' She shook her head. Her pearl earrings quivered.

'Are you sure?' he said, moving a step closer, an amused smile on his lips. 'You look as if you want to.'

'No, really,' she replied. 'It might be dangerous.'

'Not as dangerous as the front, come on,' he said and, scooping up her arm, he whisked her around the corner and into Nevksy Prospekt, where they were immediately swept up into the marching crowd.

'Bread! Bread!' they shouted. 'Down with the war! Down with the German woman!'

Prince Nicholas joined in with gusto. He linked his left arm through Nadezhda's and pumped his right fist. Since the Tsarina, the 'German woman', had had his father banished to the Caucasus just over two years ago for criticising Rasputin, Nicholas had few qualms about demanding her demise. He shouted and marched and kept Nadezhda in his tight supportive grip. It was so exhilarating, the noise, the marching, the force of will in the crowd, that she felt a quiver of adrenaline and the hairs on the back of her neck stood up with excitement. Her arms were covered in goosepimples. The energy was contagious.

'Down with the war! Down with the German woman!'

'*Marchez, marchez! Liberté, liberté!*'

To drums and the whistles, Nicholas and Nadezhda marched along with the crowd.

'Down with the war! Bread! Bread!' Nadezhda mumbled, too fearful to chant.

'And down with the German woman!' Nicholas nodded, grinning away.

There were thousands of them, tens of thousands, as many as two hundred thousand, marching up Nevsky, moving as one. They marched towards the Admiralty, the Embankment and the Winter Palace. Nicholas was becoming increasingly vocal. It wasn't his chanting that drew the attention of nearby demonstrators, but the bright, crimson colours of his officer's uniform.

'Oi!' shouted a heavy-set man, with purple cheeks and an unkempt beard. 'What are you doing here? Comrade officer. Mr My Lord. Mr Keeper of Serfs!' He showered spittle as he spoke.

'Bread! Bread!' chanted Nicholas, pumping his fist, ignoring the question.

'Oi!' spat the man again. 'Who are you? What factory are you from, Serf Keeper?'

'Down with the war! Down with the German woman!' Nicholas continued.

'Oi!' The sturdy man shoved Nicholas, hard, in the back. He tripped two steps forwards. 'We've got ourselves an imposter here, lads! An imposter!'

'Down with the war! Down with the German woman!' Nicholas stared straight ahead.

'Lads! Comrades!' came a gritty visceral cry.

'Quick!' Nicholas hissed at Nadezhda and, spotting his chance, he pulled her down a side alley. Taking her hand, they ran.

It was narrow and dark, but they ran on. Nicholas looked over his shoulder; the heavy, bearded man had not been able to follow them, he'd been swept up in the crowd, pulled along as he shouted and pointed at them, his fingers jabbing the air.

They came to the end of the passage, their shoulders heaving, their lungs burning. Fighting for breath, they found themselves in a courtyard, where four sets of double doors led up to numerous filthy-looking apartments.

'Thank goodness for that!' exclaimed Nicholas, his bright green eyes shining, his hair flopping over his face. 'I thought we were in serious trouble!' He started to laugh.

'Are you normally this foolish?' Nadezhda was doubled over, her hands on her thighs, as she coughed and tried to breathe. Wearing heeled boots, a fitted buttoned jacket and a full skirt, she was not dressed to run for her life in the snow.

'Are you normally this ungrateful?' he replied.

'Ungrateful?' She stood up and looked at him. 'What on earth do I have to be grateful for?'

'I saved your life.'

'No, you didn't!'

'I did. If I hadn't spotted the alley, then you'd have been in terrible trouble.'

'You were the one who was in trouble. I was fine.' She looked indignant. Nicholas laughed. 'He was only upset with you. In your guard's uniform and your appalling chanting.'

'And then he would have gone after you.'

'Me? Why would he have done that?'

'He'd have presumed we were married.'

'And why on earth should he presume that?' Nadezhda took a step backwards. The man really was rude. And impertinent.

'Because we shall be, one day!' he declared.

'We shall most certainly not! I'm engaged to someone else.' She blushed so deeply even her ears flushed pink. 'Or I was,' she added, before turning around to walk back up the alley.

'I wouldn't go that way!' he called after her. 'It's full of rioters. I think you'll find this is a more convenient way home.'

It's damn hard lines asking for bread and only getting a
bullet!

Bertie Stopford

CHAPTER 5

March 1917, Petrograd

The next day Nadezhda slipped out early. Dressed in an old coat she used for walking in the woods at Znamenka and a scarf she'd found at the back of her chest of drawers, she set out into the cold. And it was cold. Snowing, grey, freezing; a glacial bitterness that chilled her to the bone before she'd even closed the heavy wooden door. But this was the costume of her brothers and sisters, and after what happened with Prince Nicholas Orlov the day before, she was determined to fit in, determined to march, and determined to end the vicious war that was taking the lives of young men, workers, farmers, labourers; those crying boys, those wounded weeping souls she'd nursed all the way back from the front, but most of all Oleg.

'Brana!' Nadezhda was startled in the courtyard by a shadowy figure that appeared out of the dark. She tugged at her coat, hiding furtively behind the thin collar. 'It's not even dawn! What are you doing? Where have you been?'

'Out.'

'On the streets? All night? Where?' Nadezhda looked the

old woman up and down. She looked cold, her long nose was dripping in the icy air, her cheeks were ruddy, her felt boots were damp with snow. And what did she have in her cloth bag? 'What's that?'

'Listen,' Brana hissed through the gaps in her teeth. 'I haven't seen you and you haven't seen me.' Nadezhda was a little taken aback. 'Do you hear me?' Nadezhda looked down at the bag again. It was seemingly stuffed with sheets of paper. Or were they leaflets? 'And never you mind what's in my bag, it's none of your business. Now go! Before I change my mind and call for your mother, or shout for your brother and tell them you are intent on walking the streets on your own!'

When Militza rose a few hours later, she was surprised not to see her youngest daughter sitting at the dining table with Marina, Stana and her daughter, Elena.

'Has anyone seen Nadezhda this morning?' she asked, adding a few drops of elixir to her morning coffee.

She was running low, she noticed, holding the blue bottle up to the light. She really should try and track down that elusive Tibetan Buddhist, Dr Badmaev, or if not send a servant to his pharmacy on Nevsky to see if they had any more elixirs or tinctures or, indeed, anything left at all. Unless the Tsar had taken the lot. Dr Peter Badmaev had made himself invaluable to the court, by supplying Nicholas with copious quantities of cocaine and hashish. The Tsar and indeed the Tsarina declared Dr Badmaev's tinctures had quite cured the Tsar of all his stomach aches and insomnia. So much so that the Tsar was a huge advocate of the good doctor's tinctures; he used to declare that 'everyone needed a little cocaine every day'.

'Where on earth could Nadezhda be?' continued Militza, draining her glass.

'She's becoming quite the *feministka* these days, isn't she?' said Elena, stirring what appeared to be the last of the black cherry jam into her tea. 'She'd fit in quite well in the hospital. The Red Cross girls are all reading those sorts of magazines. You can tell who they are,' she added, taking a sip of her tea, 'because they have all cut off their hair.'

'Well, I hope she's not out on the streets,' said Stana. 'I spoke to my darling Nikolasha this morning on the telephone and even he's heard, all the way down in Tiflis, that there are marchers on the streets of Petrograd – which is saying something for the news to travel that far south.'

'Apparently, the Tsar sent a telegram to General Khabalov last night,' said Militza.

'Is he the commander of the Petrograd military?' asked Marina, flopping back into her chair.

'He is,' replied Militza. 'And he's asked him to put down the rebellion immediately.'

'How immediately?' asked Stana, stirring her tea.

'In a day.'

'A day? But you can't put down a rebellion in a day,' she said, looking a little puzzled. 'Unless you use violence. And then that would be an open declaration of war by Russia on its own people.'

Militza's hands began to sweat, and her heart raced. She closed her eyes. She really wasn't sure if this potent combination of coffee and cocaine was good for her early in the morning on an empty stomach. She put her chin to her chest and exhaled through her lips. The images, the wretched visions that kept plaguing her, came thick and fast. The red flags, the huge crowds, the noise, the drums, the whistles, the marching, the sound of hobnail on stone, the chatter of machine-gun fire, the silence and then the blood. It was everywhere. It was unbearable. When would it stop? As blood drained from her cheeks and lips, she could see it all over the streets of the city. Splashed over the cobbles, spilt on the tram tracks, the snow on the pavements turning pink. She gasped and threw her head back. Her staring eyes were as black and glassy as obsidian and a headache gripped her temples.

'Where is Nadezhda?'

Nadezhda was hurrying past the Stroganov Palace. She could hear the singing and feel the energy pulling her along the street. She was walking in the middle of the road, her arms swinging, not feeling the cold; she didn't care about the cars and the sledges whose drivers were shouting, or honking, at her to get out of the way. She narrowly avoided a *droshky* as she turned sharp left at the Fontanka River. The streets were busy, despite the stench of revolution. Children and babies in perambulators were all out for the morning with their parents. It was a Saturday, and this small moment of respite was being enjoyed by everyone.

She passed Rasputin's apartment on Gorokhovaya Street. There was still a small crowd of followers outside, mainly women of a certain age, buttoned up against the wind, holding limp flowers. A couple of jaded, bored-looking secret police, easily distinguishable by their heavy greatcoats and thick fur collars, were on the opposite side of the street. Nadezhda paused. It was hard to know what they were waiting for. A resurrection? An explanation? Or for the great *mujik* Rasputin to appear, striding up the street, bottle of Madeira in hand, a lady of dubious values at his side and for everyone to laugh at the propaganda machine that had fooled them once again. He lives! They lied! Just like before. Nadezhda crossed herself and held on to the tiny bottle of water she'd placed that morning in her coat pocket. Whatever was going to happen today, He would protect her.

The demonstrators were easy to find, for there were thousands of them, teeming through the streets. She joined them on Bolshaya Morskaya, as they chanted their slogans, waved their flags and sang the 'Marseillaise'. There was a carnival atmosphere in the crowd. One of excitement, empowerment. There was a defiance, certainly, but also an innocent enthusiasm, a giddiness that was hugely contagious.

'Bread! Bread! Bread!' they shouted, their faces turned towards the sky, red flags rippling in the breeze.

'Bread! Bread!' Nadezhda joined in, smiling at the fellow next to her. He was a young chap, too juvenile for the front, but holding an anti-war banner all the same. He nodded and shouted louder as they marched up the street.

In front of her, with red ribbons plaited through her blonde hair, was a little girl of about eight years old. Her high-pitched voice was easily discernible in the chanting. She held her mother's hand tightly as she marched, her knees rising boldly up in front of her. Her mother appeared thin and worn, her coat was ragged around the edges and her boots looked as if they belonged to someone else, but she kept smiling down at her daughter, encouraging her on.

'Bread! Bread! Bread! Down with the war! Down with the German woman!'

They were just near the Astoria Hotel when the machine guns opened fire and the singing turned to screaming.

The crowd which had been so united, marching as one, scattered suddenly, in all directions, like startled mice in a pantry. Some ran towards St Isaac's Cathedral, whose golden dome was visible through the fog-grey sky, others headed off towards the river, preferring to take their chances out on the ice. Skidding and sliding, tumbling over each other, they'd rather risk falling through the cracks of the thawing water than face the machine guns mounted overhead. High up in the roofs they were shooting the people below. The gunners had been waiting. They'd known they'd come this way. Children were trampled in the terrified rush. Others succumbed, sucked underfoot, as they fell to the stampede. Grown men lay flat on the snow, as if by playing dead they would not catch the attention of the snipers. A well-dressed young woman, probably not even part of the protest, was knocked down dead by a fleeing motor car. A sledge turned over, throwing its driver into the air. He died immediately on impact with the road. Workers flattened themselves against any wall they could find; some were crouching in doorways, others under arches, not daring to move. And still the machine-gun fire continued. And blood spilled on the streets.

Nadezhda was horrified, petrified with fear. She simply stood in the middle of the road, unable to move, shivering with her hand over her mouth. She could see the blonde hair and red ribbons of the little girl in front of her lying in the snow; the rest of her limp body was underneath a tram. Death and destruction were all around her. She wept. The short sharp machine-gun bursts made her jump. She frantically scanned the sky, trying to work out where they were located. But she couldn't move.

There was a lull in the firing and people leapt up and scrambled to safety.

'Come here!' shouted a young man in a brown cap with a red scarf tied around his neck, grabbing her firmly by the arm and pulling her along with him. 'This way!' He dragged her towards the Astoria Hotel, shoving her hard, flat against the wall. She hit her head and grazed her cheek against the sharp bricks, but managed to find enough space to stand, as he leant, panting right next to her.

'How many are there?' he hissed.

'I don't know, five, six? How many do you see?'

They fired again. Streaks of bullets sent little puffs of snow up into the air as they whistled into the ground.

'I'm not sure,' he replied.

She glanced at him. His straight nose and determined jaw made him look stronger, older, than his age. His smooth cheeks showed the first glimpses of a beard.

'There are two on the roof over there.' He nodded.

A young woman suddenly ran out from a side alley and down the street. It was inexplicable. It was madness. She ran, waving a red flag with 'Bread' scrawled across it in barely legible writing. The snipers opened fire and the bullets, puffs of snow, hailed around her. Nadezhda couldn't watch. She shut her eyes tightly, as if to erase the image from her mind.

Her toes curled in her shoes and her fingernails dug into the palms of her fists. The woman screamed as she fell; her body thumped as she hit the street.

'Dear God… bless her,' whispered Nadezhda, as the guns paused and she slowly opened her eyes. 'What are they doing? Why are they killing us? Why are they so cruel?' The young man next to her did not reply. 'Don't you know?' She turned to look at him.

His eyes were open, but he didn't speak. She pushed him a little with her elbow and slowly, to her horror, he fell to the ground in front of her. His cap in the snow, his fist still clenched, his face looking up at the sky, his chest crimson with blood. Nadezhda stared, unable to comprehend what had just happened. There seemed no reason for him to be dead. She didn't hear the shot; didn't hear him cry out. Nothing. How was it possible for a life, such a vital force, to be extinguished so suddenly and soundlessly? He'd saved her life and she didn't even know his name.

The firing started again. They were aiming into the shadows, hoping to catch the stragglers under the arches. People were screaming, yelling for them to stop.

'Bastards!' they yelled. 'Capitalist scum! The Devil is waiting for you in hell!'

The more they shouted, the more they fired. She had to move. If this young man could be taken so easily then so could she. She looked right. The doors of the Astoria Hotel were so close. Just around the corner. If she ran, if she ran fast, she could surely get inside? The question was, when should she run? When should she take her chance? She put her hand in her pocket and clutched at her small bottle of 'holy' water. 'May the Lord save me, may the Lord grant that I am invisible, may the Lord make me a shadow to fly like a bird on the wind. May the power of the *mujik* save my life,' she mumbled under her breath, her eyes half closed, her long black eyelashes fluttering. Should she run now? Or should she wait? Or would the shooting only get worse?

She hitched her skirts, rocking backwards from her heels to toes, daring herself, steeling herself for the sprint. The machine-gun fire was coming in shorter, sharper spurts – maybe they were low on ammunition? Maybe they'd quenched their thirst for killing.

She took a deep breath and went for it. With her skirts bunched up in her fists, her knees high, she ran as fast as she'd ever run in her life. The bullets whistled past, singing in her ears, smacking into the walls behind her. She made it to the corner, she slipped and fell onto snow and ice. There was no time to think; she pulled herself up immediately and ran again with huge strides towards the doors of the hotel. Then she threw herself through them with such force that she ended up falling and rolling over on to the red woollen carpet in reception.

She looked up to a sea of faces. Some were obviously marchers who'd taken shelter, others were simply about to take luncheon in the hotel, on their way for a drink at the bar and had been caught up in the mêlée. The hall and doorway were crammed, but still the gloved hand of the doorman reached down to help up to her feet.

'My lady,' he said. 'You're safe in here.'

'Thank you,' she replied, panting, her shoulders rising and falling as she caught her breath.

'Were you passing? Or here to visit anyone in particular?'

he asked, taking in the thin winter coat and the yellow flowered scarf that had slipped off her head and now hung loosely around her neck.

'Do you know if Mr Stopford is still staying here? I think I might need his assistance.'

'He is most certainly. He was here a few minutes ago. But I think you'll find him back in his room on the third floor, balcony room, overlooking the square. Room 322.'

Bertie Stopford opened his door in a collarless shirt. Nadezhda had never seen him so informally dressed.

'Goodness gracious!' he exclaimed. Her face was grazed, her hair wild and her flimsy clothes drenched with melted snow. 'I hardly recognised you! Are you all right? Do come in. Were you caught up in all the dreadfulness downstairs?' Nadezhda staggered forward. Only an Englishman could describe a massacre as a dreadfulness, she thought, as he closed the door. 'I've been trying to get outside to help for the last half an hour, but it was impossible. Sit down. What can I do? Does your mother know you are here? Would you like a brandy? I always find brandy helpful, in almost every situation.'

She took a few steps and collapsed into his arms. The poor man didn't quite know what to do with himself. Unused to emotional young ladies, he stood, stiff as a board, and gently patted her back, while she sobbed onto his starched white shirt.

'There, there. It will all be fine,' he said. Although he knew, in his heart, it would not. 'They'll come to their senses. They will. They must. It's damn hard lines asking for bread and only getting a bullet,' he added, before disengaging and immediately lighting a cigarette.

★ ★ ★

For the rest of that afternoon Nadezhda remained in Bertie's hotel room overlooking the square. It was impossible to leave, too dangerous to risk the snipers still on the roofs. She sat on a hard, upright gilt chair, nursing an un-drunk brandy at the small marble-topped table in the centre of his room, unable to comprehend fully what had just happened. Bertie stood with his long nose pressed against the cold windowpane, observing the streets below, scanning the rooftops, checking on the bodies in the snow. There were three sets of machine guns that he could see and fourteen dead bodies as far as he could make out. There were a few wounded but mostly those who were still capable had managed to crawl or drag themselves to safety. For someone normally so decisive, Stopford did not know what to do. He'd heard this was coming. Rumours were rife in the embassy that the Bolsheviks were on the march. Ready to make good use of the misery in the city, famine in the slums and the disaffection amongst the troops. They'd been gleaning intelligence on various characters for a while. Names were being bandied about. Vladimir Ilyich Ulyanov, or Lenin as he was calling himself. Trotsky. The ambassador had been warning the Tsar for months now. Bertie placed various telephone calls to the embassy, his Grand Duchess's palace and the small apartment where Oswald Rayner was staying, just to make sure they were all abreast of the situation. Nadezhda had counselled against him telephoning her mother, preferring to share the news when she arrived home. She did not want panic to tear through the Nikolayevsky Palace.

★ ★ ★

Although it already had. Militza was beside herself, pacing up and down the chequered marble floor of the Blue Parlour, smoking cigarettes and barking orders at anyone who was brave enough to enter the room. The headache that had begun that morning was becoming more and more acute. Brana was quizzed but she gave nothing away, not even the fact that she'd seen Nadezhda leave the palace before breakfast. She did however offer to walk the streets of Petrograd in search of her while Stana questioned Marina and Elena to see if they had any idea where she might have gone. It was only when Prince Nicholas Orlov called at the palace around four o'clock that afternoon, that the seriousness of the situation came to light.

'They're shooting in the streets, killing them like dogs,' he said, sipping his unsweetened tea, his legs crossed on the blue divan.

Militza was standing by the fireplace, still fighting the terrible visions that danced before her eyes. 'Does the Tsar know this? I can't believe he would ever sanction such a thing.' Her headache was now so powerful she had to close her right eye and massage her temple with the tip of one index finger.

'He gave the orders, didn't he?' replied Stana, sitting on the sofa opposite, wringing her hands repeatedly. 'What was he thinking? Ordering his police, his army against his own people? Who is advising the Tsar? Why isn't he speaking to my husband? Nikolasha would never have sanctioned such a thing. The man's mind has gone. He's taken too many of Badmaev's herbs, hashish, cocaine, he can't think straight.

Not that he ever could. He's always been a fool. A terrible fool. Weak. Fatalistic. Influenced by his wife. Paranoia and stupidity are a deadly combination.'

'Order is breaking down, that's for sure,' said Nicholas. 'You can feel it, you can see it. There's been looting, smashing of shop windows. When Nadezhda and I were marching—'

'You were marching?' Militza stopped and removed her fingertip from her temple. 'When?'

'Yesterday.'

'Yesterday?' added Marina, her dark eyebrows knitted as she sat a little more stiffly on the blue velvet divan. 'With Nadezhda?' She laughed at the ridiculousness of such an idea. 'Why? How?'

'We met by chance.'

'Chance? I didn't even know you were back in Petrograd,' she replied.

'I've just arrived,' he said, smiling.

'And you bumped into Nadezhda, of all people?'

'On the street, yes.'

'What was she doing there?' asked Militza.

'Watching the marchers.'

'I told you she was becoming quite the *feministka*,' added Elena. 'It's a cancer.'

'All the headstrong girls are,' replied Stana, looking at her own daughter. Why does comfort and privilege always breed such complacency? If only Elena knew what she and Militza had been through when they first arrived in this city. The struggles. The animosity. The blatant hatred. Maybe it was better she did not.

'Where is Nadezhda now, though, that's the question?'

said Militza, glancing out of the window and across the Neva at the gathering darkness.

'She's a smart girl, I am sure she can look after herself,' said Nicholas, taking another sip of his tea. 'But I am happy to go out and look for her if you'd like?'

'Brana is looking, and she'll be searching in places that you and I could barely imagine,' said Militza.

'You?' Marina sat back a little in her seat. 'And why would you do that? You barely know her.'

Prince Orlov put down his glass of tea. The whole family, a sea of ladies, was looking at him. 'Well,' he shrugged, 'I have some free time before curtain up at the Mariinsky.'

Outside, the streets were empty, no trams were running, there were no motor cars, no carriages and only the very occasional sledge. After the chaos of earlier in the day, the silence was overwhelming.

Prince Orlov walked slowly out of the palace, towards the centre of town, his collar turned up against the cold, his shoulders hunched and his hands in his pockets. His footsteps were dulled by the freshly falling snow. He looked across the river as he walked over Troitsky Bridge towards the Summer Gardens and the Winter Palace beyond. It was lit up like a frosted gingerbread house at Christmas. Lights were shining in the windows and twinkling out across the ice of the frozen river. He could hear nothing but the sighs of the wind and the soft crunch of his feet in the snow. It was almost as if the city were holding its breath, bracing itself, as if it knew that the next few days were to be ten days that shook the world. But for the moment, all was quiet and all was calm. The dead had been taken off the streets and the snow had covered their tracks.

He was halfway across the river when he saw a figure walking towards him on the same side of the bridge. Slight and hunched against the cold, all the strength seemed to have drained from its legs, only determination keeping it going.

It was by the light of the street lamp that he knew it was her. The shape of her shoulders, the angle of the arms, it was as if he'd sculpted her himself, and every curve and line was etched on his brain.

'Nadezhda!' he shouted. She looked up, but saw nothing. His cry was taken away on the wind. 'Nadezhda!' he shouted again. 'Here!' She stopped. He ran, shouting her name, over and over. His coat flew open, his scarf flew out either side of him as he sprinted towards her. 'There you are! There you are!'

'Here I am!' she stammered, quivering with cold.

He stopped in front of her and tore off his own greatcoat, pulling it tight around her. 'Where on earth have you been? Your family is worried about you.'

'Me!' She laughed a little. 'It's themselves they should worry about. Themselves. And every single one of their friends.'

The soldiers are now arresting officers, now setting them free, evidently they don't know themselves what they are supposed to do or what they want.

Zinaida Gippius, Poet and Novelist

CHAPTER 6

March 1917, Petrograd

That night, Militza and Stana went to the ballet at the Mariinsky Theatre to watch *Swan Lake*. They had tickets, the theatre was open. It seemed a terrible waste not to go and anyway they were looking forward to it. Everyone had said that the production was extremely good.

They took their seats alongside the slim and exquisitely dressed Princess Olga Orlov, who was on delightful form as she still couldn't believe the unexpected return of her only child, Nicholas, now sitting the other side of her. Marina and Elena were also there, only Nadezhda had remained behind. After crossing the bridge, she'd entered the palace alone and lied to everyone, complaining she had a headache and that she had fallen in the snow and grazed her face. The idea of sitting in the theatre, dressed in finery, along with the rest of the aristocracy, while the corpses of her fellow marchers froze solid in the snow, made her stomach turn. She could not make small talk; she could not concentrate or control her shaking and shivering. Oddly, Bertie hadn't made it either. He'd been detained at the British Embassy, or so he said. There had been a request from the Tsar and his family to the British government and his first cousin King George V, which regrettably had been turned down.

Militza sat in her red and gilt chair in the box, pretending to be absorbed in the dancing and the exquisite choreography, hoping Tchaikovsky's score might go some way towards silencing the voices in her head and quietening the terrible sense of foreboding in her soul. She could hear the machine guns outside in the street; they all could. But the orchestra played on and the audience pretended not to notice as the dancers tensed at the rattling of the guns, and the percussion played a little louder. Even the surprise arrival of chilled Moët & Chandon champagne during the interval didn't relieve matters. Talk of the revolution was on everyone's lips.

'Vladimir is terribly worried,' confirmed Princess Olga, referring to her gourmet-food-loving, motor-car-enthusiast husband, Fat Orlov. 'He told me a simply ghastly story about how the sailors of the Baltic Fleet killed all their officers.' She shook her head. 'I can't tell you how.' She raised a white kid glove at the horror of it all.

'They threw them onto their burning engines when they were still alive,' Elena elaborated. 'I heard about it yesterday at the hospital. No one came out alive.'

'I wonder if any of *us* will come out of this alive,' mumbled Marina, taking a sip of her chilled champagne. 'Did you hear how furious everyone was that they were feeding black bread to the city's horses? There's no hay.' She shrugged. 'How else are they supposed to keep them alive?'

'When you're marching for bread and you find out they

are feeding it to the horses rather than your children, it's not going to go down well, is it?' said Nicholas brusquely. 'One horse eats the same amount per day as ten men. And there are eighty thousand horses. That's a lot of hungry children.'

'That's also a lot of hungry horses.' Marina smiled tightly. 'Poor things.'

'Poor things, indeed,' replied Nicholas, draining his drink.

'Shall we go back in?' asked Princess Olga, who'd never been fond of tension of any kind. 'Take our seats and watch the second half?'

'I think I might just go home,' said Militza suddenly.

'Oh, really?' queried Princess Olga.

'I need to check on Nadezhda. She said she didn't feel well.'

'Would you like me to escort you?' asked Nicholas, walking towards her in the theatre bar.

'You?' said Marina, staring at him, small red patches of irritation, or perhaps jealousy, popping up on her cheeks.

'I am not a huge fan of the ballet. And you should not be travelling alone.' He bowed his head. 'I would consider it my good fortune to escort you home.'

Outside the theatre, the streets were busy and the shooting had apparently ceased. There was not a *droshky* or a tram to be seen, but everyone was out, on foot, travelling in groups, some had red banners, hanging limply, others were linking arms, talking animatedly. It was like being at a country fair, a street party, yet they were directionless, wondering what to do next.

Militza and Prince Nicholas stood, watching, seemingly invisible to the crowds.

'Are the trams on strike again?' asked Militza, as they stood on the corner waiting for her motor car.

'Most probably.'

'They have been for days, I think. Not that I have ever been in one,' she added with a wry laugh. She looked around her at the somnambulant crowd. 'It seems as if everything is falling apart.'

'Well, there's no food,' he said, shrugging. 'My mother's employing a maid to queue for bread. That's all she does. She stands all night long, waiting for the shops to open. Some people are queuing for forty hours only to find the shelves are empty. You can see why they are angry. They are hungry. And now they're shooting at them. God knows where it will end.'

'I can see where it will end.' Militza closed her eyes. 'I can see exactly where it will end. And it looks like hell.'

Militza's motor car arrived and they sat in silence, staring out of the windows at the gangs walking through the streets, gathering around the burning fires. Some were armed, wielding weapons they didn't know how to handle. The motor car proceeded slowly, past patches of snow that glowed black with blood in the streetlight, mute witness to the shootings and the killings that had occurred earlier that day. As they approached the English Embankment, they noticed some shop windows were smashed, and there was a group of young men looting what appeared to be a patisserie. Militza stared, transfixed, as they fell over each other, climbing through the shattered plate-glass window, pushing and shoving and grabbing. There was something deeply distressing about grown men fighting over cake.

'The vices, crimes and filth,' she mumbled to herself.

Driving towards Palace Bridge, it suddenly became apparent that the drawbridges had been raised to stop the protesters from coming into the centre of town. Not that it appeared to make much difference, for both Militza and Nicholas could see the frozen Neva was crawling with people, shadows, flags. They were making the crossing despite the will of the authorities, the demands of the Duma at the Tauride Palace and, frankly, common sense. The car paused at the entrance to Palace Square to let a mob of workers cross the road. Better to keep a low profile than to sound the horn. The chauffeur had already seen too many motors battered and scratched that day. Some had even been requisitioned, driven with such recklessness by those who'd never sat behind a wheel that it was a wonder there were not more corpses on the street.

Militza opened her window as the airlessness in the car was overwhelming. She stuck her chin out and inhaled the cold night air. The smell of disinfectant and the acrid, metal notes of blood were unmistakable. She looked down at the pink clotted snow by the side of the road. Someone had been wounded there and someone else had tried to save them, leaving behind the struggle and the reek of helplessness.

'Down the with the war! Down with the *burzhúi*!' A shout came from across the road.

'Down with the what?' whispered Militza, swiftly closing her window.

'The bourgeoisie,' said Nicholas.

'And who exactly are *they* these days?'

'Anyone,' replied Nicholas, counting off on his fingers. 'Anyone rich, Jewish, German, anyone who's a member of the intelligentsia, anyone who's read a book, bathed, has blonde hair, who wears spectacles to do their job.'

'Spectacles! Anyone who doesn't till the soil, then?'

'Exactly. Anyone with smooth hands and a starched white shirt.' He looked down at what he was wearing.

'I think we should drive on, at speed.' Militza tapped the chauffeur's front seat.

'Of course, madame,' he replied.

They drove past the Winter Palace, where another larger crowd appeared to be gathering in earnest around a flaming brazier. Lurking further down the Embankment were groups of Cossacks, patrolling the bridges. They appeared like visions, emerging from the white steam that rose off the backs of their horses.

'All looks quiet over there,' said Nicholas, peering through the glass at his ancestral home – the finest neoclassical palace in Petrograd, the Marble Palace, so-called because over thirty different shades of stone had been used to decorate the outside of the building.

Over Troitsky Bridge, which was one of the few bridges still open, towards the Peter and Paul Fortress, which was home to some of the capital's most violent criminals. The golden spires appeared undisturbed by the mayhem across the river. The disorder and destruction differed from street to street. Even the battleship *Aurora* with its three huge funnels glinting in the moonlit appeared still, calm, moored awaiting its refit just by the Nikolayevsky Palace on Petrovsky Embankment.

As the car passed through the wrought-iron gates and the chauffeur got out to open Militza's door, Nadezhda came tearing out of the palace. Militza had only just manged to stand up when she threw herself at her mother.

'Thank GOD!' she exclaimed, hugging her mother. 'Thank GOD, thank God, thank God!'

'Darling...' Militza held her daughter tightly. She smelt of sweat and fear. 'What's been going on? Where's the doorman, where's the butler? Where is everyone?'

Nadezhda's face was white in the moonlight, her long dark hair was tied up as if mid-toilette and she appeared half-undressed, in a chemise, a shawl, and she had nothing on her bare feet.

'What's been going on?' asked Nicholas, running around from the other side of the car.

'Nicholas?' Nadezhda looked confused.

'He was escorting me home from the ballet,' replied Militza, gathering up her daughter and heading back towards the house. 'I'd had enough, it seemed odd to be in a theatre when the streets were on fire.' It was only as she approached the steps that she realised the front door was open, wide open. It had apparently been forced and was hanging off its hinges.

'Roman!' she said, more than a little panicked as she crossed the threshold to find her son, sitting in the hallway, dressed as the cook in a white apron and white toque, nursing a balloon of brandy.

'Mother,' he replied, sitting on the hard gilt chair. 'Thank God you're here.'

'Are you all right?' Nicholas's forehead was furrowed as he glanced from Nadezhda to Roman. 'You look as if you've seen a ghost.'

'Not quite a ghost,' Roman replied, taking a very large slug of his brandy. 'But I damn near became one.'

'There were six of them with guns,' added Nadezhda.

'*You've* only just crawled out from under the bed. I had to deal with the bastards. They were hammering on the door, shouting for Uncle Nikolasha. "Grand Duke Nikolai Nikolayevich, come out!"' he imitated, shouting and cupping his hand around his mouth for good measure. 'They were yelling, over and over, and when it was obvious he wasn't here, they shouted for Papa. "Grand Duke Peter Nikolayevich, come out!" And that's when you hid.' He nodded towards Nadezhda. 'And then, they must have a list or something, as they were going through the names, shouting them all. Eventually they came to mine, and they were hammering on the door, and there was no one here to speak to them and I didn't want them to ransack the palace or shoot anyone…'

'Where was, where is, everyone else?' asked Militza.

'They've gone to watch the revolution,' said Nadezhda.

'They all have. It was easier to let them go than to stop them,' added Roman.

'And Brana?'

'Who knows where she goes every night, with her leaflets,' replied Roman. 'Anyway, they were hammering on the door, and they would not stop, so I grabbed the apron and the hat from below stairs and answered the door, pretending to be the cook. I did think about getting my pistol. But it was unclear if they wanted to arrest me, or kill me, or simply ask me where the Grand Duke was. So I opened the door, as the cook, just as they knocked it off its hinges, as you can see!'

'And then?' asked Nicholas.

'And then I spent the next hour knocking on each and every door and going into each and every room, apparently searching for myself,' said Roman, taking off his tall white chef's hat and putting it on the small marble-topped table next to the chair.

'I hope you thoroughly searched for yourself,' said Nicholas, laughing a little. 'Cupboards and everything.'

'I don't know what you find so amusing,' said Nadezhda. 'If you'd seen what I've seen today you would not be entertained.'

'Well done,' replied Militza, nodding approvingly at her son and removing her pearl hatpin and fur-lined hat. 'You confused them this time. However, we all know they will be back.'

'I am not so sure,' said Roman.

'I most certainly am,' replied Militza. 'And then, it will surely be worse.'

That night, after Nicholas had walked home back across the river and everyone else had finally gone to bed, the door barricaded, the cook's uniform returned to him, Militza lay under her sheets, staring at the white and gilt ceiling, illuminated by the light of the moon. The city was silent, save for the occasional chatter of a machine gun. What and at whom they were shooting was anyone's guess. But she could not sleep. They'd come to her house; they'd threatened her children. And her servants had deserted her, if only for one night. But after decades of loyalty on her part, not one of them had stayed back to look after the palace. And Brana? Dear, loyal Brana who'd come with her all those years ago from the mountains of Montenegro and who'd been by her side, mixing potions, burning votive candles, collecting henbane and mandrake, whispering, chanting, necromancing... where was she in all of this? Militza was truly afraid for the first time in years. She must do something to repair the vessel she had broken.

Tomorrow was Sunday, she thought, the Tsarina would be in church, with the girls, and possibly the Tsarevich, depending on his state of health. But they were always there, praying for Russia, praying for him and praying for themselves. Maybe she should go and pray and confess her sins? Come clean? Militza's mind churned as she lay there. Maybe if she told 'Little Mother' the whole story then Rasputin's curse would be no more? Maybe if she explained how she and her sister fashioned the Holy Satyr from wax, mixed it with dust from a poor man's grave and the icon of St John the Baptist; how she moulded the creature, rolling and warming the wax in her hands; how she baptised it with the soul of an unborn child, the dried-up foetus, miscarried by the Grand Duchess Vladimir all those years ago; and how they'd called on the Four Winds; and the *koldun* – the insatiable, unquenchable, licentious, duplicitous, covetous, impious, soused, drunk and self-appointed Holy Man from Siberia – Rasputin had come. Just as she had commanded.

Maybe, she could say how she killed him, or tried to, using spells and magic, all her powers, all her skills, but they had not been strong enough, and how eventually she'd smoked a gun with sage, as a saged gun never misses, and shot him through the forehead and thrown him into the river and watched him drown, his lungs fill with water as he sank to the bottom, weighed down by the fur coat of a prince. And now all of this, all this misery, this murder, this revolution was all her fault.

Maybe Alexandra would forgive her, and they could return to normal and the fighting and the shooting and the murder would stop.

Militza lay there, thinking. Thinking of all the problems she and her sister had caused. Had they opened Pandora's Box when they manifested him? Thinking of him, her semi-clad body began to grow cold. Her hands and her feet turned to stone. Despite the blankets, she shivered and shook. The temperature dropped even further. The curtains quivered with a breeze that came from nowhere.

And suddenly she could feel his presence in the room. She could smell his breath; a fug of rotting teeth and fetid alcohol overcame her. He seemed to be at the bottom of the bed, tugging at the sheets, pulling at the blankets. Was he climbing up? Or was he about to drag her down? Pull her into Hell with him. His cold hands were around her ankles, working their way up her calves. He was freezing, hard as ice, wet and damp as a riverbank, climbing on top of her, worming his way along her body, working his way up, wriggling, pulling at her thighs. Militza was terrified. She couldn't move, she couldn't scream, she couldn't breathe. Rasputin had returned as an incubus; his giant phallus was priapic. She could feel it probing between her legs, seeking her out in the darkness while she was paralysed with fear. He lay on top of her. His heavy weight on her chest, his breath puffing at her neck and his hard member between her thighs. His cold hand grasped her breasts, his open mouth wrapped itself around her nipple, his rasping tongue rooting. The smell of rotting flesh and death was overwhelming. In an instant, his haunches rose high in the air, his breath blew into her ear, he was about to enter her, penetrate her with a searing force. Militza closed her eyes, her heart pounding, her mouth dry. And then, suddenly, it stopped, he stopped, the weight lifted, and he disappeared. Sucked back down into the depths whence he'd come.

Militza exhaled, the terror and tension dissipated, her body grew warm once more, her skin tingled back into life. She closed her eyes and lay on her back, her hands in prayer, like a bride of Christ.

Would she ever sleep again?

The Russians are one of those nations which seem to exist only to give humanity terrible lessons.

Petr Chaadaev, Philosopher

CHAPTER 7

March 1917, Petrograd

Militza barely spoke in the motor car on the way to Tsarskoye Selo. She was exhausted after the night before and deeply anxious. She could not remember the last time she'd spoken to Alexandra. She'd seen her at the burial, of course. From afar. She remembered her drawn face, the slate greyness of the day and the pale crisp whiteness of the flowers she'd thrown onto the Devil's grave. The Devil who taunted her at night. Whose face mocked her and whose cock tortured her. The Devil who was never going to leave her alone. Was all this tragedy really because of him? And had she really been the one to ignite the flames of revolution? He had come through her house, that was certain. She'd introduced him to both Nicholas and Alexandra, and she'd encouraged the relationship, used her creation to keep her powerful position at Court, and when Rasputin had counselled against her, when he turned on his mistress, his creator, she'd killed him.

Militza felt engulfed by a wave of nausea so profound

she made the chauffeur stop the car. She had to get out, she had to breathe, she wanted to scream; but Stana, Marina and Nadezhda were in the car, and she didn't want to let them into her thoughts, her dreams. Her terrors.

They pulled up by the side of a road in a small village about a ten-minute drive from Tsarskoye Selo. It was quiet. One row of simple, brightly coloured wooden houses lined either side of the road. The sloping roofs were heavy with snow, the few haystacks that were visible were white like Christmas plum puddings. A dog barked at Militza as she stood in the snow, breathing in the fresh, cold air, exhaling white clouds like a steam engine. The dog's bark was muted by the fat flakes falling silently around. It moved closer and growled, baring its blunt yellow teeth.

'Who are you?' demanded an elderly woman who appeared from behind a turquoise-painted wooden gate. 'Leave my dog alone.'

'I'm just travelling through,' replied Militza, suddenly conscious of her silver fox stole, her golden necklace and the diamonds glinting around her wrist.

'Travel on, whore. We don't want your kind here.'

'I am only getting some air.'

'Plenty of that stuff here. No bread. Just air. And,' she nodded up the road, 'if you're going to see the German bitch, you can tell her she'll be a long time dead.' She coughed. Her sharp blue eyes shone with hatred and she smiled a little, her gummy grin rapidly turning into a leer as she coughed again and spat through a tube-shaped tongue at Militza's face. She missed, but the gob of phlegm landed on the hem of Militza's dress. The woman laughed as Militza hurried back into the car, shaking her silk skirts, trying to remove the stringy saliva. 'Fuck off!' the woman shouted. 'Fuck off and never come back!'

'What did she say, Mother?' asked Nadezhda, moving along the red leather seat to make room. 'She sounded angry.'

'I didn't like the look of her face,' said Marina peering over her shoulder. 'She looks like a hag.'

'She is old,' replied Stana. 'I imagine her life has not been easy.'

'It was nothing,' said Militza, her face flushed as she slammed the door of the car. 'Let's drive on, hurry, let's get out of here!'

'But what did she say?' asked Marina.

'Nothing important,' she told her daughter and herself at the same time, even though she was shocked to the core. She hadn't heard language like that since she'd listened to labourers picking grapes back in Montenegro as a child.

A few miles later, in Tsarskoye Selo, a large crowd of soldiers and civilians were just leaving the train station. Shoulders hunched against the falling snow, scarves wrapped tightly around their necks, they set off slowly in the direction of Feodorovski Sabor. It was a thirty-minute walk from train station to the cathedral; the more affluent waited by the roadside for one of the sledges that queued up to ferry the faithful to the steps, the rest had no choice but to walk. Sitting in the motor car, travelling along the wide boulevard that led from the station to the church, Militza could see rows of mounted Cossacks standing guard on either side of the road, with various pockets of policemen stationed at each corner. If they were expecting trouble, it wasn't noticeable, it didn't feel as if there was subversion in the air. The atmosphere was subdued, as if everyone was watching their step, not wanting to catch the eye of a Cossack or feel the heavy leaded ends of his whip.

'It feels odd to be back here, don't you think?' said Stana. 'I wonder if any of the girls will be in church today, bearing in mind they're all supposed to have measles.'

'Do they *all* have measles?' queried Marina. 'I know the "Bigs" haven't been at the hospital for a while, and you know how much they love their nursing.'

'It's all that training Alix gave them,' said Stana.

'It's all the men!' laughed Marina. Militza looked shocked. It was unlike Marina to be so coarse. 'What?' she laughed, seeing her mother's face. 'Everyone knows they are in love with all the soldiers. It's the only time they ever get to speak to anyone outside the family. I'd fall in love with the first man I saw if I'd been locked up in a playroom with my irritating little brother all the time. Everyone thinks butter wouldn't melt because he looks like an angel, but as soon as all your backs are turned, he's so annoying.'

'That's not true,' said Stana.

'Alexis is fine,' added Nadezhda. 'He's a child.'

'Some of the time he's fine, the rest he is annoying, and you know it,' Marina replied. 'Anyway, I'm looking forward to seeing them, it's been a while.'

The motor car stopped just near the church at the edge of the park, on the road which the Emperor and his family used to travel from the Alexander Palace. It was always swept clean of snow and today was no exception; there was a small team of uniformed servants busy with brushes, determined not to fight a losing battle, pushing the falling flakes into neat piles along the roadside.

They all got out of the car and made their way towards the steps of the church. In the shadow of the large golden dome with its even larger golden crucifix, a child on skis was playing in the snow, throwing fistfuls in the air and catching the white crystals on the tip of his tongue.

Militza looked up at the white tent-shaped roof with its green copper tiles and curved towers. She remembered Tsar Nicholas excitedly sharing his plans for the church with her. He and her husband, Peter, had talked late into the night about each turret and window. There was nothing Peter liked more than discussing architecture. She remembered also how excited the Tsar was about the laying of the first stone back in 1912. Five years ago. It made her feel wistful. How she wished she could turn back the clock.

Looking up at the ornately carved church door and the wall of saints whose halos glowed golden despite the poor light, Stana, Militza, Marina and Nadezhda made their way up the steps and paused, waiting for the people to make way for them. Their faces were perhaps not immediately recognisable, but their superior social status was obvious, and this granted them access to the front of the church. They stood, waiting, but the crowd didn't move.

'Excuse me!' declared Marina, pushing forward.

Militza touched her daughter's arm and nodded. 'Wait.'

'But—'

'We can't just push past everyone to get in the front,' hissed Nadezhda. 'There's a queue. They're ahead of us.'

'Ahead of us?' Marina's pretty mouth curled.

'They are,' agreed Militza.

They slowly walked in with the rest of the courtiers and worked their way to the front of the church. It seemed that, despite it all, no one was brave enough to take up the royal position. The spot normally reserved for the Imperial family, just to the right of the icon screen, was empty. Militza and her party stood close by and waited for the Tsarina.

Their arrival was preceded by a hush, and then, a slow parting of the crowd. Alix was in front, dressed demurely, no plumed hats, no fox furs, no diamonds, no glinting stones, just pearls, a neat grey coat with a velvet collar and the simplest of fur-lined hats. She looked tired, her face was pinched, her mouth was thin, and her pale eyes were entirely expressionless. Her shoulders sloped, her body stooping, and it was clear by the way she was walking that her lower back hurt. She was accompanied by two of her daughters – the Grand Duchesses Tatiana and Olga. They were, as usual, identically dressed. The same coat and hat as their mother, but what was truly shocking, and what made the whole of the congregation stare in total silence at the bedraggled gang of three, was that the Grand Duchesses had no hair. Their heads were shaved, they had nothing but brown stubble visible around the temples, all their golden locks, their curls, their crowning glories were gone.

Marina could not believe it. It was brutal, all their femininity and sophistication had disappeared. They looked so childish, so vulnerable. Like urchins with their thin white necks on display. They looked as if they'd just stepped out of the slums around Sennaya Ploshchad. 'What have they done?' she whispered.

'I am not sure,' replied Stana. 'I'd heard rumours but the reality is...' She ran out of words.

'It's measles,' said Militza under her breath. 'It can make

you lose your hair; they have clearly decided to shave it all off.'

'What a thing!' said Marina, unable to stop staring. 'They look awful.'

'They've been ill,' corrected Nadezhda. 'What did you expect?'

'Don't start pretending to know about measles,' Marina spat under her breath. 'You might have been to the front, once. But you don't know anything. I'm the one who's been working in the hospital.'

'Working? You've visited three or four times,' retorted Nadezhda. 'I'd hardly call you a qualified nurse!'

'Be quiet!' Militza's heart was beating heavily. The evident animosity between her two daughters was as irritating as it was upsetting.

'So that's why they couldn't leave then,' said Stana. 'When the British asked them to London. I heard Sir George suggesting it the other day. George the Fifth had initially refused to offer them sanctuary just in case their presence made things difficult for the royal family back in Britain. But in the end the King was persuaded to back down and asked them. They are cousins, after all. But they couldn't leave.'

'That's an opportunity missed,' said Marina, staring at Olga so directly that the Grand Duchess turned to look at her and smiled. Marina smiled fleetingly back. 'Are they still contagious?' she asked.

The church service began and the Tsarina resolutely failed to catch Militza's eye. She must have seen her, Militza concluded, as she scanned the church for anyone else she might know. Bertie Stopford was often seen in the crowd at

Feodorovski Sabor, but then Bertie Stopford was often seen everywhere. Sadly, he was not amongst the congregation today. There was no one of significance there. Not only did the members of the court mostly have their own private churches to worship in, but the Tsarina was so unfriendly these days, so cold, so distant and aloof, it was impossible to work out what was to be gained by making the great journey out of town on the off chance she might deign to talk to you. There was simply no social reason to travel there any more.

Militza was beginning to doubt the reasons she'd come. Was she really going to go through with this and confess her crimes? To tell the Empress about the charlatan she was clearly still in mourning for? The burden was heavy, it weighed on her shoulders, and he only had fleetingly to plague her thoughts for her to feel the very sharp pain of guilt. She stood listening to the rattling of the chain as the priest swung the incense burner around the church. Back and forth it flew, filling the air with its heady, sickly aromatics. The choir began to chant, the sweet angelic notes reverberating around the domed roof of the church. The sounds, the echoes, and the smell; it was hypnotic. Archpriest Belyaev was gliding, his black robes billowing, his crucifix catching the light of a thousand smoking beeswax candles. Frankincense, myrrh, burning wax, she felt heady and nauseous. The smell was overpowering, and Militza swooned, collapsing in a pile of fur and silk on the floor.

She came to, arranged on the mauve sofa in the Mauve Boudoir opposite the white enamelled J Becker upright piano she knew so well. Cluttered with porcelain figurines, framed family photographs and hundreds of knick-knacks collected over the years, Alix's private room with its 'ashes of roses' walls and pistachio coloured Axminster carpet was exactly as she remembered. She sat up with a start. Sitting opposite, stirring a glass of tea, were the Tsarina and the Grand Duchesses Olga and Tatiana. All three were staring at her.

'Are you all right, Mama?' Nadezhda was by the window, looking out across the park.

'Feeling better?' asked Alix. Her voice was soft and familiar but contained not one note of friendship.

'Yes, much.' Militza sat straighter, her feet on the floor, her ankles together. What on earth had happened? It was so unlike her to collapse under the smell of incense. The lack of sleep? The visit from him?

'Would you like me to send for a doctor?'

'No, no, I'm fine. I can't think what happened.'

'The heat, maybe?' suggested Olga.

'The noise?' said Tatiana.

'Nerves?' added Alix.

'What would Mama be nervous about?' asked Nadezhda. 'Other than what is happening on the streets.'

All three sat in silence.

'Tea?' asked Alix, slowly leaning forward to pick up the silver teapot in front of her. 'Sugar? Or jam?'

'How spoiling.' Militza smiled.

'We ran out of jam this week,' announced Nadezhda flatly, walking away from the window. 'And there's not a bag of sugar to be had in the whole of the city. Even if you do queue up all night.'

'Sugar or jam?' Alix repeated, her voice clipped, her irritation evident.

'Neither, thank you,' Militza replied. 'Thank you,' she said again, as Alix handed over the glass of tepid tea. 'Are *you* two feeling better?' she asked Olga and Tatiana.

'Much improved,' replied Olga, nodding her shaved head. Her large pale blue eyes were even more beautiful, more prominent than before. 'But the Littles are still very ill, and Alexis is unwell, but not as bad as the girls. It really is a nasty illness.'

'And you?' Militza asked Alix.

'As can be expected,' she replied. 'What with the war, the measles, Nicky's absence and the terrible loss of Our Friend.'

'Is it bad in the city?' asked Tatiana.

'Hush,' said Alix.

'Everyone says it's bad in the city.'

'Tatiana!' Alix looked furious.

'People are dying in the streets. They are being shot by the soldiers. They are crying out for bread, but are getting nothing but lead,' declared Nadezhda, pacing up and down the mauve and pistachio patterned carpet. 'It's bad.'

'Enough!' said Alix, raising a thin shaking hand.

'And it's all on the Tsar's orders,' Nadezhda continued, becoming more heated, more animated. 'There's blood on the streets – I have seen it with my own eyes. A young man was shot standing next to me, he went out like a light, not a sound came from his lips.'

'Stop! I command it!' Despite her ailments, Alix sprang out of her chair. 'First of all, Nicky would never order such a thing against his own people, and secondly, all is most certainly well in the city. It's just some silly nonsense. Some workers being bad mannered. The Russian people love their Little Father and their Little Mother and that's the end of it.'

'But—' Nadezhda took a step forward.

'Be quiet, my child, or I shall have you removed from my house.'

'Where is the Tsar at the moment?' asked Militza, glaring at her daughter. Willing her to behave was as futile as trying to calm a storm.

'He's at the front, leading the war effort.'

'Maybe he should return to the capital to talk to the Duma? Speak to the commanders in charge of the police and the army, tell them to go a little easier with the rioters?'

'Are you trying to meddle in politics again, Militza?'

'I only thought—'

'Well, don't think.' Alix dismissed her with a wave, brushing her away. 'There are enough people who *think* they know better around here.' She turned to look witheringly at Nadezhda. 'Too many hot little heads. Hot little heads, with too many little ideas. If they are rioting for bread, then tell them not to. It's easy.'

'Or give them bread?' snapped Nadezhda.

'Hot little heads don't get us anywhere, now do they,' replied Alix, with a tight little smile.

'But, if he could—' began Militza.

'No,' she said simply. 'We have worries of our own here, especially since He is gone.'

'I wanted to talk to you about something...' Militza tried.

'And I have no real desire to talk to you,' she said. 'Now, if you are feeling well enough, perhaps you should return to Petrograd? Your sister and daughter will be bored of walking in the grounds by now.' She smiled again. 'Oh. Just before I forget.' She walked slowly over to her mauve and white bureau in the middle of the room and opened a drawer. 'I believe these are yours?'

She held up a pair of gloves. She held them between her finger and thumb, as if there was something unpleasant about them. They were black kid. Monogrammed. In golden thread. Militza's distinctive initials were sewn into the backs of the wrists.

Her heart skipped a beat.

How?

She could feel her face blanch. Her mouth turned as dry as the Turkmen desert. 'I have been looking for those gloves everywhere.'

'Have you?' She knew.

She knew.

'How very kind.'

'Are you not going to ask where I found them?'

She knew. Maybe not what she had done, but that she'd been there, that fateful night. The night He was murdered.

'It's not what you think.'

Alix raised her hand. 'Don't. Please don't bother to explain. It's beneath… me. Now go.'

And that was it. No discussion, no wringing of hands, no weeping, no confession, no forgiveness. No kiss goodbye. A dismissal. Two decades of friendship. Over.

Little did Militza know, as she hastily made her way out of the Alexander Palace to her waiting motor car, her head spinning, her heart pounding, followed by her hot-headed, defiant daughter, that she would never see the Tsarina or any of those beautiful, ethereal Grand Duchesses, or even the blue-eyed boy-angel Tsarevich, ever again.

Even she, with her second sight and her premonitions, could not have predicted their incarceration at that house with the special purpose in Ekaterinburg. No one could have foreseen the airless, windowless cellar where they were led. The screaming and the clouds of dust and the twenty minutes of constant shooting they endured, that would fail to kill them outright. Who could have predicted the bayoneting of the girls and the boy through their bullet-proof vests made of the diamonds they'd studiously sewn into their underwear. Not even a witch could have imagined the hideous cart, loaded with bodies some, like Anastasia, still alive. It broke down on the way into the woods, where they were pummelled with rifle butts, their skulls stove in, just to make sure they were dead, and that no one could recognise the corpses. They were then stripped and doused in acid and gasoline, anything personal, or useful, or valuable was, of course, looted. They then set fire to the bodies. Their charred remains were thrown into two separate burial pits. The mine shafts that had been originally chosen as the dumping ground for the Imperial bodies had proved to be too shallow.

No one knew what fate had in store for them, any of them; no one knew what terrible vices, crimes and filth would emerge from the broken Russian vessel. But they were coming, they were coming, and there was nothing anyone or anything could do to stop them.

Back in the capital, the Countess Kleinmichel was having a small dinner with friends. Militza, Stana, their children, the Orlovs, Bertie Stopford and a few other stragglers were invited. After the shock of her meeting with the Tsarina, the return of her gloves and Alix's evident malevolence, Militza was hugely reluctant to attend. She was exhausted, worried, fearful, but no one could turn down a dinner with Countess Maria Eduardovna Kleinmichel. She was, after the Grand Duchess Vladimir, perhaps the grandest of *grandes dames* in the city, a 'lady', so they said, to the very tips of her fingers.

Well-connected in the spheres of poetry, writing and the arts, Countess Maria knew, quite simply, everyone. Widowed in the sixth year of her marriage with more money than she could possibly ever spend, despite her best efforts, she had made it her mission to host the most spectacular parties, the most memorable of which was the Night of a Thousand and One Stars, the Persian Ball, the last dance to be held in Petrograd before the outbreak of war, where the costumes were designed by Lev Bakst, and Militza had had the good fortune to befriend Oswald Rayner.

The Countess had two residences in Petrograd; one was a bohemian dacha on a wooded road on Kamenny Island, where the dancing would go on till dawn and the motor cars would queue up all night waiting to collect their increasingly inebriated owners. The other was a more staid, traditional and grander palace on Sergeievskaya, just near Tauride Gardens, where she was entertaining that evening.

The second-floor gold and white salon was already busy by the time Militza, Stana, Marina and Nadezhda arrived. Elena was working overnight in the Anglo-Russian hospital and Roman had elected to stay at home. He'd invited some members of his regiment over to drink fine wine and play cards, but truthfully, he was worried about the palace and felt someone needed to be in charge in case the soldiers returned.

'Champagne!' suggested the Countess as she spotted them all from across the room. Bejewelled, bedecked and befeathered, she looked as if she might be about to attend one of her many balls, rather than an intimate soirée for some twenty friends. 'I mean, what a to-do,' she continued, kissing Militza and Stana on the cheeks. 'All this.' She waved towards the streets below. 'Eat, drink and make merry, for tomorrow... well, who knows what happens tomorrow,' she laughed. 'I bumped into the Countess Sheremetev earlier today, and do you know what she said to me? "Isn't it wonderful!" "Isn't *what* wonderful?" I asked. "Why, the revolution, of course!" she exclaimed. I replied, "Well, Countess, you're hardly one to rejoice. It is precisely people like us who stand to lose everything!" What a fool that woman is.' She smiled and raised a glass. 'Your health! Now tell me, how are you all?'

'Have you been marching today?' asked Nicholas Orlov, approaching Nadezhda and Marina as they stood in the middle of the room, each holding a glass of champagne. Dressed in his guard's uniform, a smile on his lips, he was clean-shaven, his hair smoothed down, and he smelt of citrus.

'Me?' Marina looked appalled, taking a large sip from her glass. 'I'd sooner eat flies. And anyway we've been busy.'

'Oh?'

His question was directed at Nadezhda, but she resolutely looked over his shoulder.

'We went to see the Tsarina,' declared Marina with a small, tight smile.

'Down with the German woman!' he whispered in the direction of Nadezhda. 'Down with the war!'

His lightness irritated her, and his tone was patronising. 'I did try to tell her how incredibly unpopular she was on the streets of the city. But she didn't listen.' Nadezhda put down her full glass. 'Mr Stopford!' she said, walking to the other side of the room. 'How are you? And thank you so much for the other day.'

Nicholas Orlov's head hung a little as he watched her go.

'Nadezhda! How delightful. Are you quite recovered? What a terrible scene to witness. Today has not been quite so bad. Although I hear the Duma is in terrible disarray. What have you heard? I saw a simply frightful thing,' said Bertie, smoothing the corners of his greying moustache. 'I walked past what I thought was a pile of logs in the snow this morning, all stiff and white, and I was marvelling at how organised and immaculate it all was, piled up neatly, until on closer inspection I realised it was the bodies of policeman, all dead, stacked up, frozen solid and waiting for collection. Awful. Can you believe it? But you are all right? You made it home safely, obviously!' He laughed and, throwing back his long nose, he drained his drink. 'Have you met the Countess Kleinmichel's nephew, Dmitry? A guard in the Hussars.' He nodded at the handsome young man. 'Husband material,' he whispered in her ear.

'Good evening.' Dmitry smiled. His large grey eyes blinked behind his round wire-rimmed spectacles.

Nadezhda was on the point of replying when the butler announced that dinner was served.

The guests were gathering their things, their evening bags, their cigarettes to move next door to the dining room, when the doorman from downstairs burst through the double doors and yelled, 'RUN!' No one reacted. They were shocked to see such an uncouth man in the salon at all. 'RUN!' he hollered. Still no one moved. 'RUN for your lives, the back door has been broken into by a band of armed men, they are tearing through the house! RUN, I tell you. RUN! Run for your lives!'

'Good Lord!' exclaimed the Countess Kleinmichel to the stunned silence of her guests. 'Let's go!'

Abandoning their belongings, they were led by the Countess, at a pace, straight down the front stairs of the palace and out into the street. Standing in the snow, devoid of coats and outdoor shoes, the guests all looked towards their hostess for their next move. And, judging by the crowd, armed with rifles, axes, sticks and bayonets making their way towards them along the pavement, they needed to move fast.

'My house!' declared a rather rotund fellow whose luxuriant moustache enveloped most of his face. 'Right here!'

Fortunately, Bogdan Bogdanovich lived right across the street, and in a matter of seconds he managed to hurry the Countess and her guests into the building, firmly bolting the door behind them.

For the next few hours, they all sat in state of total astonishment, watching the scenes which unfolded in the palace over the road. The rabble illuminated every room in the house, including the ballroom where the chandelier had not been lit since the start of the war, and from there, it was easy to see them move from room to room, pulling curtains off the walls and dragging more chairs into the dining room, where the table had been laid, for a significantly different type of guest. The gang of men sat down at the table and were waited on by the Countess's own staff who not only laid extra places for their unexpected visitors, but then proceeded to bring in the steaming soup tureens, the serving dishes laden with roasted meats, boats of gravy and unctuous sauces as well as large plates of delicately prepared sautéed vegetables. The Countess's chef was French and famous in the capital for his exciting menus and skilled techniques. She'd found him in Paris.

'This is an abomination,' said Bertie, as he sat at a darkened window, watching the show, smoking a cigarette.

'Who on earth are these people?' asked the Countess. 'And what are they doing in my house?'

Bogdan Bogdanovich did his best to serve some sort of refreshments to his thunderstruck guests as they all huddled around the first-floor windows, horrified, transfixed, watching what was happening in the palace.

'Is that my wine?' the Countess queried, as bottle after bottle appeared at the dining table, only to be opened by her servants who then proceeded to sit down and join in the party, raising their glasses repeatedly in increasingly long and elaborate toasts. 'They are emptying the cellar; this is unbearable,' she whispered, witnessing her butler of twenty years standing up at the table and saying something so rousing that they all cheered and threw their glasses, her glasses, against the wall. 'I can't watch,' she said, unable to look away.

'Surely there is something we can do?' asked Militza,

fighting a growing feeling of terrible impotence and injustice. 'Call in the soldiers? Alert the police?'

'Are there any police?' asked Bertie. 'And can you be sure they would be on your side and not join in, drinking the burgundy?'

'I have never seen anything like it,' said Stana, watching as they smashed the necks off the wine bottles, making them quicker to drink from. 'The lack of vodka on the streets is what's kept them civilised, so far. This is only going to make matters worse. Inebriation is the curse of the Russian soul; it strips away all manner of decency and control. It releases the worst, the Devil itself.'

'I am not sure you could call the last few days civilised,' replied Bertie. 'Hundreds dead, possibly thousands, blood on the streets, enough to stain the snow.'

Militza turned to look at him. 'I disagree. That was civilised. The worst is yet to come. We are surely on our way to anarchy.'

There are lots of armed hooligans, here and there they are shooting... cars go past with red flags, carrying people in shabby outfits and some soldiers. The crowd is generally good-humoured, but I think there will be carnage.

Konstantin Somov, Artist

CHAPTER 8

March 1917, Petrograd

The soldiers of the Volynsky Regiment were the first to turn their weapons on their commander. They entered his quarters where he sat, unarmed at his desk, and put a bullet through his head. The Pavlovksy Guards then gathered up their weapons and went into battle against the police, who they accused of mounting as many machine guns on as many rooftops as they could access. The Cossacks were remaining loyal, so far, but could turn, would turn, at any moment, refusing to use their *nagaikas* on the demonstrators who'd stuffed padding and paper in their clothes against the blows.

Overnight, in total some 160,000 soldiers crossed over and joined the rebels. They looted their base and turned their attention on the Ministry of the Interior building, burning as many documents as they could find. One gruff man in the marauding crowd was heard to shout at an elderly fellow who was wringing his hands at so much destruction: 'Don't worry, Granddad, we shall be able to divide your houses and land among the people without the help of any of your precious archives!' They broke into the city's arsenal and armed themselves with more weapons. They robbed shops and ransacked food stores and started to bang on doors, looking for policemen to kill.

Forty were found, cowering in the basement of a church, where they were all lined up, shot and left where they fell. Without so much as thump on the back of head to dull the pain, another thirty were forced into the freezing Neva, pushed under the ice, and were swept away by the current to drown like rats.

The city was awash with the stories of brutality. Policemen were kicked to death by the mob, hounded, hunted, shot, bayoneted and stabbed. They were left in the street as food for the hundreds of ravenous stray dogs. Even the genteel ladies of the sewing circle at the British Embassy were affected. As they rolled bandages and stitched pneumonia jackets, they swapped eyewitness accounts of young policemen being trussed up and dragged through the city by their feet. Another was simply shot in the doorway of his own house. One of the young ladies, sewing in the red and white ballroom, described walking past a blazing bonfire in the street, only to discover they were burning a sergeant.

The revenge knew no bounds. They set fire to some twelve police stations, destroying records, fingerprints and decades of bureaucracy. Any building associated with the police and the judiciary was considered fair game. Even their private houses were ransacked, the clothes and possessions of their wives and children, toys, bonnets, underclothes were thrown through the windows, raining down on the streets like confetti, only to be looted by passers-by.

They stormed the prisons and released the inmates.

The Krestovsky on the northern bank of the Neva, near Finland Station, was one of the first. Built in 1893 to house a thousand inmates, the population had doubled and prisoners – both political and criminal – shared the same filthy, dank, rat-infested windowless rooms. After shooting the commander and opening up the cells, they released the stunned and blinking prisoners out onto the streets. Blinded by the daylight, terrified by their unexpected freedom, some simply stood there unable to move, some held on to each other for physical support and others just knelt in the snow and wept. Other liberations were less successful. At the Litovsky prison, while most of the prisoners were freed, a small selection who'd been housed underground were burnt alive in their own cells, after the keys to open the metal grilles were lost in the chaos and confusion.

By lunchtime that Monday, the streets of the city were teeming with prisoners who joined the rebels in borrowed or stolen clothes, too big, too small, whatever they could find. They moved as a pack, looting shops, taking supplies, stealing weapons, sweeping through streets like dervishes of destruction. The atmosphere was becoming increasingly volatile. Each minute was more unpredictable than the last. It was as if a beast had been released, broken free of its shackles, and the city was about to be deafened by its roar.

But when Nadezhda woke that morning on the divan in Bogdan Bogdanovich's first-floor salon, she was more perturbed by the fact that she appeared to be wearing a gentleman's hussar jacket that smelt of citrus.

'Well, at least someone slept well,' said Marina, stretching in her armchair, still dressed in her peach silk evening dress from the night before. 'I was bitterly cold sitting here by the fire all night long. In my damp shoes.' She gave a little shiver by way of demonstration. 'This rug was of little use at all.'

'Where did this come from?' Nadezhda rubbed her eyes, confused.

'Oh! Don't pretend you don't know,' Marina hissed, throwing her hands in the air with exasperation. She glanced around the room for eavesdroppers, but the salon was empty, the dinner party guests were in the dining room, having breakfast.

'Know what?'

'Orlov, of course.'

'He lent me his coat?'

'Of course he did. He sat by your side most of the night, watching over you, making sure you were warm, like some sort of loyal lapdog.' She could not have spat the last two words with greater venom.

'He did no such thing!' Nadezhda's face flushed as she stood up from the divan and pushed the coat off her and on to the floor.

'He did. And Bertie Stopford was next to him, whispering all night about how we should all leave Petrograd, how it's too dangerous for us to stay, we should go, go quickly and go south. As if he knows anything. He's English. And he's in trade. He's a salesman. How can he pretend to understand anything to do with Russia? Or the government or the political situation. It was beyond tiresome; I barely slept a wink.'

Downstairs in Bogdan Bogdanovich's modest dining room, with its highly polished mahogany table, hard-backed chairs, dark panelled walls and heavy bronze chandelier, there were slim pickings for breakfast. The poor man had not expected such an illustrious array of overnight guests, especially as he was living alone, except for his servants, because his wife and two teenage sons were currently in the south of France. He'd been advised by an astute lawyer friend of his, some weeks back, to take his family and his possessions out of the country. He was only back in the capital for a few days or so, to pick up the rest of his wife's jewellery and to tie up some loose ends.

'How long do you think they'll be in my house?' asked the Countess Kleinmichel glancing out of the window as she heard the sound of gunfire. She was looking a little less bejewelled and bedecked than she had the night before.

At least she had managed to sleep. Unlike the others, she had been given the master bedroom and a proper bed for the night. Militza and Stana had shared, just as they had in childhood, for the first time in thirty years. Whereas the young and the gentlemen had fallen asleep in the salon, where they'd been sitting.

'Are they still there?' asked Marina as both she and Nadezhda entered the dining room.

'They are,' confirmed Bertie, cracking open a boiled egg that, along with a few slices of bread was all Bogdan's cook had managed to find in the pantry at such short notice.

'Would you like to sit here?' asked Nicholas, looking up from his slice of buttered bread and leaping out of his seat. His hair was a little dishevelled, he was dressed only in his white shirt, his army breeches and red braces. 'Please,' he added, pulling out his chair, indicating for Nadezhda to sit down. 'Did you sleep well?'

'Yes, thank you,' she replied, looking nervously at the floor, a little disconcerted by his attention.

'When do you think they will leave the Countess Kleinmichel's palace, Mr Stopford? You are a man of the world, who might know such things,' asked Marina a little sarcastically, walking past her sister and sitting down in the seat offered up by Nicholas. She was the eldest, after all.

'In my limited experience of thuggery, madame,' replied Bertie, still looking immaculate despite four hours' sleep, bolt upright in a chair, 'I imagine when all the alcohol has been drunk and the cellar is bone dry, they will move on to pastures new.'

'How long do you think that might be?' she asked, picking up Nicholas's buttered bread.

'Judging by the generosity of the Countess, I imagine her cellar is well-stocked, so one or two days?'

'And in the meantime, we are to stay here?' asked Marina with a hint of panic in her voice.

'Dimitry and I should re-join our regiments,' declared Nicholas, looking down into the street. 'They'll be needing reinforcements.'

'Absolutely,' agreed the Countess Kleinmichel's nephew, cleaning his spectacles on a napkin. 'They'll most certainly be needing our support.'

'And we should return to the palace,' added Militza, 'before it is too dangerous to travel the streets.'

'I fear you are too late there, Grand Duchess,' replied Bogdan Bogdanovich from beneath his moustache. 'I spoke to my lawyer friend this morning and he says it is chaos out there already. He told me they've stormed the prisons and raided the arsenal and there has been a mad rush to arms. He witnessed a child shoot a soldier this morning, not out of malice, but by mistake. The child was warming himself by a street fire, playing with a gun. He also saw children throwing bullets into the fire, delighted when they exploded, only to notice a few seconds later that they had killed a man. There are people shooting in the air, people shooting each other. People killing one another over bread. It's more than dangerous out there, it's mayhem.'

'They've emptied the prisons? It's just like the French, storming the Bastille. Well, at least we are all still alive,' said the Countess. 'And I can always buy more wine.'

'But how are we supposed to get home?' asked Marina. 'I want to go home.'

'It may be too dangerous,' suggested Bogdan.

'Not if you tie a red scarf around your arm and put something red around your neck. I am sure they will leave you alone then,' replied Nadezhda.

'Do you mean join them?' asked the Countess.

'Or at least make it appear as if you had.' She shrugged.

'Isn't that cowardly?' asked the Countess. 'Claiming to be something that you're not. It's what spies do.'

'Excellent idea,' asserted Bertie. 'A truly excellent idea. Mr Bogdanovich, would it be possible to see if your housekeeper has any red cloth?'

The housekeeper was dispatched, eventually returning to the dining room with a bag of scarlet ribbons and an old scarf belonging to Bogdan Bogdanovich's wife. She sat at the table, with spectacles on the end of her short fleshy nose, needle and thread in hand, her sleeves rolled up to reveal pink spotted forearms, as soft as the belly on a rainbow trout.

They stood in line, Countesses first, being measured for

their revolutionary colours. Rough greatcoats had been found, jewellery removed, and any visible finery had been disguised. It was too dangerous to take a car and anyway, they were all being requisitioned, or repurposed, depending on your point of view, so they would have to travel on foot, like shadows through the city, hoping not to arouse suspicion or indeed any interest at all.

'Is it visible enough?' asked the Countess Kleinmichel inspecting her armband, after the housekeeper snapped off the thread with her little brown teeth. 'Do you think? Can you see it? Do I look like a revolutionary? Do I?'

Militza smiled despite herself. The Countess was moving around, studying herself in the looking glass above the fireplace, as if she were modelling the latest couture from Worth. 'It's very fetching,' she said. 'All you need to remember now are the chants.'

'Chants?'

'Don't worry,' replied Nadezhda. 'They are not that complicated.'

'Of course they're not, if workers can remember them,' replied Marina.

Nadezhda looked at her sister. It was difficult not to answer back.

'"Down with the war. Down with the German woman", is popular,' she suggested,

'I couldn't possibly say that about dear Alix,' said the Countess, still tweaking her red armband. 'We've been friends for years.'

'Oh, you can,' said Nicholas, looking away from the window. 'Most of this is her fault. If she had not been so in thrall to R—'

'He-Who-Shall-Not-Be-Named!' replied the Countess, her hand in the air.

'Well, you can say "Down with the war",' whispered Nadezhda. 'That's easy. Down with the war that is doing nothing but killing thousands and thousands of young men, turning the fields of the west red with their blood. This bitter, evil war that is starving the mothers and babies back home, because there is no one to bring in the harvest, or sow the seeds of the future. This hateful, evil, pointless war that is breaking all our hearts, killing our beautiful blue-eyed young men and sending them back to the people they love in coffins covered in flowers. This horrible, horrible war...'

She looked up, to realise everyone in the room was staring at her. She looked back down at her shoes and held her breath in the silence; all she could hear was her broken heart still beating in her ears.

'Well, I think we can all agree with that,' replied Nicholas, gently. 'Down with the war.'

'Absolutely, down with the war,' agreed Bertie, who hated silence almost as much as he hated social awkwardness. 'Although don't tell Sir George I said that, because British foreign policy is very much pro the war... of course.'

An hour later, after much discussion and sewing and planning, the group of overnight diners ventured out, one at a time, onto the street with red bands around their arms, scarves on their heads, and boots and coats borrowed from the servants.

The first to leave was Bertie Stopford. It was decided that, as he was a British citizen, it would be easiest for him to test the water with the drunken rebels and the now equally drunken soldiers who were camped out in front of the Countess Kleinmichel's palace. They were grouped around a brazier, rubbing their hands together in the cold, swaying with camaraderie and swigging from a bottle, undoubtedly sourced from the Countess's cellar downstairs. The plan was for him to slip out of the side entrance and walk up the road. He would then raise his hat if he felt it was safe. Or safe enough. And then the others would leave, heads down, armbands visible, trying to arouse as little interest or suspicion as possible.

'I'll telephone you when I return to the Astoria,' Bertie said to Militza, kissing her cheek. 'After my luncheon at Hotel de l'Ours.'

'You are going out to luncheon?'

'But of course.'

Militza was nervous that a group of four women would attract attention. In normal times ladies would have been relatively safe walking the streets of the city, but these were anything but normal times. Gangs of young men were bad enough, but gangs of men stoked with the spoils and the blood of revolution were unpredictable animals and capable of anything. The gentlemen present naturally offered to escort them across the river. But Militza knew the bigger the group, the more of a target they'd become, not only for the drunken rabble but also the machine guns still perched on the roofs overhead, whose cacophonous killing sprees continued to echo around the city.

'May the body of Spirit protect us,
May the heart of Spirit give us courage.
May the ears of Spirit make us silent as smoke,

May the sight of Spirit make us invisible to our
  enemies.'

She mumbled the spell as she stood in the doorway.
Holding on to the hands of her dear daughters and her
dearest sister, she called upon Spirit and the souls of
the witches they had burnt, the mavens of the past, the
wise women of old, to protect them and keep them safe.
Nadezhda was rigid. Normally, she would walk away
from such a show and ask her mother or aunt to stop,
pouring scorn on their pagan peasant superstitions. But
this time she just stood and bit the inside of her mouth
and tried to curb her tongue. She listened with increasing
mortification as she heard her sister join in with her
mother and pray for invisibility, for the stealth of a cat
and the cunning of a fox and for the wisp and breath of a
ghost.

And while she listened to her mother and tried to ignore
the gabbled mutterings of her sister, Nadezhda called on the
power of the holy water that was in her pocket to protect
her and her family from harm. And just as she was about
to finish her list of names for her incantation, she added
the name of Nicholas Orlov. His addition surprised her. It
was a reward, she told herself, for his keeping her warm
throughout the night.

It was well after 2 p.m. when they stepped out on the
pavement, walking swiftly, as a group, heads down, hands
clasped in front of them like nuns on the way to church.
Militza was at the front, leading the way. The atmosphere
was tense. The drunks and soldiers opposite did not turn
their heads. They were too busy working their way through

fresh vodka that excitingly had been discovered below stairs. Wine was all well and good, but what really hit the spot was strong hard liquor.

Further down the road, the ladies came across their first body. It was not a policeman, but a revolutionary, lying in the street, his legs splayed, a bullet in the chest, still clutching a fistful of papers.

'That's horrible,' hissed Marina, turning her head away, her face white.

Militza scanned the roofs. 'Can you see anything?' she asked Stana. 'Where the snipers might be?'

'They're normally on the street corners,' she whispered. 'Over there?' she suggested. 'Above the dead horse?'

'Can you see a gun?'

'I am not sure.'

'Can you?' Militza asked her daughters. 'The light is so grey.' She paused. 'Oh, to hell with it, we should not stand still for too long, let's move anyway.'

'Wait!' said Nadezhda, half closing her eyes as she squinted at the rooftops bordering Liteiny and Nevsky. 'There?' Just as she pointed, the clouds broke, a small skein of blue appeared and with it a ray of sunshine that caught the barrel of the gun as it turned and pointed in their direction. 'Run!'

The clatter was deafening. The cracking of plaster, as the bullets hit the wall behind them, sent little splinters of paint and brick into the air, that stung as they hit their hands and faces.

'Here!' barked Militza, throwing herself flat against the wall, underneath a balcony that overhung Nevsky.

'Why are they shooting at us?' asked Stana, panting as she leant heavily against the wall next to her.

'They think we're revolutionaries,' said Marina. 'It's these stupid armbands.'

'They can't see the armbands from there,' said Militza. 'They are simply shooting at everyone.'

'What shall we do?' asked Stana. 'We'll be dead before we make it home.'

'How about the Anglo-Russian hospital?' suggested Marina. 'I can see it from here.'

Militza looked at her daughter, a little astonished. 'Let's go.'

The shots kept on coming as they ran down the street. There were numerous machine guns firing from various vantage points and their fire seemed indiscriminate. Whether you were loyal to the Tsar, or part of the revolution, the fact that you were on the street was enough. And there were bodies everywhere. Militza counted at least five or possibly six, before they finally made their way through the doors of the hospital.

Inside, there were casualties. Plenty of them. The hallway to Prince Dmitry's old palace with its baroque staircase and gilt rococo cherubs stuffed into every corner was filled with bodies, bleeding, moaning, in varying states of injury and despair. They were lying on the floor, sitting in the chairs, lolling against the walls, their eyes closed, their mouths agape, civilians, soldiers, the occasional revolutionary, all waiting their turn. Meanwhile, the nurses were flitting around like butterflies from one to the other, offering bandages, sips of water, and quiet words of comfort and care.

In amongst it all was Lady Sybil Grey, a British aristocrat and philanthropist from Northumberland, who'd helped found the hospital at the start of the war. Her hair cut short for efficiency and wearing her white nurse's apron with its distinctive red cross and a small white hat for cleanliness, she was a formidable force of nature. In her early thirties, she had a pretty face, with eyes the colour of a grouse moor in winter and a crooked smile, due to a grenade injury she'd received at the front.

'Grand Duchess Anastasia Nikolayevna,' she said to Stana, sounding surprised. 'Have you come to see your daughter? She's upstairs with the wounded from the street battles today. Forgive me if I don't accompany you, but I am currently trying to work out how to use this Father Christmas coat.' She lifted up a red and white trimmed coat. 'We've been ordered by the rebels to show our allegiance to the new regime, or they will come and shoot us and all our patients, or some such nonsense, so I thought it might be easier to comply.'

'Lady Sybil, I am so sorry to bother you,' said Stana. 'We are seeking shelter from the bullets.'

She smiled. 'You and everyone here.' She looked around the huge hall. 'They've been shooting in the street for hours now. Machine guns. Pistols. And then the rebels come charging in here, scaring the living daylights out of the patients, demanding we hand over all the policemen we have hidden here. They've been on the roof twice today already, looking for machine guns. They want us to fly a Red Cross flag outside the building to confirm our neutrality, or something like that. So we have Father Christmas's coat and some bedsheets and we're hoping that'll be enough. But you never know, that's the thing.' She sighed. 'Most of the nurses slept here last night. It was impossible to get them home safely. Some of them made it back to their dorms on Vladimirsky, but the others sat up for hours watching the shooting out of the window. I kept telling them it was too dangerous to sit by the windows, because of stray bullets and glass, but none of them listened. Fortunately, they're fine. But if you will excuse me, I have a flag to put up.' She flapped the Santa costume. 'Now, where are those bed sheets?'

Upstairs, they found Elena, still dressed in her nurse's uniform from the night before. She looked tired, her face was grey and yet she seemed to be buzzing with adrenaline and excitement.

'How are you? Are you all right, what a night!' she exclaimed, putting her arms out to embrace her mother.

'My goodness,' said Stana, as soon as she saw her daughter. 'You've cut your hair.'

'Oh, I know.' Elena nodded with a light laugh. 'We did it last night, well, some of us did. We had to do something while watching the revolution. We were too anxious to sleep, too terrified to miss anything.'

'We slept the night at Bogdan Bogdanovich's. In his salon,' replied Marina. 'Countess Kleinmichel's palace was ransacked by a mob and we watched from the other side of the street.'

'My goodness, is everyone all right?'

'Everyone but the Countess, who still has a houseful of unwanted guests.'

'When will they go?' asked Elena.

'When they've drunk the cellar dry, apparently.'

'How was the rest of your night?' asked Militza. 'How are the wounded?'

'So many.' Elena shook her head. 'They've been coming in all night. Stretcher after stretcher. It's the policemen who have the worst injuries. I have never seen anything like it.'

'You have policemen here?' asked Nadezhda, looking around the ward of bandaged men. They were all dressed in white gowns, it was impossible to distinguish one from another.

'We're a hospital, we treat everyone,' Elena replied. 'We make no distinctions. I thought you'd know that, with all your equality and fraternity and marching! The *feministka* that you are!' She looked at Nadezhda's smarting face. 'Forgive me,' she smiled, 'I haven't slept.'

The discussion continued about the fighting in the streets and how it had been impossible for many of the staff to get home.

'Although,' suggested Elena, 'some people have managed to make it out in the ambulance. They seem to be leaving ambulances alone, for the moment at least.'

After further words, Lady Sybil agreed to furnish them with an ambulance. It arrived in front of the hospital just as the revolutionaries tore down Lady Sybil's home-made Red Cross flag and draped it across a motor car they had commandeered. Militza watched as it careered down Nevsky Prospekt, flag billowing, pedestrians and other rebels scattering in its path. The flag had been hoisted for little more than five minutes.

The door to the Nikolayevsky Palace was opened by the butler, still dressed in his uniform and mightily pleased to see them all, standing on the doorstep, with their red armbands, borrowed coats, and exhaustion etched on their faces.

'Mama!' Roman came running to the door, his face white with worry. 'Where have you been? I tried everywhere. I telephoned all over the city, nobody knew where you were. Least of all at the Countess Kleinmichel's house, where they failed to answer the telephone, and when they did, they simply continued to say "hello" and laughed every time I spoke. I heard gunshots all over the city all night long. I have been so worried. Do you know they have emptied the prisons? The city is teeming with criminals. They are everywhere. They want us to return to barracks, but the soldiers are no longer swearing allegiance to the Tsar. Some have already been to the Duma to say they are in support of the new legislative. I am so glad you are home. It has been the most terrible of nights.'

'We're here,' said Militza. 'We are safe, we have each other, that is the most important thing.'

'Yes,' he said. 'It is.' He embraced his mother. 'Each other,' he nodded. 'By the way,' he said, 'they have stolen the motor car.'

Our army is faithful to us, the people are loyal to us; it is only a few murderers in the capital who are making all this trouble.

Tsarina Alexandra (on the day before the abdication)

CHAPTER 9

March 1917, Petrograd

Over the next few days rumours were everywhere and facts were hard to come by. The telephones worked intermittently and there were repeated power cuts. The speed and the chaos of the revolution and the capital's precipitous descent into chaos took everyone by surprise. As the bodies of the police piled up in the streets, so gangs of bandits, drunken soldiers and revolutionaries moved through the city with impunity. Institutions were pillaged, houses and palaces were regularly broken into, sometimes three or four times a day.

After a short stint staying with friends, whose homes were also constantly ransacked, the Countess Kleinmichel eventually sought refuge at the Chinese Legation, only returning to her palace later where she was reduced to living in two rooms along with her servants, while the rest of her house was turned into a hostel for soldiers, who proceeded to use her staircase as a rifle range, make speeches and sing revolutionary songs while dancing on her tables and bashing out tunes on her grand piano. They vandalised her paintings, cutting holes in the mouths of the portraits, including one of the Empress Elizabeth, whose lips they loaded with a fistful of cigarettes. But the Countess was determined to stay, right down to her very last bottle of French champagne, to prove that she wasn't the German spy, or the German sympathiser, that everyone said she was. And she was fortunate. Many others with similarly Teutonic-sounding surnames were shot on sight. Or worse.

Militza would never forget the telephone call she received from the Countess just after they'd spent the night in Bogdan Bogdanovich's house.

'It's Dmitry,' she began. 'I almost can't bear to tell you, but I have to say it out loud to someone, just so I know that it is real.' She paused. 'The night after you left, he returned to barracks. I don't know why any one of us thought that was a good idea, but he did. Anyway, now he is dead.'

'Dead? Dmitry?' Militza's hand turned white as she gripped the telephone.

'He is,' the countess confirmed, as much to herself as to Militza.

'I am so sorry.' Militza sighed. 'What horrible, terrible news.'

'I'm so sorry too.' She paused. 'He was twenty-five years old.'

'So young, he was so kind... so charming.'

'They pulled his eyes out,' she said, her voice flat, so matter-of-fact that Militza thought she'd misheard her. 'The soldiers. They pulled his eyes out, one at a time. They ripped one out but kept the other so he could witness the murder of several of his fellow officers. Then they took out the other eye. They broke his hands and his feet and then they tortured him for two hours by holding him up on their bayonets and beating him with their rifle butts until eventually he expired... God rest his soul.'

Militza didn't know what to say. She could see Dmitry's dear, handsome young face at the breakfast table. She could see his big grey eyes – the ones they plucked out – blinking, while he polished his wire-rimmed spectacles with a napkin.

'He was such a lovely boy,' she said eventually. It sounded so meaningless. But he was. He was lovely and still very much a boy. 'How could they?'

'He was twenty-five years old,' repeated the Countess. 'Twenty-five. How can life be so cruel? How can people be so cruel? Why couldn't they have just shot him quickly, like a dog? Even a dog has a better death.'

The news of Dmitry's death and its bestial brutality made Militza catch her breath. This was it. Rasputin's prophesy had come true, the vices and crimes and filth – the sordid, evil, cruel filth – were everywhere. They were galloping through the city and dancing on the graves of young and old alike. Until now she'd been paralysed by indecision, like a deer caught in the headlamps of a motor car. She'd sensed the terrible violence of the revolution. She'd felt it, creeping up on her like ants crawling up her legs, but she'd ignored the signs. She'd been too focused on her own guilt, too focused on herself, to do anything about it. But now, now it was surely here, with all its brutality writ large. She should leave, they should all leave, without delay. She should collect up her family and run. South? The Crimea? Would that be far enough away to escape the fury of the mob?

'There's an exodus,' confirmed Bertie that afternoon over tea in the Blue Parlour. He sat opposite Militza and Stana, his legs crossed, his shoes polished, his moustache waxed. Immaculate, still, despite the chaos. 'Simply everyone is leaving town. My Grand Duchess Vladimir telephoned me this morning and has asked me to go to her palace, to her Moorish boudoir to collect her jewellery and money and take it to her in Kislovodsk.'

'How are you going to do that?' asked Stana. 'Isn't it too dangerous? There are bandits and revolutionaries everywhere. They are even patrolling the trains, taking what they want.'

'I have a few diplomatic bags at my disposal but mainly, I thought I'd use my boots.'

'Boots?' asked Militza.

'I can fill them with cash. They might be a bit uncomfortable on the train, but nothing too unpleasant. She wants her tiaras, of course, I have no idea how I shall transport them, up shirtsleeves, something like that. But it has to be done. They are stealing from every house they break into. Fortunately, they don't understand art otherwise they'd be grabbing better stuff, but jewellery is mainly what they are after. It's easy to pocket, highly transportable.' He raised his eyebrows. 'I hear Felix is back in town.'

'But I thought he was under arrest? In exile.' Stana glanced across at Militza.

'He doesn't care, he's worried about his property, his servants are busy burying the jewellery in food tins under the stairs,' he said, taking a sip from his tea. 'And apparently Anna Vyrubova has died of the measles.'

'Sadly, that's false news,' replied Militza.

'Nikolasha spoke to the Tsar this morning,' added Stana. 'He said she was well...'

'Oh, most unfortunate,' said Bertie sounding deeply disappointed. 'She really is someone I am not awfully fond of. And I don't say that very often. I find her dull, which is criminal in my book. Who knows why the Tsarina likes her so? I've also heard rumours that the guard at Tsarskoye Selo are not stable, that the soldiers might swap sides at any minute.'

'At least the Tsar is on his way back from the front, he might be able to maintain some sort of stability,' suggested Stana.

'I am not sure about that,' said Bertie. 'Nothing appears stable or certain any more. Did you hear about the Freederickszes?'

'No.' Militza leant forward.

'The rebels broke into their house and set fire to the place. They even bayoneted the dog. The Count was at the front, at Stavka, so he was fine, but the daughters and the old Countess only just made it out alive. They'd begged Sir George Buchanan for sanctuary in the embassy, as have hundreds of people, by the way, but they were refused by Lady Buchanan who said that the Countess had never invited her to her box at the ballet, so why should she help her out now?'

'Really?' asked Militza.

He nodded. 'Anyway, the old Countess died in the English nursing home last night. She never got off the stretcher they used to rescue her from the fire.' He shook his head. 'There are terrible things happening in this city. Terrible stories. Terrible violence. I shall be glad to leave it. It's like being jilted by a lover. I have been enamoured of this country, and of this city for so long. The Venice of the north. How

I have loved every golden dome, every frozen canal, every ballet, every concert, every wonderful person I have ever met. This country takes your soul, it takes it away and it doesn't ever give it back. But I am not sure I can love it any more. I am bereft. It is the total destruction of all that is civilised, and all that is beautiful, and I can't bear it.' He looked at them both, his watery eyes glazed with sadness. 'I find the whole thing heartbreaking. And the violence, I have never seen anything like it in my life. A woman died in front of me yesterday. Well, actually, more on top of me. They were shooting on Nevsky, again, and we were all lying on the ground in terror. The police shot her and she fell on my legs, trapping me for at least twenty minutes. I felt her grow cold.' He smiled, a little embarrassed – Stopford was not a chap for emotional outpourings. He coughed and lit a cigarette, feeling he'd said too much. 'Anyway, I am on the late train tomorrow night. I might be able to get a good night's sleep for the first time in weeks. It's the machine guns that keep me awake all the time and if I have to hear the "Marseillaise" again…'

That night, Militza, Stana, Marina and Nadezhda tried to work out what to take and what to leave behind. Impossible decisions. They had no idea how long they would be gone for. A few weeks? A month? A year? It wouldn't be that long, surely? Petrograd was their home. They'd be back soon. Everything would return to normal. But no one knew. Each of these decisions was overwhelming. They must be taken one small step at a time. For the moment, they were just leaving the city. They would take the servants, those who wanted to leave, to travel south to safety. But there were others who were already wearing red banners around their arms. Not that Militza or Stana felt they could say much. If they were still doing their jobs, even if somewhat reluctantly, then they didn't want to dismiss anyone, turf them out into the night for fear they might come back with a gang of friends, while everyone slept. There had been stories of servants disappearing in the night, abandoning their situations, joining the rebellion. Militza only had to think of the night at the Countess Kleinmichel's to know that those stories were certainly true. But Brana would come, they were sure of that.

Brana. Clothes. Money. Books. Should they take books? They were heavy and unwieldy but Militza could not be without them.

'We should mostly just take ourselves,' concluded Stana, sitting on a hard wooden chair in the library surrounded by papers. 'What use are these?' She waved at a pile of documents.

'I know,' agreed Militza. 'What else do we really need?'

'What is this?' asked Nadezhda, pulling a heavy green velvet-bound book off the shelves. It had a bronze, filigreed cover clipped together with an ornate bronze clasp.

'Careful!' exclaimed Militza, leaping out of her seat.

'What is it?'

Nadezhda undid the clip and sheets of yellowed paper with diagrams and writing in odd different scripts slid out from between the pages. As she leafed through, pressed flowers and herbs that had been pressed between the pages also fell out on the table. Stiff and wafer thin, they were like skeletons of their former selves.

'What is it?' she repeated, turning the pages and picking up the brittle herbs.

'It belonged to our mother,' said Stana.

'And her mother before that,' added Militza.

'It's a book of spells,' said Stana.

'Spells?' Nadezhda pushed the book away.

'I used to read them to you when you were a child,' admonished Militza. 'They're collected and perfected over centuries. There are recipes, uses for herbs, potions, tinctures, poultices...'

'I don't remember.'

'You chose not to. Labour pains, stomach aches, poor harvests, love potions, the birth of baby boys...'

'Love potions?' Nadezhda laughed. 'Love has nothing to do with a potion.'

'What do you know of love?' asked Marina. Her voice was clipped as she looked at her sister.

'A little,' replied Nadezhda.

'About as much as you know about feminism and the revolution!' Marina laughed.

'What's that supposed to mean?'

'You'd be amazed what we did mix together.' Stana smiled, glancing from one sister to another. 'We used to adore making those, didn't we, Militza? Love potions?'

'We did,' agreed Militza. 'Those and many other things besides.'

'What's the strange script?' Marina picked up a yellowed piece of paper.

'Sanskrit, mostly, Persian...'

'And the symbols?'

'The symbols are something else. Something very powerful,' said Militza. 'They take a lifetime to learn.'

'And it's yours?' asked Marina.

'Ours,' said Militza. 'Its contents should be used with caution, as Stana and I know only too well.'

'So what's in a love potion?' asked Marina.

'Rose petals, honey, lavender, bay leaves,' replied Stana. 'And you need to warm it over a red votive candle and chant "May your heart and your body and your soul be inflamed for me, and my body, and the sight of me."'

'What foolishness,' declared Nadezhda.

'What is the most powerful spell in here?' asked Marina, picking up the book.

'Manifestation,' replied Militza. 'It is more powerful than death. Death is finite. Manifestation is infinite and… the ramifications are unknown.'

'If you change the cosmic order of things,' added Stana. 'You have to be prepared to deal with the consequences.'

It is hard to work out what constitutes a life, Militza thought, sitting on the floor, surrounded by books, as she turned over volume after leather-bound volume in her hand. These were works here that she had collected over years. Decades. Works that she'd found herself, while wandering through the bookshops of Paris and Berlin. Others, rare titles, had been posted from bookshops all over the world, especially London. Watkins of London was one of her favourites; they specialised in the works of Madame Blavatsky and the Golden Dawn, necromancy, geomancy, astrology, tarot, Martinism, Qabalah, Hermes Trismegistus.

She reached into a pile and found a small crimson kid-bound version of Baudelaire's *Les Fleurs Du Mal*.

To the Reader.
Infatuation, sadism, lust, avarice
possess our souls and drain the body's force;
we spoonfeed our adorable remorse,
like whores or beggars nourishing their lice.

Our sins are mulish, our confessions lies;
we play to the grandstand with our promises,
we pray for tears to wash our filthiness;
importantly pissing hogwash through our styes.

The devil, watching by our sickbeds, hissed
old smut and folk-songs to our soul, until
the soft and precious metal of our will
boiled off in vapour for this scientist.

Each day his flattery makes us eat a toad,
and each step forward is a step to hell,
unmoved, through previous corpses and their smell
asphyxiate our progress on this road.

Like the poor lush who cannot satisfy,
we try to force our sex with counterfeits,
die drooling on the deliquescent tits,
mouthing the rotten orange we suck dry.

Gangs of demons are boozing in our brain –
ranked, swarming, like a million warrior-ants,

they drown and choke the cistern of our wants;
each time we breathe, we tear our lungs with pain.

If poison, arson, sex, narcotics, knives
have not yet ruined us and stitched their quick,
loud patterns on the canvas of our lives,
it is because our souls are still too sick.

Among the vermin, jackals, panthers, lice,
gorillas and tarantulas that suck
and snatch and scratch and defecate and fuck
in the disorderly circus of our vice,

there's one more ugly and abortive birth.
It makes no gestures, never beats its breast,
yet it would murder for a moment's rest,
and willingly annihilate the earth.

It's BOREDOM. Tears have glued its eyes together.
You know it well, my Reader. This obscene
beast chain-smokes yawning for the guillotine –
you – hypocrite Reader – my double – my brother!

She put down the book and looked up. 'I shall keep that,'
she said. 'But what shall we do with all the rest?'

'What shall we do with ourselves?' asked Stana. 'What
shall we do with ourselves?'

She sighed and looked at the piles of books and
remembered all those years ago, when she and Militza
filled their trunks to leave their wooden palace in Cetinje,
Montenegro. They packed their cheap underwear and

unfashionable clothes to arrive at Smolny Institute for Girls and then when they married and left Cetinje forever, they brought with them so very little. A few bags and a trunk with a pestle and mortar their mother had given them for grinding and blending and incantations, bottles of belladonna drops and the green velvet book of spells.

'We need to keep Mama's book safe,' said Stana. 'We can't leave it behind here. We need to take it with us. It's too valuable. It knows too much.'

'But there are so many more important things than this,' declared Marina, pushing the green velvet spine away. 'My dog, my clothes, my things...'

Marina was growing increasingly anxious at the prospect of leaving Petrograd. She disliked the Crimea at the best of times; there was too little to do, too few distractions. No balls. No theatre. No ballet. The idea of walking among the roses, clutching a tome of some description, bored her to tears. Although there was some tennis to watch and some swimming in the rock pool the Tsar had had cut out of the cliffs. Perhaps it might be more diverting if the Tsar and Tsarina came? At least she'd have the girls to talk to.

'Maybe we should give the book to Mr Stopford to take for us?' suggested Militza.

'Do you think so?' replied Stana.

'We are far more likely to be stopped than he is,' she continued. 'An Englishman on his own? He has a quick wit and a sharp eye, and he knows everyone. He can talk his way out of any situation. If the Grand Duchess is entrusting him with the Vladimir tiara, I think we can trust him with our book. The question is which one is worth more.'

The more they discussed it, the more it made sense. Bertie

was travelling to Kislovodsk, he could easily travel on to the coast. He might enjoy a small detour. Either way, it was dangerous to leave the book behind for the looters and pillagers of Petrograd, and equally dangerous to travel with it. The only question now was how to get it to him?

'I'll take it,' suggested Nadezhda. She couldn't sit there any longer, stifled by the conversation, listening to her sister, or her mother or her aunt.

'You?' said Militza. 'But you can't abide magic or incantations or spells of any kind.'

'Well, you can't give it to one of the servants,' she replied. 'As you say, it's too valuable. Roman is with his regiment going to meet the Tsar at Stavka. And Marina can't go!' Nadezhda laughed.

'What do you mean I can't go!'

'I am the only one who knows these people.'

'These people!' Marina's face contorted. 'You have no idea who they are.'

'I know more than you, sitting here with your sewing and your lapdog.' Nadezhda stood up from the floor, her hands on her hips. 'I've marched with them, I have heard their chants, I know what they want, I know why they hate us, why they hate the Tsar and why they hate the war. I have looked them in the eyes, and I have seen their sorrow.'

'Their sorrow!' Marina laughed. 'They show no sorrow for all their shooting, murdering, killing, bayoneting the Freederickszes' dog. Torturing Dmitry.'

'What do you mean, torturing Dmitry?' Nadezhda looked at her mother. At Stana. At her sister.

'You don't need to hear about that,' said Militza.

'The Countess Kleinmichel's Dmitry?'

'He's dead.' Marina's tone was accusatory. 'Oh! Didn't you know?' She covered her mouth with her hand, as if she'd accidentally let the news slip out of her pretty pink lips. Then her eyes narrowed. 'They took over two hours to kill him, they plucked out his eyes, like vultures with carrion. Broke his arms and his legs and hung him on their bayonets until he died. Those are your sisters and brothers, my dear. Those are your comrades in arms. Two hours. Both eyes. "Down with the war. Down with the Tsarina!"' Her delicate fist pumped the air. '*Vive la révolution!*'

'Be quiet!' hissed Militza.

'Why? What I'm saying is true.'

'Poor Dmitry,' said Nadezhda, shaking her head, her eyes filling with tears. 'That's awful. Why did he go back to his barracks when they'd already rebelled?'

'Maybe out of duty,' suggested Marina. 'Do you remember duty?'

'Has anyone heard from Nicholas Orlov?'

The following day it was bitterly cold. It was minus seventeen degrees and snowing when Nadezhda left the palace to walk to the Astoria Hotel. Militza had left a message with Mr Stopford the night before to ask him if he minded taking the green velvet book. He'd even offered to walk over to the Nikolayevsky Palace himself, or at least find Nadezhda some form of transport. But there was none to be had. He'd hoped he might be able to borrow a motor car from his close naval attaché friend at the embassy. But they had been attacked the night before just by the Fontanka Canal and the car had been shot at; it was riddled with bullet holes and the tyres were flat. Fortunately, neither of them had been in the vehicle at the time. But if motor cars were attracting that sort of visceral reaction, perhaps it was quicker, easier and, in fact, possibly safer for Nadezhda to walk, on her own, through the back streets. The main avenues and boulevards were too dangerous, there were too many gangs and groups marauding, firing their stolen weapons at whatever they liked. But if you kept to the back streets, kept your head and your back to the walls of the building as much as you could, then movement around the city was possible. You just never knew what was around the corner.

It was nearly 9 a.m. when Nadezhda walked into St Isaac's Square and came across a parade of soldiers and revolutionaries, flying red flags, their banners streaming in the brisk wind as they marched alongside a brass band with trumpets blaring. It took her hugely by surprise. There was quite a crowd to greet the soldiers, they were waving and cheering, like a victory party. It was a rather brilliant spectacle. Nadezhda smiled as she wove her way through the throng towards the revolving doors of the Astoria Hotel. Perhaps the worst was over? This was it. Joy on the streets. The Tsar was on his way back from the front, or so she'd heard. Once the people saw their leader, Little Father, surely everyone would come to their senses and the terrible bloodshed would be over.

She looked over her shoulder at the soldiers with their banners billowing in the wind, but just as she stepped through the doors of the hotel, there were shots. A machine gun on the roof burst into life, firing on the crowd below. Nadezhda froze, watching as the young men in the square began to fall. One. Two. Three. They were being picked off at random; some dived into the snow in front of the golden domes of the cathedral, hoping to find some sort of cover from the shooting. But mostly the crowd ran, scattering through the square, tripping over each other in their haste to escape. There was panic, chaos. Still the shooting continued, executing them, one by one. As Nadezhda watched, open-mouthed, clutching the green velvet book to her chest, she suddenly became aware of a primeval roar, a raging sound of pure fury, that came from the crowd in the square, and it was headed straight for the Astoria Hotel. The banners were gone, their weapons were shining black against the snow, their teeth were bared, their eyes were red with anger, and they were running in a wave towards the door. There was a shooter on the roof, and they were going to kill him and whoever got in their way. Someone grabbed her arm and pushed her through the revolving doors.

'Get upstairs!' yelled the doorman. 'Now!'

The guests in the lobby raced towards the lifts and the golden staircase.

Officers, journalists, foreign dignitaries, diplomats, aides-de-camp, attachés; the Astoria Hotel had rich pickings for the revolutionaries, it was rammed to the rafters with members of the *burzhúi*.

Nadezhda ran up the stairs, still holding the book. The level of screaming madness below was something to behold. Two of the huge plate-glass windows shattered in a hail of bullets from the street, sending shards of glass flying through the air. Two British officers in red jackets and white gloves appealed for calm, but to no avail. In fact, the only person who resolutely refused to join in the mayhem was a young Englishwoman who sat on her packed trunk in the middle of the mêlée, with a felt hat perched on the top of her head, smoking a cigarette.

Nadezhda bounded up the stairs two at a time, right the way to the third floor, where she remembered Mr Stopford's room to be.

'Mr Stopford! Mr Stopford! Bertie!' she yelled, hammering on the door with her fists. 'It's me! Nadezhda. Let me in!'

The shooting and the shouting below were getting louder, the mob from the street were now pouring through the broken windows and were killing anyone or anything that got in their way: men, women, the lapdogs in arms. Terrified guests were running around reception, adding to the chaos, some dressed, some half-dressed, others still in their nightgowns.

'Mr Stopford! Mr Stopford!' Nadezhda pounded the door. There was no answer. 'Please! Open up! Please. I beg of you. Please.'

The neighbouring doorway was covered in an American flag, clearly in the hope that it might protect those inside from attack.

'Here,' hissed a voice, as the door opened a crack. 'Get in here and be quick.'

Nadezhda did not need asking twice, she hurled herself through the door, breathless and terrified, gripping tightly on to her book of spells. Her saviour was a young man, half-dressed in a white vest and baggy trousers, with a cigarette stuck to his bottom lip and hair flopping over his face.

'Donald,' he said, in a deep American drawl. 'Photographer.'

'Nadezhda,' she replied. 'Princess.'

'Good.' He nodded, looking her up and down. 'Stay away from the glass, Princess.' He indicated with his cigarette. 'I warned her,' he said drily and shrugged. 'She didn't listen.'

Nadezhda looked down at a young woman lying dead on the floor. Her eyes were open, staring sightlessly at the ceiling, her mouth round with surprise. She'd been shot straight through her throat.

'There are hundreds of them,' said Donald, glancing down at the square from behind the curtain. 'I was fast asleep and got woken up by the shooting. What are you doing here?'

'I'm here to see the man in the room next to you.'

'The famous Mr Stopford!' Donald smiled. 'He left early this morning. I heard his door. A strange fellow, he keeps the strangest hours.' He sniffed and dragged on his cigarette. 'He's the best-connected man in town.'

'He deals in Cartier and Fabergé,' agreed Nadezhda.

'Of course he does.' Donald nodded and stubbed out his cigarette in his overflowing ashtray.

Outside the door, the rebels were thundering up and down the corridor, shooting at the mirrors and trying to kick in the doors. There were shouts of: 'Save the women and children!' 'Stop shooting!' 'Don't shoot!'

They hammered on Donald's door so loudly Nadezhda shrieked in shock.

'Shhhh.' Donald put his finger to his lips and indicated for her to hide in the bathroom. 'American! *Amerikanetz.* American!' he shouted at the door. 'What do you guys want? I have money, I have cigarettes.' They hammered on the door again with the butts of their rifles. 'Don't shoot! American! Don't shoot!' Donald scrambled around his room and picked up a wad of roubles and as many packets of cigarettes he could find. He opened the door and grinned broadly. 'American... *Amerikanetz.*'

'Have you seen any Russian officers?' one of the mutineers asked, plucking a packet of Winstons out of Donald's hand and placing it in his top pocket.

'Russian officers?' repeated Donald, pretending to think deeply as he handed around his cigarettes and small piles of roubles. 'Hmmm. No. I'm not sure there are any on this floor,' he said, knowing full well there were at least three of them further down the corridor. 'Why don't you try the floor above?'

And as they walked off down the corridor towards the stairs, he slammed his bedroom door. 'Princess,' he hissed, just outside the bathroom, 'you'd better run, you'd better get out of here. They've gone, but they will be back.'

'Where?' While they spoke, Nadezhda was slipping the book inside her coat for safekeeping.

'I don't know.' He shrugged. 'It's too dangerous for you to go out the front, they're shooting anything that moves.'

'What shall I do?' Nadezhda tried to control the panic in her voice.

'Through the kitchens? There's got to be an exit through the kitchens and out the back?' he suggested.

'Kitchens? Really?'

'It's the best I can do.' Nadezhda hesitated. 'Look, I'm out of cigarettes. I can't bribe them a second time.' He slowly opened the door and looked up and down the corridor. 'Clear,' he said. 'Good luck,' he added, putting his hand on her shoulder. 'Run!'

Nadezhda needed no encouragement and she scurried

as quietly and as quickly as she could towards the stairs. She flew down them at speed, sidestepping the bodies, climbing over the dead. When she reached the ground floor, she stopped, unable to believe what she was seeing. There were officers being dragged by their feet across the square, some, crying and squealing for their lives, were being shot on the ground as they lay, others were lined up in rows and dispatched like bottles on a fence. People were weeping on the floor, there was blood everywhere and broken glass, they'd even taken pot-shots at the huge chandeliers in the hallway. In fact, almost everything had been destroyed or broken.

Passing the reception desk with its shattered mirror, Nadezhda made her way down into the kitchens. She walked past a storeroom where she saw a soldier with an officer's sword cutting up the huge packets of butter the hotel had laid down for the guests. Further into the kitchen, there were groups of soldiers sitting on the floor, eating. Cheese, ham, bread, apples, herring, gherkins; anything they could find. It didn't seem to matter what it was.

Meanwhile, the one storeroom they had really wanted to break into was already occupied and destroyed. The British officers in the hotel had been one step ahead of the rebels and, realising the disastrous consequences of a bloodthirsty mob stewed in alcohol, they had occupied the cellar and smashed as many bottles of wine and spirits as they could. They'd exhausted themselves hurling bottles on to the floor until their arms hung useless by their sides, and they were knee-deep in whisky, cognac, gin, champagne, vodka and wine. A heady, but thankfully undrinkable cocktail.

That's not to say they succeeded in destroying everything,

for bottle after bottle of liberated wine had made its way into the square and was being passed around by the rebels who simply sliced the top off with their swords or smashed them open with the butts of their rifles and glugged down the contents, hoping to remain sober enough not to slice their open mouths on the broken shards of glass.

Nadezhda was terrified, but the orgy of consumption and destruction proved to be enough of a distraction for the soldiers to let her pass, almost unnoticed, apart from a few lecherous propositions and name-calling. Finally, after trying various doors, she found herself outside in the street at the back of the hotel where, for a second, she paused, leaning against the wall, breathing in the freezing cold air.

Not that the streets were any more salubrious. Drunken soldiers littered the pavements along with the dead. Some had passed out so cold, with their mouths gaping, it was difficult to work out which was a corpse and which was simply comatose.

The shooting had stopped. The man on the roof had been captured, tortured and mutilated just like all the other shooters before him. Nadezhda walked around to the front of the hotel. The wreckage was astonishing. There were pot plants in the square, cushions and chairs all over the pavements, curtains hung off their rails, there were broken pieces of china and plates everywhere, anything whole or only slightly damaged was already being scavenged by passers-by. The revolving front door was still spinning and at the foot of it was a crimson pool of blood.

'Nadezhda,' came a voice. She turned around. There, amongst the ruins and piles of shattered glass and splintered furniture, was Bertie Stopford. He had a large carpet bag in one hand and a leather portmanteau in the other. 'I seem to have missed the Babylonian hordes,' he said, slowly surveying the scene. 'What on earth happened here? Are you all right?' He turned to look at her.

'I'm fine,' she said.

'Thank goodness.' He shook his head. 'I have never seen anything like it.'

'There was someone shooting on the roof and the crowd turned and mobbed the hotel. I was rescued by your next-door neighbour. The American. Donald.'

'The handsome Mr Thompson. That's fortunate.' He sighed, overwhelmed with the devastation. 'What a tragedy,' he said. 'It is such a beautiful hotel. What were they thinking?' He sighed again. 'Have they looted the whole place?'

'They've left some of the rooms.'

'How many people have they killed?' he asked, taking in the devastation in the square. The piles of bodies, the puddles of blood. 'How many poor souls have they taken today?'

Just at the foot of the statue of Nicholas I on a rearing bronze horse, the rebels had lit a bonfire, where they were burning the dining room chairs and tables, along with piles of books from the library. Every time a book or piece of furniture was thrown on to the fire, the crowd roared their applause as they swigged their broken bottles of wine. Some of the more enterprising were drinking from their boots, having filled them to the brim in the kitchen.

Bertie Stopford felt his heart sink, his soul weep and, for possibly the first time in his life, he was lost for words. As he was staring at the bonfire and the bacchanalian orgy going on around it, he saw a figure walking slowly through the smoke. It was not so much walking as staggering, while trying to remain up right. As it lurched to the left, the figure was illuminated by the glow of the fire. He was wearing a pair of highly polished officer's boots. Bertie strained his eyes and squinted a little. The man's face was shining, not with sweat, but with blood. He looked familiar.

'Nadezhda,' he said, touching her elbow and indicating towards the fire. 'Is that...?'

'Nicholas!' Nadezhda exclaimed, shoving the book into Bertie's hands. 'Nicholas! Nicholas!' The figure scanned the square. 'Nicholas!' Nadezhda ran towards him, weaving her way through the drunken crowd. 'Here! Over here!' She ran. 'Here!' He fell towards her, staggering, like the drunks around him. He collapsed into her arms, and she crumpled under his weight into the snow. 'What's happened?' She held his face in her hands, the blood sticky and warm, she tried to wipe away with her hands, rubbing her palms down the front of her dress. 'What's happened to you? Are you all right? Please say you're all right.'

'I'm all right!' he whispered, his face contorted into a smile as he tipped his chin up towards her and tried to look through his swollen eyes. 'It's just a few cuts and bruises.'

She cupped his chin and tried to remove the blood from around his split mouth with her thumbs, rubbing it away from the corners. 'What did they do to you?' she whispered. 'What did they do?'

'They hit me with the butts of their rifles, hit me until I fell on the ground. They wanted to smash in my skull, but an old woman shouted at them and told them to stop and they just ran away with my sword.'

'Shhhhhh,' she said. 'Don't speak, I'm here now. Let's get you inside the hotel.'

With the help of Bertie and three members of staff, Nadezhda managed to get Nicholas Orlov into Bertie's room on the third floor, where they removed his bloodstained uniform. Once he was in Bertie's bed, Nadezhda immediately set about cleaning the blood off his face using the last of the hotel's hot water, a white enamel bowl and a soft cotton cloth. She was gentle and precise with her movements, desperate not to cause him any more pain. She dabbed around his eyes and touched his lips and caressed the contours of his face, while he lay there, barely breathing.

'He needs a doctor,' said Nadezhda, looking up at Bertie. 'He can't stay here, either. The electricity is out and there's no heating.'

'You're right,' agreed Bertie, lighting a candle and placing it beside the bed. 'I know there's a doctor at the end of the corridor and I will call Sir George Buchanan at the British Embassy to see if he can help. I'll be back: don't answer the door to anyone else but me. I won't be long.'

As the daylight began to disappear, the room filled with the golden light of the candle and the flame flickered and danced across Nicholas's face. His long dark eyelashes glistened with water, his battered and bruised cheeks shone in the warm yellow glow. Nadezhda began to hum under her breath. She stopped herself. It was the tune that her mother had sung to her when she too had hovered between the gates of life and death. It was a very ancient song. An incantation. She had no idea she even knew it. It felt wrong. Very wrong. The magic of her foremothers was fantasy, born out of illiteracy and superstition. She knew that, despite the book she'd risked everything to carry across Petrograd. It was ancient and unsophisticated. It didn't save poor Oleg. Why would it be useful now? She looked down on Nicholas's innocent face, so broken and swollen and covered in blood. He was at the gate. The light would surely call him if it wanted. No one else would hear her.

She dug deep into her memory. A wave came over her, a power, an energy. She began to hum, despite herself.

'In the sea in the ocean sits the most holy Virgin,
She holds a golden needle in her hand,
She threads a silk thread, she sews up the bloody
   wound,
You wound, do not hurt
You blood, do not flow
May the flesh be stitched
May the blood not flow
May the life return
May you live, loved one
May you live, loved one…
May you live, may you live, may you live…'

The effect was intensely soporific, the hair on her arms stood on end. Would it work? She had no idea. She had no idea what she was doing, playing with magic like a child. What foolishness was this! Her voice and the gentle stroking of his face would surely send him into a deep sleep. A healing sleep, that's what he needed. A sleep to repair his torn flesh and his battered bones. But instead, Nicholas very slowly opened his eyes, his cracked lips curving into a smile.

'Will you marry me, Princess Nadezhda Petrovna of Russia?' he whispered. 'I may be dead in the morning.' She stopped humming and stared at him, her hand poised in the air, still gripping the cloth. 'I worship the ground you walk on, the air you breathe and I love you, body and soul.'

'Don't talk.'

'You haunt my dreams, I can't sleep for thinking of you.' She remained silent.

'You can't deny the wishes of a dying man.' He moved his head on the pillow. His eyes shut, he winced, the pain in his head was excruciating.

'I can.'

'You may not.' He tried to smile.

'But I only have half a heart,' she whispered. 'The other half died on the battlefield, nearly three years ago.' She paused, her eyes filling with tears. 'I am in love with a ghost.'

'Then I shall take that half. I shall love it and nurture and nourish it,' he mumbled, his eyes closing. 'In the hope that one day it might… become whole.'

She leant forward and, by the light of a single candle, with the noise of the drunken rebels carousing in the square below, she slowly kissed him.

All around me there is treachery, cowardice and deceit!

Tsar Nicholas II, on the day of his abdication

CHAPTER 10

March 1917, Petrograd

That night, while Nadezhda held a vigil at Nicholas Orlov's bedside in the Astoria Hotel, holding his hands, sponging his brow, praying to whatever god that would hear her, praying for him to stay alive, praying for him to last the night, Militza was plagued by visions of burning crosses and weeping angels and the terrible images of Him, always Him, repeatedly crossing himself, crawling up her bed, pulling at the covers, only to be dragged back to the bottom of the river, weighed down by the fur coat of a prince.

She woke up to find her sheets were damp, and she was drenched in a cold, dank sweat; these were truly signs of the Apocalypse. It was coming, that was for sure; the four horses were bringing it to the city. Conquest, War, Famine and Death; they were pawing the ground, champing at the bit, rattling their bridles, ready to tear through the streets, leaving no corner, no household, untouched.

'The Tsar has abdicated!'

Roman stood in the doorway to the dining room in the Nikolayevsky Palace. His face was ashen, his hair unkempt, his unform creased. It was clear he had not slept and had rushed straight from the train station.

'There's a red flag hoisted above the Winter Palace. I saw it as I passed this morning. It's over.' He shook his head. 'Three hundred years of Romanov rule is finished. Just like that.' He clicked his fingers. 'Everything is finished. He's abdicated in favour of Michael Alexandrovich. But we all know the brother will refuse the crown. He's weak. Weaker than Nicholas, which is truly saying something. So that's it.'

'That can't be true,' said Stana, gripping the dining room table and staring directly at her sister. 'It's a rumour. Just another rumour. More false news.'

'I was there, on the train. In the camp when he signed the declaration. It was announced to the troops at the train station this morning. Some soldiers wept but mostly the others were waving their bayonets like corn in the wind. I tell you, it's over. Nicky seemed almost relieved. He had lunch with his mother, who saw him off at the station, she waved until we could no longer see her. She apparently remained on the platform on her own, weeping for hours, as we drew away. Then I saw him simply sit down and read a book about Julius Caesar in the carriage all the way back from Pskov. It was bizarre. D'you know what he said to his aide? "Now that I am free of my responsibility to the nation, perhaps I can fulfil my life's desire – to have a farm somewhere in England." England! Honestly. He's the ruler of all Russia!'

'And he wants to be an English farmer?' Marina looked horrified.

'Either that or go straight to Livadia. To watch his roses grow.'

'He's always had the parochial mindset of an English country squire,' said Stana.

'Why did he not abdicate in favour of Alexei?' asked Militza, slowly stirring her glass of raw egg with her fork.

'He spoke to a surgeon, or something, Professor Feodorov, who advised against it. Apparently, the bleeding is incurable.'

'It is.' Militza nodded, lifting her glass to her lips. 'The curse of the Coburgs.' She opened her throat and poured the eggs back in one gulp. 'No one has survived, so far, beyond the age of forty-two,' she added, dabbing the corners of her mouth with a linen napkin. 'And we know that Michael won't want the crown, unless his wife's involved.'

Stana nodded. 'She's always been energetically ambitious. But maybe even she realises it's a poisoned chalice. It's a shame the Grand Duchess Vladimir is so far away, taking the waters in Kislovodsk. This is her moment. This is what she's been waiting for all these years. She's always thought her branch of the family would be better at it than Nicky's. She'd be pushing Kirill towards the throne right now, if only she knew.'

'Kirill has already chosen his side,' said Roman. 'He is flying the red flag of revolution from his house on Glinka Street.'

'Kirill? Already?' asked Stana. 'But the ink is barely dry on the declaration.'

'There are banners and red armbands all over the place,' confirmed Roman. 'Everyone is choosing sides.'

'Of course they are,' said Militza. 'No one wants to pick the wrong one.'

'But it's typical of Kirill,' added Roman. 'He's always

been a snake in the grass, a blatant opportunist. Just like his mother.'

'So, who's in charge of the army, if Nicky has abdicated?' asked Stana.

'Why Uncle Nikolasha,' said Roman, looking at his aunt. Stana turned pale. 'I thought you knew.'

'Nikolasha? No,' she whispered. 'I haven't spoken to my husband for days.'

'He's on a train from the Caucasus to the front right now, with Father.'

'Peter?' Militza interjected. 'We had no idea.'

'Maybe he hasn't had the chance to send a telegram,' said Roman. 'Everything is so chaotic.'

'Personally, I just find it extraordinary that the Tsar didn't consult anyone,' said Militza, filling her glass pipette with the dregs of her cocaine elixir. 'The greatest political decision of his life, and of this nation, Mother Russia, and he consults no one. He speaks to no one. He makes Nikolasha commander in chief of the army without asking him. He hands over three hundred years of Romanov rule as if he was handing over a small gift from Fabergé, something that belonged to him. It didn't. It doesn't. It never belonged to him. He was only the custodian. It was not his to give away. No fight. No thought. I am not sure he quite knows what he has done.'

'Maybe if he smoked a little less hashish, he might have been able to think a little more clearly,' suggested Roman. 'I blame that Dr Badmaev friend of yours, Mama. I also blame Rasputin.'

★ ★ ★

News of the abdication stunned the city. What had started with women – mere factory workers – protesting about the lack of bread, had brought down a dynasty in a matter of days. There had not been a power struggle or lengthy negotiations, there was no tortured soul-searching. There was plenty of looting and shooting and devastation and destruction, but it was as if the mantle of government had been simply dropped, and picked up while it lay impotent on the ground.

There was a report of one aristocrat who had died spontaneously of a heart attack, but mostly the news was met with shock, silence and then a deep-rooted fear.

It took Michael less than twenty-four hours to refuse the crown. Like his older brother before him, he consulted no member of his family, least of all his ambitious wife, Countess Natalya Brassova who, as fate would have it, was out of reach in Gatchina some thirty miles south of Petrograd. Despite various officials begging Michael to take the reins – 'If you refuse, there will be anarchy, chaos, a bloody mess' – he signed power over to Prime Minister Alexander Kerensky and the provisional government. Within hours the city was covered in posters, slapped on walls and lamp-posts, proclaiming: 'Nicholas abdicates in favour of Michael! Michael abdicates in favour of the people!'

And the people's reaction was swift. They turned on the city itself, determined to rid it of all things Romanov. Up and down Nevsky Prospekt gangs of soldiers tore down the double-headed eagle crest from shops which had supplied goods to the court. The Romanov coat of arms was pulled off every building it was possible to reach, there was even talk of melting down the bronze statue of Peter the Great, erected by Catherine the Great in the Senate Square. Plaster eagles were thrown into the street. And the word 'Imperial' was scratched off the bronze plaques of every building they graced.

'They have even ruined the door of the Imperial Yacht Club,' said Bertie, drinking a stiff whisky in the Blue Salon at the Nikolayevsky Palace.

He'd come with news of Nadezhda and Prince Orlov, who was still battling his injuries, while both of them were holed up in the British Embassy as guests of Sir George Buchanan.

'The American eagle on the Singer building has been spared,' continued Bertie. 'It took a while to explain to the rebels that it was in fact a symbol of freedom and not repression. They've covered it in the Stars and Stripes to put the mob off.' He paused. 'All you can see from the street is the tiny tip of its sharp beak!' he said, laughing. 'There's been a run on red fabric as well. There's not a yard of the scarlet stuff left in the city. They've been cutting up the Russian flag and dumping the blue and white, stitching together the strips of red to swathe anything and everything in sight. Including Kirill's house, I note. He won't be the first turncoat, mark my words. Everyone will be calling themselves Comrade This, Comrade That before the end of the month. They're calling the Tsar, Comrade Romanov already. But that's probably just to humiliate him.'

'I think he's managed that all on his own,' said Militza.

'He is under house arrest, with all the children and the Tsarina at the Alexander Palace,' continued Bertie, lighting a cigarette. 'They should have gone when the British offered them safe passage. It's too late now. The Russian government is refusing to take care of their expenses. They can't go anywhere. They're sitting ducks. It's all very, very dangerous.'

'But none of the children or the Tsarina have ever done any harm, they are not political or anything like that. They are innocents,' said Stana.

'So was Marie Antoinette,' said Bertie.

'Surely it won't come to that!' laughed Stana, a little nervously.

'One can only hope,' he replied. 'But it all seems too unpredictable. I went to my Grand Duchess Vladimir's to retrieve some more of her belongings as instructed and found her faithful manservant Pavel shot on the stairs.'

'Pavel Petrovich?' Militza looked stunned. 'Dead?'

'Shot through the head, just lying there, on the stairs. I managed to gather together some of my Duchess's things, and I need to go back for more, but frankly the corpse spooked me a little. The palace was intact. Only the alcohol was gone. I locked it up. But I shall return in a few days for the rest of her jewellery, I thought it too dangerous to travel across the city with it all at once.'

'I thought you were leaving already?' asked Militza.

'That was before they stormed the Astoria and Orlov needed my help. When are you all leaving?'

'When our train is ready,' replied Militza.

'Surely the days of the personal trains are over?' suggested Bertie.

'Surely we have not come to that?' asked Stana, again.

While Bertie drank his whisky and Militza and Stana

stirred their tea, they discussed the storming of the Astoria and the terrible violence meted out to poor Prince Orlov.

After the night spent in the cold and the candlelight of Bertie's room, Stopford had returned to find Nadezhda fast asleep, her face resting on the bed, her hand still clutching the patient's, whilst his breathing was shallow but steady. They looked so content, he didn't want to disturb the couple, but the window of opportunity for movement was brief. They needed to take advantage of the early hours, the poor light and the collective hung-over slumber of the mob. So, as dawn broke, they tentatively moved Nicholas into Sir George's car and quietly drove through the snow-covered streets to Suvorov Square, the Field of Mars and the British Embassy.

Nadezhda was white with fatigue and worry, but still she refused to leave Nicholas's side. There were a few others taking refuge in the embassy, mainly secretaries and aides-de-camp who'd found it impossible or too terrifying to make it home. Unlike the Americans who'd been sleeping at their desks and on the floors of their offices since the revolution began, the British had embraced the situation with a little more aplomb and had created 'bedrooms' with cushions and soft furnishings. They had also somehow managed to requisition a samovar that boiled away merrily, just below the portrait of King George V, in the corner of the big red and white ballroom, where weekly sewing parties used to take place.

Food, however, was becoming increasingly scarce. With the kitchens of the Astoria out of business, even the dining rooms at the Hotel d'Angleterre were overwhelmed with hundreds of ex-pats caught in the crossfire, all fighting for food. Most, if not all, of the other restaurants were closed, boarded up, or looted and destroyed. So Nadezhda and her fellow embassy guests had to content themselves with whatever they could find in the basement kitchens – boxes of shortbread left over from Christmas, and a consignment of Bath Olivers that had somehow been overlooked, along with a few tins of ham and some jars of pickled herring.

Not that food concerned her. Nicholas was not making the progress Nadezhda had hoped and fervently prayed for. He was pale, his eyes were hugely swollen, his lips were dry and cracked and his breathing was becoming increasingly shallow and laboured. As she listened to his chest rise and slowly fall her anxiety increased. The British doctor who'd visited in the early hours had only shaken his head and muttered something along the lines of 'hoping for the best'. The hospitals were full, they were impossible to get to, her options had run out. If only her mother were here. She would know what to do. She would breathe life back into his soul. She'd open her trunk of tinctures and pound some powders with her pestle and mortar. She'd tell Brana to light the votive candles and she'd chant him back to life. Nadezhda shook her head. She was above that. Witchcraft. God would look after him. God would save him. She made another cross on his forehead using the cloudy brown water from the Neva that she still carried in her coat pocket.

But his hand was growing colder by the minute. His lips had lost all colour and were crusting together at the corners of his mouth. A waxen sheen glistened on his forehead. Nadezhda was seized by a sudden panic that caught her by the throat and squeezed her heart. Perhaps it was the lack of sleep, food, water, or the sheer overwhelming despair of the situation, but as she stared at his pale, waxy face, it transmogrified from Nicholas into Oleg, Oleg into Nicholas.

'Oh deary me,' whispered Lady Buchanan as she approached the bed. 'He is not looking well, is he? Very sick indeed.'

'God is looking after him,' replied Nadezhda, nodding firmly. 'God will provide.' She sponged his increasingly cold forehead.

Lady Buchanan picked up Nicholas's limp hand. 'But he's cold. He feels damp. I think he needs more than the Holy Father at this point, don't you? What has the doctor said?'

'The doctors are all busy, the hospitals are all full.'

'Then how about your mother?'

'My mother?'

'Isn't she good at this sort of thing?'

'What sort of thing?'

'You know what I mean. I've heard things. Strange, weird things. Didn't she save the Grand Duchess Vladimir's life?'

'Rumour has it.'

'Well, rumour is all you have now, dear girl. What are you waiting for? Go! But hurry!'

Outside on the street, the weather was bitter. It was minus twenty degrees and the wind stung like a Cossack's whip. This was surely the longest winter to linger in the capital since 1808. The Neva was still solid as a rock, ships were unable to move, suspended like ghosts in a state of eternal limbo. The walk across Troitsky Bridge was short but bitingly cold so when a crowded tramcar came trundling up the road and opened its doors in front of her, Nadezhda stepped in. If she kept her head down, she would be fine. She just needed to get home.

However, no sooner had the doors closed and the tramcar begun to move than a young woman let out a piercing scream.

'Thief! Thief! Thief!' she cried, pointing at a relatively well-dressed young man who was standing right next to her. 'You've stolen my fifty roubles! Look!' She opened her bag and displayed its empty interior to her fellow travellers. 'He's stolen my money! My purse! It's not here! Thief! Thief!'

The young man began to protest. He stammered and tugged at his hair, pushing his cap from one hand to the other. He had not stolen her money. He had no idea she had any money. He had plenty of his own, and if she wanted fifty roubles he had a note in his pocket.

But the young woman was not satisfied. The tramcar was stopped in the middle of the bridge and the young man was forced out. He looked up at the bus, with his feet in the snow, and repeated his innocence. His eyes wide, his hands clasping his cap. And then suddenly, someone shot him clean through the head. He fell on the pavement, where he stood. The man with the gun, wearing a thick leather jacket and a leather cap, gave orders to search him. Two workers leapt out of the bus and began to go through the dead young man's pockets. Cigarettes and a lighter were immediately requisitioned, but no purse was found.

'Are you sure he was your thief?' demanded the leather-jacketed man of the young woman. 'Take another look.'

The young woman rifled her coat pockets, hands shaking dramatically, pink lips quivering.

'Oh, here!' she said, with a little laugh. 'How foolish of

me. It must have slipped through a hole in my pocket into the lining of my coat.'

Maybe it was the laugh, or the way she waved her purse in his face, but she was ordered off the tramcar immediately, and as she turned around to step over the body of the young man, the man in the leather coat shot her clean in the back. She didn't fall but appeared to swing a little in the air. So he shot her in the back of the head and she fell on top of her suspected thief.

Nadezhda held her breath; she looked down at the floor and did not say a word. So, this was the new justice. Execution: without trial, justice or recourse.

Militza and Brana came as quickly as they could. They brought with them votive candles, a pestle and mortar and a carpet bag full of small bottles of multicoloured liquids that only they knew how to mix and administer.

Lady Buchanan gave the study over to the witch and her old nurse and firmly shut the door. She'd heard so much about the talents of the so-called Black Princesses, or the Black Crows, or the Black Peril, whatever you wanted to call them. Militza and Anastasia of Montenegro, the Black Mountains, where superstition, the occult and medicine combined. And now here they were. In her study. Frankly she found it all rather 'below stairs'. But even so...

Nadezhda overheard her whispering in English to a sturdy-looking woman called Edith.

'I quite enjoy having my tea leaves read. And I have to admit I have seen ghosts. But this gives me the creeps. It's like a couple of peasants from the village turning up with lucky heather. I mean, one of them actually is a peasant, the other... who knows?'

But Nadezhda didn't care. She couldn't. She didn't have the energy. This was her only hope. Her last throw of the dice. She sat on the small wooden chair outside the study, with her eyes half closed, her head resting against the wall, praying to herself, whispering under her breath, hoping against hope that her mother and Brana could halt the fever, stem the flow of blood and make him well. And as she sat with her eyes half-closed as if in a trance, she saw him. Oleg. Walking through the Elysian Fields, with his arms outstretched, his face in the sun. His father was beside him, his beard was long like Jesus's, next to him a dog was bounding through the poppies, the cornflowers, the ears of waving wheat. Behind them both, running a little to catch up, was the young man from the bus. He was still holding his cap, passing it from hand to hand, but he was smiling. He waved and shouted, and Oleg and his father stopped, waiting for him. And Oleg smiled. What a smile it was. Golden and shining and beautiful, it lit up Nadezhda's heart.

'Are you all right?' asked Lady Buchanan, who suddenly appeared before her, blurred. 'Would you like a cup of tea? Help dry those tears.'

Nadezhda had no idea she had been crying, or indeed for how long. But her mother now also appeared at the door, accompanied by a whirl of sweet-smelling smoke from the herbs she'd been burning in the room.

'He should be well now,' she said, wiping her brow with the back of her hand. 'The fever has left him.'

'Thank you,' said Nadezhda, embracing her mother and placing a kiss on her cheek.

'He's not out of the woods yet,' Militza warned. 'But at least he now knows the way.' She paused. 'Olga would never forgive me if I let her son, her only child, die in such a way. Attacked in the street and robbed of his sword, that's no way to go.'

'How did you know about the sword?' asked Nadezhda.

'Oh,' her mother looked puzzled, 'his spirit must have told me.'

... silent and motionless, they gazed in horror-stricken stupor at the sacrilegious holocaust which was slowly devouring the martyred staretz, friend of the Tsar and Tsarina, the *Bozhy Chelovek*, 'Man of God'.

Maurice Paléologue, French Ambassador

CHAPTER 11

March 1917, Tsarskoye Selo

All plans were on hold. The sands were constantly shifting. And the changes were swift. The national anthem disappeared overnight, to be replaced by the 'Marseillaise'. No one was asked to pray for the health and the happiness of the Tsar and his family at Mass any more. In fact, priests themselves were no longer safe – as obvious members of the *burzhúi*, they became targets of abuse and violence. Whole regiments were leaving the front, downing their weapons and simply walking off home. Food was now in acutely short supply. There was only a little black bread to eat, white bread had been so polluted and diluted with chalk and wood shavings, it was dangerous and inedible. Newspapers were published erratically, the post was even worse; over one million letters had been destroyed at the general post office in the last week alone. The Tsar had unquestioningly and unresistingly placed himself in the hands of the revolutionaries and he was now sweeping the snow off the paths of the Alexander Palace to keep himself occupied. Accompanied at all times by a guard, he showed no emotion at all. The Tsarina was calm, simply relieved to have her husband back by her side. And the rumours were correct that Anna Vyrubova did indeed have the measles. And although there were many who fervently prayed for her speedy and not entirely painless death, it was sadly proving not to be terminal.

Nikolasha, along with his brother Peter, took the train to Stavka at the front, from the Caucasus, to take up the reins as commander in chief of the army. They were joined by Roman from Petrograd who, along with his father and his uncle, all swore allegiance to the provisional government. Nikolasha's hands shook as he signed his written oath, little knowing he had already been dismissed. The order from the capital had been delayed. No one wanted a Romanov in charge of the army. No one wanted a Romanov in charge of anything. So Nikolasha's first order was confirming his arrival at the front and his second was to announce he was stepping down in his role as commander in chief, in favour of General Alexeev.

Nicholas Orlov was sitting up in his makeshift bed at the British Embassy. The swelling around his eyes was beginning to recede. Whatever incantation or spell Militza and Brana had chanted, or cast, had brought him back from the white light he'd seen at the end of the tunnel. How he'd desired to walk towards it. He could feel its balmy heat, see its joyful glow right in front of him, just out of reach. But he'd been pulled back from the light by a force so strong he could not resist it.

Lady Buchanan arrived with a tray of tea, rattling with

glass cups. 'I'm afraid there is no milk or sugar or anything like that,' she sighed as she placed the tray down on the small table beside the bed.

'It's perfect,' said Nadezhda, sitting on the other side of the bed. A blush of hope blossomed across her cheeks. 'I am just so happy to see him sitting up.'

'We all are.' Lady Buchanan smiled. 'It's a huge relief. I managed to speak to your mother last night.' Nicholas turned to face her; his eyes just barely open. 'She's been desperate for news. She is so happy you're making progress.' He tried to smile but winced again with the pain.

'We all are,' said Nadezhda, standing up to move a curl of hair from in front of his eyes.

'How is love's young dream?' exclaimed Bertie as he burst into the room, clutching a huge bouquet of red roses. Nadezhda snatched back her hand as if she'd been burnt and sat swiftly back down in her chair. Her cheeks flushed the colour of Bertie's flowers. 'These are for you, Nicholas!' he continued. 'Don't ask me where I got them. Actually, I'll tell you. My Grand Duchess Vladimir's. They were in her little hothouse. I spotted them from her boudoir window, and I thought I'm not leaving them behind for the rabble, they won't appreciate them at all, but I thought of you, you two. Here!' He smiled, incredibly pleased with himself. 'We need water and a vase.'

He turned around. Standing right behind him was Militza.

She stood in silence and looked at the flushed, flustered face of her daughter and the half smile on Nicholas Orlov's bruised and battered face. Why had she not noticed? She was normally so astute; she could smell love as soon as the spark lit up the heart. It was as sweet and fragrant as the taste of happiness. But this, this she had missed.

'Why don't I go and find something?' she said simply, and left the room.

Bertie sat down on the bed next to his flowers and continued to recount his news. He'd been to the ballet the night before and they'd played the 'Marseillaise' in the *entr'acte* which he'd found truly shocking. The Imperial box had been initially empty but two people, a man and a woman, in 'citizen's clothes', had sat in the Emperor and Empress's seat for the second half. Most of the other boxes that were more usually occupied by the Grand Dukes and Grand Duchesses were also taken, by soldiers in their dirty uniforms, spitting sunflower seeds all over the floor. At the end of the ballet, half the audience joined the dancers on stage and sang the 'Marseillaise', again.

'And do you know the irony of it all?' he said. 'The ballet was *The Sleeping Beauty* and the King, the Queen and of course the Princess, danced by the brilliant Smirnova, were all wearing tiny little crowns.'

'What on earth were you doing there?' asked Lady Buchanan. 'Isn't it far too dangerous?'

'This whole is city is dangerous, my lady,' he replied. 'Life is dangerous. But you can't let that stop you.'

'How is the patient?' asked Sir George Buchanan, standing in the doorway.

'Better,' replied Lady Buchanan.

'Improving,' confirmed Bertie.

'Good, good, that's what we like to hear,' said Sir George. 'Ah, Grand Duchess,' he added, turning to Militza, who'd appeared clutching a vase. 'Is your husband still at the front?

With Grand Duke Nikolai Nikolayevich? Who is refusing to leave, I hear, despite being relieved of his post. No sooner had he got his feet under the desk than he was told to go.'

'You seem remarkably well-informed,' replied Militza.

'I try.' Sir George smiled.

'He doesn't want to desert his country in its time of need, that is all. He's as much a general as the others. He's the most senior Romanov and he wants to do all he can. He also says it is hard to know who to trust when all they say about him is lies; how can you believe what you hear about anyone?'

'This is true. One always needs reliable sources. Do you have any news from Tsarskoye Selo?'

'Only that they are under house arrest.'

'The Emperor is learning to play Patience,' added Sir George. 'And various loyal subjects have placed themselves under house arrest along with them. Sydney Gibbs is refusing to go.'

'The tutor?'

'Yes, and the doctor, Dr Botkin, is also refusing to leave.'

'And the soldiers?'

'They are loyal for the moment. But you can feel it. I was granted a short audience the other day. I had to stand. No chair was offered. I wasn't there for very long but the soldiers, the footmen, are just a little slower to react. They didn't open the doors very quickly and now they look you in the eye. It's brazen and frightfully rude. But everyone is complaining about staff everywhere.'

'Oh, I agree,' added Bertie. 'At the Hotel D'Angleterre, it's appalling. They are all demanding higher wages and shorter hours. Barely anyone is working at the Astoria. The place is hardly open. Only old regulars like me are there. There's no food in the kitchen either. My room maid won't clean my room daily any more. I have to beg her to turn down at all. Everyone is demanding higher wages but if everyone gets paid more, then everything is just more expensive. That's capitalism. Not communism.'

'We've heard that there'll be a moratorium on exiles in the next few days, which is good news for Prince Yusupov and Prince Dmitry Pavlovich,' said Sir George. 'But less helpful for the stability of the capital.'

'There'll be a fresh batch of anarchists from abroad pouring in to stir up trouble and we can barely cope with the ones here at the moment,' declared Bertie.

'Are you referring to that ghastly little German agent, Lenin?' asked Lady Buchanan, her nose curling. 'Didn't you say he was planning to come here to stir up trouble? He keeps advising his followers, whoever they are, to kill anyone who has property and refuses to divide it up. Madness.' She laughed lightly.

'It certainly is,' agreed Sir George. 'I even heard a rumour there's a gang planning to exhume the body of Rasputin.'

'Exhume Rasputin?' Nadezhda looked aghast. 'Why would anyone want to do that?'

Would the Devil never sleep? Would he never leave them alone? The idea of him being dug up, shown the Light one more time, made both of the sisters' stomachs churn. What would they do with the body? Would they make him a martyr? Canonise him? Or would they parade him through the streets of the city? The whole body? Or just his head?

What if his corpse was not in the grave? What if he wasn't dead at all? What if they'd buried a ghost?

They drove themselves mad with questions. The mere mention of his name was enough to cause them both palpitations.

'We should go,' said Stana, pacing up and down in the Blue Parlour, wringing her hands over and over again.

'What would that achieve?' asked Militza.

'I don't know. But I can't just sit here. My mind won't rest. I have visions of his rotting corpse standing outside our house. Pointing his fingers. Jangling gaoler's chains. Accusing us of his murder. River water pouring out of his shoes. The idea of exhuming him fills me with horror. We can't let it happen.'

Militza didn't dare share her visions, or the details of his nightly visits which were becoming increasingly heightened, as if he was toying with her, unable to leave her alone. Only the night before, she'd lain helpless, pinned down, unable to move, as he'd clawed at her with his rough, damp, calloused hands. He'd run his coarse leathered tongue up and down her legs, across her stomach, licking her skin. She'd woken, covered in sweat and moist between her thighs.

Militza's footman managed to find them a motor car to drive them out to Tsarskoye Selo. It was small and uncomfortable, driven by a sturdy taciturn gentleman who sweated garlic and gherkins and smelt heavily of tobacco. Sir George had informed them the soldiers would rob the grave that night so there was little time to formulate a plan. As they set off in the darkness, they crossed the bridge and were forced to stop by the Field of Mars. There appeared to be flares and torches and hundreds of people standing around. Suddenly there was a cacophony of explosions, one after the other, illuminating the night sky.

'What are they doing?' asked Stana.

'They're preparing to bury the dead,' said the driver, his voice monotonous and matter-of-fact.

'What dead?' asked Stana.

'The heroes of the revolution,' he replied. 'But the ground is too hard, no one can dig it. So, they are blowing it up with dynamite.'

'They're burying the dead in the park?' asked Militza.

'They were going to bury them outside the Winter Palace,' he continued, with a sniff. 'But they decided they'd put them here in the end in the Field of Mars. The morgues are full. They've got to do something. The cold has kept them frozen solid so far, but they're saying there's a thaw on its way. And you can't have all those corpses rotting around the place.' He sniffed again. 'It's unhygienic.'

'How many do you think they are burying?' asked Militza, watching through the window, as gangs of workers started digging at the soil, moving the piles of mud that had been sprayed all over the ground.

'Thousands of them, or so they say,' replied the driver. 'A mass funeral. They'd planned it before, but there are no police left to deal with the crowds. All dead, of course. They're worried about disorder, but they can't wait any longer, half of the corpses haven't been washed or anything. Very few have been laid out properly. Not enough money, no one to pay them. Some people have been throwing a few kopeks down when they go to the morgue. But it's not enough. Half the people don't know who the dead are. Some have names pinned to their chests. But the others, well, who knows? They smashed the skulls and stove in heads, makes them unrecognisable. And you can't even tell by their clothes, half the time; not one of them has a pair of boots to their name.'

'No boots?' Militza leant forward, towards the driver, frowning a little.

'Nicked,' he replied. 'No one wants to put a good pair of boots in the ground.'

Finally, the roadblock was opened, and they were allowed to continue on with their journey. They drove in silence. The further out of the city they went, the more Militza and Stana grew fearful. Maybe they should have asked Roman, who had just come back from the front, to come with them. They didn't even have a gun.

'At least Nicholas Orlov is getting better,' said Stana into the darkness.

'Much better,' agreed Militza, staring through the window at the thick snow and the moonlight reflecting against the dappled bark of the rows of silver birch trees.

'Nadezhda seems to be a little enchanted. He certainly is with her.'

'Yes.'

'Well, I think it's wonderful news. After all she has been through.'

'I never thought I would see her happy ever again,' said Militza turning to look at her sister in the darkness. 'After Oleg. I had never seen a soul so devastated, so broken and still capable of rising in the morning.'

'Nothing breaks like a heart,' said Stana, patting her sister on the knee. 'But nothing mends like it either.'

'To have loved and lost makes you scared to love again.'

'But she is young and wilful—'

'And brave.'

'I wonder where she gets that from!'

'"There is no fear in love, but perfect love casteth out fear",' said Militza.

'Absolutely. 1 John 4:18,' replied Stana.

It was around midnight when the motor car drew up at the church where, several months previously, they had both witnessed the burial of Rasputin. As they approached the church, Militza suddenly ordered the driver to stop. There, ahead, was a small gang of soldiers carrying torches; next to them was another group, hunched over, spades and picks in hand, digging up the soil.

'There!' said Militza pointing. 'It's happening already.'

'What shall we do?' asked Stana.

They sat in the car as the group slowly excavated the grave, neatly piling up the soil as they went. They didn't appear to be a drunken rabble intent on destruction, it was more like an organised group, following orders. This was planned.

'They don't want him to be a martyr,' whispered Militza under her breath. 'They want him to disappear. No grave, no focus. No focus, no Rasputin. No martyr.'

She exhaled with relief.

It took them about an hour to dig up the casket. It was heavy, sodden with mud and difficult to haul out of the earth, but they managed it and, as it broke through the soil and was lifted high in the moonlight, Stana grabbed Militza's hand. Neither of the sisters knew what they were expecting to see or hear. A howl from hell? A primal scream? A spray of molten lava? But there was nothing. Nothing but silence and darkness. Even the soldiers stepped back from their work momentarily to stop and stare. The most famous man in all of Russia was lying in that wooden box.

They picked up the coffin and carried it to the truck they had parked up nearby.

'What shall we do?' asked Stana.

'Follow the truck,' said Militza, instructing the driver.

Driving through the forest, down increasingly narrow and potholed roads, the sisters were careful to keep their distance. But the further their journey, the deeper into the woods they went.

'Do you know where we are going?' Militza asked the driver.

'This is the dead forest of Pargolovo,' he replied.

'Why "dead"?' asked Stana.

'The trees don't produce leaves here in the summer, and nothing falls in the winter. They are like sticks, twigs. They appear dead, but still they grow.'

An involuntary shiver went down Militza's spine.

The truck stopped and the soldiers climbed out, carrying the heavy coffin with them. They moved off to the right, down what appeared to be a track in the woods.

'Shall we follow them?' asked Stana, holding onto her sister's arm.

'Of course,' she replied, instructing the driver to stay where he was. 'We won't be long.'

It was easy to find the track. The snow had been well-trodden and stained with the clods of mud that had fallen off the coffin. It was also illuminated by what appeared to be a bonfire burning briskly up ahead. There was shouting and cheering, there were more soldiers. Militza and Stana came to a clearing and immediately hid behind the trees, peering through the bare twigs. They could see about thirty soldiers all standing around the fire, some with bottles of wine or vodka in their hands, others smoking and flicking butts into the fire. The bonfire was piled high with pine logs and next to it was the coffin, placed on a stand, making it easier to open. It took them about ten minutes of banging and chiselling before they managed to prise off the lid. It came off slowly, sliding away to the left, and was pushed into the snow. They all peered into the coffin and then immediately recoiled, some of them covering their mouths, others retching on their shoes. The smell was clearly revolting. After a few minutes, they returned, curious for a second look. The expression on their faces was one of fascination and awe. Here was the Holy Satyr, the Mad Monk who'd captivated the Tsarina and the whole of society combined. Here he was, lying in a box, with a bullet hole through the head.

No one wanted to pick up the body; it was as if they were scared to touch him with their bare hands. Someone pushed a plank down into the back of the coffin and slowly they raised the corpse. As his face caught the light of the fire, Militza gasped.

He looked alive, dressed in his black monk's robes, his hair parted and smooth, his beard brushed, a cross glinting around his neck, his arms folded across his chest.

'He's been embalmed,' whispered Stana. 'He looks as he did in life.'

The soldiers recoiled. Astonished, appalled, terrified. Horror-stricken.

'Bastard!' yelled a voice.

'The Devil,' shouted another.

A hand swooped in and pulled the cross off his chest. The pine plank slipped, and the corpse fell out of the coffin into the snow, Rasputin's black robes billowing up as it did so.

'Cut off his cock!' boomed a voice. 'Cut it off and send it to the Tsarina!'

'A little memento to keep her happy!'

'A present from the front!'

And they all started to laugh, guffawing and slapping each other on the back. The next few minutes were almost unbearable to watch, but Militza and Stana could not turn away. They stood quiet as statues behind the trees, transfixed as the soldiers sliced through Rasputin's genitals and, laughing, threw them into a bag. They then proceeded to douse the body in petrol and hurl it onto the fire. The corpse ignited into a fireball, sending a fountain of sparks shooting into the sky. The smell was overwhelming, even from this distance, petrol, embalming fluid, putrefying, burning flesh. Militza finally turned away, covered her nose and mouth with her hands and put her head on her sister's shoulder.

'Mother of God forgive them, Father of God forgive them, for they know not what they do. May the Four Winds take him, may the earth bury him, may he never walk this land...' she muttered into her sister's soft neck.

Stana gasped. Militza looked up and, in her sister's large black pupils, she could see the reflection of the flames and a vision of hell. For as the fire burnt the corpse, it moved. It rolled. It turned. The arms rose, the hands expanded, the fingers splayed and, slowly but surely, Rasputin sat bolt upright.

'Jesus Christ!' screamed a soldier. 'Don't tell me he is still alive!'

There was panic around the fire. There were cries and screams.

'Kill him!' shouted another.

'Kill the Devil!' yelled another.

They ran around in fear, prodding at the fire with sticks, too scared to get close.

'Oh my God,' said Stana, covering her mouth in horror. 'Don't look.'

'I shan't,' replied Militza, staring deep into her sister's eyes while the whole scene was mirrored in her irises, black as obsidian. 'I know he is dead, for I killed him myself.'

'You killed and you drowned him and he shall never be made a saint.'

'And he rises from the flames simply because he has not been hamstrung,' whispered Militza. 'You must hamstring a corpse before you burn it. Just ask all the witches they murdered at the stake and the widows they burnt in India. He is dead and he shall never rise.'

The most striking thing was the utter unexpectedness of it, like a train crash in the night, like a bridge crumbling beneath your feet, like a house falling down.

Alexander Blok, Poet

CHAPTER 12

March 1917, Petrograd

The thaw took them all by surprise. Overnight the snow became slush, the slush became water, and the streets began to flow with a fetid river of filth and rubbish. The destruction from the revolution, the mud, the mire and the misery, had all previously been covered by a heavy layer, a blanket of crisp white snow. Refreshed almost nightly, it covered a multitude of the city's sins. However, with the arrival of the first rains, the snow receded to reveal the dark grey stench of death and decay underneath. Forgotten bodies that had lain uncollected for weeks began to appear. Like snowdrops breaking cover at the merest whiff of spring, they rose up, some in clusters, near a previously mounted machine gun post, others, like the city's drunks, had simply fallen and been forgotten, iced like figures on a cake during the early hours, only to reappear finally with the melting snows. You could smell them down the street, along with the dead dogs. It made everyone long for the winter.

Not that the slush and the filthy water seemed to dampen the spirits of the crowds gathering at the Field of Mars to watch the mass interment of those who'd fallen in the first few days of the revolution. There were hundreds of thousands of mourners crowding the streets, carrying huge red banners with slogans such as: 'Heroes Who for Freedom Fell', 'Hail to the Democratic Republic', and 'Eternal Memory to Our Fallen Brothers'. Dressed in red sashes or armbands they moved slowly through the streets keeping in time to the lugubrious melody of Chopin's 'Funeral March' or a slowed down version of the 'Marseillaise'.

'Everyone in the kitchen is asking for the day off,' said Brana as she stood in the doorway of the Blue Parlour, wearing what appeared to be an outdoor coat.

'What for?' asked Stana.

'To pay their respects to the fallen.'

'Fallen?'

'Their fallen brothers.'

'What? All of them?' Stana glanced out of the window at the gathering crowds below.

'The footmen have said they'll stay,' replied Brana.

'How very kind of them both.' Stana spun around to face the old woman. 'Bearing in mind I have employed them for years and I've educated all six of their children. They can all read and write, you know. And one of them does the books at the Hotel D'Angleterre. Anyway, since when were you in charge?'

'I'm not,' replied Brana.

'It sounds as if you are.'

'No one is.'

'How very egalitarian.'

'They should go.' Militza nodded. 'But be back by six o'clock, before it gets too dangerous on the streets.'

'Dangerous for who?' asked Brana, her pointed chin raised a little out of her thick black scarf.

'Run along now,' said Stana, waving her hand as if dismissing a child. 'Before I change my mind.'

'Tell them they can go,' agreed Militza.

'Back by six.' Stana smiled.

The salon door slammed. Militza and Stana looked at each other. Neither of them said a word. Militza walked towards the window and stood, watching the crowds pouring over the bridge, crossing the Neva and marching on towards the Field of Mars.

'Thank goodness they'd organised to do that now. If that taxi driver was telling the truth, there are thousands of unclaimed souls thawing in warehouses all over town.'

'It makes me ill just thinking about it,' said Stana, pressing her forehead against the cold windowpane. 'Almost as ill as the other night.'

Neither of them had told anyone else about the horrors they had witnessed. How they'd stood until the early hours watching Rasputin's corpse smoulder out in the woods. How they'd watched him collapse, limbs first, leaving nothing but his torso, complete with his charred head, his mouth open, baring his teeth, screaming at the sky, his fatty lips having long since disappeared. It was around 6 a.m. when he disappeared into dust. The soldiers were reduced to kicking the corpse back into the fire to make sure everything did burn. Then they stamped out the embers and kicked the ashes around the woods. Who knew what was pine ash, or what was satanic priest? By then no one cared. The effects of the alcohol had worn off. The blood lust had abated and any fear of the man himself had died along with the flames.

Militza had slept soundly that morning for the first time in months. Perhaps it was exhaustion? The night spent in the woods? Or perhaps demons can be slain?

The sea of red banners and sashes crossing the Neva was something to behold, as was the stream of coffins covered in red flags processing towards the burial ground.

'Where are all these people coming from?' asked Stana. 'Just when you think that must be the end, they keep on coming.'

The noise, the drumming, the marching, the low-level singing reverberated around the city. It was as if the buildings themselves were marching; such was the pounding, the beat rattled the windows and shook the floor of the palace where they stood. Down in the street they teemed past, old women, servants, labourers, children; those who had no coffin to bury, their dead having been interred somewhere else, carried planks of wood, also festooned in red. Tears streamed down their faces as they marched, their lamentations rising above the sound of the music. Militza had never seen such a solemn and dignified crowd.

'It is almost as if they are showing the authorities that having got rid of the police force, there was no need for them in the first place,' she said.

The procession lasted all day. Many of the mourners stood for hours, knee deep in filthy icy water, unable to move, unable to release the coffin they were holding. As each coffin was placed in the ground, a shot was fired by one of the cannons from the Peter and Paul Fortress. It was around 10 p.m. that the last of the coffins was placed in the communal grave in the Field of Mars, leaving the crowd to disappear into the freezing dark night.

The next morning, they began to pour concrete on the graves, covering them all with the hard, impermeable material.

'Can you believe my whole household went?' said Stana as she sat drinking tea in the Blue Parlour. 'And not one of them came back before ten. We had to endure a cold supper, but at least the footmen were here.'

'There was no priest, no religious ceremony at all,' added Bertie Stopford, putting down his glass of tea. 'I heard the Cossacks refused to take part – because there was no mention of God, and no figure of Christ, they said it was a pagan burial. And it was. Do you know what Maurice said?'

'The French ambassador?'

Bertie nodded. 'I wrote it down as it was so moving. "No priest, no icons, no prayers, no crosses. The only anthem was the Workmen's *Marseillaise*… I reflected that I had perhaps witnessed one of the most considerable events in modern history. For what has been buried in the red coffins is the Byzantine and Muscovite tradition of the Russian people, nay the whole past of Orthodox Russia."' He looked across at Militza who was deep in thought.

'He is right,' she said, looking up. 'Yesterday was the day the Church died. It won't return to Russia for over seventy years.'

'What do you mean?' asked Stana.

'Just that,' said Militza. 'This is now a godless country. To have buried the dead without so much as a prayer would have been unthinkable, even a few weeks ago.'

'Well, no one in the government attends a daily *Te Deum* any more, that's for sure,' added Bertie, taking a sip of his tea. 'It really does feel like the beginning of the end.' He shivered. 'I'm glad I shall be leaving tonight,' he declared. 'I am booked on the midnight train to Moscow and then on to the Caucasus and Kislovodsk.'

'How did you get a ticket?' asked Stana.

He smiled. 'I had to pull a lot of strings. But my Grand Duchess can't wait any longer, she's run out of funds, and been placed under house arrest.' Bertie looked at the astonished faces of Militza and Stana. They clearly had not heard the news. 'Can you believe it! A woman of her ranking and distinction. But it seems the revolution has spread beyond the confines of this city and Moscow and out to the provinces. Two men from the Provincial Government turned up at her villa and searched the house. They went through her private letters…'

'Her private letters!' Stana was astonished.

'Her private letters,' he repeated. 'And having found something compromising, I can't imagine what, she was placed under house arrest. She is allowed visitors, but she can't leave.'

'How awful,' said Stana.

'I agree,' acknowledged Bertie. 'Never in her life has she been denied anything. Can you imagine how that feels? Poor woman. So, I leave tonight with your book and a thousand revolutionary roubles in my boots. Diamonds in my pockets, rubies in a cocoa tin and the Vladimir tiara in my carpet bag, which I am declaring as a diplomatic package.'

'That sounds dangerous,' said Militza.

'I have done much worse.' He smiled, tapping the side

of his long slim nose. 'I shall be like the Scarlet Pimpernel, entirely invisible.'

Militza couldn't help but think as Bertie Stopford kissed both her and Stana goodbye, how unlikely and how brave a fellow he was. Charming and utterly trustworthy, there was something so quintessentially British about the man – she could quite see why the Grand Duchess Vladimir absolutely adored him.

'Adieu,' he said from the doorway. 'And I promise to keep your precious green book totally safe.'

Within days of Bertie's departure south, the situation in the capital deteriorated fast. Grand Dukes Peter and Nicholas had thought of returning, having been dismissed from the front, but they were refused safe passage. They might garner respect from the generals at the front, but the provisional government didn't want them anywhere near the city. The idea that either of them might prove to be a rallying point, a lightning rod of popularity, meant they were told to go south, right away.

Militza was disappointed because she missed her husband hugely. She greatly valued his opinion and judgement and dearly wanted his help in packing up the palace. Stana was horrified that her husband, the once proud general who'd led armies, was now running south as fast as he could, with his tail between his legs.

The subdued funeral procession at the Field of Mars proved to be an odd hiatus, the idea that the violence of mob rule was over, incorrect.

Elena returned from a shift at the Anglo-Russian hospital

which had been raided and ransacked more times than any of the nurses could remember, to find that the house of Mathilde Kschessinska, the Tsar's former lover and principal ballerina of the Mariinsky, had been taken over by the rebels and they were getting it ready for Lenin, who was travelling on a sealed train to the capital, arriving any time soon.

'I am not entirely sure who he is,' she said, taking her coat off in the hall and handing the footman her hat. 'But no one speaks well of him in the hospital.'

Elena went on to say that she'd also heard that Sandro, the Tsar's brother-in-law, might be organising a train.

Militza glanced across at her sister. 'A train? Do you have any idea when?'

It was 10 p.m. the following evening, when Militza and Stana found themselves back in the hall surrounded by bags, people, one small dog, Nadezhda and Roman. Marina, who was overwrought with anxiety, was pacing up and down the marble floor, shouting orders at the servants, trying to find important hats, important trinkets, endless trivial necessities. No one wanted to leave; they were desperate to stay – it was as if by leaving they'd admitted defeat. They'd lost control of the situation. But it was clear tensions were still mounting. And if Sandro and the Tsar's sister, Xenia, were leaving and there was a train with spaces, they would be mad not to grab the opportunity with both hands.

Militza felt right to the marrow of her bones that decisions made at this time would prove to make the difference between life and death. Her sixth sense was talking to her, it wouldn't stop talking to her, and she knew she should listen. Anyone who stayed now might live, or they might live to regret it.

'Has anyone heard from the Orlovs?' said Nadezhda, standing beside a small bag, wearing two coats and extra stockings, her pockets full of pearls.

'They're coming,' replied Stana. 'I know they are. They're just a little worried about getting Nicholas on the train, but now he can walk they're hoping it won't be too hard.'

'Has anyone seen Mignon?' asked Marina, looking around for her little French bulldog.

'Over there?' suggested Stana, bent over a bag.

'I'm bringing Augustus,' announced Nadezhda, walking back into the hall holding a Persian cat.

'No cats on the train,' said Stana. 'That's what Sandro said. Dogs are only allowed if they can sit on a lap and be quiet. No Borzois, no birds, or anything like that.'

'Oh, but I can't leave him!'

'Brana, tell her: there are no birds or cats on the train.' Stana turned to look at the old woman, wrapped in her black scarf.

'There are no birds or cats on the train,' Brana repeated.

'Where's your suitcase? Brana? Where are your things?'

'I'm not coming.'

'What do you mean, you're not coming?' Stana was buttoning up her coat. 'Don't be foolish.'

'I am not.'

'What? Madness! Tell her, Militza!' Stana looked at her sister.

'Tell her what?' Militza was distracted by the dogs, the noise, the chaos.

'Tell her to come. She has to come. She always comes.'

'Who?'

'Brana. She has to come to the Crimea.'

'Of course she's coming to the Crimea.' Militza looked up from her bag and gazed at the woman. 'Of course you're coming to the Crimea. You come everywhere with us. You have done for almost thirty years!'

'Not any more.' Brana's face was expressionless and yet determined.

Militza laughed. She was incredulous. 'What do you mean?'

'I'm staying, I'm staying with my brothers and sisters.'

'Your brothers and sisters! What brothers and sisters?' replied Militza. 'You're from Montenegro!'

'My brothers and sisters of the revolution.'

'Them?' Marina pointed towards the street. 'You're joining *them*?' She walked slowly towards the old woman, growing increasingly red-faced. 'The murderers? The people who killed Dimitry? Who've imprisoned the Tsar and opened the prisons and released the criminals and the beggars? The rebels who attacked Prince Orlov? After all we've done for you. After all we've given *you*. All this!' She waved her hand around the hallway. 'All this and you're leaving us!'

There was silence as everyone stared at Brana who stood surrounded by suitcases and dogs and servants and Militza and Stana and their children and all she had known for the past thirty years.

'They need me,' she declared, tugging on her black knitted shawl.

'We need you,' whispered Nadezhda. 'Nicholas needed you.'

'Then you should go,' declared Militza. 'You should go.'

'With your blessing?' asked the old woman.

'Not with my blessing,' snapped Stana. 'Never with my blessing. With my curses following you like arrows in your back till the end of your days! Which with any luck won't be long.'

Brana turned and looked at Militza; Militza stared back as she fought her tears. The old woman's sharp grey eyes and long bent nose were so familiar, the way she shuffled as she walked, the way she coughed, the rare times that she laughed, her incredible knowledge of herbs and tinctures and mantras, chants and incantations; Brana had known Militza for her entire life and now the woman was leaving. Militza was hurt, she was furious. The woman wanted her blessing?

'I think it's probably best you simply go.' Militza spoke quietly and gestured towards the door. 'Good luck,' she managed to say as the old woman turned and left.

'Go to the devil!' spat Marina.

'Go to the devil,' barked Stana. 'In fact, you are already halfway there!'

The silence after the old woman had walked through the large wooden door was deafening. It was the first time in her life that Brana had used the main entrance, and she closed the door carefully, precisely and quietly behind her. No one knew what to say. Nadezhda wanted to cry.

'Right!' declared Militza, her hands in the air. 'Let's sit on our suitcases and be silent. We need to placate the house spirits and wish them well, so we do not have any more trouble today, and they do not come after us, and make us return to collect things we have forgotten.'

It was traditional to do this before a long journey, but somehow tonight as they sat and said their goodbye to the spirits and contemplated the vast unknown lying before them, and Brana's dramatic departure, it seemed all the more poignant. The silence lasted a full minute before they left the house, getting into two cars which took them to a siding just outside Nikolayevsky Station.

Militza, Stana, the children and their dogs stumbled across the railway tracks towards what they hoped was their train. There were no lights, and it appeared deserted as they picked their way towards it in almost total silence. Stana looked across at her sister.

'Are you sure it's here?' she hissed. 'And this is not a trap.'

And what a trap it would be, half the Romanov family, a significant group, the majority, all captured together, at once.

'Militza!' came a call out of the darkness. 'Is that you?'

'Xenia?' Militza walked, blinking, towards the voice of the Tsar's sister, placing her feet carefully as she went.

'Yes,' Xenia replied, standing on the tracks, shivering in her nurse's uniform.

'You look freezing, where's your coat?'

'I left without one. We're being watched, the secret police follow our every move. I had to make it look as if I was just leaving work. And now all I have in the world is this uniform and a small dressing case.' She held it up in the moonlight. 'I'm hoping Sandro's remembered to get me a coat! In fact, where is my wretched husband? We're in here,' she said, pointing at the door to the darkened carriage. 'They're promising to turn the lights on when we leave the station. We just don't want anyone to see us leave. I'm terrified of trouble. Do you know they won't let poor dear Nicky leave Tsarskoye Selo? They're well enough to travel now, since the measles, and all he wants to do is come south with us, meet Mama in Kiev and then off to the Crimea. I know it's out of season and we normally don't spend Easter there but who cares? Needs must. Anywhere has got to be better than here.' Xenia's teeth were chattering. She wrapped her arms tightly around herself to try to keep warm. 'Come on, hurry up, everyone,' she hissed into the darkness. 'We should leave as soon as possible. The longer we wait, the more dangerous it becomes.'

Nadezhda was first into the dark carriage, carrying her small bag, wearing her extra coat, her stockings, her pockets full of pearls. 'Nicholas?' she whispered into the darkness.

'Shhh!' came a reply.

'Nicholas!' she asked again, walking up the carriage in the blackness, sliding open the compartment doors, scanning the darkness, trying to make out his face.

'Shhh!'

'Nicholas who?'

'Orlov?'

'Shhh.'

'Do you want to get us all killed?'

The smell of clothes, breath and bodies, of dogs, old coats, boots and stale brandy and cigarettes was cloying. The compartments were airless and stuffed with people, pets and luggage; it was overwhelming. There was little room for passing in the corridors. But Nadezhda was determined, and despite the cold she began to sweat underneath her coats.

'Nicholas,' she hissed into the last compartment but one.

'We are soldiers,' came back the reply.

'Soldiers!' Nadezhda was taken aback.

'To guard the train.'

'Oh, of course,' she replied quietly. Sliding the door shut, she leant back against the window in the corridor. There were soldiers on the train! What if they turned? What if they massacred them in their sleep? And where was Nicholas? 'Nicholas?' she whispered once more.

'We are in here.' It was Princess Olga Orlov. 'How ghastly this all is,' she said, pulling back the carriage door. 'How ghastly to be running away in the dark, like a gang of common criminals. It's so humiliating.'

'At least we are leaving,' said Nadezhda, peering into the darkness. 'Nicholas?' she asked.

'Here,' came his weak response.

'Poor Nicholas,' said Olga. 'He's been so brave. It was agony for him to get here. If it hadn't been for the morphine, he wouldn't have managed at all.'

'I am fine, Mother,' he mumbled in the darkness. 'And so much better now I know my darling is here.'

'I'm here,' said Nadezhda, fumbling towards him in the darkness. 'And I am not going anywhere.'

It took about half an hour for everyone to climb aboard the train, with their bags and dogs and their coats stuffed with precious stones, trinkets and as much money as they could carry.

'I have so little with me,' muttered Xenia, still shivering in the corridor. 'Mimka, you know my maid.' She nodded down the other end of the train where all the servants had been sent. 'She's offered to come back once we are settled in the Crimea to collect my jewellery.'

'I hope you've hidden it!' exclaimed Stana.

'Under the floorboards on the back stairs. I thought they'd never look there.'

'They'll look everywhere,' said Militza, staring into the blackness.

'Olga's sewn some of her diamonds into the hem of her skirt,' declared Xenia. 'Her lady's maid spent days doing it.'

'Let's hope she did,' replied Stana. 'And didn't stitch the skirts with glass beads.'

'No one is trustworthy any more. Even Brana's gone and joined the revolution,' said Militza.

'What, that old hideous nurse of yours? Best place for her!' Xenia sighed. 'What are we to do? My heart is crying tears of blood when I think of my brother and his beautiful children trapped in Tsarskoye Selo. Why are our cousins taking so long to help him? Their silence is lamentable. Where's King George? What's King Christian doing in Copenhagen? They've all gone quiet. No one is offering safe passage. The government is refusing to let them go. They are prisoners. Prisoners in their own country. He rules by divine right. How can this no longer be the case? I don't understand. I shall never understand. I am ashamed of my country. I am ashamed and embarrassed that everything has crumbled so quickly and nobody has realised and is standing up for Nicky! No one.' She shook her head in the darkness. 'What must he think? That we have all abandoned him?' She shivered. 'Oh, where is Sandro with my coat! I can't understand why he is so late. Well, actually, I can. He's coming by horse-drawn cab. All our cars have been stolen.'

Sandro finally arrived amid a flurry of suitcases, dogs and servants, with three of their six sons, and thankfully a coat for his wife. They were shouting, bickering, hauling bags and suitcases up and down the train. Somehow their ebullient presence made everyone else feel a little foolish. The previously silent passengers came out of their compartments to talk to each other, and as the train prepared to depart, Xenia suggested they might turn on the lights.

'No, no,' said Sandro. 'Let's wait until we leave the city.'

'And the soldiers?' asked Xenia. 'Are they really necessary?'

'Trust me,' he replied. 'We shall need them.'

It was pushing midnight as the train left the station. Militza and Stana stood looking out of the windows at the city beyond. The moon and the stars were out, there was little or no wind, an apparently tranquil night. In some parts of the city the electricity was working, there were lights in the windows, there were a few fires in the streets, braziers lit to keep the rebels warm, with smoke curling up into the sky. The skyline was so distinctive; Militza could draw it in her sleep. She sighed. Her breath fogged the window. Both she and her sister had arrived here, all those years ago, with nothing except a trunk and some poorly fitting clothes. And now they were leaving. How she loved this place, the birthplace of her children, her husband. She looked at her sister in the darkness and Militza leant over and gave Stana's hand a hopeful squeeze. Little did they know they would never see the city, never walk its streets, skate its canals or breathe the chilled air of the Neva. They would never see Petrograd again.

The lights went on in the carriage and Sandro opened a bottle of champagne.

... a colony of Grand Dukes and Grand Duchesses and one fine day they will all be arrested and sent to different places.

Grand Duke George Mikhailovich

CHAPTER 13

April 1917, Crimea

Sandro was proved correct. They did need the soldiers. At every station during the four-day journey south, the train was overrun with refugees trying to force their way aboard, their faces pressed against the windows, their palms and fists hammering on the doors, their children crying, their babies screaming; it was terrifying.

The first time it happened, it was 3 a.m. and most of the passengers on the train had just fallen into an uneasy, fitful sleep. The gentle, soporific rocking of the carriages had finally overcome the anxiety of departure and the crowded conditions. But as they pulled into the first station after Petrograd, held up by a signal, the noise and the shouting were overwhelming. The banging on the doors and the cries from the platform woke the whole train. The dogs began to bark, and the younger children cried, as soldiers ran up and down the corridor brandishing guns and shaking gleaming bayonets.

'What's going on?' demanded Xenia, standing in the corridor, still wearing her coat.

'Where are we?' asked Marina, clutching on to Mignon who was snarling with fear. 'There are faces at the window!'

With scarves pulled tightly around their heads and huge imploring eyes, they put their palms together in prayer, begging to be let on, desperate to escape. They had no idea where the train was headed, but clearly wherever it was going was better than where they were.

'Let us on!' they pleaded.

'Help us,' they begged.

Some held up their children. 'Take them!'

It was appalling. Militza had never seen anything like it. 'What is this?' she asked Sandro, who was standing next to her in the corridor, wearing his red velvet dressing gown.

'It's the war, my dear. The wretched war and the revolution. It's creating a lethal combination of fear and starvation. I thought you knew?' He turned to look at her. 'A clever woman like you, you know everything.'

'I have barely been out of the city for months.'

'It will get worse, believe me. I've seen trains crowded with people, clinging on for dear life. The tracks are littered with the fallen.'

'Fallen?'

'The ones on the roof who drink too much and slide off in their sleep. The lines south are full of them. You hear the thud of bodies as they slip off and hit the tracks. It's impossible for the trains to avoid them in the dark. It's only during the day that they stop to haul the bodies off the line.'

'How terrible,' Militza replied, closing her eyes to the hands slapping at the windows.

He sighed. 'It's as if all the vices, crimes and filth of our nation are writ large.'

She turned to look at him, her blood running cold. 'Why did you say that?'

'Mama!' implored Marina, still clutching her dog. 'Do something, this is awful.'

'From now on,' declared Sandro with a wave of his hand, 'I think it's better that we travel with the curtains closed. That way we won't see the faces at the windows and better that they don't see us either.'

For the next three days and nights, the train made its painfully slow way south. It stopped at numerous train stations along the way and each time the reaction was the same. The hammering on the windows, the pleas coming through the glass, the cries of children, wailing, at all hours of the day and night. While the soldiers appeared in the doorways, their bayonets fixed, their eyes increasingly glassy, the passengers on board slowly began to lose interest in what was going on outside. They would sit in their compartments playing cards, reading books, working their way through their well-packed picnics, while their dogs amused themselves chasing each other up and down the corridors. Occasionally someone would flip open a curtain to report on the weather, or to ascertain where they might be. Some of the landmarks were familiar as this was a well-trodden route for most members of the party.

Not that Nadezhda and Nicholas noticed anyone other than each other. He was now well enough to sit up for longer periods and they spent most of the day talking quietly, reading to each other or playing rounds of bezique. Princess Olga found herself stepping more and more often outside her carriage for fear of disturbing the couple. Nadezhda obviously returned to the compartment she shared with

Marina at night, but as soon as the pale light of dawn penetrated the white muslin curtains of the train, she was knocking gently on Nicholas's door, asking if he'd like some tea from the samovar at the end of the corridor.

'I do so hope you don't mind me sitting here,' declared Princess Olga on the second day of the journey. 'It's just that I don't want to intrude.'

'No, I quite agree!' laughed Stana. 'We all remember being young. It's as if the air itself is enough to keep you alive.'

Olga smiled weakly. 'And that's what worries me. I know I have your daughter to thank that he is still with us, Militza. But life is so fragile.'

'I'm not sure it was Nadezhda, actually,' corrected Stana.

'Oh, but he so nearly died.' Olga shook her head.

'She's a good nurse,' declared Militza.

'An amazing nurse, by all accounts. Even on the train to the front, with the soldiers she was the one who made all the difference. She has inherited more than your dark hair and eyes...'

'Mother nature is a powerful thing,' said Stana. 'Her ability to mend flesh and bones is beyond our understanding.'

'But Nadezhda has something else.' Olga smiled.

'She makes Nicholas very happy, that's for sure,' added Stana. 'But as for anything else, I am not so sure.'

'And to think we had supposed him for Marina,' said Olga, glancing out of the compartment at Marina who was standing in the corridor, playing with her dog. 'That would never have been a love match.'

At the other end of the carriage, Nadezhda dozed, with her head resting gently on Nicholas's shoulder. He could

feel her soft breath against his cheek. Its warmth was
unbearable, for it had only recently escaped her lips. Her
soft lips, those lips that had kissed him once as he lay on
the edge of life, crawling towards death. How he longed to
feel them once more. Their sweet softness, their rose-tinged
taste. But he didn't dare. He'd seen her in his dreams and
felt the weight of her as she sat on his bed, next to him, so
close and yet so out of reach. As the train rattled slowly
along the tracks, a lock of her hair tickled his forehead. He
wanted to touch it, take it, wrap it around his finger. His
soul was burning with desire. It took all his willpower not
to take her in his arms, right there, on the banquette, in the
half-light of the afternoon.

He was holding a small leather-bound volume of
Alexander Pushkin's poetry, and reading it quietly, so
quietly, like a lullaby. Or so he hoped.

'I loved you: and perhaps that love
still burns within my soul today;
But do not let it trouble you;
I would not sadden you in any way.
Silently, hopelessly I loved you,
Sometimes jealous, sometimes too shy;
May God grant you be loved by another,
As sincerely and as tenderly as I.'

It was as if Oleg was talking to her. Nadezhda was
asleep but she could still hear the words of the poem,
whispering to her heart. There he was, reciting them, yet,
weirdly, she could no longer see his face. She knew it was
him, his voice, she knew what he looked like, of course

she did, but somehow the golden hair, the Siberian blue eyes, were less bright, less sharp, as if she were looking at him through smeared spectacles that needed polishing. He smiled and waved at her and then he walked away and was gone.

'... I pray God grant another love you so.'

Nadezhda woke with start. Her throat felt strangulated as if she was gasping for air, as if she'd swum up from the very depths of the ice-cold Neva.

'Oh, my goodness!' she exclaimed, looking around the stuffy carriage, devoid of light and air. 'We need to open some windows. Open some windows and let the soul out.'

'The soul?' Nicholas was confused and put down the leather-bound book.

'I can't hold on to his soul any longer! Open the windows!'

'What are you doing? We can't.'

'We can do anything, anything we want.'

'But it's dangerous.'

'Not as dangerous as this.'

She leant over and kissed him full on the mouth.

After four days of travelling behind curtains, unable to stop or get out at any station, the train slowly, finally, drew into Sevastopol. And the party held its breath. This was the end of the line, their splendid, or indeed not splendid, isolation could last no longer, and it was time to step back into the world. But what sort of world it was, no one had any real idea and the terror and the confusion of their journey did not instil in them any sort of confidence.

Their approach seemed oddly quiet. There were no

crowds, no refugees, there was nowhere else for them to travel. It was disconcerting.

'Where is everyone?' asked Xenia, tweaking back the white curtain. 'The place is deserted.'

'It shouldn't be,' replied Sandro, pulling back the curtain a little more. 'I ordered my officers to be in attendance.'

'Your officers?' asked Militza.

'From the military aviation school near here.'

'Are they still loyal?'

'Last I heard,' he said, smiling.

'Oh, my goodness!' Marina declared, her face flat against the glass. 'Look! We've got motor cars!'

'See? Officers and motor cars. It's all fine. There's no revolution here!'

Despite Sandro's optimism and the officers and the motor cars lined up waiting for them at the station, the atmosphere as they disembarked was odd and strained. There was little fanfare, none of the usual gentle applause, or even a band, to welcome some of the most important members of the Imperial Romanov family. Their arrival was treated with disdain, suspicion.

As they walked down the steps blinking into the sun, they were met by a group of sailors who'd been dispatched to carry their luggage, such as it was. Not one of them saluted and not one of them smiled.

'They are so unkempt and untidy,' whispered Xenia to Militza. 'And why are they staring at us? These sailors have been mine and Nicky's friends since we were children and now they look at me with hatred, as if we are the enemy.'

'Maybe we are,' suggested Militza, moving slowly towards the line of cars.

'Why do they hate us so much?' asked Xenia. 'What have we done to deserve this?'

Glancing up and down at the sailors' surly faces, Militza felt as if any sudden movement would be unwise. She just wanted to get to her house, to Dulber – Crimean Tatar for 'beautiful'. Tucked away between the sea and the mountains, her husband had found the perfect spot on which to build his dream house, a magnificent ode to Middle Eastern architecture. With its imposing white walls and silver cupolas, its huge turquoise mosaic arches, and fountains and courtyards, it was more like visiting the majestic city of Samarkand than a 100-room palace just south of Yalta. But Peter had designed it himself, meticulously sketching every room and hallway. It had been a labour of love that had taken him over five years. As Militza sat in the car, surrounded by luggage and dogs, squeezed up next to her sister and her eldest daughter, she closed her eyes and prayed. She mumbled under her breath that all would be well, that their house had not been looted, their servants had remained loyal and that there would be roses in the garden, fruit on the trees, that the herbs would still be there, that they would soon be going home to Petrograd. She felt sick with anxiety, but mostly she prayed that Peter and Nikolasha had made it back from the front. Four days on a train without news was enough to make even the most rational of minds race.

The two and half hour journey from the train station to Dulber through the Crimean countryside was breathtaking. The grey, grim, appalling misery of the longest and coldest winter since 1808 had suddenly given way to lush greens, pale pink blossoms and hillsides of wildflowers – daisies, poppies, bright pink campions, wild geraniums and electric blue cornflowers. Militza didn't know where to look. It was an assault on the senses. She and Stana opened the windows and inhaled the warm, heady, sweet-smelling air. After four days locked up on the train, it made them both smile; they almost laughed, a little giddy with the oxygen and the plentiful freshness of it all. It felt as if they had escaped, they were free from the shackles of death, war and revolution and all the awful visions they had seen. Stana stretched in the back of the car, her arms high above her head.

'I feel I have been released from a prison,' she said. 'I feel I can breathe. I want to laugh. I want to sing! I want to dance! Do you think it's over?'

'I feel there is hope,' replied Militza. 'I feel there's life.'

'How beautiful it is to be here!' exclaimed Stana, leaning forward to engage the driver of the motor car. 'Has anyone else arrived yet? Or are all the houses still empty?'

'They are empty, madame,' came his curt reply. 'All empty save for Livadia.'

'Has the Dowager Empress Maria Feodorovna arrived from Kiev?' asked Stana, her eyes half closed in the bright sunshine. 'I thought she was coming a little later this week?'

'Comrade Romanov's mother is not here,' replied the driver, glancing up at his mirror to see her reaction. 'And their old palace has been requisitioned.'

'Requisitioned! By whom?'

'I'm not sure.'

'For whom?'

'I'm not sure of that either. Rumour has it, it's for Yekaterina Breshko-Breshkovskaya.'

'The so-called Grandmother of the Revolution?' It was

Militza's turn to laugh a little. 'I shouldn't think so, she was last seen in a Siberian prison in Irkutsk.'

'She's out,' he replied. 'Kerensky freed her.'

'Why on earth?' asked Stana.

'I am not sure, Comrade,' replied the driver slowing down a little. 'But she was welcomed by a large crowd. It was in the newspaper.'

'Then it must be true,' replied Militza.

'Well, that's what they said,' he replied, his eyes narrowing.

'As I said, then it must be true.' Militza smiled.

The revolution might not have quite arrived here, but its spirit certainly had.

However, as they reached Dulber in the dying light of the afternoon, Militza was thankful to see a line of servants and estate workers along the drive to welcome them. It was not all of them, she noticed, as they circled the fountain at the front of the house. She was used to so many more. A few had clearly chosen the same route as Brana. But it was enough. They were loyal, they looked pleased to see her and Stana and the rest of the entourage, even if their welcome was a little muted. Militza smiled and waved as she saw them; she was comforted to see the garden in flower, the grass cut, the windows intact, the proud cypress trees still stretching towards the turquoise blue sky – but most especially to see her husband and brother-in-law Nikolasha standing at the door. They were there! They had made it back from the front, limbs and life intact.

'How was your journey?' asked Peter, stepping off the threshold towards his wife. He looked different. He was still handsome. But he was thinner, he'd shaved off his beard, leaving just a simple moustache, and he was wearing civilian clothes. Militza had rarely seen him out of uniform – it was odd, a little jarring even, as if he couldn't wait to throw off the shackles of power.

'You look…' She paused.

'I know,' he agreed, smiling. 'They pushed me out of the army, what am I supposed to do?'

'But…' She looked across at Nikolasha who was still determinedly wearing his uniform, including his medals and the Cross of St George, along with a golden sword for valour.

'He asked to be allowed to go on wearing military uniform and the provisional government conceded.' Peter shrugged.

He'd never been fond of his military role. Peter wasn't the sort of man who enjoyed shouting orders or punishing people, he was too mild-mannered for that. When his brother had addressed the troops on the front only a few days ago with the words: 'You do your duty to the utmost and I am with you: steal and I will hang you, every one,' Peter had been a little taken aback. He wasn't sure how to motivate troops, but he was fairly certain there were other, more positive ways of doing it than that.

'I like the lack of beard,' said Militza smiling, and kissing him on the cheek. He smelt so delightfully familiar, so calm and kind, she felt her shoulders relax a little; she'd had no idea how much she'd missed him.

'You do?' He nodded with apparent delight. 'I was worried you wouldn't.'

'You look younger.'

'That's always a good thing. Ah!' Three other motor cars were coming up the driveway. 'Here comes the cavalry.'

Behind, in separate cars, came Roman, Nadezhda, the Orlovs and the few of their close retinue, including Militza's and Stana's lady's maids. Peter was delighted to see his children, and hugged them all while Mignon barked for attention and danced in circles around his feet.

'Come in! Come in!' he declared. 'We have fresh lemonade… Where's Brana?' He paused on the threshold and looked at his wife.

'She decided to stay behind,' Militza replied.

'Behind? And look after the palace, good idea.'

'Behind. And join the revolution.'

'The revolution?' Peter stopped in his tracks and looked again at his wife, this time with astonishment. 'Well,' he shrugged, 'I never really liked her.'

'You didn't? It's been over twenty years.' It was Militza's turn to be astonished. 'You never said.'

'Well, you liked her,' he replied, taking his wife's arm. 'And that was enough for me.'

Nikolasha was more formal with his wife, standing in the doorway. He looked oddly stiff and rigid. It was obvious the last few weeks had taken their toll. The arduous journey to the front, and then the return, his loss of rank, his fight to prevent his cousin the Tsar from abdicating, the abdication itself, the death of the Empire, the end of three hundred years of Romanov rule weighed heavy on his shoulders. His large grey eyes were filmed with tiredness, his moustache, normally so carefully waxed and smooth, was wispy and untrimmed.

'My darling,' he said, planting a small kiss on Stana's cheek. 'How are you? And how are the children?'

Stana's heart slowed as she took in what the past few

weeks had done to her husband. He was such a proud man, powerful even. Other men stood to attention when he walked into a room; he drew focus. She could see him dancing at that Imperial ball all those years ago, when he'd secretly dragged her away from the crowd and they'd made love in the gardens on the roof of the Winter Palace. How handsome and masculine he had been, and so very tall.

Now he stooped, he was thin, rubbing his eyes as he spoke to her. 'Is Elena here?' he asked, searching the milling group for a familiar face.

'Over there.' Stana pointed towards the fountain.

'Oh, my adjutant, Count Stefan Tyszkiewicz, will be pleased to see her. He asks about her all the time.'

'You still have an adjutant?'

'For the moment, at least.'

'What a joy to be here, though, all of us together, in this beautiful weather, with the sea, the mountains and family.' She smiled.

'Entirely cut off from the outside world,' replied Nikolasha. 'We have removed ourselves from the order of things. We shan't be able to influence anything, change anything. We have entirely isolated ourselves from any of our relatives abroad. It worries me.'

'Let's go inside,' said Stana. 'It's been a tiring journey.'

The next few days were ones of readjustment. Militza and Stana began settling in at Dulber along with their families, dogs and the Orlovs who were staying in one wing of the house.

At Ai Todor the mood was a little more tense.

Less than a five-minute drive away, the sweeping neoclassical palace of Ai Todor was a little smaller than the hundred-roomed Dulber Palace and so, for the first time in years, Xenia and her husband Sandro had to share a bedroom. For several years they had lived entirely separate lives, which had rather suited them both. For them to be together now, especially under such stressful circumstances, proved to be rather a volatile mix. The rows were plentiful, and their children were finding the proximity of both their parents uncomfortable, to say the least. Added to that, the Grand Duchess Olga, the Tsar and Xenia's youngest sister, was also lodging in the palace. Pregnant with her first child, she was accompanied by her much-despised husband, the commoner Nikolai Kulikovsky. In addition to all that, there was the imminent arrival of the Dowager Empress, who had been forced to leave Kiev much against her will. She had been refused access to the deposed Tsar, who she had not seen in over six months, and had not been allowed back to Petrograd to collect her things or pack up her palace. So, with no other options available to her, she was journeying to the Crimea, of which she had an innate dislike. Quite apart from the fact that the Imperial Romanov family always celebrated Easter, the most holy and important day of the year, at Tsarskoye Selo, it was here she'd nursed her dying husband Alexander III, a giant beast of a man who had expired in her arms from the great pain and putrefaction of nephritis.

However, the glorious weather did help lift everyone's mood a little, and news that the Yusupovs were on their way also made for conversation, while they walked, gardened, fished, played tennis and went on picnics to try to fill the time.

For Nikolasha, the inertia was proving very difficult. A man used to making important and difficult decisions with speed and precision, he was increasingly frustrated by the lack of anything to occupy his time. Peter was content with reading his books about architecture, Sandro was endlessly examining his currency collection, but Nikolasha was used to being a man of action. And after the first few days of pacing the marble floors of the palace, he took to spending his time walking to the beach with his hunting rifle to shoot birds. Quite what birds they were, Stana did not know, for he never brought anything back for the kitchen.

And food was a problem, despite the orchards. Apricots and wild strawberries were available, but almost everything else was in short supply. As indeed was any news from the north. Contradictory snippets made it through; the situation at the front was depressing. There were rumours of the collapse of the army and the fleet, and there were defectors everywhere. Insubordination was growing by the day. The few newspapers that arrived at the summer palaces made for miserable reading.

At the beginning of Holy Week, the Dowager Empress arrived from Kiev, as did the Yusupovs from Petrograd; the tales of their journey south, the crowds, the refugees trying to board their trains, all had a familiar ring to those who were already there. The Yusupovs, Felix, Irina and their two-year-old daughter known as Bébé, moved into their summer residence in Koreiz, and the Dowager, her entourage, a Cossack bodyguard and two ladies-in-waiting, as well as Princess Irina Dolgoruky and her husband Sergei, all moved into Ai Todor.

Easter Day was also Sandro's birthday and although the

morning was a little damp and a mist had rolled in from the sea, the residents of the Imperial enclave of the Crimea were determined to celebrate. In Ai Todor the children spent the morning painting Easter eggs. While at Dulber, Militza and Stana, along with Marina, Roman and Nadezhda, spent the night before Easter in church, where they walked around the outside of the building, waiting for the sun to rise before pronouncing, 'Christ is risen!'

But the highlight of the day was a luncheon, to break their fast, at Ai Todor. Everyone was invited to celebrate the resurrection, and Sandro's name day, all at once. Presents were hard to come by, but wine was not – every palace and every estate on the coast had their own vineyard.

It was around 2 p.m. as the Dulber party were walking up the drive.

'I can't believe it,' came a cry through the open windows of the palace. 'How is this possible on such a day! Happy Easter,' Xenia declared through tight lips as she opened the front door. 'Christ is risen. And it appears so is our cook. Risen and disappeared. He's gone to join the army. Been called up, apparently. But only after he's stolen all the flour, sugar, butter and milk in the whole damn house. And he hasn't cooked a thing. Gone.' She waved a hand. 'Disappeared in a puff of smoke with the contents of the kitchen. We have nothing, nothing to eat at all.'

'Happy birthday to me!' proclaimed Sandro, walking up behind her with a glass of champagne in his hand. 'Fortunately, he's left behind the contents of the cellar, so we have something to celebrate with.'

Although no one felt like celebrating, something of a steely determination set in with the idea that the revolution and the actions of one wayward cook were not going to spoil their day. So with the help of the remaining loyal retinue, they decided to conjure up some sort of picnic from the cherries and the apricots the Dulber party had brought with them, the asparagus growing at Ai Todor and the boxes of Turkish delight the Yusupovs had produced for Sandro's birthday.

Militza had braced herself for the arrival of Prince Felix Yusupov. His extrovert flamboyance and desire always to be at the epicentre of everything scared her. Having made his dislike of her evident from the very beginning, they were the most unlikely co-conspirators in the death of Rasputin. Plus, there was the Dowager Empress, whose history of antipathy to both Militza and her sister was well known. It was a heady mix of guests for luncheon.

'Grand Duchess.' Prince Yusupov greeted her. 'How very charming to see you after so long, oh, and the sister in tow too.' He smiled at Stana, tipping his head.

His pale hair was slicked back, his slightly tanned face was clean-shaven, he wore a white shirt and cream-coloured trousers with polished riding boots, giving the impression of a man *en vacances*, rather than a murderer escaping punishment.

'You appear well,' replied Militza. 'Not tired by your arduous journey? Or your stay on your estate?'

'The most arduous thing about our journey was the dogs,' he replied. 'They ran up and down the train and people kept treading on them. That and the people clamouring to get on board. You?'

'Something similar,' replied Militza.

'As for my stay at Rakitnoye, well, actually, I enjoyed it.

It's not an estate that I get to visit much, it's a bit out of the way, but it was lovely to walk, look at the woods, at the Dnieper River, read some books, and contemplate my crime, of course! I think I have fared better than poor Dmitry, stuck at the edge of the empire for a crime he didn't commit.'

'I saw him before he left,' she said, smiling tightly. 'He was accepting of his fate.'

'Was he now...? I don't believe you have met *ma petite* Bébé?' he said, gathering up the beautiful blonde cherub of a child toddling at his feet. 'Here she is.' He balanced the little girl on his hip. Dressed in white frills, with a baby blue sash around her waist, Bébé Yusupov was quite enchanting. 'Bébé, this is Grand Duchess Militza, say hello.'

'No!' replied Bébé, shoving Militza in the face with her chubby little hand. 'Go away!'

'Ha, ha, ha – I see my charming great-grandchild is already a most discerning character,' came the distinctive voice of the Dowager Empress, walking slowly across the white marble terrace. 'She has Nicky's eyes and Xenia's temper.'

'Your Imperial Majesty.' Felix Yusupov bowed.

'I think we're all called Comrade now, aren't we?' she replied. Taking a sip from a tiny glass of cherry brandy, she looked him up and down. 'I suppose we are to congratulate you. You're a hero.'

'Me?' He shook his head a little.

'For ridding us of that terrible vermin.'

'It's awfully kind of you,' he said, putting his daughter back down on the ground.

'You've saved us all from that ghastly man. Saved my son and his fool of a wife from that awful influence.'

'One does what one can.'

'I don't think I have ever been this close to a murderer before,' replied the Dowager, putting the glass to her thin, elderly lips. 'It's quite exciting.'

He smiled and looked Militza directly in the eyes. 'No, I don't suppose you have.'

'We are all in your debt,' she replied and raised her glass in the air. 'Your good deed will never be forgotten.'

'You're too kind. I was simply doing my duty to Mother Russia.'

'Well, She is eternally grateful. To Prince Felix Yusupov, saviour of Mother Russia!' toasted the Dowager.

'To Felix!' toasted the rest of the party.

'Saviour of Mother Russia,' added Militza, taking a small sip of her champagne.

The sun came out during the afternoon. The smaller children played on the lawn overlooking the sea, while the rest of the party drank delicious Galitzine champagne from a nearby estate, ate cherries and discussed what was happening at Tsarskoye Selo. The other, more delicate subject – that of their impending penury – was politely, if not directly, alluded to. The truth of the matter was, since the abdication all members of the Romanov family had ceased to be beneficiaries of the Imperial purse, and they had no money, and no access to money, except what they could raise from their estates. And since most of their estates had been requisitioned or were now nothing but muddy fields on the frontline, the income was minimal to say the least. Looking around the room, the only one unaffected by the abdication was Prince Yusupov himself, whose funds appeared to be limitless.

While the conversation swung from pity towards Nicky and the children (the plight of Alix was seldom mentioned), to fury at the abdication, Nicholas and Nadezhda slipped off down the end of the garden towards the footpath and the beach beyond.

The footpath was narrow and edged with long grasses, foxgloves and poppies, as well orange and white oleander bushes and the occasional majestic cypress, pointing up into clear blue sky. Nicholas's health was much improved. Although he still walked with a stick that he often swirled around in the air when trying to express himself, he now strode along the path with determined vigour. Below was the shimmering sea, in the most perfect of bays, a sliver of pebbles, framed by foaming white horses. It was completely deserted.

'Christ is risen!' he proclaimed to the cliffside. 'And so have I!'

'Like Lazarus!' laughed Nadezhda.

'Exactly like Lazarus!' he laughed back. 'I am honestly indebted to you for my life.'

'And you for mine.' She smiled, turning circles on the path, disturbing a cloud of small blue butterflies. 'Isn't it beautiful here, this time of year. All this!' She spun around, her arms outstretched.

'Truly,' he replied, staring at her, her white dress billowing in the breeze, her long dark hair falling out of its pins as she danced along the path ahead of him. She was like a feather in the wind, light and lithe and entirely impulsive.

This must be true love, he thought, for it made him feel invincible, vibrant, free, alive and truly happy.

'Marry me, Nadezhda Petrovna!' he shouted after her, through the grasses.

'What?' she asked, turning in the air back towards him.

'Marry me!' he yelled so loudly the whole bay could hear it. The proposal bounced off the cliff and echoed around the cove. 'Marry me, marry me, marry me.' The words ricocheted and repeated themselves, like an ecstatic chorus of joy.

'Yes,' she replied. The shock of her response caused her to stop in her tracks. 'Yes,' she said quietly, almost to herself. She looked back at him, dressed in his loose white shirt, thin cream cotton jacket and baggy dark trousers, at his tousled hair and broad grin. 'Yes, I will.'

He ran down the hill towards her, hobbling a little in his haste to seal his love with a kiss, to make sure she would not change her mind.

'You will? You will?' He could not believe it. 'I have loved you so much, Nadezhda Petrovna, from the day we first met,' he said as he cupped her face in his hands and kissed her. Never had lips tasted so sweet, or skin felt so fair. Once he'd started, he could not stop; he kissed her cheeks, her forehead, the backs of her hands, he kissed her lips again, once more. They were still so soft and sweet, like the cherries she had been eating. He kissed her eyelids. He stroked her face. 'You said yes, you said yes,' he whispered, staring deep into her dark eyes, like pools for him to drown in.

'I said yes,' she agreed, smiling.

'Then I am the happiest man that has ever lived!' he said, throwing his jacket on to the ground and himself on top of it. 'Come, lie here with me and look up at the sky.'

They lay on his cotton jacket, hidden from the world by the long waving grasses and the flowers and butterflies. And as they lay there, he kissed her over and over, cupping her bosom under her white cotton dress, and she kissed him back, her back arching a little, her passion more forceful that it had ever been. She rolled on top of him, the buttons on her dress a little undone. He could see the shape of her, under her chemise, the whiteness of her skin, the paleness of her bosom. His desire was overwhelming. Here, on a cliffside overlooking the sea, there was nothing he wanted more.

After all the death and the misery and the war; this was life, this was love.

'I love you, Nadezhda.' He kissed her passionately, his tongue in her mouth, his arms tightly wound around her, his body hard against her. He forced himself to stop. 'I must ask your father,' he said suddenly, sitting up. 'And your mother.'

'My mother?' laughed Nadezhda, lying in the grass, her hair loose, her pale cheeks flushed.

'I think little happens in your house without her approval!'

'And when shall we marry?' she asked, looking up at the clouds drifting by in the sky.

'As soon as possible,' he replied. He turned to look at her. 'Nothing is certain any more.'

'Nothing is ever certain,' she said. Tugging at a blade of grass, she curled it around her fingers. 'I never understand why we think it might be.'

'One thing is certain... we shall have children,' he declared.

'Lots and lots!'

'How many?'

'Six.'

'Four.'

'Seven!'

'Oh, please don't let this be our first argument!' He bent over and kissed her.

'And we shall return to Petrograd.'

'Of course we shall. Of that I am also certain. We shall live in the Marble Palace, overlooking the Neva.'

'And I shall skate.'

'And you shall skate, and I shall watch you from my window.'

'And how happy we will be.'

All round and everywhere, there is only anxiety.

Bertie Stopford

CHAPTER 14

April 1917, Crimea

Back in Petrograd, Brana opened the doors of the Nikolayevsky Palace to her brothers and sisters of the revolution. There were so many rooms, so many supplies, so many comfortable beds, it seemed a travesty to let such a cornucopia go to waste. She'd dismissed the other servants the night Militza and the rest of the family had left. She'd given them an ultimatum to join the rebels or leave. The majority had simply upped and left. Despite their lack of money, or breeding, they knew their shiny fingernails and their polished manners would have them singled out as members of the *burzhúi* in no time. Only the old woman from Montenegro and a few of the stable lads and some of the below-stairs maids could walk the streets amongst the fetid masses and not be accosted. Besides, few of the servants were from the capital itself. Most had been born and brought up near Znamenka, the old country estate on the Gulf of Finland, so it was to there they returned, leaving Brana in the big palace, with two men from the stables and one of the old footmen who simply couldn't leave.

The Neva was thawing. There was an open stream some twenty yards wide alongside the banks while the centre still remained frozen. And along with the filth swilling through the streets and the slush came the rats and the rebels. No one was working. No one wanted to work. No one was being paid. It was anarchy. Nearly two million had now deserted the front and they were loitering in the city with nothing to do. Starving, cold, penniless and angry, they were ripe for the plucking. All Lenin had to do was reach out and take them.

On 16 April, the night after the Romanovs left to travel south to Crimea, Lenin arrived in a sealed train at Finland Station festooned with garlands and red banners to a rapturous welcome. And Brana was there, standing in the crowd, illuminated by giant searchlights that swept their brilliant beams just above the heads of the masses that had gathered to hear him. They waited, necks craned, on the tips of their toes for the arrival of the new messiah. It didn't matter that the Germans themselves had helped Lenin cross the border. They'd been only too delighted to give him free passage through their own country so he could release his toxic brand of revolution behind enemy lines. Anyone could have stirred the crowd, but Lenin did much more than that. His rhetoric was sublime, his delivery mesmeric, his oratory skills enough to raise the dead, but they had simply been sleeping, and he did more than raise them; he called them swiftly to revolution.

'The people need peace; the people need bread; the people need land,' he cried to appreciative roars and raised fists. 'And they give you war, hunger, no bread... We must fight for the socialist revolution, fight to the end, until the complete victory of the proletariat. Long live the worldwide socialist revolution!' He cried again, 'Peace, bread, land!'

It was a simple mantra and the chant worked its way right to the back of the crowd and out into the streets beyond.

'Victory for the proletariat. Peace! Bread! Land!'

It made perfect sense to Brana. She'd seen the injustice, the privilege. She'd spent enough time at court to realise the contempt in which they held the common man, the peasant, the serf. She'd heard them talk, she'd seen the way they'd looked at her. She was nothing but a crone in their eyes. She was a shadow of a person, a cipher, whose opinions, ideas and talents were barely, if ever, recognised. Militza and Stana might have been different, but they were not different enough. They still took her entirely for granted; they never asked her where her own family might have been, where they were living, subsisting, back along the pirate coasts of Montenegro. A place where she was born and to which she would never return. So she shouted. She punched the air with her fist, with decades of sadness and frustration, decades of injustice, of invisibility, resentment and disappointment, all the way back to the Blue Parlour that overlooked the Neva and the Winter Palace.

News of Nadezhda's engagement to Prince Nicholas Orlov was met with a certain amount of surprise. For the older gentlemen, who had been so preoccupied with the revolution, the abdication and the war, the idea that there could possibly be room for affairs of the heart was something of an anathema.

Peter was so shocked when Nicholas asked for his

daughter's hand in marriage, he had to sit down in the library. He had been waiting for some sort of romance to build between Nicholas and Marina, who was nearer his age.

All the same, he was delighted, of course. He was extremely fond of Nicholas's father, Vladimir 'Fat' Orlov. They had spent months together in the south discussing the finer points of Roman architecture, while consuming bottles of Georgian wine. Vladimir was an enthusiast, he loved motor cars, food, wine and conversation, life; to have him as part of the family would be an asset to say the least. His wife Olga was more controlled and the product of centuries of aristocratic inbreeding, slim to the point of fragility, beautiful enough to be admired for her looks and painted by the famous Valentin Serov, the premier portrait artist of the day. It was said, 'No one wears a hat like Olga.' And she did have plenty to choose from.

Also, what better distraction from a revolution and an abdication than a wedding?

Dulber was abuzz. There were flowers to choose, a dress to be made, a feast to prepare, a church to find. And all in the space of their ten-day engagement. They had to move fast – the likelihood that the authorities would agree to such a gathering was slim and the situation on the estates was getting worse by the day.

At first, house arrest for the Crimean inhabitants was unofficial. The locals, and particularly those from nearby Yalta, remembered the old days very well, and their respect for the Imperial family ran deep. A large number of them were employed on the numerous luxurious estates that were only occupied for a few months of the year – so the work was light and the remuneration reasonably generous. Over the years, there had also been a process of natural selection, allowing only the most loyal subjects to take up residence on the small, beautiful peninsula, so close to the Tsar's summer house. Now that Yekaterina Breshko-Breshkovskaya, the 'grandmother of the revolution', was expected to take up residence in the Tsar's beloved Livadia, things were changing very rapidly indeed.

As indeed were the rules and regulations. The royals became prisoners and were required to tell their unofficial guards exactly where they were going, at all times. Written permission was needed to drive into Yalta, or further afield, and gatherings of any sort were problematic. No one wanted to attract the attention of the locals, who had already started to trespass, pulling up plants and driving their carts at speed along the tracks, kicking up dust in the faces of their rich residents, picnicking at their leisure, sitting on their lawns.

However, the behaviour of the house guests towards their captors was hardly compliant or conciliatory. And no one was more disobliging than the Dowager Empress, who simply refused to cooperate and infuriated the guards. They descended into even more extreme levels of disrespect, sneezing, coughing, blowing their noses to put her off her stride. But she was imperturbable. For her own peace of mind, she simply pretended they did not exist, and she went about her day, looking straight through them as if they were made of glass. She would travel back and forth to the veranda with her Holy Bible, written in her native Danish, and read it from dawn till dusk. It gave solace, reminded her of home and distracted her from worrying about her son, imprisoned by his own guards in Tsarskoye Selo.

Not that any of this bothered Nadezhda, or indeed Nicholas; they didn't want a large wedding, or a feast, or a ball, or a party. They simply wanted to be married in the eyes of God.

Marina was initially a little put out. Nadezhda was six years her junior – *she* should have been the one to marry first. She should be the one everyone was fussing over, she should be the one making clandestine trips to Yalta to find a dressmaker, to source yards and yards of fabulous white silk chiffon. She was twenty-five years old. It was surely her turn. Perhaps no one would ever want to marry her?

But, in the end, she loved her sister and wanted her to be happy, and they sat up lighting candles together the night before the wedding, just as her mother and her sister Stana had done, decades before.

'Apotropaic magic,' said Marina. 'Do you remember?'

Nadezhda was lying in bed, with her dark hair pinned in little circles around her face, ready to be curled into ringlets in the morning. Dressed in a white frilled nightdress, she was propped up on a mountain of pillows, watching her sister.

'So, we light the candle in the window,' continued Marina, striking the matches, 'to welcome in the light and good fortune and dispel the darkness.'

'Superstitious nonsense,' declared Nadezhda with a yawn.

'You say that,' replied Marina. 'But... actually.'

'Actually nothing. It means nothing. It has no power and I'd rather not.'

'But it's been passed down through generations of wise women. Look at Mama.'

'Look at Brana.'

'Let's not mention her.'

'How about Rasputin?'

'Let's not mention him either.'

'But I thought…'

'He was a man of God, that is all. Murdered by a prince,' said Marina.

'I am not so sure,' sighed Nadezhda.

'It was someone touched by the Devil, that's for sure,' replied Marina. 'Maybe they started all of this. This chaos. This revolution.'

'Anyway, go on, the candle… And if it goes out?'

'And if it goes out, it's an ill wind and your marriage is doomed!' Marina laughed, shaking her hands and wiggling her fingers as if she was casting a spell. 'Doomed, I tell you, doomed!' She leapt into the same bed.

'Of course!'

'Much like Aunt Stana's,' said Marina. 'Although I'm not entirely sure Spirit could have foreseen her first husband's numerous mistresses and obsession with one particular lady in Biarritz!' She paused. 'At least Aunt Stana is happy… now.'

'I can't see how. Nikolasha is like a bear with a sore head now he has nothing to do. He's only been trained for the army, like all the men. Take that away and Nicholas says he's like a madman wandering the coast taking pot-shots at seagulls.'

'He's bored.'

'We're all bored. But he's the only one shooting gulls.'

'Now you know why we never come here for Easter! Out of season the Crimea is simply ghastly!' Marina declared. 'Oh, to be back in Petrograd!'

But Marina would not have recognised Petrograd that spring. The embassies had mostly closed, only the British were still operating. They had a bird's-eye view of Lenin's comings and goings since he'd taken over the house of Mathilde Kschessinska which was across the Troitsky Bridge from the embassy. The house, like much of the rest of the city, was covered in scarlet banners and flags emblazoned with the Bolshevik mantra 'Bread, Peace, Land'. Instead of spring flowers and the welcome green shoots of spring, the streets were filthy with mud, leaflets and copies of Lenin's latest political organ, his newspaper *Pravda* – 'Truth' – which was being produced in Mathilde's old basement. Brana was one of its chief distributors.

Suddenly there was a guttering noise from the candle across the room; the flame flickered in the window, disturbed by a draught. Despite herself, Nadezhda held her breath, staring at the candle, willing it to stay alight. As quickly as it came, the draught disappeared and the flame shone upright and strong, like the cypress on the coast, pointing determinedly towards the sky.

They both exhaled and looked at each other.

'Do you ever think of Sofia?' asked Marina, propping herself up on the pillows.

Sofia was Nadezhda's twin, who had been stillborn.

Nadezhda lay against the pillows and stared at the ceiling. 'The one who died... so I might live.'

'I don't think it was quite like that.'

'I've always felt it was.'

'I'm sure it wasn't.' Marina squeezed her sister's hand as they lay side by side in bed. She paused. 'I saw her, you know.'

'Sofia?'

'She was tiny. She looked as if she was asleep. It was almost as if she were smiling. As Mama said, she was not made for this world. She was more fortunate than that, she went straight to the next.' She looked across at her sister. 'Sofia was so lucky, so good and so beautiful that God wanted her straight away. He couldn't resist. She was too perfect... That's what Mama said.' Marina sighed. 'I remember being a little bit jealous. Can you believe it? What was wrong with me that I had to live, and she was so perfect that she got to die straight away? And she *was* perfect, by the way, and everyone cried at her baptism, and everyone cried at her funeral which they held on the same day, one after the other. I remember it well.'

'So, she didn't die so I could live.' Nadezhda stared at the blue mosaic ceiling. 'She was simply too perfect to live in this world, anyway. Like Oleg.'

'Like Oleg.' Marina squeezed her sister's hand again. 'I know you will be happy, you and Nicholas. He loves you heart and soul, you only have to see his face when you walk into a room to know that. You'll be blissfully happy.'

'I shall.' Nadezhda nodded, sounding determined. 'And my heart will be whole... one day.'

'I know it will.' Marina kissed her sister on the cheek. 'Sleep well, for tomorrow you are getting married!'

Nadezhda lay awake, staring at the ceiling, listening to the candle at the window. She was waiting for it to gutter, waiting for it to die. For the dark to come in and take her. If Oleg didn't want her to marry Nicholas, he would blow the candle out. And if Sofia didn't want her to marry Nicholas, she would do the same. Dear Sofia. What would it have been like to have a twin sister? Someone so perfect that God stole her as soon as she was born. She never cried. She never drew breath. She never experienced the sadness of this world.

It felt as if she had been awake all night, but Nadezhda must have slept. She didn't hear the candle burn down, and she didn't hear the wax drip down the side of the wall and splash all over the floor.

'I'd say that the goodness and the light were most certainly invited in last night,' yawned Marina, looking at the wax on the floor. 'There's nothing left of that candle. Evil has well and truly been warded off!'

The wedding took place at St Nina's at Kharax, a tiny church made of white marble, with pretty arches and presided over by an elderly Georgian priest. There were sixteen guests in attendance, including Nicholas's best men Sergei Leuchtenberg, Count Stefan Tyszkiewicz and Roman. None of the guests at Ai Todor were allowed to go – this was the limit of their guards' generosity when it came to family gatherings.

Not that Nicholas and Nadezhda needed any others. As she walked into the church dressed in folds of white chiffon, clutching a large bouquet of pale pink roses, wearing a pearl and diamond tiara and a rope of pearls around her neck, Nicholas caught his breath. The curls around her face, the paleness of her throat, the elegance of her shoulders, the long white veil, he had never before seen anyone quite so beautiful, quite so ethereal. Her fragile beauty was offset by her father, her uncle, and indeed his own enormous father, all three wearing vast white Circassian coats, complete with large white sheepskin hats, rows of glimmering medals and huge, tasselled Circassian swords. They wore shiny black boots and tight black trousers, their various moustaches and giant beards covering their faces. They were quite something to behold. Nicholas's mother, Militza and Stana had also dressed in white, with large picture hats, pearls and drop pearl earrings. It was a sea of white, save for Nicholas himself, who was wearing his blue and red guard's uniform.

There was no singing, no choir, no music, just a blessing from the priest and an exchange of rings, while the best men held the crowns above their heads, before crowning them both king and queen of creation. It was a short service. But Nadezhda did not mind. She was delighted that the candles stayed lit, that the priest didn't stumble, that neither Oleg nor Sofia had intervened.

On the way out, as they walked back into the beautiful warm sunshine, their lips still damp from sealing their vows with a kiss, Nicholas heard a rustle in the bushes.

'What is that?' he whispered to his bride. He gripped her hand. 'Who's there!' he barked.

'Who goes there!' commanded Nadezhda's uncle, Nikolasha, his hand gripping the handle of his heavy ceremonial sword.

Vladimir Orlov was not far behind, but his sword was the largest of them all and dragged a little on the ground. 'Who's that!' he demanded.

'Me!' hissed a voice. 'Sandro.' Sandro staggered out of the bush, thick oleander leaves stuck in his hair, closely followed by three of his sons – Dmitry, Rostislav and Vassili.

'What *are* you doing?' asked Nikolasha, sheathing his weapon. 'I could have killed you.'

'Apologies,' replied Sandro with a little bow. 'But I was dispatched by the others to glean as much information as possible about the bride. To spy on the dress and the ceremony, since none of us was allowed to come. Xenia and her mother wanted to know what was going on, and no one turns the Dowager Empress down, now do they?' He stood up and smoothed his hair, removing the leaves. 'I'd best be off,' he said ruefully. 'Before a sailor, or a guard, or someone ghastly like that, finds us here and alerts the authorities.'

The reception was a frugal affair – champagne, smoked sturgeon, whatever Korniloff the chef could find in the Yalta shops. There were some toasts, but no dancing and only a few photographs to record the day.

'I know you'll be happy.' Militza kissed her daughter as the couple prepared to leave.

'Are you sure?' Nadezhda whispered in her mother's ear. 'But what about Oleg?'

'The candle stayed alight.' She squeezed her daughter's shoulders. 'He would have said something if he wanted to. And as for your wedding night...' Militza paused. 'Don't forget that you are supposed to have pleasure as well.'

'Pleasure?' She looked at her mother, horrified. 'I am not like you! I am Russian. I'm not from the Black Mountains.'

'The pleasures of the flesh are not a sin, they are part of life, they bring life. Life begets life, pleasure begets pleasure, joy begets joy.' Militza smiled. 'And may the experience of all the witches, the mavens, the sirens and the nymphs help you on your wedding night. May you ride the waves of passion with joy.'

'I am not a witch.' Nadezhda smiled stiffly.

Nadezhda and Nicholas left in a small horse-drawn carriage covered in white flowers to spend their three-day honeymoon in the Swallow's Nest, renting rooms above the restaurant that overlooked the ocean.

A neo-Gothic extravaganza of turrets and towers, perched forty metres above the sea on the Aurora Cliff, it had two bedrooms. The main bedroom at the top of the stairs had wood-panelled walls, a huge window looking out over the water and a four-poster bed.

Nadezhda was terrified as she stood, stiff and static, while Nicholas slowly began to remove her clothes. The white dress, the under-petticoats, the chemise, her drawers. She stood stark naked beside the bed and dared not look him in the eye. She was shaking as he stepped forward and kissed her. He ran his fingertips over the top of her shoulders and down her back and she felt her knees tremble so that she fell back down on to the bed. He swiftly unbuckled his trousers; they dropped to the floor, followed by his underwear. It was light, the sun was pouring through the window. It could not be more perfect. He lay down on her and felt the soft touch of her skin. She moved; she rose up to meet his kiss. Her sweet lips devoured his.

The more experienced Nicholas unlocked a passion in his wife that was entirely unexpected. Accustomed to the old adage that aristocratic ladies don't move, he was astonished by her thirst, her appetites; this was a physical love match that sent him into paroxysms of delight. He revelled in the way she moaned when he touched her, how she curled and curved and coiled herself around him. He knew she was fervid, but such fervour, such ardour in a woman, in a wife, was beyond his wildest expectations. It was as if she was just ecstatic to be alive, as if she'd been damming up this passion for so long and he had released the river. He was enchanted, beguiled, bewitched.

Surely the revolution could not be that bad? Surely it would be safe to leave the confines of the Crimea and journey back to the capital? The most anxious to do so was the Dowager Empress, desperate to see her son. She and her daughters Xenia and Olga took tea every day on the veranda. One afternoon, after the Dowager complained vociferously about her incarceration, her life, her son, her loves, how much she missed the Mariinsky Theatre, how she used to listen to the music every night via a tube connecting Anichkov Palace and the theatre – it was agreed that Mimka, Xenia's loyal maid, should return to Petrograd to test the water. She was to collect Xenia's jewellery, which had been hidden under the stairs, and find out exactly what was going on at the palace.

Mimka could not believe her eyes when she left the station in Petrograd. The capital was in disarray, the rubbish piled up in the streets, the shops were entirely empty, most of the palaces had been requisitioned by rebels, there were communists everywhere, the provisional government was losing power, the revolutionaries were stirring things up. Anyone who had stayed was under house arrest, or arrest in the Peter and Paul Fortress. The former Tsar was under armed guard, unable to leave the palace – all talk of him and his family being able to leave Russia for abroad was at an end. And all Xenia's jewellery had been stolen. Thieves had taken the lot. Mimka stood in the empty hallway of the palace that she had called home for the last ten years and cried. The statues at the foot of the stairs were broken, the paintings had been pulled off the walls and someone had clearly been killed or wounded on the black and white marble floor in the hall because there were dark smears and stains where a Persian rug had been. It smelt of death and misery. She could not leave the palace quick enough and in lieu of jewellery, she grabbed a few dresses, a huge hat with ostrich feathers and a kimono from Japan.

As she sat in her horse-drawn carriage wringing her hands at the misery of it all, there was a screaming and shouting in the street and, suddenly, the door of the carriage was flung open and a pinch-faced old woman shouted, 'Get out! This carriage has been requisitioned by the revolution!' Before Mimka could say anything, a large pile of newspapers tied up with string was hurled into the carriage. 'Get out!' the woman yelled. 'In the name of the revolution! We need this carriage!'

'Where's the revolution going?' asked Mimka, a terrified stammer in her voice.

'The revolution is going to the train station!' barked the old woman, climbing up into the small black leather seat opposite.

'How fortunate! I can take you,' replied Mimka. 'I am going that way myself.'

'Good.'

They sat in silence for a minute. Mimka stared at the piles of *Pravda* newspapers at her feet, too scared to look at her requisitioner. But slowly she raised her eyes. Looked at the thin face, the pinched mouth, the scarf pulled tight under the chin.

'Brana?'

'Who's asking?' The old woman stared across at her passenger. The young woman looked plump, fed – if not necessarily well – but she was most certainly a *burzhúi*, they all looked the same.

'It's me, Mimka, the Grand Duchess Xenia Alexandrovna's maid. The sister of the Tsar?'

'Comrade Romanov.'

'Comrade Romanov's sister's maid?' Mimka ventured. 'I know who you are. You're Brana, the maid of Grand Duchess Militza Nikolayevna.'

'I was never a maid,' corrected Brana.

'Oh.' Mimka paused. 'Of course not... Did you know, Nadezhda has just got married?'

'Comrade Nadezhda? No, I did not.'

'He's a very nice man. Prince Nicholas Orlov. I don't know if you remember him? He's very handsome.'

'I saved his life once,' she replied. 'More's the pity.'

Mimka carried on talking all the way to the station. Nerves and a desire to ingratiate herself with the old nurse, to placate the revolution, made her garrulous in the extreme. As they pulled up outside the station, Brana smiled. It was disconcerting.

'Can I give you a message for Comrade Nadezhda? For she was the gentlest of them all. Tell her a tornado is coming. It's powerful and it's full of hatred and it will destroy everything in its path and blow everything out of the water and everything else will be killed in its wake. She needs to leave, and leave now, with Comrade Orlov if she must.

There will be murder. As Comrade Lenin says: "Revolution without assassination is nothing." They are coming and no one is safe. And you can tell the mistress I know what she did. I was the one who found her gloves and I was the one who gave them to the Tsarina, Comrade Alix. I know she smoked the pistol with sage, and a smoked pistol never misses. I know it all and the Devil himself is coming for her.'

Two days later, while Nadezhda and Nicholas still slept in the Swallow's Nest house, Sandro was woken at four in the morning by a cold metal pistol pointing at his face. He was rigid in bed, his wife still asleep beside him, his eyes wide open, his heart pounding in his chest.

'What do you want?' he whispered.

'Get up!' barked a sailor. 'And get out of the bed! I have come to arrest you and the rest of the Romanov scum on behalf of the provisional government and the Soviet of Workers and Soldiers' Deputies! Now move!'

The next few minutes were chaos. Xenia started to scream, shots were fired in the air and the whole house awoke to find Ai Todor invaded by some fifty sailors, with three trucks of soldiers outside, armed to the teeth with pistols and machine guns.

With Xenia in bed under armed guard, her hands above the blankets so they could see them at all times, Sandro was led out with a gun to his head, and taken to the drawing room where they demanded he open the large desk in front of the window. Covered in gold leaf with a green leather top, it looked important, and more frustratingly for the sailors, there was a large drawer in the middle that was locked.

'Give us the key!' yelled the ringleader. 'Now!'

'I don't have it,' whimpered Sandro, kneeling on the floor. 'It belongs to the Dowager Empress Marie Feodorovna Romanovna.'

'Open it!' shouted the sailor. His lips were so close Sandro could smell the man had had vodka for breakfast.

'How about a knife?' he suggested.

'We're not going to break it,' he laughed. 'It belongs to the people now and we look after our nice expensive things.'

'But I don't have the key,' whispered Sandro, his hands sweating, his legs trembling and his knees hurting as he knelt on the floor.

'Wake up the old woman, then,' demanded the sailor.

No one moved. The idea of marching to the Dowager's room at this hour was a step too far.

'Move it!' he shouted. 'Move it, or I'll shoot! You!' He nodded towards Sandro. 'Lead the way!'

As Sandro led the gang through the house towards the Dowager Empress's bedroom, Xenia was negotiating with her guard, getting him to remove his hat, get her some stockings and turn around while she dressed. She was just lacing up her boots when a female soldier came bursting into the bedroom and rifled through her dressing table, stealing the last few bits of jewellery she had left. She was swiftly followed by others who ransacked the cupboards and the drawers, seizing letters, diaries, anything they could find. They even searched the still warm bed.

With Sandro outside in the corridor, they burst into the Dowager's bedroom to find the seventy-year-old Empress sitting bolt upright in bed.

'What do you want?' she asked.

'We want the letter, the secret letter, that links you Romanovs to the German swine!' the sailor spat. 'In you come!' he ordered the other sailors.

The lack of respect for the old woman was astonishing. They opened all the drawers, the cupboards and pulled her clothing out. They pulled up the carpet, they ran bayonets through the cushions and the divan to check for concealed valuables, they went through her correspondence, collected all the letters with foreign postage stamps, her diaries and, most upsettingly of all, her Bible, the Danish Bible she'd brought with her when she arrived in Russia as a young bride, the one she read every day on the veranda. She begged them to return it, she offered up her jewellery – pearls, gold, rubies. But the head sailor, with his bayonet drawn, refused.

'We are not thieves!' he proclaimed loudly. He held up the Bible. 'This is a counter-revolutionary book and a respected lady like yourself should not poison your mind with such things.'

Meanwhile, Xenia dispatched a shivering servant to warn the inhabitants of Dulber about the impending raid, but he arrived too late. Another group of sailors and soldiers had already entered the estate and were rampaging through the palace.

Roman was woken first with a torch in his face and a gun to his temple, while a gang of men dressed in red armbands searched his bedroom, turning everything upside down. Roman lay still as corpse in his bed, panicking about the fate of his mother, father and Marina. The young man with the gun at his head was surprisingly youthful, he was breathing heavily through flared nostrils as if to suppress his fear.

'How long have you been in the navy?' Roman whispered.

'Don't speak!' The young man shook his gun in Roman's face.

'You don't look as if you've been in the fleet long.'

'Long enough!' he barked back.

'Everything all right here?' asked a soldier walking over to the bed and shining another torch into Roman's face.

'Absolutely! I can handle him.' The young recruit looked down at Roman. 'This bastard doesn't look as if he's done a day's work in his life!'

They moved further into the palace, knocking on doors, waking up Militza, Stana and Peter. Nikolasha was woken last by the commissar from the provisional government. As the most senior Romanov, and former commander of the army, it was to him that the invaders dictated the new rules of engagement. While the sailors tore through the palace, stealing the solid silver knives and forks, emptying the store cupboards and removing all the pistols, revolvers, hunting rifles and bullets they could find, the new rules were barked at the old man sitting in his nightgown on the corner of his bed. All forms of motor transport were to be confiscated, all forms of written correspondence were now censored, all foreign servants were to be removed, and that included any tutors who might be educating the children, and there was to be no mixing between the households. None whatsoever.

Militza and Stana sat seething with fury as the soldiers leafed through their private letters, seemingly astonished by the different languages in which they were written: French, Russian, English, Persian – the correspondence was mostly incomprehensible. Almost as baffling was Stana's thick leather almanac where she kept a detailed list of all the plants she'd planted in the garden and the names and addresses of exotic seed suppliers that she had sourced from all over the world.

As Militza sat in the grand drawing room surrounded by the chaos, she quietly thanked Spirit and the Keeper of Secrets and the Keys, and the Queen of all Witchcraft – the three-faced Hekate – that Bertie Stopford was still taking the waters in Kislovodsk, accompanied by the Grand Duchess Vladimir, and Militza's green velvet book.

The city is unspeakably dirty. Chaotic crowds, disorder, anarchy. In one word – revolution... The most humanistic soul must now agree that Russia *cannot* live without a baton. It needs a policeman and not freedom... If a new tsar comes, he will be extremely cruel.

Vladimir Paley, June 1917

CHAPTER 15

June 1917, Crimea

Although Nadezhda and Nicholas's honeymoon had been all too brief, a lot had changed in the three days they'd spent in the Swallow's Nest on the coast.

The guard around Dulber had been doubled, as had the number of soldiers at Ai Todor. All correspondence was now monitored, censored, with thick black lines scoring out whole paragraphs, even the names on the envelopes were altered. Xenia was being referred to as the 'Former Grand Duchess Xenia', and the Dowager Empress as 'Citizen Maria Feodorovna Romanova'. But perhaps the largest change of all was that, after marrying Prince Nicholas Orlov, Nadezhda was now no longer considered a Romanov; she was not the daughter of Grand Duke Peter Nikolayevich Romanov, cousin of the Tsar any more, she was an Orlov and, as such, she was no longer a person of special interest. She was free to leave Dulber, free to leave the compound and live wherever she pleased. In fact, contact with her mother, aunt, brother and sister would be discouraged and require special written permission.

The idea of a forced separation from her family was not something that had occurred to her. But it certainly had its appeal. A fresh start. A new life as an Orlov. Out of the shadow of the Black Crows. She and Nicholas sat in the drawing room in Dulber, side by side on the divan. Her father Peter and Uncle Nikolasha sat opposite, while Militza paced around, the Cuban heels on her grey kid pumps tapping sharply on the shiny mosaic floors.

'We could take rooms nearby?' suggested Nicholas, rubbing his hands together a little nervously. Although excited to be setting up a new life with his wife, he had thought he might have a little more time to organise it all.

'Yalta,' agreed Nikolasha. 'It's close by and relatively safe, despite the soviet being the most extreme in the area. But we need you near.'

'We do,' nodded Peter. 'So we can see you.'

'You can be our eyes and ears. They mean to imprison us here for God knows how long, and we need to know what is going on in the outside world, even if we can't do anything about it.' Nikolasha tugged at his beard. 'I think that is the best strategy.'

'My daughter and her happiness are not a strategy,' snapped Militza, stopping in her tracks. Nadezhda was her youngest child, she was not supposed to leave home first, and she was not supposed to be exiled; not while she was herself under house arrest.

'But we must think logically,' said Nikolasha. 'To have them close by would be useful.'

'We could always go to Kiev?' suggested Nicholas. 'It's a beautiful city, my parents are moving there, they could help us.'

'Olga and Vladimir could be useful,' added Nadezhda.

'Kiev! Absolutely not!' Nikolasha stood up and tugged at his jacket, straightening his uniform. 'As the most senior person here, I forbid it. Kiev is not safe. It's a den of revolutionaries. The soviet has already forced the Dowager Empress to leave, and she is the mother of the Tsar! If you don't think they could turn up on your doorstep and take you prisoner with the cock of a pistol, then you are more of a fool than you look. Married or not, Nadezhda is a Romanov, and as soon as they hear she is in the city they will track her down. Lock her up and throw away the key. The Crimea is the safest place.'

The next few days were a frenzy of activity as Nicholas travelled back and forth to Yalta searching for rooms, and Nadezhda packed up their few belongings. Nicholas's journey was made all the more difficult because of the lack of motor transport. He eventually managed to persuade the chief guards' officer to drive him in one of the cars repossessed from the Dowager Empress.

Both Marina and Militza found Nadezhda's imminent departure depressing to say the least. The fact that the inmates at Dulber and Ai Todor were not allowed into the town for any reason at all made Nadezhda's departure all the more distressing. It was as if they had all been placed in quarantine for some incurable disease. There was a permanent guard of twenty-three sailors in each of the houses, while others roamed the gardens and patrolled the coast. The land between the estates had been declared a sort of no-man's-land where, occasionally, members of each household were allowed to exercise, but not allowed to meet or discuss anything.

As she packed up her things and sat in the back seat of the car, next to her husband, Nadezhda realised how torn she was. A new life, a new husband, and yet she was going to be the family's one and only lifeline to the outside world. She did her best not to cry as she watched her mother wave her goodbye. They had no way of staying in touch with one another, no means of communication. Her mother smiled. Her sister waved. Nadezhda bit the side of her mouth and tried to smile back. She had no idea what she was going to do, how she was going to live or what was going to happen.

'Don't worry,' said Nicholas, seizing her hand. 'We shall be fine. I know we shall.'

'We shall,' she agreed.

As they arrived in Yalta, about half an hour's drive away, Nadezhda felt as if she had landed in another world. The fashionable seaside resort was normally quiet at this time of year, the neoclassical streets would usually be empty save for the locals going about their business, but as Nadezhda and Nicholas drove down Autskaya Street towards the coast, past the house where Chekhov had lived and had written *The Three Sisters*, they saw a riot of red bunting, with scarlet flags flying everywhere. The pavements were packed with flag-waving citizens, all sporting red armbands. There was a party atmosphere in the streets, and everyone was smiling.

'I see she's arrived then,' said the driver.

'Who?' asked Nicholas leaning forward in the seat.

'Yekaterina Breshko-Breshkovskaya.'

'The grandmother of the revolution,' mumbled Nadezhda, staring out of the window at the waving flags. 'Is that her there?'

Walking along the street, dressed in a simple black cotton dress with a round white collar, her grey hair pinned up in a loose bun, was a diminutive, elderly-looking woman. She was surrounded by an entourage of some fifty to one hundred people all waving flags and chanting. 'Long live Napoleon, long live Napoleon.'

Nadezhda narrowed her eyes. The old woman turned and looked at the passing car and fixed Nadezhda in her icy gaze. They stared at each other for a few seconds; Nadezhda had never seen, or felt, such a cold determination, such hardened resolve, such calculating detachment. She shivered. Rumour had it that Yekaterina had spent forty-two years chained to a stockade for dissent, and no one in the penal labour camp could break her. She'd escaped from prison numerous times – the last one involved her making a 620-mile journey on horseback across the Siberian steppes, only for her to be recaptured seven miles from her destination, Irkutsk. She was seventy years old at the time.

'Why are they chanting?' asked Nicholas.

'She's promising to give them all land and not draft them to the war,' replied Nadezhda, still looking at Yekaterina.

'Bribing them then,' said Nicholas.

'Bribing them,' agreed Nadezhda. 'Or throwing them a lifeline. It depends on your point of view.'

'But what's Napoleon got to do with it?'

'She's supposed to be the daughter of Napoleon the First and a shop assistant in Moscow.'

'A shop assistant in Moscow? From the occupation of Napoleon the First?' asked Nicholas, incredulously. 'That would make her extraordinarily old. Napoleon died in 1821.'

'Facts are boring, when there is a much better story to tell.'

'Well, that is true,' he agreed, smiling as he looked at his wife. How he loved her proud features and sharp mind.

Their apartment on Autskaya Street was on the second floor of a neoclassical building painted white and lemon yellow and sporting large windows at the front and a small balcony with a fat white balustrade. From one of the windows, if you craned your neck, you could see the sea, and from another, the peaks of Ai-Petri. It was clean, had three bedrooms, a study, a parlour, a kitchen area and a small bedroom for a maid. Nadezhda had never been anywhere quite so modest in her life. It felt very different from the exotic Dulber Palace, or the sprawling estate of Znamenka where she'd grown up, with its huge gardens and views out onto the Gulf of Finland. But none of it really mattered – she had her freedom, she was able to come and go as she pleased, without the prying eyes of the guards. That night, as she lay in bed, listening to the sound of the sea and the gentle snoring of her husband, she resolved to stay firm and determined, if only for the sake of the other prisoners. They needed her help. Self-indulgence at this time would only help the enemy.

And what they needed most was food. Ever since the early morning visit and subsequent looting and emptying of the storerooms in both Dulber and Ai Todor, there was very little to eat. There was no flour, no sugar, no meat, no potatoes; all they had were the vegetables from the estate, which they would try their best to make into as many exciting dishes as possible, such as a 'wiener schnitzel' that was actually made of shredded cabbage and carrots.

Nadezhda's main preoccupation, or indeed occupation now, was trying to get as many supplies as possible to the captives. She'd scour the markets, and beg for bread from the baker, who mainly had black bread but occasionally she'd manage to find a few loaves of white. And then she had to get her supplies to one of the houses, with or without the permission of the guards.

But morale among the prisoners was low. Information was so scarce. Letters were being intercepted all the time. The Dowager Empress received a letter from her cousin in Denmark that had taken over three months to arrive and when she opened it, she found it had been almost entirely redacted.

Princess Irina Yusupova tried as hard as she could to keep in contact with the Dulber and Ai Todor households. She was on her own. Prince Felix had returned to Petrograd, worried about the palace on Moika and their immense number of treasures, leaving his wife and baby daughter behind. But the guards followed Irina's every move. Their house, Koreiz, was monitored but she was not under house arrest, so she and Nadezhda tried to work together, bringing in as many letters and telegrams as they could. Irina employed various ruses. She would call one of her many little dogs, pretending to have lost it in the no-man's-land. It was the signal for either Sandro or Peter to approach the closed gate, where she'd slip them a letter, or a newspaper hidden in a hollowed-out book. But in the end the guards grew wise to their tricks, and she was no longer allowed to walk in the no-man's-land or shout out the names of her dogs.

It was Nadezhda who came up with the plan of using beautiful blonde Bébé.

'She is so adorable no one will suspect her,' she said to Irina, while sitting on the veranda at Koreiz.

'You're right and Bébé goes everywhere, she is allowed to visit whoever she wants.'

The plan was bold and brave and required them to sew telegrams and letters into the lining of Bébé's coat. Then the delightful babbling toddler was instructed to go and visit Granny Xenia, or Great-Granny Empress, or Great-Aunt Militza. Then, while the child sat in the kitchen, swinging her plump little legs and munching on an apple, her coat was cut open, the contents read and replied to and all sewn back up again, before she was sent back to her nanny, who crouched the other side of the gate. It wasn't ideal and sometimes Bébé had other ideas about where she might like to wander, distracted by a dog, a kitten, or a butterfly, while Nikolasha or Sandro sat anxiously on the veranda, waiting for news from the outside world.

Nadezhda and Nicholas were in their parlour wrapping up the loaves of bread Nadezhda had managed to purchase before the bakery opened at 5 a.m., when there was a loud banging on the door. They both froze and stared at each other.

'Who is that?' whispered Nadezhda.

'Are you expecting anyone?'

'No. If we keep quiet, they'll go away.'

The knock came again.

'No one knows we are living here,' said Nadezhda.

'Ignore it.'

Another knock, more loudly than the first and the second time, and then the door rattled.

Nicholas moved. 'Shall I?'

'No. You stay here.'

Nadezhda's hand was trembling as she opened the door a crack. Anxiety, fear, nervousness, terror: she, Nicholas, the inhabitants of Ai Todor and Dulber ran the full gamut of these emotions every day. She placed her foot firmly against the door so no one could push it further.

'Who is it?' she asked through the gap.

'It's me! Bertie! Open up!'

'Stopford?'

'Of course Stopford! How many Berties do you know?'

'Bertie! Mr Stopford!' Nadezhda swung open the door. 'How lovely to see you! What are you doing here?'

'Are you going to invite me in?'

'Of course! Please.' She stepped aside. 'Darling,' she called, 'it's Mr Stopford.'

'Mr Stopford! Mr Stopford,' exclaimed Nicholas, walking excitedly towards him. 'How are you? How very unexpected. What a delight!'

'Let me take your coat and your hat,' said Nadezhda. It was the first time in her life she'd ever offered to do such a thing. What a world she now lived in. Answering her own front door, taking guests' coats... it was not something she'd ever thought would happen to her.

'Here,' said Bertie as he watched his hostess fumble with his hat and coat. 'Let me help you.'

'How on earth did you find us?' asked Nicholas, shaking Bertie's hand. 'No one knows we're here.'

'Ah!' Bertie smoothed down the corners of his moustache. 'I had the very good fortune to bump into Prince Felix Yusupov on the train south. He is not the most discreet of fellows. Quite apart from regaling the whole carriage with the minute-by-minute story of how he murdered Rasputin, he told me you had married, for which congratulations, and that you'd moved into town.'

'He told the whole train about how he murdered Rasputin?' asked Nicholas.

'Several times over,' confirmed Bertie.

'What a thing to admit to,' said Nadezhda, shaking her head.

'He's a hero in their eyes,' said Bertie. 'The story was met with rapturous applause, every time he told it. He's a hero.'

'Of the most unlikely sort,' said Nicholas.

'I couldn't agree more,' added Bertie. 'I pointed him out to a great friend of mine in Petrograd the other day. She said, "Nobody would be able to pick this man out in the crowd as an assassin. With his fine features, dark melancholy eyes and ivory skin he might almost be called effeminate. One sees such men only in very old families where the vigour has begun to run low."'

'Maybe he didn't actually kill Rasputin?' suggested Nadezhda, walking into the parlour. 'I have always thought it odd, I can't imagine Felix pulling a trigger. Maybe it was someone else, like Dimitry? Would you like some tea?'

'Perfect,' he said, sitting down on the wooden chair. 'Oh, look, you can see the sea… Almost.'

'If you stand on one foot and look through there, you can see a small sliver,' added Nicholas, with a light laugh.

'Anyway, Felix told me you were here,' said Bertie. 'So I came to you via the Obolenskys.'

'The Obolenskys – are they here as well?' asked Nadezhda.

'Simply *tout le monde* is here,' replied Bertie. 'Felix is

having a little breakfast at the Café Florens and then he's coming over here to take me to see your mother.'

'My mother?' queried Nadezhda.

'I promised I would deliver her book, remember?' He patted the small leather case he had at his feet. 'And I always keep my promises. I also have letters from my Grand Duchess Vladimir to the Dowager Empress and others for Grand Duke Nikolai Nikolayevich and a few others from the embassy, including one from Queen Alexandra.'

Nicholas frowned a little. 'You travelled with all those on your person?' Bertie nodded. 'But what if you got caught?'

'Why would anyone stop me?' he replied with a shrug.

'And what are you planning to do with them all?' asked Nadezhda.

'Why, deliver them, of course.'

'You can't,' replied Nicholas. 'They are not letting anyone in or out.'

'But even my Grand Duchess Vladimir was allowed visitors,' exclaimed Bertie, leaning back in his chair and crossing his legs. 'What a terrible state of affairs this is. It seems the infection is spreading south more quickly than we expected. Mutiny is everywhere. Officers are being killed at their desks, in their beds. It's all too ghastly. And the new Soviet in Sevastopol are a nasty bunch, but I did think that they'd show some respect for the Tsar's mother. She's an old woman, for goodness' sake!'

As they drank their tea, Bertie talked about his trip to Kislovodsk, how well the Grand Duchess Vladimir was faring, how anxious she was about her son Kirill's leaving Russia for Finland, having declared his allegiance to the revolution, and how her country palace at Tsarskoye Selo had been requisitioned.

'The housekeeper had left the electric light on all night,' explained Bertie. 'And the military police came in and decided to make an inventory of the whole place. They went through everything. They even opened the safe, which was thankfully empty of valuables, but inside was a book, written in German, which they confiscated immediately. The newspapers reported that it was a German code book and she was a collaborator and spy. But they have since had to apologise,' he smiled, 'as it was merely the handbook for the safe, written in German!'

'I heard that awful revolutionary woman has finally arrived in town,' he went on. 'Yekaterina Breshko-Breshkovskaya.'

'She arrived a few weeks ago,' said Nicholas.

'I met her once,' said Bertie, smoothing down the leg of his cream linen trousers.

'What was she like?' Nadezhda leant forward in her chair.

'She wasn't very charming. In fact, I didn't like her at all. Revolutionaries are normally quite charismatic, like Lenin for example. You can appreciate his oratory even if you don't like what he is saying. But she, she was just a rather gruff peasant, who had nothing to say for herself whatsoever.'

'She is certainly making waves down here,' said Nadezhda. 'She has a fervent following.'

'Best to stay out of her way, though, if I were you.'

Just then there was another loud knock at the door. Nadezhda and Nicholas both froze again.

'That'll be Prince Yusupov's driver,' said Bertie. 'He promised to collect me by motor car and drive me to Ai Todor.'

Nicholas opened the door. 'Prince Yusupov!' he declared.

Dressed in a pale cream woollen suit, with a crisp white shirt, a round-necked collar and with a peach silk scarf placed carefully in his top pocket, his fair hair oiled flat, his face freshly shaven, Felix looked dapper and well-rested, despite his long journey from Petrograd. He marched straight into the apartment, holding a rolled tube of some description and a brown paper bag.

'I had to come and say hello!' he said, grinning. 'Congratulations on your wedding, Orlov. Congratulations indeed. I hear you married one of the daughters of the Black Peril.' He laughed. 'Excellent idea. Clever, beautiful and gifted! I have brought you a little something, not a huge amount, as I have spent weeks trying to hide most of my things but here.' He handed over the brown paper bag. 'Congratulations on your wedding. Ah,' he stepped into the parlour, 'how are you, Princess Nadezhda? You are looking well. Especially under the circumstances.' He gestured around the apartment. It was unclear whether he meant the rooms themselves, or the revolution outside.

'Thank you.' She smiled at him.

'It's just a little cigarette box, something for,' he looked down, 'the table. Anyway...' He rubbed his hands and, flapping his heavy cream baggy trousers, sat down in Nadezhda's wooden chair. 'So, all well, Bertie?'

'Very well. I see you have your paintings with you.' Bertie glanced at the rolled-up tube.

'Shhh!' Prince Yusupov playfully placed his finger to his lips. 'I am not leaving the Rembrandts in the motor car for any old fool to steal.'

'Rembrandts?' asked Nicholas.

'Here.' He nodded down at his feet. 'I've carried them all the way from Petrograd on the train.'

He tugged at the elastic band wrapped around the tube and slowly, carefully, unfurled the two canvases. They were exquisite, so beautifully, artfully painted that Nadezhda took a step back to admire them and held her breath, as if inhaling and exhaling would break the spell. They were so lifelike, the energy in each painting was extraordinary. The wide black hat and the flat collar, the feathers, the pearl brooch and the curled hair were sublime and flawless.

'*Portrait of a Man in a Broad-Brimmed Hat*, from 1665, and this is *Woman with an Ostrich Feather Fan*, painted in 1656. Pretty, aren't they?' He smiled proudly. 'Anyway, I'm not leaving *them* behind for those ignorant animals to slash and daub.'

'Too right,' agreed Bertie. 'It would be an utter sacrilege.'

'Along with the very many others,' agreed Felix, snapping on the piece of string. 'I have just come from Café Florens and tea with Countess Betsy Schuvalov and she tells me there's terrible news from Ai Todor.'

'What news? No one hears anything, they can't get to them, they are completely shut off,' said Nicholas. 'Have they been raided again?'

'No.' He shook his head. 'Princess Dolgoruky has died.'

'Irina?' Nadezhda covered her mouth in shock.

'Suicide, apparently.'

'Suicide? Surely not!'

'A Veronal overdose. She's taken days to die. In agony. Been depressed for weeks.'

'Everyone is depressed there,' agreed Nadezhda. 'There is nothing to do, nothing to eat, and they are being kept as prisoners in their own homes. It is terrible.'

'I think she had her reasons,' said Yusupov, plucking a cigarette from a gold and lapis Fabergé cigarette case in his top pocket. Across the lid ran a snake made of diamonds.

'Oh?' asked Bertie, who never missed a moment. 'Poor thing,' he added, just in case.

'Well, if my husband had been having an affair with Xenia and the authorities now insisted I had to live in the same house as the lovers, watching, waiting for them to disappear off for furtive moments of intercourse, and then having to pretend I hadn't seen or heard anything, I might reach for the sedatives.' Felix flicked his ash into a little silver tray once used for sugar almonds.

'Indeed,' agreed Bertie, also lighting a cigarette.

'But she has six children,' said Nadezhda, sitting slowly down on the yellow divan. 'That is terrible news.'

'Terrible news,' agreed Felix.

'Is there to be a funeral?' asked Nadezhda.

'Tomorrow,' said Felix. 'In Koreiz.'

'Is it close family only? I would like to show my respects,' said Nadezhda.

'No,' said Felix. 'All the families are allowed to attend. Everyone. The Dulbers, the Ai Todors. I hear all of Yalta is going.'

'Well, that is excellent news,' smiled Bertie, inhaling his cigarette with evident satisfaction.

'Really?' Nadezhda looked a little horrified. 'How so?'

* * *

The requiem began on the dot of 10 a.m. It was in a small church, near Koreiz, surrounded by oak and laburnum woods, right by the sea, and everyone was there, dressed in black, hands clasped in front of them, heads bowed. Everyone, that is, but Bertie Stopford. Dressed in an immaculate black suit, with a white shirt and black tie, his head was not bowed, and his eyes were constantly glancing around the church, locating the Dowager Empress, Militza and Nikolasha, for his pockets were full of letters and telegrams and, inside his black coat, tied by a belt, was the green velvet book. He'd been up half the night before, planning how he might distribute the mail, but now he was in the church itself it was looking to be a little more problematic. There were guards in the pews and milling around at the back. The only place which remained unsupervised was the open coffin itself.

Princess Irina Dolgoruky lay half-covered in a silver pall, surrounded by a bed of pink roses. With her marble-white face, her closed eyes, her hands folded in prayer, she was an intimidating sight for a lapsed Roman Catholic like Bertie, who'd never seen an open casket in his life. As the procession began and the Princess's six children went to kiss their dead mother for the last time, Bertie seized his chance. He joined the stream of people walking towards the coffin, knowing he must be quick. Then, as he passed the Dowager Empress, he deftly dropped a letter in her lap. The old woman glanced up in shock. Postmarked from London, this would be the first uncensored letter she'd received in months. Bertie stood with his back to her, and then bent down to tie up his shoelace.

'Should you need to reply, Your Excellency, I shall be beside the grave,' he whispered.

She simply smiled and nodded, and all the while her black-gloved hands pushed the stiff envelope up her left sleeve.

Next was Nikolasha, right near the front; sitting stiffly as only a military man can, he didn't notice when the telegram fell into his lap. It was Stana who jabbed him in the ribs and made him look down. He, too, squirrelled it rapidly away in his jacket sleeve.

The green velvet book was more difficult. He could hold on to it and hope to see Militza beside the grave. He could walk up to her and hand it over in full view, as if it were nothing. But he could not, would not take the chance. Bertie was at a loss. Militza was a little ahead; he could see her straight back, her dark hair pinned up under a large black-brimmed hat. She, too, was heading towards the coffin. He pushed past a few elderly ladies, much to their irritation, and slid two places in front of Militza. He didn't have time to speak to her; the guards were watching.

He bent forward in front of the corpse, tugging at his coat; he pursed his lips, trying to get the book out from under his jacket, but it would not move. There was nothing to be done, try as he might, he could not pull it loose. So, Bertie stood up straight and, with a dramatic wail as if riding a tide of terrible grief, he grabbed the book from under his belt, threw his arms up in the air and in one swift adroit movement, sobbing loudly, he planted a kiss on the Princess's hard, white cheek. Then he slipped the book between the pink roses around her face. He stepped back and caught Militza's eye. Militza frowned, he nodded at her again and then back at the coffin. He was hugely relieved when she also threw her arms in the air, as if to embrace her dear departed friend, and slipped the green velvet book deftly under her cape. It was not the smoothest manoeuvre Bertie had ever pulled off, but certainly one of his more macabre.

And it was fortunate that he had taken the risk, because the burial where he'd hoped to be able to hand over the book was postponed due to the appalling rain. It was too wet to finish the service, all the mourners were stuck in the mud, slipping and sliding down the banks of the hill that descended towards the graveyard. Everyone was drenched to the skin and departed rapidly, leaving only the immediate family under a tree beside the unburied coffin.

'What a miserable day,' said Bertie, as he sat in the hired motor car with Nadezhda and Nicholas on their way back to Yalta.

'Poor Sergei,' agreed Nadezhda. 'Imagine not being able to bury your wife. How long do you think the coffin will remain under the tree? Until it stops raining? My mother would see that as a sign.' She stared out of the window. 'Not burying the dead.'

'There really is nothing worse,' agreed Bertie.

The family of Romanovs had been issued with food vouchers by the Vyborg Food Committee. Only those members of the former royal family who are unwell will receive flour.

6 October 1917, *Petrogradskaya Gazeta*

CHAPTER 16

July-October 1917, Crimea

Perhaps it was the rain? Maybe she caught a chill? Either that, or the news in the letter from Queen Alexandra had not quite been what she'd hoped for, but after the funeral, the Dowager Empress's health took a turn for the worse. She retired to her room for most of the day and, instead of reading her beloved Bible, she knitted gloves until the wool ran out.

Supplies were still extremely low. They were expensive and difficult to come by. What they did have was of extremely poor quality and had often been adulterated. The butter looked like Vaseline and tasted like petrol, the bread was hard and coarse, the coffee was made from ground acorns and the tea from dried rosehips. The boredom was unbearable; everyone was fractious, especially the younger children, who had read all their books four or five times over and knew them by heart. Xenia was finding things particularly difficult, and looked worn, exhausted and pale, although plenty put that down to a guilty conscience, having to sit down every night with her lover, now a widower, and his six motherless children.

But the worst of it was living in limbo and a constant state of fear. The idea that they could be arrested or murdered at any point was enough to break the strongest spirit.

There was a tension between the two nearest soviets. In Sevastopol they wanted to keep the Romanovs as prisoners, so they did not become a rallying point, a cause célèbre. In Yalta they simply wanted them dead.

One early midsummer morning, while scouring the empty shops, Nadezhda stumbled on a large crowd gathered around a stage erected on the seafront. There were red flags flying in the breeze and a small brass band playing the 'Marseillaise'. Everyone seemed excited. There was a buzz in the air.

'Who are you waiting for?' asked Nadezhda, smiling nervously, edging her way into the crowd.

'Babushka,' replied a leather-faced old man, a smack of broken blood vessels across both cheeks. He looked her up and down.

'Yekaterina Breshko-Breshkovskaya?'

'Yep, Babka.' He sniffed, turning away. 'She should be here any minute.'

And right on cue, an elderly, diminutive, white-haired woman in black coat and black small-brimmed hat took to the stage.

'Babka! Babka! Babka!' the crowd shouted, punching the air in unison.

There were whistles and applause and cheers before she managed to the silence the crowd, simply by raising her hands.

'Comrades!' she began. They all cheered.

'Napoleon!' someone shouted.

'Napoleon! Napoleon!' Others took up chant.

'Comrades!' she shouted again. 'I have news from our brothers in the capital and Comrade Lenin!' The crowd hushed. 'The fight for freedom is working! We are throwing off the shackles, we are destroying the *burzhúi*! We are stopping the war! What we need is faith! What we need is peace, what we need is bread! What we need is land! Claim back your land! Take what is yours! And don't let anyone stand in your way, for revolution is coming here. It's coming, I tell you, and we...' She paused and raised her arms in the air again. 'And we shall overcome, and we shall prevail. All of us!'

They crowd cheered. 'Bread! Peace! Land!' they chanted. Over and over.

'Do you know why we have no bread, no land, why *we* are poor!' Babushka demanded, her face growing redder. 'Because *they* want you to be!' She jabbed her finger in the air. 'They *want* you to be!' Nadezhda looked in the direction the old woman was pointing. 'They want you to be poor, they want you to starve, they want you to have no land, they want you to have nothing! They even stopped the railroad from coming here, from bringing progress and trade. It stopped at Sevastopol! Why? To save the views from their precious bloody houses! They didn't want to hear the noise. The noise of progress!' Nadezhda's heart skipped a beat as she realised the old woman was pointing up the coast towards Dulber, Ai Todor and Livadia. 'They hate you! They want to keep you as slaves. Serfs! Indentured! They privatised the beaches, so you can't land your fish – they don't care about you, or your families. All they want is to keep their nice pretty houses and nice pretty gardens and you, you lot can go to hell! Forget the train, serf! Take your horse and cart instead!'

The crowd erupted. 'Down with the Tsar! Down with the German spy! Down with the Romanovs!'

Nadezhda pulled her shawl tightly around her shoulders and walked swiftly away.

But it was not the increasingly anti-Romanov rhetoric that was bothering the captives further along the coast, but the health of the Dowager Empress and their total lack of supplies. The truth of the matter was that they had run out of money. There was little money for food, which was expensive and scarce. There was no money for clothes, which had to be darned and mended, and there was no money for sewing materials, which were also expensive and in short supply. There was no leather to resole their shoes, which they now repaired using squares of linoleum. It was no wonder the Dowager Empress never left her room and most of the prisoners never slept.

Meanwhile the war continued, the death toll mounted, the Germans were making progress and the troops were deserting in droves. Soldiers were now equal to their officers, weapons were controlled by committees, no one needed to salute anyone, and discipline was collapsing. Posts were abandoned overnight, and soldiers returned home, only to find the situation in their towns and villages was even worse than at the front. Many took to highway robbery, or that default position of the Russian – drunken debauchery.

Sandro was fortunate enough to receive an unredacted

letter from his brother, Sergei Mikhailovich, discussing the level of madness sweeping the country.

> *A Russian is so uncivilised, so much of a savage, that now he can lead only two kinds of life: either under the baton of a strong authority, fearing punishment, or in a complete anarchy under the motto 'Grab everything which does not belong to you.' This behaviour is now being demonstrated on the railroads. How do people understand freedom? ... The trains are not running – kill the station manager; the train goes too slowly – unhook the car carrying food.*

'I'd say we are better off here,' declared Xenia, digesting the contents of the letter. 'At least we are a little safer, because of our armed guard.'

'Except they could kill us at any time,' Sandro laughed. 'It's just the Sevastopol soviet that is stopping them.'

'What a comforting idea,' she replied, savouring one of the black, red and white cherries that had been harvested from the garden.

And still there was no news from Tsarskoye Selo; no one knew what was happening to Nicky, Alix and the children. The Dowager Empress could talk of nothing else. She was beside herself with worry and would not stop asking when they were coming home to the Crimea.

Eventually, as the temperatures rose and the unrelenting sun beat down, it was decided that Felix Yusupov and his wife Irina should travel back to Petrograd, to plead with Kerensky and the government to relax the rules of the arrest of those in Ai Todor and Dulber. They were also instructed to find money and jewellery, anything that might be easily and readily sold.

Or indeed smuggled out of the country. Following the raid on both their houses, the prisoners had become increasingly adept at hiding what remained of their jewellery. Squirrelled away in doorframes, chair legs and under the stairs, it was like playing a game of cat and mouse with the Bolsheviks, each testing the other's skill and ingenuity. Ladies soon learnt that cold cream jars were no defence against probing soldiers' fingers, although hollowed out bars of soap fared better. But nothing seemed more secure than Bertie's boots.

One afternoon, just before he set off back to Petrograd, Bertie met Militza and the Dowager on the beach. Both had managed to slip their guard to discuss taking some pieces out of the country and safely to England. Militza had brought the necklace she'd worn when she first involved the Tsar in necromancy at Znamenka all those years ago. Dressed in her dark green silk dress, her bosom heaving with rubies, she'd called up the ghost of Alexander III, who'd warned his son about the stampede at Khodynka Field, where thousands died trampled underfoot as they ran for free beer and gingerbread to celebrate Nicholas II's coronation. If only he'd listened, if only he'd not gone out to a ball at the French Embassy, he might have looked as if he'd cared a little more about the corpses in the field, and those killed underfoot. But he didn't. He drank champagne, while they counted the dead.

'I can take that to London for you,' Bertie agreed, holding the string of dark crimson stones up to the sun. 'Beautiful... Pigeon blood rubies. From Burma?'

'They are,' said Militza. 'How did you guess? And can

you take these for Nadezhda?' She held up a large pair of drop diamond and pearl earrings.

'Didn't I give you those?' asked the Dowager Empress, her pale blue eyes narrowing as she inspected the earrings. 'On your wedding day?'

'You did.'

'I remember it well, unlike your sister's wedding, which was a ghastly affair I choose whole-heartedly to forget.'

'Oh, do tell,' said Bertie, his lips pursed in wry amusement.

'I shall not,' snapped the Dowager, scanning the stone beach. 'Now, can you see a dog's skull sitting on a rock? It's my marker, all my jewellery is buried in a cocoa tin, under the skull. Where on earth is it?' Her voice was sounding a little panicky. 'They can't have dug up my tin! My cocoa tin! No one knew it was here!'

'Is that it?' exclaimed Bertie, pointing much further down the beach towards the shoreline. 'I can see a little skull from here.'

'But that's not where I left it!' She sounded rattled. 'That's not where I left it at all. It was here. Don't tell me they discovered the tin and threw the skull over there?'

'It was the wind,' said Militza staring out to sea.

'What wind?'

The Dowager regarded her just as she had done all those years ago, with irritation. Militza's throat tightened; all it took was one look to take her back to those miserable days at court, when no one would talk to her and Stana, and they'd whisper behind their backs about how they smelt of goat. The Goat Girls, they'd called them. So poor and lowly born, despite their brand new silks and diamonds, they sweated the stench of goat through their very pores.

'The wind blew it down the beach,' she replied, pointing up to the cliffs. 'It comes from the east. If you look up, all the trees are bent that way.'

'I buried it around there.' She pointed a shaking, veined hand. 'Near those rocks.'

'Let me have a look,' offered Bertie, with a small bow, before bounding rather athletically over the rocks in his leather-soled shoes. 'Around here, you say?'

He began rattling his walking stick down every hole and crevice he could find while the Dowager looked on in silence. The tension grew as rapidly as the sweat on Bertie's brow. Every so often he'd look up and smile and mop his forehead with his handkerchief and carry on. Then, at last, he came across something resembling a cocoa tin.

'I have found something!' he declared.

'Thank goodness!' The Dowager clutched her chest.

'It's heavy,' he added, pulling it out and giving it a rattle. 'It seems to have been undisturbed.' Thankfully, as he opened the tin, the pile of gems within caught the sun and lit his face in a kaleidoscope of colours. 'There's quite a lot in here.'

'I should hope so too,' replied the Dowager. 'I'm a Former Empress.'

As the summer wore on, the feeling of isolation and anxiety grew. The lack of news from Tsarskoye Selo was troubling everyone.

One blisteringly hot afternoon in late July, while Militza was lounging in the shade underneath a large white picture hat, wearing a white gown that had yellowed a little with age, she heard the pitter-patter of footsteps along the path towards the fountain.

'Beware of small children bearing gifts!' said Stana.

They both watched as Bébé toddled towards them, wearing a boater with a large pink sash and a white frilled dress.

'She looks better turned out than the rest of us,' said Stana, with a stretch. 'Here, Bébé, Bébé, Bébé.' She called her as she might a small dog or a cat. 'Here, Bébé, Bébé, Bébé, I have sweets!' she said.

'You never have sweets,' the seemingly angelic child replied, placing her plump little hands on her hips.

'Who are you supposed to see?' asked Militza.

'Nik-Nik,' she replied, kicking a leg in the air.

'Nikolasha? The Grand Duke?' asked Militza, sitting up.

'Nik-Nik.' She screwed up her face and walked over to the fountain. The cool water was much more inviting than any of those ladies.

'Let me help you!' said Militza, getting out of her chair. Now where could it be hidden this time? She swiftly picked up the little girl and carried her over to the shade. 'Let's take that hat off immediately.' Within a few minutes Bébé was playing happily in the fountain in her drawers, while Militza and Stana painstakingly searched her clothes. There was nothing in the hat, or her shoes, nor in the frills of her dress.

'That's odd,' said Stana, sitting back a little. 'She was all dressed up, looking so smart, with a hat and her sash, you would have thought she was carrying something.'

'The sash!' said Militza, unfurling the pale pink silk. As she lifted it up, a heavy envelope fell into her lap. Addressed

IMOGEN EDWARDS-JONES

to Dowager Empress Maria Feodorovna, it had already
been opened. 'Shall we?' she asked.

'Certainly,' replied Stana.

They both sat in silence as they read the extensive
collection of letters from Nicky, Alix and the children,
describing what life was like at Tsarskoye Selo, how
appallingly they had been treated, with little food and
no heating. How they'd spent their days chopping wood
and playing cards and pacing the corridors of the palace,
trying to humour their guards. Then came talk of them
packing, packing to come to the Crimea, how excited they
were to come to Livadia at last, to see the sea, and their
cousins, to play tennis and swim, breathe the air, see the
sky. They'd been given a week to organise it all, which,
as Alix complained jokingly, is never enough. After four
months of total confinement, they could not be more
excited. But at the last minute there was a change of plan,
they were forced into a closed train, marked 'Red Cross
Mission' and sent to Siberia. To Tobolsk. Where the Tsar
himself had sent criminals, murderers and revolutionaries
to die.

'Dear God,' said Stana.

'Dear God indeed,' replied Militza.

The news was enough to take away all hope, suck all
the spirit from the prisoners in the Crimea until there was
nothing left except total despair. On reading the news, the
Dowager struggled to breathe, for they had all secretly
believed it was only a matter of time before her son and the
family were allowed to join them on the coast.

Now they knew what it was like to be totally
disenfranchised, like their servants, and their serfs.

★ ★ ★

Some two weeks later, Militza woke suddenly to the sound of tapping on her window. The heat of the night was stultifying so she had left her curtains open and the moonlight was pouring in through the window. The tapping came again. She held her breath and lay rigid in bed. Her moment had come. They were always going to come in the night. It was a full moon, the perfect night for maleficence, the perfect opportunity to kill them all… She closed her eyes and began to pray.

'Militza!' It was more of a hiss than a whisper. 'Wake up! We need you!' Militza opened her eyes and exhaled. 'Please come quickly. It's Xenia, we need you! It's an emergency. Olga's in labour. She's thirty-five, it's her first baby, we can't have her die in childbirth on top of everything else.'

A few minutes later Militza and Stana were running through the trees in their nightgowns, up to their knees in long grasses and wildflowers, carrying the green velvet book and a small bag of herbs and poultices. Xenia was lighting the way with her torch.

'I'm sorry to wake you, I just didn't know what to do. No one in Ai Todor has delivered a baby. Olga is so old, and this is her first, and I can't wake Mother because I don't want her to see her youngest daughter die in front of her.' Xenia was babbling with nerves. 'I know you know, and I'm terrified, and she's terrified, and we're all terrified. And you were so good with Alix when Suzanna was born.'

'Suzanna?' Militza stopped in her tracks. What was Xenia talking about? How did she know anything about a child called Suzanna? 'I don't know what you're talking about.'

Xenia stopped and looked at Militza in the darkness. Stana was up ahead, and carried on running, the bag of herbs swinging by her side.

'I know,' said Xenia.

'I don't know what you're talking about,' continued Militza, thankful for the darkness so that Xenia couldn't see her face.

'Nicky and Alix's fifth daughter, the one you rescued and sent out of the country. Suzanna. Who lives in Holland, with Leendert Johannes Hemmes. That one. That baby. That daughter nobody wanted.' She was beginning to raise her voice. 'That daughter who will never know who she really is. Who her parents really are. That one!'

'There was no fifth daughter,' replied Militza as steadily as she could. 'There was no fifth baby girl. That was a phantom pregnancy. It was an ovule.'

'Don't take me for a fool, Militza Nikolayevna. I know what you did. I know it was your idea. To take a child away from its mother. She wasn't even two days old, snatched from her mother's arms, packed off in the middle of the night, smuggled over the Finnish border in the care of a man who was a charlatan and a fraud. With five million roubles in his back pocket for his trouble. Everyone said it was to save the monarchy, save the Tsar; the people could not cope with another daughter. Well, that went well, didn't it! Where are the people now? Where are they!' She was shouting in the woods, her arms outstretched, her hair loose around her shoulders, and by the light of the moon, Militza could see she was crying. 'That poor little baby.'

Militza stepped forward in the darkness and put her arms around Xenia, who sobbed. And as Xenia cried, the full moon came out from behind a cloud. Its clear pale light shone into the darkness: the illuminator of secrets, the bold, silver beam of truth. 'Don't worry,' soothed Militza. 'Don't worry.' She stroked her hair, as if she was talking to a child.

'We're lost,' replied Xenia, looking up into the eyes that were blacker than the woods around them. 'We are all totally and utterly lost. And I'm scared.'

'Hurry up!' came a shout through the trees. 'This baby is not going to deliver itself!'

Arriving via the terrace and through the open French windows, Militza and Stana slipped through the house like ghosts. Outside Olga's bedroom, the much-maligned commoner Nikolai Kulikovsky was pacing the corridor, running his hands through his hair, pausing every now and then to listen to what was happening on the other side of the firmly closed door.

'Oh, thank goodness!' he said, as soon as he saw Militza and Stana. 'The cavalry has arrived. Please tell me she'll be all right. Please.'

'She'll be fine.' Stana squeezed his shoulder. 'She's not the first woman to do this.'

'But she's thirty-five,' he exclaimed.

'And strong as an ox,' said Stana.

'You still haven't told her mother she's in labour?' he asked Xenia.

'No.' She shook her head. 'There's no point in worrying her.'

Inside the hot, sweaty room, with its drawn curtains and

closed windows, Militza and Stana felt immediately short of air. Coming through the cool of the woods into this stifling room was enough to make the sturdiest soul faint.

'Open the windows, let in the air, the poor woman can't breathe!' Militza marched around the bed to find Olga already moaning and writhing around on the bed with her legs apart, flat on her back. 'I think you should stand up, if you can,' suggested Militza. 'Or roll over. You might find it easier.'

'Like an animal?' said Xenia. 'She's the daughter of the Tsar!'

'I promise you,' nodded Stana. 'It's easier.'

'But it's undignified.'

'Not half as undignified as being dead,' snapped Militza, pushing up her sleeves. 'Now is there any warm water, soap, towels? Anything?'

'You can scream if you want,' said Militza, pressing a damp towel to Olga's forehead.

'But Mama is down the corridor,' said Xenia. 'And her husband is outside.'

'He'll be glad she is still alive,' said Stana. 'And the Dowager is as deaf as a post!'

Olga laughed from the bed and then bellowed like an ox as she pushed herself up on all fours on the bed. Her back arched and she yelled even louder as a rush of liquid burst on to the bedsheets and the floor.

'Good girl!' encouraged Militza. 'Keep going, you're nearly there! Push, push, push and when I tell you, stop. And then you push again. Is that clear?'

'Yes!' Another contraction tore through her body, making her cry out in pain.

'Push!' yelled Militza. 'Good girl.'

And then, in a flurry of shouting and pushing and moaning and hot water and towels, there was a silence, as the whole room held its breath. Total silence. Followed by the most perfect cry Olga had ever heard.

'Hello,' she whispered as she collapsed on to the bed.

'Congratulations,' said Militza gathering the baby and laying it on Olga's breast. 'You have a boy. A perfect baby boy.'

'A boy.' Olga smiled as the baby latched on to her plump bosom and immediately began to feed. 'Oh look,' she said, looking down.

'He's been here before,' said Militza. 'This is not his first time.'

'I do believe I am the first Grand Duchess ever to suckle her own baby,' replied Olga. 'I shall most certainly do this again. I think I like having babies!'

The birth of baby Tikhon went some way to ease the monotony and the misery; that, and the fact that a few more letters made it through. Apparently, Kirill had escaped to Finland. The red banners flying above his palace in Petrograd were not enough to deter the Bolsheviks and he'd crossed the border with his wife and children. He was safe, but should the winds change he was also close enough to make a grab for the throne, something his mother, Grand Duchess Vladimir, had always dreamed of. Others were not so lucky. Lobbying the British for sanctuary seemed to be a road to nowhere. Despite hundreds of years of offering refuge to the needy, Sir George Buchanan was told by the Foreign Office that: 'The presence here of Grand Dukes is not desirable at present.'

Meanwhile, Irina Yusupova returned to the Crimea without her husband and with none of the jewellery or money they were hoping for.

'There was nothing there,' she whispered through the hedge as she pretended to walk her dog. Both Militza and Xenia were standing behind the oleander, their eyes glancing left and right for guards. 'Whatever you have hidden, whatever you had, is no more. Felix and I went through our Moika Palace, hiding what we could. But it's chaos. I have La Pelegrina pearl on me at all times, but everything else they find and steal. I can't tell you,' she said. 'Nothing is how you remember. The soldiers have no boots and are wandering the streets shooting. It is all such a mess. There's no food. Rations are so low, people can't eat. And there's a man called Leon Trotsky who is constantly stirring up the crowds. They seem to love him. They hang on his every word. But there are strikes and the peasants are looting and burning manor houses. You can see the plumes of smoke from the train, all the way from Petrograd to Moscow. Estate after estate is being torched. Moscow is just as bad. There are thugs and gangsters everywhere. It's almost as if they have forgotten we are at war with the Germans. They are most happy killing each other. What are we to do? What does Nikolasha think?'

'He doesn't think much,' said Militza. 'His spirit is broken. A military man without an army, he is miserable. And what did Kerensky say about the Dowager Empress? Is he going to help?'

'I spoke to him at length, I went to the Winter Palace and begged—'

'The Winter Palace?' asked Xenia.

'Oh, please don't tell the Empress but he is living in the royal rooms, Nicky's suite, like the Tsar. They all are.'

'Good God!' said Xenia.

'The rebels are everywhere,' continued Irina. 'They have occupied every palace they like – the only person still in their palace is the Countess Kleinmichel.'

'She is?'

'She's put a sign on her door saying it's the property of the Petrograd soviet and trespassers should keep out.'

'She's always been rather fabulous,' said Militza, smiling. 'Is she well?'

'No one is well. And Felix has insisted on staying. I don't know why, I am terrified for him. It is so dangerous. People are being killed all the time.'

All the time.

Prince Yusupov was hugely anxious while walking the streets of Petrograd that early autumn. He'd dispatched his wife almost as soon as he could. This city, that had once breathed elegance and sophistication, was no place for a woman; it had entirely collapsed and was nothing short of a cesspit. And it certainly smelt like one. Unfortunately, he still had business to do. Too late to save most of his jewels, he was determined to ensure that the one pile of diamonds he had left would make it out of the country. However, as the government got weaker every day, so the level of violence rose. But despite the hardships and the brutality it was extraordinary to realise there were some people who still remained in the city. The Grand Dukes George Mikhailovich and Dmitri Konstantinovich were heard to be dining at Donon's on a regular basis, although what they had to eat was anyone's guess. Grand Duke Nicholas Mikhailovich, otherwise known as Uncle Bimbo, called in at the Moika Palace for an evening along with the recently returned Bertie Stopford, who'd just made it back from Kislovodsk and the Grand Duchess Vladimir's, where he'd been to deliver her money.

'She is much better,' declared Bertie, over a flute of fizzy champagne. 'Now she has been released from her three months' detention and is taking baths for her heart. She has a few old servants and is very happy at the idea of getting some Cossacks from the village, all from the same family, to protect her.'

'Are the Cossacks still loyal out in the villages?' asked Uncle Bimbo, as he sat down in one of Yusupov's fine silk-backed chairs. At six foot three, he was a beefy, bald bear of a man and he made the chair seem particularly small.

'Some,' replied Bertie. 'I can't think why you are still in the city.'

'You know Uncle Bimbo,' laughed Felix, filling up his glass of champagne. 'He's a political liberal, he's a socialist – these are his people!'

Just as all three of them chuckled, there were shots fired in the street.

'Not again!' Felix stared at the open window.

'Not more,' added Bertie.

'The days, the nights, the pillaging, the murdering, when will it stop?' Felix suddenly looked exhausted.

The noise from the street below was appalling. There was shouting and kicking and shooting, then screaming and squealing, like pigs in an abattoir. The three men remained immobile, frightened and revolted by the sounds below.

'Enough!' declared Bertie striding towards the window.

'Enough,' agreed Felix, joining him.

'Comrades!' Uncle Bimbo bellowed out of the window. 'Leave that man alone!'

Below in the street lay the battered body of an elderly man who had been set upon by a band of sailors, clearly drunk enough to fancy some sport. They'd pummelled the old man with their rifle-butts and kicked him with their hobnail boots. The man was crawling along the pavement on his hands and knees.

'Leave him!' Uncle Bimbo repeated.

The old man looked up at the window from where the cries had come. Blood was streaming down his face from two gaping holes where his eyes had once been. Yusupov stepped back in horror as the final blow was swiftly administered by an old woman from the crowd. Murder or mercy, it was hard to decide.

'Dear Lord,' whispered Bertie. As he watched, his eyes narrowed a little. 'I think I know that woman.'

'Oh, yes?' said Uncle Bimbo, his face contorted with the horror of what he'd just seen.

'I think that's Grand Duchess Militza's old woman servant.'

'What?' replied Felix. 'The Black Crows' old crone.'

'Brana?' said Uncle Bimbo.

'That's her name,' confirmed Bertie. 'I remember her well. We took a train together, once, to the front.'

All three of them looked back through the window just as Brana looked up.

'Things really are taking a turn for the worse,' replied Uncle Bimbo.

In Petrograd, the coldest winter since 1808 had given way to a dank and damp summer which had been swiftly succeeded by the bitter rains and storms of a dank and dismal autumn. Mud was everywhere, it covered the streets and caked the pavements and with no one to clean them, no one to sweep and hose and maintain any sort of decorum, everything was grinding to a halt. All was poised. All was primed. Ready.

In Yalta, as Nadezhda had witnessed, Babushka's followers were growing by the day; red armbands were as ubiquitous as the lack of civility on the streets. You could feel it. She could feel it, it was fermenting, growing like a bacterium, a virus that was working its way through everyone, and it made her uneasy. Access to her parents and her siblings was now nigh on impossible. And the rain, the rain just wouldn't stop.

It was 4 a.m. on 25 October 1917 when Nadezhda and Nicholas were woken by violent hammering on their apartment door. They went rigid with fear. Who was this? What was this? Who was calling at this ungodly hour?

'Leave it,' he whispered.

They hammered again.

'I can't.'

'Let me go.'

Nicholas slowly made his way towards the door, his heart pounding, his mouth dry. Was this it? Were they to be taken in the middle of the night like so many others? Terrified, he listened at the door. He could hear heavy breathing. The rise and fall of another man's chest, just the other side. He was poised by the handle, too frightened to speak. Suddenly an envelope was slipped under the door. Nicholas swiftly pulled back the locks and flung it open, but the messenger had disappeared.

'What is it?' asked Nadezhda shivering next to him in the darkness.

'A telegram, I think.' Nicholas walked towards the light in the bedroom. He opened it. 'It's Bertie.' He stopped and turned to look at her, the colour draining rapidly from his face. 'It's happened. We must tell the Dowager, your mother, Nikolasha, all of them. They must be prepared.'

The rain was horizontal as she and Nicholas battled along the coastal road to Dulber. Normally such a calm driver, Nicholas was screaming at the one horse he'd managed to find, smacking his neck with the reins. The thunder rolled in from the sea, lightning cracking out of the sky. The wind had churned the waves into a stampede of white horses crashing on the rocks below.

'Hurry up!' shouted Nadezhda. Her voice was carried on the wind. 'Please! We must get there before the soldiers, before they murder them all in their beds! Hurry up!'

Nicholas lashed the horse again and lightning shot once more across the sky, illuminating the path. Nadezhda closed her eyes, terrified of what she might see. Would there be guards, with guns, pointed at her and her husband as they stormed the gates of the estate? But who stands guard on a terrible stormy night, especially when there's vodka to drink and no one's getting paid? Pulling the cart up in front of the fountain, Nadezhda leapt out of her seat and ran to hammer on the door.

It was hard to make themselves heard above the noise of the storm, but she would not stop. Her face was flat against the door, her hair dripping with water; it ran down her cheeks and off the end of her nose. But she kept on hammering. Both fists, then one at a time, until finally, eventually, Militza appeared in the doorway with a thick woollen shawl tied around her shoulders.

'Oh, Mama!' Nadezhda cried as she staggered through the door. 'It's revolution! They have taken the Winter Palace, stormed the building, drunk the cellars dry, smashed everything, Kerensky has escaped, dressed in women's clothes and Lenin is in power. All is lost. We are lost. We must prepare to die.'

She promptly fainted on the cold marble floor.

'Darling!' Nicholas ran into the house and fell on to the floor beside her. 'My darling, my darling.' He kissed her cheeks, her lips, he stroked her wet face, kissed her hair. He looked up at Militza. 'She is all right, isn't she? She'll be fine?'

'She'll be fine,' smiled Militza. 'I can hear your daughter's heartbeat from here.'

I feel very anxious for the safety of the emperor... If he once gets inside the walls of the prison of St Peter and St Paul, I doubt he will ever come out alive.

George V, King of England

CHAPTER 17

February 1918, Crimea

The news from the capital swept through the two households, creating a blind terror. What was to happen to them? What was to happen to the Tsar? The Bolshevik party was now in power, with Lenin and Trotsky at its head. There was no news of the Tsar, no news from friends and family abroad and what news there was chilled the blood.

Caught in the capital, as the rebels stormed the Winter Palace and gorged themselves on the cellars of fine wines and Armagnacs, Felix's escape from the city was nothing short of miraculous. Little did he know that he had the Black Crows and their daughter Nadezhda to thank for it. For no sooner had the revolution been declared than a distraught Irina had appeared on the other side of the garden gate, wringing her hands and begging for help: her husband was in Petrograd, there were guards at the Moika palace, and soldiers sleeping on the marble floors, he was wanted by the Bolsheviks, his apparent arrest and imprisonment in the Peter and Paul Fortress had already been celebrated in the newspaper, he needed to escape as soon as possible. Militza managed to get word to Nadezhda who was then instructed to contact Madame Ignatiev who had run the Black Salons back in the day, when the beau-monde of St Petersburg had embraced the black arts with a fanatic fervour. And through her, the Freemasons had come to his rescue. They supplied false papers, and access to a private locked carriage, on an otherwise crowded train with broken windows and torn blinds, and a safe passage to Kiev. There, the hotels were full, but he was given lodging, then met in the Crimea by a Delaunay-Belleville car, flying his family crest at the train station before he was ferried with apparent ease directly to Koreiz. Unfortunately, he had none of the jewellery he had been intent on saving, including a substantial collection the Dowager Empress had asked him to rescue. It had already been relocated to Moscow, on the orders of the new government.

Orders from the new government were coming thick and fast. Within days of taking the Winter Palace, there was a change of guard at Dulber and Ai Todor.

Militza and Stana were deadheading roses in the gardens of Dulber when they saw the trucks arrive. The roar of the engines, as they tore up the driveway lined with cypress trees, was enough to make both their hearts beat ferociously and their palms sweat. Having spent months going to bed at night, unsure whether they would wake again in the morning, this sudden invasion was enough to bring on a state of panic.

'What new hell is this?' whispered Stana, holding her sister's arm. 'I am not sure my nerves can take any more.'

Standing with their secateurs in their hands, wearing sturdy leather gardening gloves, the sisters watched as an extraordinarily tall man leapt out of the truck, wearing a long leather coat, and a peaked cap pulled down over his face.

'Citizens!' He nodded in the direction of Militza and Stana as they stood staring at him. 'Comrade Zadorozhny, from the Sevastopol soviet.' He nodded again. 'I am here to speak to the owner of this household.' He looked down at a piece of paper. 'Under the orders from Lenin himself, you are under the strictest house arrest.'

'But we have been under strict arrest for months already,' said Militza, walking towards the apparent beast of man, who at first glance looked like a murderer, but on closer inspection seemed like a more gentle soul.

'It shall be stricter still,' he replied, through his thick moustache.

'Stricter still?' Militza felt her shoulders sink.

'It is for your own safety,' he stated, looking down his large nose at her. 'The Yalta soviet – under Babushka – want you dead, the Sevastopol not so much. And Comrade Lenin himself does not want you shot, not right away, anyway. He wants to save you from our comrades in Yalta. So for now, my soldiers and I have been told to guard you. And you are not allowed to leave the compound. Not for any reason at all. Not to go to the beach, or for a walk, or a swim, or play tennis or whatever you do... with your time.' He waved his hand dismissively. 'You are not allowed in town. Ever. For your own good, Yalta is too dangerous for you. Visitors are by invitation only... And I also have your correspondence.' He raised a giant fist, full of envelopes, all of which, Militza could not help but notice, had already been opened. As he handed over the bundle of letters, a unit of armed guards poured out of the back of the truck and dispersed across the property. 'I also have another order,' he said, towering over the two women. 'For all of you, including, especially, Citizen Nikolai Nikolayevich Romanov, to surrender your weapons. All guns, all pistols, all swords, should be handed over to me. All the better to protect you, obviously.'

If the idea of handing over their few weapons and their renewed incarceration were not enough to depress Militza, Stana, Nikolasha and Peter, the news contained in their letters was beyond distressing. Their estates had collapsed, their fields were being burnt and ransacked and their farming equipment destroyed. Herds of oxen, workhorses and thoroughbreds had all been killed in an orgy of desecration and carnage.

'They have broken and smashed the hothouse at Znamenka,' said Militza, looking up from her letter from their lawyer at the breakfast table, where she whipped up one solitary egg in her glass. 'All the orchids have gone.' She paused, her hand shaking a little. 'They have set fire to the books in the library.' She looked up at her husband. Her black eyes filled with tears. 'There is only a pile of grey ash to show what was once there.'

'It is almost as if they are punishing us for keeping them illiterate and ignorant for so long,' said Peter. 'Anything we treasured or touched, they have destroyed.'

'Any news of the Nikolayevsky Palace?' asked Nikolasha.

'He says he has not managed to get inside, only Brana has gone.' Militza put down the letter. The description of the betrayal was too much.

'Gone?' asked Stana.

Militza sighed. 'Yes, apparently. Mimka did say that she was working at *Pravda* but I still did think she might be looking after the house. But no. It's gone. It's been handed over to the revolution. Lock, stock and barrel. According to my lawyer, they have even taken all our clothes.'

'I suppose you can't blame her,' said Peter.

'What do you mean?' Nikolasha looked horrified.

'After all we have done for her!' exclaimed Stana.

'What did you do for her?' Peter sat back a little in his chair. 'Exactly.'

'She came with us from Montenegro, and she came to the city and lived in the court,' said Stana. 'And—'

'And she was still illiterate and a servant. She never married. She never had children, she had no life outside the one you gave her.' Peter's voice was quiet and measured.

'Well, there's no need for her to have taken all our clothes,' replied Stana. 'And anyway, how are we to survive? Without the income from our estates, we have no money. No money from the court. There is no court. We are the ones who have nothing now.'

'How will anyone survive?' asked Nikolasha, taking a sip of his acorn coffee. 'Our climate is most badly suited to political and social mismanagement. In the summer we lay down resources for the winter. We pickle, we plant, we store, we manage our supplies with care. We have to. We cannot be profligate. We cannot waste things. We polish our apples and pile up our firewood, for the winter is long. And this winter,' he sighed, 'will be very long, very long indeed.'

★ ★ ★

Nikolasha's prediction was, of course, correct, although even he could not know quite how difficult the winter of 1917–1918 would become.

Within weeks of his arrival, Zadorozhny issued an order that was to have an impact on them all. The *whole* royal party should move into Dulber, with immediate effect. For their own safety. It would be easier for him and his troops to defend the inmates if they were *all* in one place, and Dulber with its high walls and turrets was already built like a Persian fortress. The news was not well received by the prisoners in Ai Todor. Little did Zadorozhny know that Peter's palace had for years been the subject of ridicule in the higher echelons of the court. Its interior design had been mocked, his unusual taste criticised and its architecture viewed with disdain, and indeed horror. All the other palaces in the area were of Italianate design; Dulber was a little too Tartar for Western tastes. Mostly they blamed his wife for his poor architectural choices. Being from Montenegro, she clearly knew no better. He'd been unduly influenced. Again. The poor, weak, easily led man that he was.

The Dowager Empress's fury on her forced incarceration with the Black Crows, their husbands, and their children in the 'hideous' Dulber Palace was evident as she thundered across the threshold, pursued by Xenia, Sandro, their six offspring, Olga, her baby son Tikhon and her husband, and the remaining tiny handful of loyal servants.

The rest had gone. Some had flown in the night, others had simply walked out of the gates, unwilling to work for no money, with little or no food.

'We have put aside the finest room in the house for you,'

declared Militza, by way of appeasement. 'It has views of the sea and of the Ai-Petri mountain. It is my favourite room in the house.'

'And what a house,' exclaimed the Dowager, walking straight past Militza into the heavily mosaiked hallway. 'If I didn't have a headache already, I would surely develop one quite soon.'

Following a servant slowly up the stairs, breathing heavily as she went, the Dowager Empress walked into her exquisitely positioned bedroom suite, with expansive coastal and mountain views, seen through elegantly draped arched windows, and promptly slammed the door.

'What are we to do?' whispered Militza to her husband, on hearing the crash upstairs.

'I think a luncheon and perhaps a dinner might restore everyone's humour,' suggested Peter, smiling at his remaining guests. 'I think we should ask Korniloff to do his very, very best.'

So, after weeks of their living on little but buckwheat and pea soup, with a few mildewed potatoes, the chef, Korniloff, did his absolute best to ease tensions by serving meat, twice in one day.

'I have to say,' remarked Sandro, dabbing the corners of his mouth with his napkin, after polishing off his dinner with a hearty gusto. 'Old Korniloff really has surpassed himself tonight. I have not felt this full for months.'

'Well yes,' agreed Peter. 'A little red wine?' he added, offering one of the many vintage bottles that still remained in the well-stocked cellars of Dulber.

'Most kind,' replied Sandro.

Peter sipped his wine in silence and looked down the

length of the linen-topped dining table at his twenty or so other guests, scraping the last of the food off their plates, their faces dulled by boredom. After months of 'boiling in their juices', as Xenia put it, there were few topics for conversation except, of course, what was really happening to Nicky and the world beyond their walled prison, which was far too painful to discuss.

'How long do you think they'll keep us here?' asked Xenia, eventually, looking across at her mother, who had dressed for dinner, with pearl earrings and a little diamond choker around her neck.

'Not long,' she replied with a tight smile. 'The world will come to its senses soon enough, and everything will return back to normal. Just as we were. You'll see. We'll be back in St Petersburg by the spring.'

'I have a feeling the world is changed forever,' replied Nikolasha from further down the table.

'Nothing is forever,' replied the Dowager, with a little shake of her earrings. 'Changes come and go, but Romanovs, we remain the same.'

'I think this change might be a little bigger than most,' suggested Nikolasha. 'Seismic, I'd say.'

'And we all know who's to blame for that, don't we?' replied the Dowager, briskly slicing the meat on her plate.

'Lenin?' said Nikolasha.

'Don't be foolish.'

'The Tsarina?'

'Your household,' she shot back.

'Well, I wouldn't—' started Peter.

'Oh, please, do take some responsibility for your wife and her sister and your actions,' she interrupted, placing her knife and fork down and picking up a goblet of heavy Crimean red wine. 'We all know that Rasputin came through your house. You introduced him to my darling Nicky and that woman, and all this, this terrible tragedy, this terrible injustice, is your fault. If it had not been for you, and your Friend, none of this would have happened. The revolution, the end of a three-hundred-year dynasty, is all your fault. *You* will be remembered for this.' She took a sip of her wine. 'And history will not treat you kindly.'

'And it's nothing to do with the Tsar?' asked Militza.

Everyone turned to stare at her.

'It has nothing to do with Nicky,' the Dowager Empress replied slowly. 'Nothing at all. It is all to do with *that* man and *that* woman and *your* household. And I shall never forgive you for it,' she whispered, looking down at her food. 'In fact, the only person who deserves fine praise in all of this is Prince Felix Yusupov, my gallant son-in-law and the true hero of Russia.'

'How so?' asked Stana.

'For shooting your *Muzhik*, for murdering the man, for poisoning him, feeding him with cakes and shooting him through the head and drowning him in the Neva.'

'Oh, yes, of course,' Stana snarled. 'How could any of us forget? He tells everyone that story and it gets bigger and more elaborate every time. You would actually think he was the one to pull the trigger!'

'He was,' replied the Dowager. 'And the world is a better place for it.'

'I think this subject should be closed,' suggested Peter, 'while we are all under my roof.'

'And what a roof!' Xenia laughed drily.

'You are very welcome to leave it, should you so wish,' replied Peter.

'Well, we all know none of us can do that,' said Xenia, stabbing the last piece of meat on her plate and popping it into her mouth. 'We'll be shot by the first opportunist that sees us.'

'Oh, don't say that,' muttered the Dowager, shaking her head. 'I worry so much for Nicky and the children. What are they doing out there in Siberia? So far from home. It's a place for criminals. Why can't they come here to the Crimea where they belong? At least we would all be together.'

'We would,' agreed Xenia. 'Imagine how delightful that would be.'

Nikolai Kulikovsky smiled. 'And then we could all play proper happy families.'

Before anyone could respond, the double doors to the dining room swung open and Korniloff appeared still wearing his chef's whites, with his hat slightly askew on his sweaty forehead.

'You called for me, Grand Duke?' He smiled at Peter, who was sitting at the head of the table.

'Yes, indeed.' Peter nodded. 'We all just wanted to thank you so much for the incredible food you have managed to serve today. It has made our first day together so much more... palatable.'

'It has certainly made a delightful change from porridge, that's for sure!' laughed Sandro, helping himself to some more wine. 'The stew at luncheon was delicious.'

'So, you like the billy goat?' Korniloff nodded enthusiastically. 'It's a strong flavour but if cooked long enough...'

'If that's what it was.' Sandro smiled. 'Excellent meat, goat. Not at all tough. Not at all like you would imagine.'

'And dinner?' the Dowager enquired, tweaking the meat with her fork.

'Hee-Haw!' He grinned, looking around the room, delighted with himself. 'Donkey!'

'Donkey?' The Grand Duchess Xenia released her fork with a clatter on to her plate.

'Donkey,' he said, still grinning. 'A strong flavour but if cooked long enough…'

'Very palatable,' agreed Peter. 'Who knew? Donkey. Delicious.'

That winter, starvation and typhoid, brought back by lice from the trenches, killed more than the bullets, or the Germans, or the Bolsheviks had managed to do so far, and added to that, Spanish influenza had swept in from Asia, killing millions more. Criminal gangs were terrorising the cities, pillaging and taking what they wanted. It was common to wake up with a muzzle at your face while the rest of your house was being ransacked by a bunch of hooligans who didn't even bother to wear masks. With no firewood to burn in the cities, they began chopping down the trees that lined the boulevards, burning fine furniture from the homes of the affluent and, of course, their books, hundreds of thousands of them, to feed the small cast-iron stoves, known as the *burzhúi* because of their pot-shaped bellies and fondness for literature.

In Petrograd the lights were out, and the starving were stalking the streets looking for anything they could eat. They rummaged through bins that were crawling with rats; all the cats and dogs had disappeared. At night, as the corpses of the horses lay rotting by the pavements, shadowy figures emerged to carve off pieces of meat, which they ate raw by the roadside. After just a few months of Bolshevik power, the city was at a standstill, the factories were shut, with no fuel to keep them open, their assets stripped by their workers for cash. The ration cards issued by the Bolsheviks provided little in terms of food or petrol or kerosene. All the private shops were shut, their windows boarded up or clouded with chalk dust. An anarchic underclass had crawled through the broken windows and front doors of the foreign embassies and abandoned palaces, only to avail themselves of the luxuries inside. Enjoying glugs of cognac while playing cards, their lady-friends sported scarlet lipstick, wearing the increasingly foul-smelling dresses and undergarments of the former mistresses of the house.

Brana was now living in the Blue Parlour on the second floor of the Nikolayevsky Palace. She liked the big fireplace, the old chandelier and the views over the Neva. She had indeed, as the lawyer's letter suggested, sold all the mistresses' clothes and the paintings and any little bourgeois knick-knacks she could get rid of, so she could feed the other families that had moved into the many other rooms in the palace. She'd also burnt quite a lot of the furniture. She was a Bolshevik and all riches should be shared equally. But there were fewer and fewer riches left in the city and the situation could not get any worse. Even at the Bolshevik headquarters where she worked during the day, packing and then circulating the newspaper *Pravda* around the city, the atmosphere was becoming increasingly fractious. Paper stocks were low and so was morale and they were fearful.

'Nothing is moving fast enough,' complained a small, bearded man with a thick head of hair and round glasses.

Brana had met him before in the offices upstairs. He was head of the Petrograd soviet and had been leading the rebels against the Cossack counterattack at Gatchina. She liked him. Leon Trotksy was dynamic, exciting, highly intelligent and popular with the rebels. Despite being Lenin's number two, he spent time talking to the workers in the basement.

'We need to spread the message faster, move faster, get the word into the countryside,' he added. 'We need volunteers to travel north, south.' He was pacing round between the piles of newspapers, his right hand moving up and down, reiterating his point. 'East, west, taking newspapers and ideas with them.' He stopped and looked. 'Anyone here? Anyone here volunteer? To help Babushka, for example, in Yalta?'

'I can,' said Brana, a stack of newspapers under her arm.

'You?' He stared through his small round spectacles.

'I know it well. I used to spend every summer in Yalta.'

'You summered in Yalta?' His voice a little high with incredulity.

'Right next door to the Livadia Estate.'

As the pipes thawed in the cities, the sewage that had been frozen, due to lack of heating in the winter, burst forth, releasing a heinous deluge that flowed through the streets unchecked. The stench was monstrous and the spread of disease appalling. The revolution shifted to the countryside, and it became a battleground between the Reds – the Bolsheviks – and the Whites – the newly formed resistance. Roaming armies scavenged from village to village and, like locusts, stripped them of anything of value or use, leaving the inhabitants to starve and shiver to death. Anarchists, bandits, warlords; they swept through the steppes, acting with impunity, shooting at random anyone who looked affluent, intellectual, bourgeois, bespectacled or simply educated, raping and looting as they went. The rules of battle were increasingly barbaric, verging on the medieval and, as the supply of pistols and guns dwindled, sabres, knives and bayonets were increasingly used, appalling injuries sustained, with no hospitals or medics to deal with them. Death was often slow, protracted and painful.

In Yalta, for Nadezhda and Nicholas it was a daily struggle to survive. As the baby in her belly slowly grew, the reality of their situation became starker. The Yalta soviet under the charismatic influence of Babushka was by far the most bellicose. All around them was danger, hunger, disease. Every day Nicholas left the apartment to find food, firewood, kerosene for the lamps. The lights were out all over the city, people were surviving on what they had managed to store during the relatively fecund summer months. News was sparse, the civil war was gathering apace, the government in nearby Kiev was changing hands from the Reds, to the Whites, to Poles and even the Germans.

The Germans were advancing; they were making progress. Nadezhda was terrified of bringing a baby into this world. It was almost as if nature were playing a joke, the cruellest of tricks – new life was growing inside her, just as all hope was dying. Hunger gnawed at her from the inside, grinding its sharp teeth inside her belly. The bread, the water, the thin millet kasha were not enough; while her baby appeared to feast on her flesh, her belly grew bigger as she grew thinner and thinner, increasingly pale. Her huge dark eyes were growing larger, as her cheeks slowly hollowed.

Nicholas lay awake at night, staring at the ceiling, churning with worry that his wife appeared to be fading away before his very eyes. He'd heard rumours that at the other end of town they were selling horsemeat, someone had mentioned there were dogs' tails, which tasted just like veal. Or eggs. What wouldn't he sell for eggs? His father's watch. His mother's portrait in its Fabergé frame. Anything. Beside him, Nadezhda tossed and turned, holding her belly, rolling from one side to the other, seemingly beset by the most terrible dreams of drowning and a man crawling up through a hole in the ice. She muttered in her sleep; she cried out in the pitch blackness, and he could hear what she saw in her nightmares. It was as if she was being dragged under, hauled away by her ankles, back under the ice.

He rose early. He was determined to find something to eat, his wife was slowly slipping into the next world, taking his unborn daughter with her. Nadezhda was sleeping as he penned her a note and slipped out of the door. She was, at last, at rest. He sighed a little with relief as he slowly closed the latch.

It was 5 a.m. and outside on the street it was dark but busy; with supplies such a scarcity, only the tenacious could survive. Nicholas turned his collar up, put his hands in his pockets, his head down and started to walk. The pavements were covered in a thin film of ice, sleet came down at an angle of forty-five degrees, but it wasn't far to the woman with a supply of meat, just at the edge of the city. It was just over an hour's walk, possibly more in these inclement conditions. He picked up pace. His stomach grumbled, he hadn't eaten for the last thirty-six hours, and his body felt weak, but his resolve was strong, determined. The atmosphere on the street felt tense. Everyone was on edge. No one knew what was going to happen, there was danger everywhere. All it took was a wrong look, eye contact, a disagreement, and you could lose your life.

The moon still shone, the sleet eased off and the beginnings of a rusty pink dawn gently blushed the sky. Underfoot the streets were filthy, a recent thin fall of snow had grown grey and gritty and none of the rubbish from the past few months had been cleared. Bottles, cans, rotting food, pamphlets encouraging revolution, horse manure, dead rats filled the roads – it was hard for the few motorcars and carts to make their way.

On he walked. His feet were painful, his mouth was dry with thirst, his thin backbone was rubbing up against his shirt. Everything hurt. His hips, his shoulders, the soles of his feet. Hunger did strange things to the body, it ground it down, suffocating it with lethargy and weakness. He looked up to find that the houses were thinning out and the side streets were turning to mud – it couldn't be far. He took out a small piece of paper.

'Olga,' he mumbled. 'The end of the road. Past the church. Turn left at the old oak tree.' Was this the road? The church and the old oak? He stood and slowly looked around. 'Excuse me?' There was a man, wrapped up in what appeared to be a cloak on the steps of the church. 'Excuse me?' he asked again, as the rags stirred. 'I'm looking for Olga?'

'Olga?' mumbled the man, raising his head and opening his eyes. One was dark and the other was entirely white. It shone like a gull's egg in the dawn light.

'Yes, Olga,' said Nicholas, taking a step back.

'Have no fear of me,' said the one-eyed man, raising a hand. 'I'm a priest.' He opened his torn cloak a little to reveal ripped black robes. 'I lie here to protect my church from the mob, they've attacked it once before. They almost took my sight, but I shall not be defeated. God is great, God is merciful.'

'Indeed,' agreed Nicholas, his head bowed. 'Most merciful.'

'Olga, you say?' asked the priest, staring at Nicholas. 'Olga the Meat?'

'My wife is with child...'

'There,' he pointed a long, gnarled finger, 'to the right of the tree, the big wooden door.'

Through the pale grey light, Nicholas could see a short queue of some seven souls waiting in line outside the wooden door to what appeared to be a barn. His relief was palpable as he walked over and took up his place at the back of the queue, careful not to make eye contact with anyone else.

Once he reached the front, the barn door slowly swung open and an overwhelming smell of rotting flesh hit him. High, sweet, acrid, it punched him at the back of the throat so hard it made him cough and his eyes water. The old crone squatting on a haybale in front of a low table covered in carved up animal parts didn't appear to notice.

'I've got pork, some sausage, *kielbasa*, dogs' tails and some cat?' She sniffed, rubbing her calloused hands up and down her muddied, bloodied terracotta skirt.

'Cat?' he asked, a laugh floating through his voice. 'What tastes better?'

'Taste?' Her face crumpled as she looked up along her nose at him. 'Are you a *burzhúi*?'

'No, Citizen,' he replied hastily, his heart pounding. 'I am a citizen, too. Just like you.'

'Of where? Cos you don't sound like one of us.'

'Kiev,' he said quickly.

'Kyiv.' She sniffed, looking him up and down. 'Show me your money.'

He pulled out a portrait of his mother in a Fabergé frame. She leant forward and had a good long look.

'Umph!' she scoffed, sitting back on her haunches. 'Where d'you get that?' There was a rustling in the shadows behind her. Men? Rats?

Nicholas's palms began to sweat. 'I stole it. It's expensive… so I'm told.'

'That's useless to me. Got any gold? I only want gold.' Nicholas patted his own pockets, searching them for non-existent sources of gold. 'Hurry up,' she said, looking over his shoulder. 'Don't waste my time.'

'Ummm.' Nicholas hesitated.

'Get on with it.'

'Here,' he said, over the clatter as it landed on the brass plate in front of her. 'My wedding ring.'

'There's a good boy.' She grinned. 'I like a wedding ring.'

★ ★ ★

Nadezhda woke to a gentle but persistent knocking on her door. Hauling herself off the divan and wrapping herself in a shawl, she walked over slowly and quietly and held her ear to the door. Better not to answer, better not make a noise.

'It's me,' hissed a voice. 'Bertie!'

'Bertie!' she exclaimed, throwing open the door. Never had she been more pleased to see anyone in her life. 'Oh, Bertie,' she cried and fell into his arms.

'Goodness gracious!' he said, holding her. 'There is no need for that! No need for that at all! Look how magnificently... um, with child you are.' He looked down. 'I had no idea. If I had, I would have brought more.' He held them aloft. 'Oranges!' They shone luminously bright in the dim light of the corridor. 'Only two, I am afraid. All there were.'

She covered her mouth. 'Where did you get them?'

'A little old lady was selling them on the platform in Sevastopol.' He looked her up and down again, taking in her grey face, her thin hair and her shaking hands. 'Why don't you eat them now? I could peel them for you.'

'Come in, come in,' she said, smiling. 'There might be some tea, I could light the samovar. How are you?' He picked up his carpet bag and followed her in. 'Where have you come from? Have you seen the Grand Duchess Vladimir? What is the news?'

As Bertie peeled an orange, filling the room with its extraordinary perfume, its bright intense zest, he spoke of where he'd been and what he'd seen. Twenty-six generals had been massacred at Vyborg. It had all been witnessed by an English lady-friend of his. They'd been thrown into the river and pelted with logs and stones for hours, until they died. Poor Prince Vyazemsky had been murdered by his own peasants, his eyes plucked out while his wife was forced to watch. He thought he'd seen Brana in the street with a gang of hooligans, but he was probably mistaken. Grand Duke Kirill's baby Vladimir had been baptised, and Grand Duke Boris was a godfather. They were living in Finland, having made a speedy escape. Rumour had it that Kirill carried his pregnant wife across the ice to safety. Although the Gulf of Finland was not frozen at the time, so how could that be true?

'Here,' he said, handing her a segment of orange. 'I hope it's sweet.'

Nadezhda closed her eyes as she bit into the orange, its rich delicious juice bursting into her mouth and trickling down the back of her throat. She had never tasted anything quite so extraordinary in her life. The vitamins, the sugar, the taste coursed through her body, making her shiver and the baby kick with delight. Some juice dribbled down her chin, she licked her fingers, all sense of decorum gone.

'Thank you,' she whispered, as he passed her another piece.

Donon's was, apparently, against all the odds, still open. The house band had long since been dismissed, so it was a bit dreary on Sundays. Despite it all, there were still pockets of hedonistic resistance. You know what Russians are like, there might be no bread, but there are still bottles of champagne hidden in some dining room across town and anyone with money was spending it, as if there was no tomorrow. Indeed, there was no tomorrow. The Tsar was still in Tobolsk, under house arrest, with conditions getting worse by the day. There was a rumour they were going to be moved to somewhere more secure. Ekaterinburg? He wasn't sure. He'd seen his Grand Duchess Vladimir. He'd managed to smuggle her diamond and pearl tiara out of Russia a few months ago and hidden it in London, but he had a bag of cufflinks and cigarette cases in a pillowcase in his carpet bag, there on the floor, which she'd asked him to take back to England, if he could, but he might have to deposit them in the Swedish Embassy if needs absolutely must.

'Shall I peel the other one?' he asked, looking down at the ball of sunshine on the table.

'We should leave it for Nicholas,' Nadezhda replied, placing her hands firmly on her lap as she stared at the second orange.

'If you're sure? What he doesn't know won't hurt him.'

'I'm sure.' She smiled.

'I have a letter for your mother,' he continued, opening up his coat. 'From Oswald Rayner.'

'Mr Rayner?' She looked puzzled. She had not heard his name for a while.

'My old English friend, the diplomat.'

'The spy?'

'This is for your mother, and is hugely important, so he says.'

'It's not opened.'

'Can you deliver it in person?'

'Well...' She looked down.

'Or maybe Nicholas? Where is he?' He looked around the poky, dark apartment, expecting him to walk through a doorway.

'He's out looking for food.'

Bertie Stopford frowned. 'He needs to be careful. There's

something going on in the town today, I've been told, and I don't like the look of it at all. In fact, to be honest, I don't like the look of any of it very much.'

'It couldn't get much worse,' she sighed.

'It could, and it will,' he insisted. 'Did the Tsar learn nothing from the French apart from a love of Cartier and champagne?'

It was a little after 2 p.m. when Bertie slipped out of Nadezhda's apartment, leaving behind him the sweet smell of citrus and the letter for Militza. He was anxious to try and find transport that might eventually take him to Moscow and beyond. Little did Nadezhda know, as she hugged his slim shoulders and looked into those watery eyes the colour of the English Channel, that she would never see Stopford again, and that he would never again set foot in Russia. Or, indeed, that dear Bertie would end up incarcerated for two years in Wormwood Scrubs Prison after an 'unfortunate episode' in Hyde Park, only to end his days living a peripatetic life in Europe.

And although she was sad to see her friend disappear, she was more worried about her husband.

It wasn't long before the noises coming from outside were frightening. There was shouting and shooting and screaming, as gangs of sailors ran amok, up and down the street, their hobnail boots pounding the pavement, dragging what appeared to be their officers tied up, like slaves, their hands bound together in front of them, their heads pushed forward, staring at the ground, as they staggered towards the seafront. Nadezhda clutched her belly, shaking with fear, as she watched through the half-open curtain. There seemed to be an old woman in charge, barking commands, shaking a walking stick, urging them on. Babushka. The old hag was on the street with her gang of rebels. Killing. Beating. Fanning the flames of revolution. Where was Nicholas? Why was he taking so long? He was only supposed to go out to buy meat. Nadezhda was beginning to panic. Her legs were shaking so much she had to lean against the window sill. The baby, her imagination, the terror, the cries from the street below were a hideous combination. Was he dead? Lying in ditch? Like Oleg. Not Oleg. She retched. She gripped on to the wooden sill, breathing heavily, fighting the desire to pass out. Where was her holy water? The bottle of mud? Where was her God when she needed him most?

Two shots rang out below and a man was screaming, yelping like a dog, high-pitched, unbearable. The noise was enough to pierce the soul. Where was Nicholas? Dear Nicholas with his bright green eyes. Please God don't say that was him. Dear God, can you hear me? Can you hear me? She pressed her forehead against the cold windowpane, her eyes tightly shut, not daring to look down. Dear God...

'The Lord's my shepherd...' she started. 'The Lord's my shepherd...' The words stuck in her throat, her throat that was dry and rasping with fear. 'The Lord...' She felt nothing. No comfort, no succour. She stopped. What she needed was a miracle. What she needed was magic. And then, from seemingly nowhere, from the very pit of her stomach, from her soul, she began to mumble the battle protection chant her mother had shown her once, all those years ago, in the green velvet book. How she had hated that book and all it stood for. And yet now, as she closed her eyes she could picture the page, the black ink, the spidery writing. She could see it in its entirety.

*'The child came from the womb: it had no mind,
no reason, no eyes, no words, no wicked heart. So, my
revolutionaries have no mind, no reason, no eyes, no
words, no wicked heart against my beloved, Nicholas.'*

Over and over she chanted, her body swaying with the
rhythm, her mind focused on his face. She called upon her
sisters to help. She called upon her mother, her aunt; she
could feel the power tingling all over her skin as the hairs on
her arms stood up and shivers ran up and down her back.

*'The child came from the womb: it had no mind,
no reason, no eyes, no words, no wicked heart. So, my
revolutionaries have no mind, no reason, no eyes, no
words, no wicked heart against my beloved, Nicholas.'*

The clock struck 5 p.m. She was exhausted, white, the
blood had drained from her lips, but she carried on and
on, until the door to the apartment was flung open and
Nicholas staggered into the hall, clutching a bag. He was
covered in blood.

'Oh, my darling! Where have you been? Where have you
been?' she asked, frantically wringing her hands, tugging at
her shawl.

'Hiding,' he replied, gesturing towards the streets. 'From
the mob, who seem to be rounding up everyone. I came
through the back streets. Through the mud and the scum,
through the filth and the misery.' He shook his head. 'I hid
behind a broken-down cart and, by some miracle, they
didn't spot me cowering there. I don't know how. I just
closed my eyes and prayed and then she found me.' Out of

the shadows now stepped an old woman, hunched, with a thin woollen scarf tied tightly around her face. Nadezhda stared. It couldn't be. Here? In Yalta?

'She helped and brought me here.'

'Brana?' whispered Nadezhda.

'Good evening.' Brana smiled.

'How?' was all Nadezhda could say.

'I spotted him, cowering like all cowards.' She smiled again, a little wider this time. 'And I recognised his face. I pulled him back from the light once before and I heard you calling.'

'Me?'

'So here he is.' She shrugged. 'Normally I'd leave him to the mob. A *burzhúi* like him. They're fair game. But it was your voice. "The child came from the womb"... I know it well. It's a powerful voice.' She nodded. 'So, I did as I was told. As I was asked. We come from a long line you and I...'

'Oh, Brana, thank you! Won't you come in? We don't have much but I have tea...'

'No...' she paused, 'thank you.'

'Are you sure?'

'Perfectly,' she replied. 'I've got work to do. The Babushka needs my help. I've wasted enough time here as it is. I don't want to regret my decision.' She sniffed at Nicholas, his cowed face, his hands covered in blood. Her lips curled with contempt. She turned and then turned back. 'Good luck with your daughter.' She looked down at Nadezhda's swollen belly. 'And I shall see you, when I shall see you. Not in this world, probably, but certainly in the next.'

'I shall tell Mama I have seen you!'

'Don't.' And she turned and left.

* * *

'You're safe! Are you hurt?' She took hold of his bloodied hands.

'I'm fine, had that woman, Brana, not come along when she did... who knows?' He leant forward and kissed her forehead. 'Let me wash my hands and face, I am not sure if this is even my blood. And then we shall drink tea and I have meat!'

'Meat?'

'Veal,' he said. 'Or is it venison? I am not quite sure. It was hard to see in the dark barn where I bought it.' He pulled a small cloth bag out of his pocket, containing two thin tails, one from a dog and the other from a cat.

'And I have an orange.'

'An orange?'

'Bertie Stopford came while you were out.'

'He did? He's still alive? Of course he is. He'll out-live us all... And he brought oranges.' He picked it up and, holding it just below his nose, inhaled the sweet heady smell of citrus. 'You should have this, my darling.' He offered it back to this wife.

The shouting, the shooting and the screaming carried on well past the boiled venison, or veal, supper and into the night. Meanwhile Nadezhda prayed for the souls of the young men she'd seen, and Brana. She lit candles and burnt some herbs from the kitchen. It was not to God that she was talking.

The next morning, perhaps revived by the meat and the orange, Nadezhda decided she could not bear the claustrophobia of the apartment and, despite Nicholas's pleas, she insisted on walking down to the sea for a stroll along the harbour wall.

'I need the air, my darling, I can't sit here any more,' she replied, putting a pin in her hat. 'The riot seems to be over. Listen. It is quiet on the street. We must seize the moment. A quick walk, some fresh air. I can't breathe in here.'

Finally, he agreed, but only if he could accompany her. The sun was shining a little, and the air was cold but relatively still; a gentle breeze, when they reached the harbour wall. They stood, side by side, looking up at the sky, inhaling the fresh air, dreaming of freedom, thinking of happier times. Anywhere, but here.

'You see?' She smiled at him, gesturing across the harbour. 'No one ever breathes in the sea air and feels sad. Look, look at all that lovely seaweed bouncing and swaying in the water.'

As they watched the seaweed ebbing and flowing with the gentle waves, they both began to suspect all was not quite what it seemed. It was Nadezhda who frowned first, then Nicholas; they both gasped, covering their mouths in horror. For the seaweed bobbing around on top of the water was, in fact, the raised swollen fingertips of the officers who been thrown in the sea. They stepped closer and looked down into the clear water. Below, they could see rows of corpses weighed down by the rocks tied to their feet. As they swayed, coats billowing in the current, they looked like a ghostly army, with their arms raised in defeat.

To us, Marie Feodorovna is an old reactionary woman and her fate is of no interest to us.

Trotksy on the Dowager Empress

CHAPTER 18

March-May 1918, Crimea

As the temperatures outside began to rise and the snows receded on the summit of Ai-Petri, to be replaced by the pale blossom of citrus trees, so relations in Dulber grew ever colder. In fact, the only person apparently warming to conditions was the burly guard Zadorozhny, who was beginning to develop a close affinity with his prisoners. He treated them badly in front of his staff before conversing with them in private. He was particularly fond of the Dowager Empress. He'd go out of his way to provide extra provisions, including some sort of afternoon tea and, very occasionally, bottles of milk. Little did he know that the bottles were used by the Romanov prisoners to pass messages to the outside world.

Not that the outside world was listening or inclined to help. Russia was losing the war, the Germans were taking more and more territory by the day, Ukraine had fallen and joined the Germans in fighting the Red Army. They were making inroads south towards Crimea. The soldiers from the Yalta soviet were prowling around the walls of Dulber, their heavy carts rattling with machine guns, as they demanded Zadorozhny hand over the Romanov captives, or they'd inform Lenin of his counter-revolutionary tendencies.

But Zadorozhny stood firm. He mounted his men on the roof, armed with machine guns and searchlights. They combed the undergrowth below for signs of ambush, waiting for personal orders from Lenin to dispatch the hostages. No one was quite brave enough to disturb the status quo. But the tension was palpable, with Sandro asking the guards every evening on his way up to bed: 'So, will you shoot us tonight?'

Meanwhile, they all gathered every evening for dinner, at the behest of the Dowager, in the main dining room. After a few weeks of imprisonment, Zadorozhny had decided that in order to protect the remaining members of the Romanov family, the Yusupovs should also be forced to live under the same roof.

'My son tells me you're dead,' declared the Dowager, looking up from a letter she was straining to read by candlelight. She was taking an aperitif before dinner and had only just received an opened envelope, written by her dearly beloved Nicky at least two months before.

'Who's dead?' asked Sandro, taking a sip of claret. In lieu of the terrible rations, lack of kerosene, money, or anything else to do, Sandro had taken to opening a very pleasant bottle of red wine earlier and earlier during the day. Deprived of his books on astronomy and numismatism, as well as his extensive coin collection, Sandro was at a loss as to how to fill the hours that dragged interminably.

'Not you... Felix,' replied the Dowager, a little irritated by her son-in-law. She was a little irritated by everyone. Irritated by the situation, irritated by the guards who followed her every move and invaded her privacy, irritated by a revolution she simply could not comprehend. But she was *desperate* to see her son. She talked and thought about little else.

'Me?' enquired Felix Yusupov, plucking a cigarette out of his mouth. 'Was that before or after my imprisonment in the Peter and Paul Fortress?'

'After, one would presume,' said Sandro.

'What does he say? Is he sad? So fascinating to hear about oneself in the past tense, don't you think?' He paused and took a quick puff on his cigarette. 'Is he weeping as he writes? Overcome with grief? Poor Felix, how I loved him so!'

'You'd enjoy that, wouldn't you?' replied Sandro. 'A period of national mourning after your demise?'

'Wouldn't everyone?' replied Felix, flicking ash into a small silver saucer.

'Oh, darling, don't be so crass,' said Irina, who had dressed for dinner in a flowing midnight blue silk dress, with a tight silk turban and a long rope of pearls. She too was smoking, using a long black holder made of jet. 'You're such a showman.'

'"The death of Metropolitan Vladimir, my good old General Ivanov, and Felix was a great shock to us,"' read the Dowager. '"Dear Lord! Hasn't enough blood already been spilt! And all these insane killings of officers by people who are allegedly tired of War! Sometimes one really does think that one is going out of one's mind." Poor Nicky.' She shook her head. 'I know how he feels.'

'That's it?' Felix huffed. 'It's a wonder though,' he added, 'that the man is so misinformed. He seems to know and question so very little. He merely repeats what he has been told. What else does he say?'

'That he is in Tobolsk and they read his letters,' she sighed. 'And their funds have been reduced, again, and they've had to dismiss eleven staff.'

'Eleven? It's fortunate he is not with us. There are forty-five of us here and barely a valet between us!' Felix laughed and stubbed out his cigarette. 'I believe it is time for our porridge and peas to be served. Or is it potato porridge tonight? Or simply plain old porridge?' He rubbed his hands together. 'The excitement!'

The dining room was lit with as many candles as the household could muster. Militza and Peter sat at either end of the shiny table (the linen cloth had long since been put away). They had started sitting there months ago as host and hostess of the house, and had remained there ever since, with other members of the family taking their usual, well-worn spots. The rituals of human beings were extraordinary, Militza thought as she sat down once more to a bowl of hot steaming whatever-poor-Korniloff-had-managed-to-find-in-the-kitchens. Very occasionally he managed to pull something out of the pantry, or the garden, but one of the best chefs of his generation, who would open a hugely glamorous restaurant in Paris after the revolution, was forced to slice and dice potatoes in water with a little salt and pepper or possibly some foraged herb for seasoning.

However, even more problematic than the food were the recent arrivals at the palace. For Militza had Prince Felix Yusupov on one side of her, and his father, the Count, on the other. His wife Irina was a little further down on the right and opposite was his mother, Zinaida, who after a few glasses of champagne liked nothing more than to boast her son was the murderer of Rasputin.

'Can you imagine how brave he was?' began Zinaida, again. 'I do find it extraordinary that he was the only one to stand up to the Devil, don't you?' She smiled at the Dowager. 'I know you always disliked the man and the aura of evil surrounding him. But it was my son, mine, who did something about it.' She took another sip from her flute. Her huge blue eyes shone in the candlelight which also danced on her pale grey hair. Her smile was thin and tired, after months of strain.

'I agree,' nodded the Dowager. 'If only one had acted sooner.'

'Or indeed acted at all.' Zinaida laughed a little.

'While you are in my house, though...' said Peter at the other end of the table.

'Well, you didn't like him either,' quipped the Dowager. 'I know *you* didn't. He banished you to the Caucasus,' she nodded towards Nikolasha, 'and ruined your life, Stana, and he constantly briefed against you,' she finished, smiling at Militza. 'It's a wonder you didn't all kill him yourselves. I would have done if I'd had the chance.'

'Really?' asked Stana.

'Except I was the one who did,' declared Felix. 'Me! With poison cakes and madeira and I shot him. Bang! Like a dog and threw him into the river!'

'All on your own,' added Militza. 'A heavy man like that.'

She couldn't help herself. The images of that night played out constantly in her head, among them one of Felix Yusupov, passed out in the snow, his fine face in repose, his delicate eyes shut, while everyone else was frantically trying to remove the body, wrap it in a curtain, push it into the boot of a useless motor car that stalled and stuttered along the canal-side in the early hours of the fateful morning.

'Turns out he wasn't that heavy,' Felix declared, exhaling a cloud of cigarette smoke in her direction. 'And anyway, I had some help. Dmitry, he was there. But it was I, Felix, who pulled the trigger.' He positively quivered before her eyes. Was he daring her to say something? To call his bluff? Maybe he'd told the story so many times, he'd begun to believe it himself. We all tell ourselves lies, sometimes so often they become the truth.

'So brave,' cooed his mother opposite.

Only his father remained silent. Count Felix was a little deaf these days and perhaps all the happier for it. More of a military man, fond of parades and pageantry, his will had been broken by the stifling nature of his incarceration. Even his visceral dislike of Militza and her sister was waning. He was, after all, a guest in her husband's unfortunate-looking palace, but at least he was alive, drinking a broth of some description. He'd lost quite a few friends to this war already.

'What are they talking about?' he mumbled through his large moustache, its corners sodden with soup.

'The murder of Rasputin,' replied Militza.

To mention his name out loud, even in the company of others, sent a chill up her spine. It was almost as if she could feel the intensity of his gaze boring into her back. She glanced quickly over her shoulder. How foolish she was. He was dead. Under the ice. She'd watched him drown, the tiny bubbles floating out of his open mouth as he sank. She'd then watched him burn and turn to dust, stamped into the ground by soldiers, drunk on cheap wine and vodka.

'How tiresome,' said Count Yusupov. 'Surely there are other things to discuss? Like how on earth are we to get out of here and where we'll go? I fancy a return to Petrograd, to sort the buggers out, let them know what's what, get those soldiers out of the palace on the Moika.'

Just then the doors to the dining room burst open and a terrified servant stood there, his hands clasped in front of him, his head whipping left and right as he looked up and down the table.

'Some sailors are here, they've stolen horses and somehow broken through the perimeter. I have no idea where Zadorozhny and his men are, they are demanding wine and food and "Death to the Bourgeois" and "Death to anti-revolutionaries", and "Death to the landlords!"'

'We should hide!' declared Felix, leaping out of his chair.

'How many are there?' asked Nikolasha.

'Five, sir. Six. Ten?' the servant stammered.

'Well then, invite them in,' said Militza.

'Do what?' replied Felix, staring at her, his mouth hanging open.

'Far better to look the enemy in the eye than cower behind the curtains!' said Militza.

'I couldn't agree more,' said Count Yusupov, smoothing down his moustache.

The old Count stood up, as did Nikolasha, and Militza made her way to the door. 'I think as I am the hostess, I should do the inviting?'

'Be careful, my love,' said Peter. 'The naval cavalry are famed for their cruelty.'

'To men, maybe, but not to women.'

In the dark, Militza held her candelabrum aloft. It was

hard to see how many they were or what their intent might be. She caught glimpses of horses, a flash of a sword and the shine of a boot.

'Gentlemen!' she announced. 'You must be tired after your ride. Do come in, we have some wine and what little food we have we shall share.'

'Death to the landlords!' yelled a sailor.

'Food, you said?' asked another.

'Would you like some wine?' she replied. 'We have red and white wine?'

'Which one is stronger?' hollered a voice from the dark.

'Why don't you come in and find out?'

A few minutes later, the most feared unit in the navy was sitting at the dining table, drinking wine and eating what few slices of bread and sausage could be found in the empty kitchen. Their elbows were on the table, their pistols by their sides, their uniforms covered in blood. A few of them were wearing the spoils of war: a brooch, a diamond bracelet. A small string of pearls peeked from the pocket of a particularly brutal-faced young man.

The Dowager was transfixed. She sat rigid, her back straight, her lips closed in a tight line as she watched. Irina Yusupova smiled sweetly, slowly, almost imperceptibly, removing the lengthy rope of pearls from around her neck and quietly putting them under her seat cushion. Nikolasha looked tense; he knew what this gang of increasingly drunken sailors was capable of.

'Have you come far?' he asked.

The apparent leader looked Nikolasha up and down, pulled the hair on his chin and curled his lips. 'You commander in chief of the army?' he asked.

'I was.' Nikolasha nodded.

'You should still be,' he said, nodding back. 'That was their first mistake – to get rid of someone who knew what that were doing. Good health!' He raised his glass and drained it in one before lurching across the table. Xenia recoiled, Sandro smiled stiffly and slowly handed over the bottle of red wine he'd been working his way through all evening. The commander grabbed it and without saying a word filled his own glass to the brim, sloshing and splashing as he went. 'You!' He pointed his thick short finger up the other end of the table. 'You! Yes, you!' He jabbed at Felix Yusupov. 'Who are you?'

'I'm Citizen… Felix Yusupov.' He smiled and waited for his name to resonate.

'And what do you do, Citizen Yusupov?' he asked.

'I killed Rasputin,' Felix replied.

'What, every day?' The commander laughed. He took a swig of his wine and grimaced slightly.

'Rasputin!' repeated a sailor next to him, before spitting on the floor.

'Rasputin!' agreed the leader, before also spitting on the floor.

'Um, well…' ventured Felix glancing around the table. 'I…'

'Let me shake your hand. Shake his hand, lads, shake his hand, the saviour of the nation! You have nothing to fear from us!' He walked up to Felix and slapped him so hard on the back that Felix fell forward in his chair. 'Lads! This is the guy! Come on, let's drink to him! Drink, drink, drink!'

So, while the rest of the royal party sat stiffly in their seats, terrified a sudden movement might spark some sort of riot, the sailors drained every bottle on the table and demanded more. One of them arrived in the dining room with Felix Yusupov's guitar and the evening ended with the prince serenading the rabble while they sang bawdy drinking songs, raising glasses variously to the death of Rasputin, the success of the Revolution and the victory of the Red Army. Finally, at 3 a.m., they left. Brandishing their flags, they took off on their stolen horses and headed for the hills.

After that evening, the Dowager only ever took supper alone in her quarters. She would appear at the top of the stairs if there were a roll call taken by the guards and she would appear at the balcony to take some air, but she did not come downstairs again. The guard on the palace was doubled at the insistence of Zadorozhny, who placed a twenty-four-hour watch on the roof. But that did little to ease the terror within the palace as they lay awake in their beds listening to the sound of machine-gun fire.

There was no respite, no relief, even as Easter approached and the rules of Lent remained unobserved. What was the point of giving up flour or sugar when one hadn't been able to eat it for more than forty days or nights anyway? And still they weren't allowed to leave, not even to attend church.

On the morning of 1 March, Nadezhda stood alone in her kitchen drinking a cup of cold acorn coffee while Nicholas was out scavenging in the streets, looking for food.

Suddenly, she doubled over in pain. This was it, no waters, but her baby would wait no longer; she would have to do this entirely on her own. No mother, no sister, it was two days before her twentieth birthday, and she was terrified.

Crawling on her hands and knees, bellowing and moaning like the animals she'd seen as a child at Znamenka, she slowly made her way towards the bedroom, leaving a trail of thin blood in her wake. The pain was overwhelming; she cried out, arched her back, clawed at the rug on the floor, pushing down with her all strength. What did her mother say? What did the sisters say? What did she know, what could she remember? Breathe, breathe, gather yourself ready for the next one. Open a window. Let in the new soul. 'Just as a chicken lays an egg quickly, so may I, sister of sisters, give birth quickly.' Again it came, the pain tore through her and she threw up all over the floor. Bile. Yellow water. Grasping at the chair legs, she crawled up to the edge of the table, growling as she lay across it, her knees open, more bloodied liquid pouring down her legs. Breathe, breathe. This was the time to rest, inhale, exhale, inhale, gather your strength. She staggered towards the divan and lay back slowly, her legs apart, her knees in the air. The wave hit her with such force, she threw her arms back and grabbed the arm of the divan, pushing until she could take no more. She ripped at her shirt, her buttons flying off, she wanted to get naked, take all her clothes off, she hated the material, the feeling, she was suffocating in cloth and sweat. How much more could she take? Here on her own. Where was Nicholas?

One final wave, one final push, bosom exposed, legs apart, belly contorted, it appeared to come from the very depths of her soul, she bellowed, the bellow became a roar, she felt herself tear open with the full force of life and then, then, there was silence. Total silence. She made as if to sit up, and passed out, where she lay.

She came round to find Nicholas crouched on the floor, with a damp towel in his hand, that he pressed repeatedly, annoyingly, on her forehead. His face was white, his eyes rounded with horror and full of tears.

'Wake up, my darling, wake up, please, please, wake up,' he whispered over and over, patting, pressing the towel.

'The baby?' mumbled Nadezhda. 'Where's the baby? Where's the baby?' She sat bolt upright, frantically searching. 'Where's the baby?'

Nicholas glanced at the divan. 'I'm sorry. I'm so sorry.' It was all he could manage to say.

Nadezhda stared. On the divan was a balloon and inside appeared to be a tiny form. 'Quick,' she said. 'I need scissors, a knife, anything, she's in caul, undisturbed, she's magic, she's perfect, she's full of fortune. She's one of us.' Nadezhda snipped and pulled and tore open the sack. The fluid drained and the baby coughed. Nadezhda paused and stared and took in the full beauty of her daughter. 'Welcome to the world.' She kissed her soft, sweet-smelling head. 'My little witch!'

'Oh, my darling.' Nicholas was overwhelmed. Not only was his wife alive, so was his baby daughter. His eyes filled with tears as he squeezed his hand. 'How are you feeling?' he whispered.

'Whole,' she replied.

★ ★ ★

At Dulber, Militza heard of the birth of her granddaughter from a message delivered by one of the servants. She silently crossed herself and looked towards the heavens to thank God and Taweret, 'The Great One' – the ancient Egyptian goddess of childbirth – for the safe delivery of Princess Irina Nikolayevna Orlova. Born in caul, never to drown, always to be fortunate. Militza allowed herself to smile. She knew. It was written. Princess Irina Orlova would have deep black eyes.

Survival was on everyone's mind when, two days later, Russia and Germany signed the Treaty of Brest-Litovsk, which meant that Soviet Russia ceded vast amounts of territory to the Germans. Finland, Estonia, Latvia, Lithuania were all handed over, Ukraine was recognised as an independent country and the Crimea was to be occupied by Germany.

Panic swept through the palace. What were they to do? Where were they to go? They were sitting ducks, awaiting their own execution. The Red Army was waiting to kill them, the Yalta soviet had been sniffing at the gate for months. Nikolasha took command: the prisoners needed to defend themselves, an around the clock vigil was organised. Nikolasha would sleep outside the Dowager's bedroom on the floor in the corridor and the rest of the Grand Dukes would stay on the roof, keeping lookout, watching the Yalta Road. There was only one problem. Their lack of weapons. Zadorozhny was summoned by Nikolasha to the small turquoise-tiled study off the hall. But before Nikolasha could open his mouth the fearsome-looking giant spoke.

'You're in grave danger, Yalta want you all dead,

Sevastopol are merely waiting for the orders to come and kill you. I keep thinking I should tell them you are all going to Moscow soon for trial, to buy you some time. I have heard there is a gang coming tonight. They plan a raid to kill you all. A large party of sailors – they are awaiting transport.'

Nikolasha was stunned. He expected as much, but hearing it said to his face was enough to chill the blood. 'We need weapons,' he said. 'And we need to guard the Empress, for she will be the one they most prize.'

'I have your weapons,' he replied. 'I have hidden them on the roof. You may have them, they are yours to do with as you wish. I have a plan to buy some time.'

'I'd like to hear it,' said Nikolasha.

'I shall go now to Sevastopol to find reinforcements. If the rabble comes while I am away, I am confident my troops will hold the line – in the absence of a commandant, they cannot force my men to surrender. They will stick to their orders. And then I shall come back and guard you and your family to the bitter end, they will have to drag me out, by my feet, my soul having long since departed this world. That is my solemn promise, to you, the Tsar and God. Long live the Tsar!'

Good as his word, Zadorozhny mounted his horse and left at speed for Sevastopol. He was expected back later that evening. But Yalta lay closer to Dulber than Sevastopol...

No one could sleep. Militza sat on her balcony, overlooking the road, her eyes strained, looking for any movement, any sign of troops approaching the palace. How ironic, she thought. Here were forty-five souls all staring out of their windows, watching for the enemy. How much they'd all laughed at this house, how much they had sniggered at her romantic husband for creating such a palace, and now they were depending on its thick walls, its Persian ramparts, for their very lives.

It was Peter who spotted them first from the roof.

'There!' he hissed. 'Coming up the road.' The bandits from Yalta were heading towards them. Nikolasha took out his binoculars and scanned the route. They were armed, heavily armed – he could see rifles and bayonets glinting in the moonlight. 'Wake the men, man the machine guns and don't let anyone see us. You! Yusupov! Put out that cigarette, pick up a pistol and guard the landing.'

'But I couldn't. I can't,' Felix replied, fumbling around with the pistol and dropping it on the floor.

'Pull yourself together,' barked Nikolasha. 'It's not as if you haven't killed a man before. In cold blood. At least this lot are expecting it. Now hold the weapon properly and get downstairs!'

'Of course, of course,' said Felix, stubbing out his cigarette with his boot and picking up the weapon. 'Downstairs.'

'Machine guns! Are you ready?'

'Ready!' came the response, followed by the loud click of engagement.

'Trust in God's grace and mercy!' declared Nikolasha, before taking up his rifle and his position on the roof.

The rabble closed in and started hammering on the gate.

'Let us in, in the name of the Soviet Russia!' They discharged their rifles in the air.

'Shoot over their heads!' commanded Nikolasha.

A heavy volley of shot rang out. The bandits fell on their knees. Militza watched from her balcony.

'May the light of the moon blind them, may their weapons cease, and their horses go lame, may they run back whence they came.'

'Let us in, in the name of Soviet Russia, on the Order of Lenin, we have come to rid the world of the Romanov plague!'

'Fire!' barked Nikolasha, and another volley of shots flew over their heads.

'Surrender your hostages or be damned!'

'We have no commander! We have been instructed to keep the gates closed and the hostages under guard!' shouted a soldier at the gate. 'Anyone who crosses the threshold will be shot!'

'Fire!' commanded Nikolasha, and the machine guns on the roof burst into life.

The bandits from the Yalta soviet fell to the ground in fear.

'Keep firing!' encouraged Nikolasha, as the gang upped and fled.

'We shall be back with more men, come sun-up!' shouted the leader. 'Be afraid, be very afraid, for tomorrow you shall all die!'

That night was the longest any of them had ever lived through. They stood on the ramparts, looking out for the rebels and praying Zadorozhny would return with a battalion to rescue them. As the night wore on, their hopes began to fade; it was simply a question of which horde would make it to Dulber first. The ones who wanted them immediately dead, or the ones who were prepared to wait a little while before killing them. As the Grand Dukes paced the roof, all that could be heard from below was the mumbled, terrified noise of prayer. Passage after passage was being read out loud from the Bible. Meanwhile, in her bedroom, Militza lit her votive candles and called upon the Four Winds to confuse the enemy, put their plans in disarray, to save their souls.

'How long before he comes back?' Peter stood on the roof, smoking.

'How long does it take to raise a small army?' replied Nikolasha. 'How long does it take to raise any army and march them back?'

'We're doomed,' said Peter simply. 'Well,' he exhaled, 'at least I am dying with the people I love.'

'There!' said Nikolasha pointing towards the Sevastopol Road. 'There's a convoy!'

Peter grinned with relief. 'Here they come!'

The two brothers watched as the convoy drove closer, hope springing eternal in their pounding hearts.

'They're here!' hissed Peter, giving the dozing Roman a gentle kick. 'We are to be rescued after all.'

Then, suddenly, without explanation, the convoy of trucks drove past.

'They've missed the turning,' said Nikolasha, his voice incredulous. 'Now what are we to do? Shout? Wave? Beg?'

It was only as dawn broke that they realised all Zadorozhny's company of soldiers had fled. They were on their own, on the roof, with a few pistols, a couple of rifles and a ceremonial sword to protect them. Nikolasha turned back.

'Can you hear that?' he asked his brother.

'What is it?' Peter replied.

'Boots.'

Hundreds of them, marching along the road, pounding the track, down the Yalta Road towards them. And all they could do was watch as the army approached.

They hammered on the gate. Dulber held its breath.

'Open up in the name of the Kaiser,' came the shout. 'On the orders of Majesty Kaiser Wilhelm the Second, you are free! All of you. We are in charge now.'

'Saved by the enemy,' said Nikolasha.

'A solution to our difficulties no one could have foreseen,' replied Peter. 'Except perhaps my wife.'

Thou shalt leave everything loved most dearly, and this is the shaft which the bow of exile shoots first. Thou shalt prove how salt is the taste of another man's bread and how hard is the way up and down another man's stairs.

Dante, *The Divine Comedy*

CHAPTER 19

June 1918-April 1919, Yalta

The summer of 1918 was glorious in the Crimea. The sun shone, the flowers bloomed, and the Germans brought order to the streets of Yalta. Shops opened. Banks reopened. Trains to Sevastopol began to run again, on time, and supply lines were re-established. The hotels and restaurants took bookings, the citizens of the city promenaded along the harbour front, no one looking too closely into the water.

The inhabitants of Ai Todor gratefully moved back into their more luxurious accommodation, the Yusupovs returned to their estate and Nadezhda, Nicholas and baby Irina left their dark apartment in Yalta and were welcomed back with open arms to Dulber. Militza was shocked to see her daughter looking so thin and so pale, shocked by her drawn face and her huge dark eyes. She was also a little wrong-footed by the fact that her own daughter, Olga, had not employed a wet-nurse for the baby. They were impossible to come by these days – no peasant woman wanted to breastfeed the child of a Romanov. There were plenty of other new things to get used to.

Firstly, everyone found it difficult to bury their anti-German feelings. Having spent the past few years swearing allegiance to Mother Russia and ridding themselves of anything that could remotely be perceived as pro-German – the name of their capital city notwithstanding – suddenly to be in thrall to the enemy was disconcerting to say the least. The Dowager Empress refused to meet the German commander, because she regarded Germany and Russia as still at war, and when the German ambassador to the new independent Ukraine did arrive to pay his respects, breast gleaming with medals and self-importance, he was shooed away with a broom. The Germans were keen to offer the Romanovs protection and the Romanovs were determined not to accept it. A genteel sort of stalemate reigned, where everyone politely got on with it, while trying to stay out of each other's way.

The only time the ex-prisoners really did intervene was to prevent the execution of Zadorozhny and his soldiers. The Germans were truly astonished to witness the captives embrace their former captors with kisses and tears, wishing them bon voyage and safe passage out of German-occupied Crimea.

Secondly, having spent months eating little but potatoes and water, they found the abundance of food overwhelming. Eggs, flour, sugar, meat, cheese! Despite it still being the period of Lent, no one refused a thing, there was gourmandising and feasting on every morsel that came, hot and steaming, out of the kitchens.

And thirdly, of course, they were free. Free to travel into Yalta, free to shop in Koreiz, free to swim and play tennis and free to visit each other's palaces, to have lunch, dinner, afternoon tea. Pick flowers, cultivate their roses. They could walk wherever they wanted.

There was also news. News coming from all sorts of sources. Grand Duke Michael had been exiled to Perm in Siberia. Ella, Alix's sister, and Oleg's brothers, Igor and Ivan Konstantinovich, as well as Sandro's brother Sergei, had all been taken to Alapayevsk in the Urals, and the Tsar and his family had been moved to Ekaterinburg to the Ipatiev House. Ekaterinburg was closer to Moscow, closer to the Crimea, which was a good thing. The hyacinths were out, their perfume was intoxicating and everything looked quite beautiful.

'Oh, Mother,' said Nadezhda, entering the turquoise study just off the hall, with Irina swaddled tightly in her arms. 'I completely forgot; I have a letter for you from Mr Rayner.'

Militza froze at her desk, her fountain pen still in her hand. 'Rayner?' What could he possibly want from her? A confession? Surely not. Not now that Felix was happily taking all the credit for dispatching the Mad Monk. 'Where on earth did you get that from?'

'Bertie Stopford. He came to the apartment a few months ago now, just before Irina was born, on his way back to London.'

'Dear Bertie.' Militza looked wistful. 'How was he?'

'He had a pillowcase of the Grand Duchess Vladimir's jewellery and cigarette cases he was smuggling out for her. Anyway, he gave me this.' She handed over the envelope. 'It's unopened.' Militza stared at the letter. There was a pause. 'Are you not going to read it?'

'It can wait,' replied Militza, turning back. 'If that's all,' she said brusquely.

'Well, actually, now that I have you on your own, I did want to say one thing.'

'Oh yes?' Militza looked up from the letter she was writing.

'Sorry.'

It took Militza a little by surprise. 'What do you mean, sorry?'

'Sorry for everything. Sorry for what I have said, what I have done. How I belittled your gift, your knowledge, the lineage, the sisters who came before you, before me...' Nadezhda's pale face flushed with emotion. 'Ever since I had baby Irina, it all makes sense. How all you ever wanted was to help me. To do your best. I understand. I understand it all. Maternal love. All you want to do is protect them and love them and make sure nothing terrible ever happens.' She looked down at her baby sleeping in her arms. 'How did you not laugh at me? How did you not shout and scream and tell me I was an ignorant fool? I am so sorry.' Her face crumpled. 'I really am.'

'Oh, darling.' Militza stood up from her desk and hugged her daughter and kissed the silky forehead of her granddaughter. 'I loved you. And I love you still. No one can make you believe. No one can force you. You have to get there on your own. I knew you would in the end. I just had to be patient.'

'Thank you, Mama,' Nadezhda whispered in her mother's ear. 'Thank you for giving me life and thank you for saving my dear devoted husband. I am forever in your debt.' She kissed her once more on the cheek and slowly left the room.

★ ★ ★

After her daughter had gone, Militza sat her desk, overcome with emotion. At last, she smiled. At last, Nadezhda knew. She looked down at the letter on the desk, swiftly closed the door and, leaning against it, tore it open. Her hands were shaking as she scanned the pages – what did he want? He enquired about her health, asked after her husband, hoped the weather was pleasant in the Crimea. So far, so English... And then, she saw a name. It stopped her in her tracks. She had to read it twice.

We know about Suzanna.

How? How did the British know this? Bertie? Did he know? Who else knew?

We have known for a while. And I wanted to reassure you that she is safe. Safe in Doorn in Holland... she is nearly 15 years old now... safe with her 'father' Leendert Johannes Hemmes...

Militza sat down in her chair and clasped the letter to her chest. She shut her eyes. Was it really fifteen years ago that she, Stana and Maître Philippe had smuggled the Tsarina's fifth daughter out of Russia? Fifteen years. The child that never was. The phantom pregnancy. The ovule. That was how they'd explained it. How did they manage to keep that secret safe for so long? How long had those five million roubles lasted? She remembered them all piled up, crisp and flat and in sequential order, straight from the

Tsar's private bank. How they waved goodbye, as Philippe drove off to the border with Finland so as not to arouse suspicion. How the Tsarina cried, how she shivered with misery, her white face etched in sadness. But there was no other choice, the Russian people would not stand another daughter. Four was enough. Five would never be forgiven. They needed a son and heir. The daughters were useless, they counted for nothing without succession. Militza laughed a little at the irony. Alix could have as many daughters as she wanted now. Imprisoned in Ekaterinburg, with no throne, no country to run, no one would notice another girl now.

> *But just in case... in case of the worst. I am not sure the Russian populace is capable of regicide, but that 'plague baccillus' Lenin is capable of anything. As he has often said: 'Revolution without assassination is nothing.' So I am fearful. Fearful for the Tsar, but I think even he might draw the line at women and five innocent children. Quod fors feret, Suzanna is safe...*

That was it. He said nothing else. How astonishing it had not been opened. Should she keep it? Destroy it? She looked around the room. What to do with something as important and incendiary as this? And then she saw the green velvet book, the book of incantations and spells, and slipped the letter quickly between its yellowed pages.

Initially, it seemed odd to play tennis and eat strawberries while the rest of the country was tearing itself apart. The elder members – the Dowager, Nikolasha, Militza, Stana, Xenia and Sandro – were anxious to let their guard down, but remained a little tense, tinged with uneasiness. They were consorting with the enemy and yet, the enemy was more benign than their last prison guards.

The young, however, had no such compunction. They drank their champagne, swam, hiked and danced as if the last few years had not happened. They even decided to publish a weekly magazine of all their exploits. The *Merry Arnold* had sixteen correspondents, who wrote about subjects of their own choosing. Mostly they were escapist, fabulous adventures, journeys to far distant lands, captured by the imagination of the young authors; sometimes they would write stories of the week, about walks into town and closely fought tennis matches. There was a gossip column, full of tittle-tattle and tales of intrigue and potential love matches. Each editorial meeting finished with the reading out loud of the articles, followed by the correspondents all singing a song to the glory of the magazine, serenaded by Prince Felix Yusupov on his guitar. Proceedings were often brought to an abrupt halt by the cutting of power at midnight, although they did sometimes sing late into the night by candlelight.

But most popular of all were the picnics in the flower-carpeted meadows that stretched out between the mountains and the coast beyond. These were complicated affairs that required planning and forethought with chairs, tables, rugs, gazebos and parasols, and that was all before anyone had discussed the food, the wine, or the champagne. The champagne and the wine were not hard to come by; the food was a little more problematic, but each household brought its own, taking care not to duplicate, so there was usually more than enough for everyone.

Towards the middle of July 1918, the Dowager had planned a rather large picnic of all the families in the grounds of Ai Todor; the excitement had been gathering for days, who was bringing what, how much champagne was required, how big was the basket of wild strawberries that Xenia's children had gathered on the hillside?

However, the night before, 18 July, the heavens opened in a way unprecedented in the region. Militza lay in bed, staring at the ceiling, listening to the rolls of thunder and watching the lightning illuminate her room. For hours and hours it circled above them, refusing to move on, like a boiling cauldron. And the rain lashing at the windows and pounding the ground was of such magnitude that she imagined the Lord himself was weeping. For the first time in her life, she felt truly afraid. Anxiety gripped her with a force so powerful she struggled to breathe. What was happening? Some abomination was in progress, something so evil that even God could not look on without tears. She kept on expecting to see Rasputin, prowling around at the foot of her bed, illuminated by flashes of lightning, dressed in his black robes, with his fetid beard and long hair, the glint of a crucifix around his neck. She awaited the tight grip around her ankles and the feeling of his sodden corpse as he climbed on top of her. But even he was not there.

White, drained, exhausted, she rose the next day determined not to attend the picnic. Something was horribly wrong, and she could feel it. The ground would be wet, and the grass damp; it was enough of an excuse not to go. But Nadezhda was insistent.

'The Dowager will be furious,' she said folding a white knitted blanket to keep her daughter warm. 'She's been planning it for days. She's chosen the spot. There'll be no end of drama if you don't come.'

So, against her will, Militza accompanied Peter, Stana, Nikolasha and all the young to the flat field at the bottom of the hillside overlooking the sea. The servants had gone on ahead, taking the tables, the carpets, the white canvas gazebo and a collection of canvas chairs. In the middle of it all sat the Dowager, sporting a white dress and large picture hat, a glass of champagne in her hands as she surveyed the scene.

'It's just like old times, isn't it?' she said, as Militza stooped down to kiss her smooth, cold, damp cheek. 'No Nadezhda?' she asked, looking over Militza's shoulder.

'She's running a little late,' replied Militza. 'The baby was crying.'

'Babies are always crying.' The Dowager took another sip of her champagne.

After the storm, the sun was shining in a cobalt blue sky and the crowd of young flopped on the rugs and carpets, smoking cigarettes and laughing. Nadezhda approached, clutching her daughter to her chest. Even from a distance, Militza could tell something was wrong. Her body was stiff, her footsteps were quick, and she was walking straight towards the Dowager.

'Excuse me,' she said, leaning over. The Dowager looked at her and Nadezhda leant over and, ashen-faced, whispered in her ear.

The Dowager laughed. It was an odd, hard, sharp laugh of disbelief. 'Don't be so ridiculous,' she boomed, getting out of her chair. 'I have never heard such rubbish in all my life. I would know! I would feel it! Here!' She clutched her chest. 'It's simply not true! This is fraudulent news. Fraudulent news indeed.'

Everyone stopped what they were doing and turned to look at the Empress Marie Feodorovna.

'She is telling me – *me!* – my son is dead. The Tsar is dead, shot, murdered, last night along with his wife and *all* his children. All five of them. Shot, bayoneted in a basement. What sort of fool do they take me for?' She paused. 'It's simply not true. My son is alive. I would know if he were not. I would feel it in my heart. And in my heart, he lives. I know. *I know.* He's alive, they are *all* alive.' She sat slowly down in her chair. 'He's alive,' she whispered.

'Would you like us to pack, your Imperial Majesty?' ventured a servant.

'No! You fool! Carry on, carry on with the picnic.'

And more bad news was to follow.

The prisoners were awakened and driven in carts on a road leading to the village, where there was an abandoned iron mine with a pit 20m deep. Here they halted. The Cheka beat all the prisoners, striking them on the head with their rifle butts, before throwing their victims into this pit, Grand Duchess Elizabeth being the first. Hand grenades were then hurled down the shaft, but only one victim, Fyodor Remez, died as a result. Following the explosion, Grand Duchess Elizabeth and the others were heard singing an Orthodox hymn from the bottom of the shaft. A second grenade was thrown, but the singing continued. Finally, a large quantity of brushwood was shoved into the opening of the mineshaft and set alight. Half an hour later, the singing finally stopped.

Peter put down the letter and no one spoke. What was there to say? Grand Duchess Elizabeth, once the most beautiful woman in Europe, the Tsarina's sister, a woman who'd given her life to the nuns at the Convent of Saints Martha and Mary, where she was their abbess, had been thrown down a mineshaft and burnt alive? For what? For being married to Grand Duke Sergei Alexandrovich of Russia? A Romanov. A man who'd been assassinated, blown up, thirteen years previously. A man whose body parts she'd collected, bit by bit, off the street after the bomb attack in Moscow so he could be buried in as much of his entirety as possible. Had she not suffered enough already?

'Were there no survivors?' whispered Nadezhda, tears in her eyes. Her father shook his head. 'So, all of Oleg's brothers have died too? Ivan? Ygor? Konstantine?'

'All dead. The whole Konstantinovich family.'

'All burnt alive in the mineshaft?'

'It seems so.'

Later, it was discovered, when they exhumed them from the mineshaft, that one of the princes had a wound dressed by a handkerchief, tied around his head. It appeared that the Grand Duchess Elizabeth, with broken limbs and terrible injuries, tried to tend to him, before dying in the flames.

But the Bolsheviks had only just begun. All of the Grand

Dukes foolish enough to have remained in Petrograd were shot. Arrested, imprisoned; they killed four Grand Dukes in one day. They died praying on their knees in the Peter and Paul Fortress; those too ill to stand were shot on the stretchers where they lay. The big and burly Uncle Bimbo was executed with his favourite Persian kitten in his arms. He fell backwards into a pit already containing thirteen other bodies.

Nobody could be quite sure of anything any more. There were religious services held all over Europe for the murdered Tsar and his family and yet, in the Crimea, any suggestion of a Mass or a Requiem in his honour was shut down by the Dowager Empress Marie. What was the point of praying for the souls of her son and his family if they were still alive? Far better to carry on, playing tennis, having picnics and reading passages from the *Merry Arnold* to pass the time.

Undoubtedly, Lenin was ridding Russia of Romanovs to stifle any counter-revolutionary ideas, but that didn't stop contingent after contingent coming to Dulber in the hope of persuading Nikolasha to front up the White Army and lead a counter-attack up from the south. There was talk of Nikolasha becoming the next Tsar, which would make Stana and, of course, her sister Militza the most powerful women in all of Russia. If they ever managed to take back the throne, of course.

'I see old habits die hard,' said Felix, late one evening in October, after yet another delegation of officers had left Dulber in the afternoon.

Xenia had thrown a cocktail party at Ai Todor, anything to fill the hours and help with boredom. Normally, at this time of year, the royal party would have left the sunny climes of the coast for the cut and thrust of the city. This was about to be their third winter in the Crimea. Apparently, there was no end to this genteel incarceration.

'I am not sure what you mean,' replied Militza.

'You've always wanted to be Tsarina, ruler of Russia,' he said, smiling. 'It's just a shame there's no throne left for you to seize. The "Black Plague" strikes again.' He laughed. 'It's a bit like this Spanish flu, it's everywhere.'

'I think my husband and his brother are more interested in saving the country than ruling it.'

'Do you ever wonder if the events of the last few months are, as some people have claimed, the result of Rasputin? Whether the calamities which have overtaken our unfortunate country are down to him?'

'I simply can't see how those two things are related,' replied Militza.

'That the person who brought down Rasputin also brought down a 300-year-old empire?'

'I wouldn't know.'

'I went into Yalta this afternoon,' he said. 'To meet a crone called Mother Evgenia. She is supposed to have the power of prophecy. She was stricken by some mysterious disease that made her half-paralysed and not able to rise from her bed for nine years. They say she also has a deep-rooted horror of fresh air, she never allowed a window to be open, yet her room, instead of smelling like some fetid hell hole, smells only of fresh flowers.'

'And did it?'

'Smell of flowers? Yes, but I didn't manage to discuss that, because as soon as I entered her hovel, she threw her arms in the air and exclaimed, "You have come! I have been expecting you! I dreamed of you as the saviour of the country!" Can you imagine?' He smiled and lit a cigarette. 'She kissed my hand and then said, "Don't be unhappy. You are under the protection of God. Rasputin was a fiend, whom you slew like St George did the dragon. Rasputin himself is grateful to you and protects you, for in killing him, you prevented him from committing even greater sins."'

'I am sure he's very grateful indeed.' Militza nodded, the image of his face, underwater, flashing through her mind.

'She said more. "Russia must go through terrible trials to atone for her sins. Many years will pass before her resurrection. Few of the Romanovs will escape death, but you, you will survive. You will take an active part in the restoration of Russia. Remember that he who opened the door, must be the one to close it."' He smiled at her. 'He who opens the door, must be the one to close it.'

Militza smiled briefly back at him.

A month later and the war was over. According to the terms of the Armistice signed on 11 November 1918, the Germans were to evacuate all the territory they had gained during the war, including Crimea. And with them they took all sense of stability.

The civil war was raging, the fight between the Reds and the Whites had broken out all over the country. Half of the young men in Dulber and Ai Todor offered their services. Xenia's elder sons, Roman, even Nicholas Orlov volunteered to swell the ranks of the White Army and fight for the freedom of the Motherland. But they were all refused. In the few months since the delegations had come to the Crimea, the landscape had changed. Anyone with any connection to the Romanov family was considered undesirable.

Needless to say, Nikolasha found it insulting and hammered the table with his fist on hearing the news.

'Then what are we to do? Sit here and wait for our own destruction?'

'We could leave?' suggested Militza, sitting at the other end of the table.

'And go where?'

'Our sister, Elena,' began Stana. 'Queen of Italy.'

'I know who she is!' snapped Nikolasha.

'Well, she's offered her yacht, the *Trinacria*.'

'Are we to run away on a yacht to Italy? I, commander of one of the greatest armies in the world, am to run away from thugs and bandits and Lenin, on a yacht, to Italy?' He was shouting, his fist banging the table with each word he spat through his bushy moustache, his cheeks growing scarlet with fury. 'Italy!' he scoffed. 'What sort of country is Italy! It has no power, and no army to speak of. What would we do there?'

'The British have offered to rescue the Dowager Empress,' said Peter.

'And SHE has refused to go!' yelled Nikolasha at his own brother. 'I can't leave! I can't run away. Am I the coward? Am I to be humiliated by a little old woman? A little old woman who still believes her murdered son is alive, despite his death being announced on the front page of every single newspaper in the world! No!'

'But we could ask the British? Just in case?' suggested Nadezhda.

'In case of what?' He smiled so unpleasantly she had to look away. 'They're not going to help us, despite being on the same side during the war, they're frighted of their little democracy, they're scared of revolution, they think we might infect them with our disease. They don't like us, the British, they only want to save the Empress because she's their cousin. The rest of us can rot in hell. For Christ's sake they've just refused Sandro a visa.'

'They have?' asked Peter.

'They have, dear brother. We are on our own. That's for sure.'

Then came the news that the Red Army was marching south, the smell of blood in their nostrils, their bayonets sharpened and glinting in the sun, and the Whites were not holding them, they'd been overcome. They'd started a new offensive; they were now approaching the narrow entrance to the Crimea and there was little or no resistance. The picnickers were trapped. They had nowhere to go, but still Nikolasha and the Dowager Empress refused to go. If they left, what sort of message would it send to the country? That the Romanovs were defeated? That the fight for Russia had been lost? Lenin and his Bolsheviks had won?

Militza and Stana sat in the turquoise drawing room taking tea and listening to the boom of the approaching guns. With each explosion, each blast, the chandelier above their head quivered and little snakes of dust escaped from the cracks in the ceiling.

'How far away do you think they are?' asked Stana, looking anxiously towards the hills.

'A few miles, maybe more,' replied Militza.

'Is this what he meant? Do you think? Rasputin? The filth and the vices?'

'Even *he* could not have imagined this. Even *he* was not this evil. Millions of people are dead and for what? Nothing. I don't think I have ever been sadder in my life.' Militza drank her glass of tea. 'I am crushed with grief.'

'And resigned to death?' said Stana.

'What will be, will be.'

'Mama!' said Nadezhda, walking into the drawing room. 'The British have a boat at Sevastopol, and they have asked the Empress, again, to leave. She, of course, is refusing but I can't take this any more. I can't. I have Irina to think of and my whole life ahead. I'm twenty-one years old. I can't stay here to be murdered, shot, burnt alive at the bottom of a mineshaft. I can't bear this! I won't bear this. I want to leave. I want to live. I want my daughter to live.' She started to cry.

'Darling, don't worry.' Militza leapt out of her chair to put her arms around her daughter. 'Please don't cry.'

'I'm going to Xenia's birthday party right now to persuade the Dowager to leave.'

'She won't change her mind,' said Stana.

'But she has to. Otherwise, we shall *all* die. We shall all die and it's just a question of how painful our deaths will be. It's that simple.'

'She won't, she's stubborn and old and weighed down by her sense of duty.'

'Even if it means death for all her family.'

'She won't change her mind,' said Stana.

'Not unless we make her,' Militza said.

'What are you going to do?' Stana watched her sister walk towards the blue study off the hall.

'I am going to close a door that I opened a long time ago. Come,' she said. 'Both of you. I need both of you.' She picked up the large green velvet book and started to leaf through the pages, looking for the spell. 'The Dowager is stubborn, and her sense of duty runs deep. I can't do this alone.'

'What, me?' asked Nadezhda.

'Yes, you,' confirmed Militza, looking up from the book. 'It's impossible otherwise with someone this truculent, someone this stubborn. Stubborn enough still to believe her own son is alive, when the whole world knows he is dead. Are you one of us? Or are you not?' Nadezhda looked at her mother and into her black eyes.

'We need you,' added Stana. 'We don't have the power on our own.'

'What are you?' Militza paused. 'Who are you?'

'I am a witch's daughter.'

In the middle of Xenia's birthday party, the Empress was called to the telephone. It was Captain Charles Johnson from HMS *Marlborough* calling to say that the Red Army was less than five miles away and he considered this fact called for her immediate departure. For some reason, this time, the Empress did not refuse. Maybe it was the sound of gunfire drowning out the singing at her daughter's birthday?

390

Or was it the smell of smoke that was turning the blue sky black? Or was it the chanting she heard in her head, three voices, like sirens, telling her the time had come to leave? She should flee as soon as possible. Fly like a bird, run like the wind, sail away. She immediately wrote a note to Grand Duke Nikolai Nikolayevich in which she informed him of her decision to evacuate and urged him to join her in leaving as soon as possible.

They had less than two hours to pack. HMS *Marlborough* would collect them off the beach at Koreiz at five o'clock that evening. Ai Todor and Dulber were thrown into chaos. What to take? What to pack and what to leave behind? Photographs? Letters? Jewellery? All the money they could find. Mementoes, treasures. What does constitute a life?

Militza was swift and decisive, Stana was a little more discombobulated. The real problem was they had no idea how long they would be away. Just as they had already left the capital at speed, so now they were leaving the Crimea. The question was when would they return?

By 4.45 p.m. the Dulber household were all gathered on the beach in silence, anxious, more than a little terrified, awaiting the arrival of the Empress and the rest of the Ai Todors. The sun was already sinking and dusk was gathering; there was the continuous sound of rifle fire approaching the shore. Speed and secrecy were vital, any move that betrayed the evacuation to the Bolsheviks could be fatal.

'She's late,' hissed Nikolasha, dressed in his military uniform, complete with a lambskin Astrakhan hat. He was an imposing sight, especially for the British who'd never seen anyone quite so tall and exotic before.

'She said she'd be here at 5 p.m. and not a minute before,' replied Stana. 'You know what she is like.'

Half an hour later the Empress and Xenia and her children had still not arrived. The sound of gunfire was getting louder, and the fires were turning the evening sky to scarlet as they tore along the coast. Nikolasha was pacing the beach, while sailors from HMS *Marlborough* sat in their tenders, waiting, scouring the cliffs for any signs of the royal party.

'Send a car!' ordered Nikolasha. 'To her estate to see what is happening. She might have been captured already, taken, shot. Why isn't she here?'

Militza and Stana tried to calm him. It wasn't unreasonable for her to be a little late. Two hours is a short time in which to pack up a life. But he was extremely anxious. They had so many people to load, so many trunks, so many dogs and children, and the Bolsheviks could discover their plan at any point.

Finally, eventually, the Dowager was spotted on the top of the hill making her way slowly down to the shore. In her hands she held two small dogs and next to her walked her grandson, Vassili, carrying his pet canary in a cage. The gunfire grew louder, but she didn't flinch or seem to hurry, she took her time, said goodbye to her staff, offering them her black-gloved hand to kiss. She paused. Her daughter and her five children all bent down and took a handful of soil from the cliff edge and placed it in their pockets before they walked slowly towards the beach and the tender that was to take them to the warship.

But word went out. The Empress was abandoning Russia, it was all over, the Reds had won and the Empire had fallen. Within hours, panic had spread up and down the coast; thousands of refugees started to pack what they could and head for the beaches. By the time HMS *Marlborough* had moved further along the coast to pick up the Yusupovs, there were hundreds of them, sitting on their suitcases, crowding the shoreline, dazed, heartbroken, desperate, terrified, all looking at one warship for help.

HMS *Marlborough* was overwhelmed. They had been instructed to pick up only key members of the royal family, around twelve of them in total, but still they kept on coming. Thirty, forty, fifty, and some forty-odd servants and trunks and boxes and numerous little lapdogs. Captain Charles Johnson was worried for his ship; he was also worried about accommodating such illustrious guests. However, it was the request from the Empress that wrong-footed him most. Just as they were about to weigh anchor, she refused to leave. With so many refugees on the beaches, so many people running up and down on the shore, shouting, waving, desperate to board, she could not go without them.

'But I can't take them all, your Imperial Highness,' replied the captain, his head bowed.

'Then get some more ships,' she replied.

By the following morning, four more British destroyers and one French ship arrived to gather up the remainder off the pier in Yalta. The Dowager's departure had released a tidal wave of people who'd abandoned their houses, their possessions, their lives, and hurried to the waterfront in a frantic effort to board the Allied ships. As the Red Army tore through the last few miles towards the coast, many families were separated in the chaos, hundreds of children boarded the ships in the clothes they were wearing, with nothing but handfuls of Russian soil in their pockets.

By midday the gunfire was so close to the shore the flotilla simply had to set sail. Like a mother hen leading her chicks, the Empress finally left. The royal party all stood on deck as they stared at a scarlet sky. The hills behind Yalta were aflame. Militza held her breath and her husband's hand, the grief of leaving was overwhelming.

'What are those little black things all along the shore?' asked the Empress.

Prince Felix Yusupov stood next to her, his rolled-up Rembrandt in his hand. He looked down the long tube and declared, 'I think you'll find that's your silver, madame.'

The servants had packed and brought it to Yalta in the hope of getting on board the warship but they had been so afraid they'd be left behind, they'd abandoned the fifty-four cases of silver on the quay.

'And look,' he added, pointing his long fine finger, his left eye closed. 'I'd recognise that stooped, scarfed figure anywhere. Militza!' he said. 'I do believe that's your old nurse, on the beach, all on her own. Do you think we should wave goodbye?'

They continued to watch on in silence. No one could speak. What was there left to say?

A few minutes later HMS *Marlborough* pulled up alongside a Russian ship bound for the coast. On it was a contingent of some four hundred fiercely loyal young officers of the White Army, on their way to a certain death.

They recognised the Dowager Empress, a slight figure beneath the White Ensign and the tall distinctive figure of

Grand Duke Nikolai Nikolayevich and they saluted and began to sing the Russian Imperial anthem to a member of the Russian Imperial family within the boundaries of the empire, for the very last time.

The rich harmonious voices rolled across the waves towards the warship and, as she stood and listened, large tears silently, slowly streamed down the Empress's cheeks.

'God save the Tsar,' they sang. 'Strong and majestic... Let him reign for our glory... God save the Tsar!'

But the Tsar was dead.

And little did they know, as they sailed slowly away to exile on the Black Sea, this would be the last glimpse any of them would have of home. Never again would they see Russian soil.

'I can't believe it,' whispered Stana, her hands shaking as she stared at Yalta all aflame. 'The destruction, the death, the loss of life. A generation destroyed. A country in ruins. A future turned to dust... Who could have ever predicted all of this? What are they doing?'

'What were *we* doing?' asked Militza.

'Nothing will ever be the same again,' said Stana with tears in her eyes. 'Nothing. It's over. It's finished.'

'What fools we all are,' said Militza. And as the sky turned a blood red, she slowly gathered her shawl around her hunched shoulders and went below deck, into her cabin.

EPILOGUE

Militza, Nadezhda, Peter, Stana, Nikolasha, and Nicholas Orlov and all their children survived the 1917 revolution. They escaped off the beaches of the Crimea with some of their fortune, rescued by the British on HMS *Marlborough* in April 1919 along with Prince Felix Yusupov, his wife, Princess Irina, plus his parents, Princess Zinaida Yusupova and her husband, Count Felix Yusupov, as well as Grand Duchess Xenia and her mother, the Dowager Empress Maria Fyodorovna.

After a somewhat protracted journey, some were deposited in Turkey while others continued on to Malta, Militza and Stana and their families ended up living in the South of France, where Grand Duke Nikolai eventually died in 1929, followed by Grand Duke Peter in 1931, and Grand Duchess Anastasia in 1935.

Militza lived on, only to become caught up in the Second World War. She left France for Italy to stay with her sister Queen Elena. But the situation became very unstable, and as the king and queen went into hiding, Militza ended up seeking refuge in a convent close to the Spanish Steps in Rome. A few months later she managed to escape to the Vatican, where she received sanctuary within the walls of

Vatican City for three years. Eventually she travelled, along with her sister Elena and the rest of the Italian royal family, to Alexandria, Egypt, where she lived along with a myriad of other deposed royals, including King Zog of Albania, as a guest of King Farouk of Egypt. Grand Duchess Militza died in Alexandria in September 1951, aged eighty-five.

Nadezhda went on to make her home in France. She and Nicholas had another daughter, Xenia, however they were to divorce in 1940. Nadezhda lost her daughter Xenia in 1963. Irina, the youngest passenger aboard the HMS *Marlborough*, only outlived her mother by one year. Nadezhda died in 1988 aged ninety years old. She is buried in Chantilly, France.

ACKNOWLEDGEMENTS/ AUTHOR NOTE

First there was *The Witches of St Petersburg* and now there is *The Witch's Daughter*, which continues the story of the 'Black Princesses' from Montenegro – from the murder of their old friend Rasputin, to their ultimate rescue off the beaches of the Crimea. Of course, they survived, while millions of their peers, friends and fellow countrymen, tragically, did not. They were tenacious women; they were brave and they were brilliant. And although this is a work of fiction, the majority of the story is true, and I am deeply indebted to my dear friend, the journalist and ridiculously talented war correspondent, Nikolai Antonov, who first told me about the 'Black Princesses' all those years ago, in 1992, as we sat around his kitchen table in Moscow drinking strong vodka and eating stronger pickles.

His eyes shone as he wove a magical tale about these two beautiful, young princesses who arrived from Montenegro, married into the Russian Court, introduced Rasputin to the Tsarina and brought down an empire. 'Power, magic, sex!' he laughed. We charged our glasses and I promised him I'd write it as soon as I got home.

I didn't of course, I ended up writing other things, but Nikolai would not give up. He'd called me often from Moscow sharing little bits of information he'd found. They were hard women to track down. Being neither the victors, nor male, they were usually consigned to the footnotes of history. But I do remember one telephone call from Nik some ten years later and just days, in fact, before he died. He'd just found out the most fantastic fact and he had to tell me right away.

'The reason they were called the Black Princesses.' He paused, for dramatic effect, static cracking down the line. 'It was not because they had black hair, or because they liked black magic, but because they had black eyes! Black eyes,' he repeated. 'Black eyes!'

And I have been haunted by their black eyes ever since. Their black eyes, their visions, their powers and what drove them. And the more I read, the more convinced I became of their crucial involvement in this extraordinary part of Russian history. The story of the succession, the tragedy of little Alexei; they were there. They supplied the gurus, the drugs, the spells, the incantations; they were there in the bedchamber, they were there at the parties and the balls. Confidantes, friends, allies and supporters of a Tsarina who must have carried guilt around with her like some toxic burden, every day. Mother and murderer of her own son, there's nothing to ease that sort of pain. Not even Rasputin. And then, they were caught up in the revolution, as everyone was, but they were the ones who made it south, they survived on their wiles, their charm and, of course, their magic.

And then there was Militza's daughter, Nadezhda, torn between two worlds, torn between two loves, two ideals, two different dreams for the future. Buffeted by history, it takes character and strength to make it out and a certain romantic fortitude to fill your pockets with soil and pearls and stay alive. But mostly it takes a huge amount of luck.

Firstly, I would like to thank Katya Galitzine. Her knowledge of all things Russian is unsurpassed, her friendship is boundless and her patience endless. I have bored her with my questions, raided her bookshelves and sat for hours in the stunning Prince George Galitzine Memorial Library in St Petersburg, where I researched a lot of this book, taking notes from its volumes of incredible and rare books. She has sent me photographs, extracts and priceless snippets of information. Thank you. And thank you for fuelling my obsession with the beautiful soul that was Prince Oleg.

Secondly it has to be the Witches – Angela Janklow, Eleanor Tattersfield, Susan Campos, Delphine Le Dain, Pippa Hornby, Johnny Hornby, Sarah Manley, Simon Dunlop, Alex Michaelis, Susanna Michaelis and Nicholas Laing – what a trip! What a gang. Never to be forgotten.

The wonderful Daisy Waugh, who kept me going, plied me with wine, pizza, life-affirming good advice and supportive tarot!

The beautiful, witty speechmaker extraordinaire Santa Montefiore, whose salmon and vodka and turns of the tarot have made several hundreds of evenings all the more glorious.

There are many others who have listened to me endlessly discuss the witches and their daughter – I thank you: Candace Bushnell, Claudia Winkleman, Sarah Vine, Libby Ferguson, Sarah Ferguson, Anne Sjimonsbergen, Sean

Langan, Ciara Parkes, James Purefoy, Sebastian Scott, Peter Mikic, Jennifer Nadal, Joanne Black, Clare Atkinson, Katie Walker, Tina Cutler. Your wit, wine and wisdom were gratefully received.

And, of course, the Book Club Queens: Assia, Brigitta, Claire, Emma, Emily, Jenny, Justine, Kate, Phoebe, Pippa, Yasmin and elusive Charlotte! Your love and joy are bounteous!

My sister, Leonie, my mother, Scarlett, my brother, Marcus. My wonderful, handsome husband, Kenton; for listening to yet another anecdote or idea like you've never been asked the same question before.

Special mention goes to my agent, Eugenie Furniss, who walked with me every step of the way with this – nearly fifteen years in the writing of both books and she read and re-tweaked and re-read and edited and advised – thank you! You are a very good friend.

To my incredible editor, Rosie de Courcy, who made it better and understood what I was trying to say. You are utterly fabulous in every way. To ALL at Head of Zeus – thank you.

Also Joth Shakerley who was there that night at the kitchen table in Moscow and who has been there always. I love you. Your positivity, support and deft swipe with a salted fish move mountains. You are the best of friends.

I would like to thank the London College of Psychic Studies for their joyful and inquisitive approach to life. I am extremely grateful to my teachers for their kindness, knowledge and patience, most especially Robin Lown, who has put up with me in his palmistry class for the last four years.

And lastly my children, Allegra and Rafe (whose knowledge of Rasputin in now encyclopaedic). Thank you for your love and understanding. I promise I am now out of the office, for now.